THE LAST KEEPER

THE LAST KEEPER
Book One of the Warminster Series

J. V. Hilliard

Paperback ISBN 978-1-77400-041-0
Electronic ISBN 978-1-77400-042-7

Printed on Acid Free Paper

DragonMoonPress.com

PROLOGUE

*"The blade of betrayal, the sharpest of weapons, is
wielded not by your enemies, but by your friends."*
—Warminster, the Mage

THE SUN WAS BEGINNING to show red over the horizon,
as the wooded hollow in the shadow of the Dragon's Breath
Mountains stirred. Light streamed into the valley, illuminating
the dew that clung to the long blades of grass and turning it
into a sea of little stars. The first song of the morning echoed
out of the trees and was soon supported by a chorus. The soft,
steady rush of a stream lay beneath the sound of the birds; it
was a new one that had survived the flood of the last rain and
that might someday carve its own valley out of the mountain.
Overhead, a breeze gently rustled the leaves of the treetops,
seeming to whisper wordless secrets over the forest.

In an instant, a single, ear-splitting sound drowned the
valley in a thunderous clap. A white-hot blaze of magic twisted
the air, charring the ground beneath it. Birds fluttered into
a frenzied cloud, while woodland creatures scattered in all
directions. A human figure, hunched and bleeding, tumbled
out of the rift and onto the blackened ground.

After a long moment, the figure—a man—finally stirred.
His burnt hands pressed into the scarred landscape, and with
excruciating difficulty, he forced himself into a seated position.
He drew a long breath before lifting his head.

The man's face was dirty, his countenance heavily obscured
by soot and ash. From his slow movement and hunched
posture, he could have been taken for an old man, though in
truth he was barely beyond forty. Two dark rivulets of blood
flowed over the grubby mess of his cheeks, dribbling like tears

from hollow eye sockets.

The man's head cocked abruptly to the side, alerted by some instinct, and he listened intently. The faint sound of horses' hooves and the shouting of men's voices issued from his magical portal, which still hung in the air. He cursed to himself and lurched unsteadily to his feet. The man swayed briefly, as if unsure of his balance, and then began stumbling deeper into the woods. He reached out with his hands and felt his way between the trees.

The loud whinnying of a spooked horse suddenly echoed through the valley, followed by more shouting and the noise of armored feet hitting the ground. The man in the woods slowed, his shoulders slumping. This was a confrontation he wished to avoid if he could.

"We couldn't get them through," a voice called from behind him. "The horses. Nervous beasts, horrible with magic. I suppose you knew that would slow us down."

The man came to a halt, his head turning. He made no reply.

"Then again," said the other, more quietly, "I suppose you also knew that we wouldn't need horses to catch you. What a state you're in, old friend."

"Still better looking than you, Captain," the man answered.

His pursuer sighed. "You can stall all you want, Graytorris. We have to take you back to the cathedral, and you're in no state to run any farther."

"Do you see me running?" Graytorris replied, and with a sharp gesture, he uttered a single word and the door in the air disappeared. "At least your horses can run free without you."

"Why are you trying to force my hand?" The captain was beginning to sound frustrated. "We can reopen the portal at need. You're only drawing out the inevitable."

"Oh, is Radu there? Poor fellow. You ought to be back with

your books," Graytorris said, raising his voice and turning his blind eyes toward the crowd of men flanking their leader. There was no reply. "Really, Rhron, he's always been rubbish with a sword. The great keeper must be desperate."

"I volunteered," Radu replied, revealing himself. His voice trembled, and Graytorris sensed fear and adrenaline in his words. "What a piteous fiend you've become."

Graytorris shook his head and cackled. The words stung true, but he refused to let them know it. His old teacher must have been pushed to the edge to ride here in his condition.

"You should have stayed there, Precept," he said, pushing himself defiantly away from the trunk and taking a blind step in the direction of his pursuers.

"You know I have orders to kill you if you refuse to come," Rhron said. His tone had turned clipped and professional. "I'm asking you one last time, Graytorris. Don't make me do this. Don't make my *men* do this! They're as much your friends and fellows as I am."

Graytorris just stood silently, resolute despite his weakness, his mouth flattened into a proud, angry line. Rhron's armor rattled as he jerked his head and his troops moved to flank and surround their target, drawing their swords with a cacophony of hissing steel.

"It's over," Rhron told him. "You must surrender to the will of Erud."

At this, Graytorris's expression hardened further. "You know," he said, "an all-knowing god such as Erud ought to have seen this coming and resolved it before it happened. Erud *has* no 'will.'"

"Heresy," Radu snapped from the ranks of soldiers surrounding him.

"No, Radu, it's true," Graytorris went on, unbothered. "Because if Erud had a will then one would think, logically speaking, that they'd do something to stop what I'm about to do."

The knights shifted toward Graytorris as Rhron raised his gauntleted hand to give the kill order. All of them moved a split-second too late. Only Radu, quick-witted and poor with a sword, had either the cowardice or the presence of mind to stammer out a protection spell.

"Drenering uderforer dodt," the blind man uttered.

All the men surrounding him winced in agony, grabbing at their chests and throats. A pain grew in Graytorris's arms, pulsing through his veins. A magical necrosis drained the energy from the trees and grass around him. The wave of energy inside him morphed from life to death, temporarily becoming one. The spell was working.

"Drenering uderforer dodt," he repeated, with some difficulty.

The troops writhed and collapsed to their knees, as did Rhron, though Radu had evidently escaped. Graytorris did his best to ignore their groans, as well as the brutal, scorching pain that racked his entire body as the spell took effect.

Almost unable to stop himself, Graytorris repeated the incantation one final time, completing the spell. He fell to his knees, trying not to faint, but the spell had taken something from him, too. He realized that Rhron's knights were dead, as much from a rising stench as through his own magical senses. But the spell kept moving on to the valley itself, leaching life out of the flora, stilling the limbs of insects, seeming to even deaden the noise of the nearby stream.

He felt the stolen strength of the living things in the hollow rush into his limbs. The pain was still there, but as seconds passed it became less intense and he found he could stand tall.

Before he knew what he was doing, he made his way to his former friend's corpse, where it lay in the grey and ossified grass. The plants, once green and pliant, now crunched harshly under his feet, and once or twice even broke his skin. Graytorris knelt among them, feeling for Rhron's body.

When his fingers found the mail-covered torso, it rose slightly under his hand.

He started. One hand flew to Rhron's mouth to check for breath, and he felt the faintest gust touch his palm. Stunned, he sat back. The captain was clearly on the edge of death, but by all rights he shouldn't have survived the first wave of the spell, let alone the last.

Graytorris paused, listening to Rhron's quiet, labored breathing. Apologies and explanations sat just under his tongue, but his lips twisted against them.

"You brought this on yourself," he told the dying man.

The two of us must make a grim picture, he thought, *sitting in the middle of a stillness born of death rather than peace, surrounded by petrified trees and scorched earth. This hollow will never be a natural place again.*

His heart skipped a beat, then slowed to a deathly pace as the spell continued to exact its toll on his body. The pain returned with a vengeance, searing through his flesh like hellfire.

In his agony, a single, wild thought suddenly entered his brain, and he quickly spoke the incantation of another spell—one that would both save and damn Rhron. One that would preserve their friendship, even if only in its most twisted possible form. In that moment, his only wish was to not be alone.

Though still unconscious, Rhron drew in a harsh breath, followed by a loud, keening scream. The cracking of bone met Graytorris's ears as the man beside him began to transform. At the same time, his own pain intensified so that he too was unable to keep from crying out. His strength finally drained to its limit by the necrotic ravages of the spell that had petrified the hollow, Graytorris lost consciousness and collapsed to the ground.

Moments later, the nameless beast that had once been Rhron Talamare stirred and whuffed quietly, sat back on its haunches, and waited for its master to awaken.

CHAPTER ONE

"...and so, the blinded man shall pass
through the fog and walk on the water."
—The Tome of Enlightenment

DAEMUS ALARIC WAS DREAMING again. This wasn't unusual. He was both blessed and cursed with oneiromancy, or the powers of the Sight—visions imparted by Erud, the sexless Ancient of Knowledge. Only those few who were gifted with the Erudian Sight could see events that had not yet come to pass, omens that were interpreted by his sect, the enigmatic Keepers of the Forbidden.

It was the same dream he had every night. It would always begin like any normal dream: odd yet ordinary, vague, and soft. Daemus never remembered the first dream, but he always remembered the second, the one that arrived in the early hours of the morning and left him only after his eyes were already open.

He wandered through fog, aching from the coldness of the Sight, a damp chill pressing through his skin and into his bones, his constant companion since childhood. Daemus shivered, more violently so than usual, but remembered to send his ritual prayer of thanks to Erud. He was much better at that in his dreams than he was during his waking hours.

He paused for a moment to catch his breath and look around. The fog seemed to have grown even closer, and when he lifted his hand unbelievingly in front of his face, he could barely make out its silhouette. He took a couple of deep breaths, steadying himself and choking down the urge to panic. There was a sound from somewhere to his right, the cawing of a carrion bird perhaps, and the chilling touch of an unseen breeze that did little to blow the fog away.

Gathering himself, Daemus struck off, choosing his path almost at random. He walked slowly, carefully, expecting the ground to give way at any moment or for something to loom up in front of him. But there was nothing, just a sweeping, impenetrable field that seemed to stretch on into eternity.

He felt as though he'd wandered aimlessly for hours, finding no landmark of any kind. He sweated despite the cold, and his legs ached. His throat burned from thirst, and he felt ready to collapse. His weary limbs trembled uncontrollably, and every torturous step felt as though it could be his last.

At the very moment he knew his strength would fail, a massive expanse of still, clear water melted out of the fog, glassy before his feet. Distant mountains hugged the far edge of the pool, darkened by the night sky. Daemus paused, suddenly remembering that he wouldn't get the chance to drink. He never did, for this was when the blinded man appeared.

He watched as an ethereal figure emerged from the mist, hovering over the water's surface and meandering closer to him. It was a man, hunched and cloaked, his eyes hidden by greying bandages stained with blood—familiar, but only from his dreams. His face seemed to twist and change from night to night, growing darker and more haggard, though Daemus knew it was the same man each time. He always seemed unable to sense Daemus and was certainly unable to see him. Yet when the man was near, Daemus never felt safe. He looked like terror and death and emptiness. It was all Daemus could do not to scream.

As though tied to the same puppeteer's strings, both Daemus and the man grew still at the same moment. Distantly, Daemus registered that something new was coming. His dream had never taken him this far, and that knowledge was terrifying. He didn't want to know what would happen next.

His mind moved sluggishly, as though he was being slowly trapped in hardening amber. Perhaps the fog itself had clouded his mind when he was breathing it while desperately seeking his way. Panic crept up his spine, his eyes diluting as the fight-or-flight response kicked in. The man was so close that Daemus could smell the tracks of fresh blood crawling down his cheeks. It smelled of rusted swords and the bile of ruptured organs.

The man raised his head, his bloody countenance impassive, his robed arm reaching out for Daemus. It weaved through the air mere inches in front of him, as though the blinded man was looking for a stitch in the fabric of reality. Somehow, he seemed to be unaware of Daemus's presence, though his gnarled finger was so close to the young man's face that Daemus could see the dirt caked beneath the beds of the nails.

Daemus tried to move again, but his body refused to obey his mind's desperate commands. He swallowed, his dry throat savoring the precious saliva, and fought back the tears that threatened to overwhelm him.

He opened his mouth and screamed.

The shrill sound ripped through the silence like a bell ringing in a sleepy village. Daemus's hands flew up to his face as though to force the sound back in, but it was too late. Daemus knew in that moment that he'd made a fatal mistake. The figure had been unaware of him… until then.

The stranger turned.

"Finally," he said with an evil cackle. "You've come for me, Daemus Alaric."

Daemus opened his mouth to scream again, but the mist was sweeping back down from the mountains and swallowing up everything around them. Even the blinded man was no exception, and he melted away from Daemus along with everything else. Darkness overcame him, swirling into the blackness of unconsciousness as the stranger's harsh laughter continued to echo in his ears.

"DAEMUS, WAKE UP!" A FARAWAY voice cried to him. "You're having a nightmare."

His mind began to swirl, and he fought the urge to succumb to the terror, concentrating instead on the soft voice that was calling to him. A calming hand took him gently by the shoulder and Caspar Luthic, his roommate, drew nearer.

He felt an uneasy pang in his stomach at the transition from dream to consciousness. His vision slowly returned, his eyes roaming around the cloister as he looked for signs of the blinded man. It was only then he noticed he was standing, and that he'd soiled his undergarments.

"You're safe," Caspar assured him, gesturing for Daemus to sit. "We're here, in our room. You were sleepwalking again."

"The blinded man," Daemus murmured. "It was the blinded man."

"Take some water." Caspar forced a clay mug into Daemus's trembling hands. Daemus chugged the water as if it were a life-saving potion. When he finished, he wiped his brow and gathered his thoughts.

"Thank you, Caspar."

"Let's get you to the infirmary." Caspar reached for his cloak and boots.

"No," Daemus begged, "I can't."

"Why?" Caspar asked. "I'll make sure no one sees us this time. The other Low Keepers are asleep."

"Please, no more embarrassment. I'll change and clean up, but let's keep this to ourselves. Our classmates are relentless."

"We all have growing pains," Caspar reassured him. "The

Sight comes to each of us differently."

Daemus found little solace in those words. The Sight had cost him more than it had cost Caspar and the other Low Keepers combined.

"Very well," Caspar relented. "Let's get you cleaned up and back to bed."

"I shan't sleep a wink more tonight," Daemus confessed.

"Precept Radu will know if you don't," Caspar said. "He always does. At least try."

As Caspar quietly left the cloister to retrieve more water, Daemus dropped to his knees and leaned heavily against the wall. He wept softly, the specter of his prophecy lingering in his mind, the words of the blinded man clutching at his soul.

TRUE TO HIS WORD, Daemus didn't sleep for the remainder of the night, peering instead from the small window in his cloister and out into the vastness of the heavens. He watched the patient movements of the Ancients as they made their nocturnal progression through the Great Hall of the night sky. He tried to note their changes, knowing that Precept Radu would likely ask his astromancy class about the celestial events the next afternoon. But fatigue tugged at him, and their starry travels were easily forgotten.

"Caspar," Daemus whispered, trying to subtly wake his friend, but his cloistermate had found a deep slumber, wrapped tightly beneath his woolen blanket. He wanted to stir him, to share his thoughts and talk to someone other than himself. But Caspar was far off somewhere, stealing the rest he'd told Daemus to find for himself.

His gaze returned to the blanket of stars. From his window, he could see the outlined buildings of the town of Solemnity, just outside the gated walls of the cathedral, and little else.

Low Keepers had the worst accommodation of all the Divine Protectorate of Erud and, of course, the worst of the chores. His livestock-feeding and stable-sweeping duties awaited him once the Great Hall gave way to the dawn.

The Ancients' glowing faces were his friends, and silent ones at that. They never answered him, save for one. His Ancient, the Ancient venerated by his order: Erud.

He often wondered why the great Erud cared so much for the goings on in Warminster, a land of mortals so far away. And why had the Ancients left the land for their place in the heavens if it was so important to communicate with them? It seemed as if the Great Hall wasn't that far away, so why leave at all? Was it so they could watch over their children from afar while escaping a realm that they'd helped to birth? If Erud cared so much, why leave and instead send cryptic messages about the future from a vast distance?

As far as Daemus knew, only one Ancient had refused to leave Warminster, and that was Trillias, the Ancient of Sport and Tests. A cousin of Erud, he'd remained behind on his island, offering magical rewards for those who could overcome his challenges.

So far, few had.

Daemus readjusted the blanket on his shoulder and scrunched himself into the window's alcove, resting his legs on the cold, stone ledge. He propped his head against the window and watched as Solemnity's first lights began to appear in the distant windows. It was nearly dawn.

He closed his eyes and heard his uncle's voice in his mind. "If you're afraid to sleep," his Uncle Kester would say, "at least close your eyes and rest." He knew now it was a ruse that he'd used to trick Daemus into falling back to sleep after a nightmare when he was younger. Perhaps there was some wisdom in it. It worked more often than not.

He closed his eyes and listened to the sounds of Solemnity waking up. Horses neighed and faraway voices fell softly into his ears.

The next thing he felt was Caspar's hand, shaking him by the shoulder.

"It's time, Daemus," Caspar said. "I'm glad you got some sleep."

Daemus looked out the window and saw the darkness of the Great Hall diminishing. He couldn't have slept for more than fifteen minutes.

Daemus smiled in gratitude and groaned when he stood up. His uncomfortable perch had taken its toll. He washed his face in their basin, then stared uncertainly into the shard of mirror that lay unceremoniously beside it. His white eyes had a hollow, haunted look, their unusual hue offset by the dark bags that surrounded them. He'd been teased mercilessly because of his eyes for as long as he could remember. When he was younger, he'd hated them for making him different. Now that he was older, he liked them for the exact same reason.

He hid his soiled undergarments in his satchel before they left. The pigs needed feeding before class, and he'd thought it was a perfect way to hide his own stains from the other Low Keepers who were assigned laundry duty that afternoon.

He was drained, but he willingly traded the peril of his powers for the fatigue of another day.

CHAPTER TWO

"A hunter who knows how to hunt knows
how to hunt without his falcon."
—Faxerian proverb

SIR RITTER VALKENEER WAS daydreaming of a new pair of boots. He'd torn a hole in the sole of his current pair after deftly escaping a snare trap set by the trollborn tribes that hunted close to his ancestral home at this time of year. They'd been hoping for small game, but instead he'd left them with shoe leather.

He was on the hunt with the Longmarchers, his team of rangers and scouts, moving noiselessly from tree to tree, deep within the forest of Ravenwood. The Longmarchers had been given their moniker by Ritter's father, Lord Hertzog Valkeneer, because he felt it perfectly befitted the scouting element of his small retinue of rangers. They operated outside of typical military protocols and spent extended periods of time in the field.

Ritter leaned against a tree and followed his mind to Storm, his war falcon, surveying the forest from high above. He saw through Storm's eyes, heard through his ears, and could command the bird to watch, fly, or attack with a quick thought. It was an affinity to animals that he'd inherited from his mother, a Raven elf and sorceress. It would shorten the hunt, but Ritter enjoyed the simplicity of the link. There were no politics, no hidden meanings, but a shared existence impossible to describe to those who didn't possess the same ability.

Juxtaposing the falcon's vision with his own, Ritter watched a stag bounding in from the south. The stag, unaware of Storm and Ritter, was climbing the mossy rock formations below the hunter. It was soon within range.

Ritter slowly and quietly adjusted his body against the tree, relaxing his bowstring and moving his longbow from one side of the trunk to the other, anticipating the coming shot. He took a long, deep breath to calm the excitement before the kill.

The stag bent to drink at the stream not fifty yards away from him, then raised its neck as though it had been alerted somehow to his presence. It paused for a moment, then leapt forward in an unpredictable burst, fleeing the stream in a blind sprint.

Ritter felt the tension rise as adrenaline surged through his veins. His heartbeat echoed in time with the stag's own hurried pace. With his bowstring drawn back and begging to be let loose, it was time for the shot.

He turned to his right, where his lieutenant, Wilcox de la Croix, stood below him, his longbow also drawn. Ritter knew he had the superior shot lined up while Wilcox was still nocking an arrow to his string. He smiled to himself, tweaked his aim to the left and let fly, his arrow whistling within a foot or so of the stag. The stag turned and raced through the underbrush toward de la Croix, whose arrow was finally nocked and who released the string just in time.

The arrow flew true and hit its target, downing the stag on impact.

Ritter turned to face his friend from his perch in the tree and said, "Good shot, de la Croix. It's about time you feathered us a nice meal."

"Ha!" de la Croix boasted, beaming with pride. "The famous Bull's-Eye Bowman of the Bridge, beaten again. If you keep this up, someone will take your title at the next Crossed Arrows Tournament."

"Perhaps," Ritter replied, smiling enigmatically. "But fifty silver laurels say it won't be you."

By now, more of the Longmarchers had arrived, their

progress through the forest as silent as a squirrel. Ritter turned to look at them and then pointed at the downed animal.

"Someone cut his throat and truss him up," he said. "We dine well tonight."

WHEN DARKNESS FELL, RITTER ordered his men to set up camp on the outskirts of the forest. His Longmarchers dug a firepit and created a rudimentary spit using a spear and a couple of downed trees. De la Croix's kill was skinned, prepared, and impaled on the spear, and once the meat was cooked and camp had been struck, the men set about it with their knives until nothing remained but bone.

Unless they had time to forage, the Longmarchers ate what they brought with them, but today was different. They were close enough to the town of Valkeneer to lower their guard and enjoy a hunt. Roasting wild game on an open pit would bring unwanted trouble in the far fields, but the Longmarchers felt free of the dangers of the Dragon's Breath Mountains.

"So, no trace of the bandits?" Marr Larkin said. A Raven elf from the nearby forest, though still a subject of the crown, Marr sat amongst the huddled group. "A fortnight searching for them and nary a hoofprint."

"If the rumors are true," de la Croix replied, "and Veldrin Nightcloak has come to Ravenwood, we'll find him."

The Longmarchers were used to tracking the trollborn tribes of the north, and on rare occasions, the cryptid creatures of the nearby wilds. Cryptids were the not-so-mythical beasts that plagued their borders every now and then.

"Confident, are you?" Til Aarron, the group's unofficial bard, said subconsciously, strumming the notes of his newest song on his lute. "Shall I start composing 'The Ballad of Wilcox de la Croix'?"

The Longmarchers chuckled at the lieutenant's expense, and even de la Croix found humor in the jab as he took a swig of his ale.

"If the Cloak was truly the one who pillaged the villages in Queen's Chapel, he shouldn't be hard to find," Rufus Crag offered while taking a drag of his pipe. "You can't hide the trail of a hundred horses in the woods so easily."

Crag, like Ritter, was a trollborn. While Ritter was born of a human father and elven mother, Crag was born part-human and part-huldrefolk, on his mother's side. The huldrefolk were half the size of humans, and depending on their lineage, they made quick and vicious warriors. Crag's human blood made him taller and even stronger than the average huldrer, to the benefit of the Longmarchers.

"Are the Raven elves searching too, Sir Ritter?" Marr asked.

"Aye," Ritter replied, after taking a bite of his venison. "My mother assured me that she sent word to the coronel."

"Then you doubt the reports from Queen's Chapel, sir?" de la Croix asked.

"Someone raided those towns." Ritter stood and spat into the firepit. "But if the rumors are true, the Cloak vanished into the Dragon's Breaths as if he was never there."

"Horses and carts laden with treasure always leave tracks," de la Croix observed.

"Yet we found none," Ritter said, starkly. "Our adversaries, whoever they may be, are skillful."

"Then let's drink to the lad or lass among us who finds the first hint of their path," Marr pledged, raising his tankard high. "To the bastard's trail!"

"The trail!" the group toasted.

They sat up talking and drinking for the rest of the night, picking the remainder of the bones clean and going about their business in the bushes. There was safety in numbers and the troop knew they were close to home, so the camp had a relaxed atmosphere. Ritter, ever careful, doubled the night watch anyway. They slept in their leather armor and kept their weapons close at hand.

THE MORNING CAME TOO soon for Ritter as he was awoken by his war falcon. Storm's imperceptible thoughts rushed through Ritter's mind, coaxing him from his slumber. It was near dawn, and Ritter reflexively grabbed for his longbow.

His sharp senses detected no disturbances, save for his guards at the perimeter of the camp and the waning embers in the firepit from the night before. He breathed a sigh of relief and cleared his mind to better connect with Storm.

As he calmed, he looked through the eyes of the falcon. At first, Ritter saw only trees and foliage, but as he concentrated, he found what had alerted the bird.

A line of horses was marching through the forest along the Tavastia Bridleway, the road to Valkeneer, outside the nearby hamlet of Gossamer End. The bridleway was the main road to and from the castle, but it rarely saw the likes of the royal retinue that traveled it today.

Twenty knights held lances high, striding atop armored steeds toward Valkeneer. The front row of lancers bore pennants decorated with the purple and gold of Thronehelm, Warminster's capital city. Pennants of powder blue and yellow from the barony of Queen's Chapel were mixed amongst the ranks.

Ritter heard de la Croix stir next to him.

"What is it?" his lieutenant asked, his voice cloudy from sleep. "I know that look. What have your trollborn senses detected?"

The word "trollborn" was often spoken without forethought by the commoners. It was usually meant as a derogatory term and was thrown around easily to smear those unfortunate enough to be byproducts of a raped and pillaged town that had been attacked by hideous giants, trolls, or ogres.

Some trollborn mixes were more socially acceptable than others, but trollborn blood was like a scar, often hard to hide. In the case of de la Croix, Ritter knew it was said fondly, as his friend correctly attributed his connection with Storm to his hybrid race.

"It's not good," Ritter murmured. "Royals on the bridleway, heading for the castle."

"How do you know?" de la Croix asked, flashing a curious look at the young captain.

"The flags," Ritter said. "I don't like them."

De la Croix sniffed as he sat up. "Horrible, gaudy things."

"No," Ritter replied. "It's not that."

"Then what is it?"

Ritter stared through Storm's eyes at the flags, a furrow forming on his brow as though that, too, had been blown out of shape by the wind.

"In all of my short twenty years," Ritter said, "I've never known the king of Thronehelm nor the baroness of Queen's Chapel to set foot in Valkeneer. Something must be amiss."

"What are your orders, sir?" de la Croix asked.

"We must return," Ritter replied. "Immediately."

Less seasoned warriors might have grumbled or gossiped about what the royal visit could mean, but the Longmarchers were more disciplined, more determined. They filled their packs and took the camp apart in near silence, burying the animal bones and filling in the firepit to leave no trace of their presence.

Then the Longmarchers began the last leg of their march home.

A DAY HAD PASSED, AND Ritter and the Longmarchers had made their way back to town. Ritter had commanded

Storm to follow the royals from a distance, and their progress seemed peaceful but hurried. Pressing on throughout the night, the retinue reached the gates of Castle Valkeneer before the Longmarchers.

Ritter found their pace unnerving, but said nothing to his troops.

As the morning turned to afternoon, his Longmarchers appeared from Ravenwood on the outskirts of Gossamer End and traveled along the bridleway to the keep.

Even to the Longmarchers, the Bridge was intimidating. An ageless castle, its origins lost in the fog of time, it had guarded the borderlands for many centuries. It had earned its name because its front gates took the form of a bridge that linked the frontier of Ravenwood to the doors of the keep. Travelers, merchants and pilgrims alike all used the Bridge to cross the Gossamer River, which formed a natural border between Valkeneer and the wilds of the forest. The Bridge and its soldiers were the first line of defense against the occasional assaults on the rustic town and the last line of defense when times were direst. The castle was small but stalwart, pocked with scars from hundreds of repelled attacks in the distant and not-so-distant past. More of a fort than a castle, the legend went that the Bridge—or Castle Valkeneer to give it its true name—had never fallen.

As Ritter and the Longmarchers approached, they noticed the flags of Thronehelm and Queen's Chapel flying over the keep and atop the battlements, next to the standard of Valkeneer. The Thronehelm standard featured the silhouette of a shield and a helm in the center. The flag from Queen's Chapel, Ritter's home barony, was split into quarters, containing the silhouette of a chapel in the upper left corner and three gold palmettes in the lower right.

The Longmarchers entered from the rear of the Bridge and crossed through its portcullis, where Ritter heard his sisters calling out to him. Tishara, the younger of the two, squealed at the sight of her older brother, and they both raced across the flagstones to greet him. When Ritter saw Tishara, he held her briefly before turning to Aerendaris and embracing her, too. And of course, Aerendaris was with her stray cat, Aliester.

Aerendaris was the second oldest of the Valkeneer children. At eighteen, she already looked remarkably like her mother, Amandaris, possessing the same black hair that was natural for Raven elves. She was short but slender and, like her mother, she was a sorceress, a profession that was common amongst their kin. She'd lived her life in the shadow of her family, shielded and distanced from the real world. Ladylike and noble, she nevertheless shared Ritter's affinity with the woods.

Tishara was a little different, a tomboy who took after her human father. She was training to become a warrior. Like the rest of the Valkeneers, she felt at home in the forest, which was why she aspired to become one of the Longmarchers. At fifteen years old, she was still too young to take to the field, but she showed a lot of promise, even besting Ritter in some of her training. Already taller than her older sister, she possessed a more athletic build, along with a wiry strength and a determined streak. Her light brown hair, which she got from her father, was pulled back and tied in a ponytail. And unlike her sister, she wasn't wearing any makeup.

"It's good to see you again." Ritter smiled. "Tell me, what news is there?"

"The princes are here," Tishara explained, sneaking in a sideways glance at her sister. "Montgomery and Everett Thorhauer. And so are their cousins, the Viscounts Joferian and Talath Maeglen of Queen's Chapel."

"Why are they here?" Ritter asked.

"I overheard the princes talking to Father in the drawing room," she said. "Their voices were raised, as if in argument. I couldn't hear what they were saying, but it sounded important. Father has been in a foul mood ever since, and mother thinks we can't see the tears in her eyes."

"You may be correct," Ritter agreed. "When someone rides through the night, it rarely means good news."

"Spoken like a true noble," said Forbes Driscoll, the captain of the guard. He'd been with Ritter's sisters but had made his way across at a more leisurely pace.

Driscoll wasn't a typical guardsman. He was a small man, with dirty, blond hair cropped closed to his head, and he was clean-shaven. Forbes was more of an uncle to Ritter than a captain. He had a big personality, which spilled over from time to time in ways that some nobles would frown upon. But in Valkeneer, it was welcomed.

When he saw Ritter, he'd smiled warmly and greeted him as an equal, even though Driscoll wasn't a noble. It was an egregious breach of formality, but Ritter didn't care.

"We can exchange pleasantries later," Driscoll said. "We have no time to change or to engage in idle banter. The princes await us in the great room."

"What about my troops?" Ritter asked, concerned that Driscoll's usual, casual manner sounded more urgent.

"They're dismissed," Driscoll replied, waving a hand carelessly at the returning Longmarchers.

Ritter's brow furrowed.

"Come with me please, Sir Ritter. You may bring your sisters."

Driscoll led them through the keep's vaulted double doors, which were flanked on both sides with guards from Castle Valkeneer and Castle Thronehelm.

The great room was directly on the other side of the doors, which opened into an expansive, sunken chamber. The grey, stone walls were adorned with the well-preserved pelts of the region's trophy game. The Valkeneer family ate with and amongst their servants and guards at several long feasting tables in the center of the room, so it didn't contain any of the usual thrones or accoutrement for nobles.

When he entered, Ritter released Storm and the war falcon took to the air, swooping gracefully through the chamber, away from Ritter's falconhand. Storm stretched his wings and circled the room, then flew over to his perch in the far corner near the stoked hearth. It was a spectacle the Valkeneers were used to, but the young princes and their cousins, as well as their entourage, found themselves watching the bird in awed fascination.

"Sir Ritter of Valkeneer," a familiar voice echoed through the chamber. Ritter's former instructor at Halifax Military Academy, Captain Leowin Shale, approached him. "Good to see you, son."

When the captain saw his former pupil, he embraced him before shaking his hand heartily. The Valkeneers watched the reunion while their guests stared at the falcon.

"I trust you had a productive journey, Ritter," Sir Hertzog Valkeneer said. He was the patriarch of the family and father to the young ranger and his two sisters. He looked the part of a frontier noble, with a wind-weathered face and a full head of greying hair. Hertzog's voice was calm but forceful with a distinctive tone.

"It was largely uneventful," Ritter replied with a shrug, adjusting his bow, which was slung across his back. "There was no trace of the bandits that the rumors spoke of."

"Then you'll be ready for some action," his father said. "You remember Prince Montgomery and Prince Everett Thorhauer, of course. And these are their cousins, Viscount Joferian and Viscount Talath Maeglen."

"It's nice to see you all again, my lords."

"Again?" murmured Joferian, just loudly enough for it to carry across to Ritter. It seemed that the visitors—or at least Joferian Maeglen—didn't remember him.

"We spent eight years as boys at Halifax Military Academy together," Ritter reminded them.

The Maeglens and the Thorhauers stared at Ritter, a cold vexation emanating from behind their eyes. Prince Everett looked as though he was about to say something he'd later regret, but he was interrupted by Captain Shale.

"I, for one, remember your exploits all too well," Shale interjected, a wry smile spreading slowly across his battleworn face. Shale had trained Ritter, who had always been the best scout in the academy.

"Young Ritter here took point on all of our training missions," Shale continued, directing his speech to the rest of the room instead of just his young protégé. "His performance in training is one of the reasons why we feel confident that he can track these brigands. Why, I remember one of our exercises when we played capture the flag. While the other cadets waded right into battle, Ritter used the melee as a diversion to sneak around the combat and pluck the enemy flag from right within their fort. It's the only time a cadet has ever captured the flag singlehandedly, and Ritter did it all without engaging in combat. Any man who can do that is fit for a brigand hunt in my book."

"Enough of this," Sir Hertzog huffed. "To business."

He turned to look at Ritter before continuing.

"Our visitors have asked us to help deal with Veldrin Nightcloak. News of his return to Ravenrood has reached Thronehelm, and he and his brigands are pillaging near the Dragon's Breath Mountains,"

Ritter's father explained. "They have need of you and what the Longmarchers can bring to the campaign."

For several minutes, Sir Hertzog Valkeneer shared tales of raids and marauding, sparing them none of the brutality. Ritter had known of some of the attacks before their most recent expedition, but more had followed since their departure.

"The Nightcloak has become bolder," Sir Hertzog explained. "The number of attacks has grown, and we believe their numbers have swelled in recent weeks like water flowing from a burst dam. The bandits have now been reported in three separate baronies: our barony of Queen's Chapel, Hunter's Manor to the south, and Foghaven Vale to the northeast. These are no ordinary highwaymen. They operate like a militia, which leads us to believe they're being led by an ex-military officer like the Cloak."

"I see," Ritter nodded.

"The truth is, in recent weeks, the brigands have hit a number of merchant and pilgrim caravans and are no longer just striking out at defenseless villages and towns in and around Ravenwood. They've even razed the settlements of Ralsweik and Vendal in the norsemen's Kingdom of Rijkstag."

"What would the king and the baroness have House Valkeneer do?" Ritter asked.

"Ravenwood is on our borders," Sir Hertzog said. "We have a duty to aid the barony and the capital. I need you to lead a scouting party with the princes and the viscounts. Find these raiders and put an end to this."

Ritter had concerns for the safety of the princes and their cousins as they showed off their shiny armor and well-oiled swords in the fall foliage and naked trees of Ravenwood. The princes had no idea what other enemies awaited them on the other side of the Bridge. He paused to think for a moment, knowing he could do nothing about it.

Finally, but with a palpable air of doubt, he said, "Of course, Father. The Longmarchers will heed the call."

LATER, WHEN THE REUNION was over, Ritter retired to his room. He was enjoying the solitude and thinking about the task that lay ahead of him, but his thoughts were interrupted by a knock at the heavy oak door.

"Enter," Ritter called.

The door opened and Prince Montgomery Thorhauer filed into the room. He was alone, which was unusual, and Ritter wondered where his brother was. As protocol dictated, Ritter snapped to attention, standing up and turning to face him.

"To what do I owe this surprise, my lord?" Ritter asked.

"I wanted to speak with you," Montgomery replied, closing the door behind him. "I sensed some reticence in you about our task. What troubles you?"

Ritter thought for a moment, parsing his words. "With respect my prince, the borderlands are unsafe at the best of times. It's not that I don't believe in your skills as swordsmen, I just don't want the sons of King Godwin to be in harm's way. This is something the Longmarchers can handle alone."

This was part of the truth, but not all of it. Deep down, Ritter also knew he didn't want to take on the responsibility of a mission that could shape history if one of the princes or viscounts were to die. But he also knew he had no choice.

Prince Montgomery seemed to see things a little differently. When Ritter voiced his concerns, Montgomery laughed at him.

"Apologies," Montgomery said. "I meant no disrespect either. Believe me when I say that my brother and I, as well as my cousins, can handle ourselves. Why so worried? Come, let's spend some time enjoying what comforts we can. We ride at dawn."

CHAPTER THREE

"Tetrine are rare and mythical beasts that resemble black horses with a horn on their heads and should be avoided at all costs, for they can only bring doom and despair."
—A Warminster Bestiary (Fourth Edition)

ADDILYN ELSPETH AWOKE FROM her light sleep to the distant sound of neighing horses. For a moment, the scarlet, high-reaching towers of her beloved homeland stood firm before her closed eyes, wavering and vanishing with the last of her dream. She'd never been away from home for this long before.

Her eyes opened, and after a moment she reached up to rub away the sleep, taking a long breath. She'd been so excited to go on this journey, to actually *see* the places and people her diplomat father dealt with on a daily basis, that it had never even occurred to her that she might feel homesick. But in truth, even that was a kind of comfort. In dreams, she could still hear the steady thrum of the ceremonial drums bidding her farewell, a sound she wouldn't hear again until they welcomed her home. She blinked as she remembered what had woken her up.

Horses?

It seemed impossible that another group of travelers might have chosen the same route. Maybe it was bandits. Tensing, Addilyn reached for the dagger she kept under her bedroll and glanced around the tent. Oddly, her retinue were all still asleep—even Eiyn, who should have been up by this hour for morning prayers, eager as he was to ensure them an auspicious journey. Once, he'd even woken Addilyn to pray with him, before being gently reminded by one of her two faithful maids that the princess was unused to life on the road and would need her sleep.

The sound came again and Addilyn jumped, shivering a little in the chill air. None of her companions stirred even slightly, and she felt a strange intuition that the guard on duty would also be asleep at her post outside.

Unsure what else to do, she got up slowly. This certainly didn't seem auspicious, but sometimes the blessings of the Ancients came in strange forms. Surely there had to be some reason why she was the only one to wake at the sound, some current of fate trying to sweep her along, whether for good or for ill. It was this thought alone that caused her to leave the tent.

There was the guard, Mir, asleep on her feet just as Addilyn had suspected. She'd be deeply ashamed to find that she'd slept through part of her shift, but Addilyn couldn't fault her.

The noise came again, closer this time—not from the direction of the road, as Addilyn had thought, but from the woods on the other side of the camp. She was even more convinced that something strange was afoot. The logical part of her brain, which was beginning to wake up, told her it was more likely to be travelers or merchants if it had come from the road. For one last moment, she hesitated.

Movement flashed in the corner of her eye and Addilyn glanced over at their white stallions, which were picketed not far from the tent. All of them were awake, it seemed, and had bowed their heads in the direction of the forest. It was an oddly familiar image, though not one she'd seen before. As she began moving past them toward the trees, Addilyn struggled to recall the source of the memory. It certainly wasn't bandits; bandits didn't have mages, and a mage wouldn't bother to put all the people to sleep while leaving the horses alone.

Everyone except me, she reminded herself. This was something else, something she *knew* if she could just—

A massive shape stood out in the darkness to her elven eyes. As she drew toward it, she saw there was more than one. It was a crowd of imposing black horses, each with a single horn, surrounded by a bizarre energy that practically screamed its presence to even her barely trained magical senses.

These creatures weren't supposed to exist. As a child, she'd been told all about the tetrine—that they were black unicorns, ten feet tall, that brought death with only a look. For centuries, they'd been thought to be a product of mere legend, and even those who didn't dismiss their existence as apocryphal held them to be so vanishingly rare that seeing just one was considered the worst of all possible omens.

And here was a herd of them, emerging from the woods at almost the same time, like a phalanx of soldiers marching to battle. They weren't quite ten feet tall, but they weren't far from it either. And one of them was looking right at her.

She hadn't died yet, so perhaps the legends weren't true.

Addilyn couldn't help being captivated by their beauty. The smoothness of their dark coats reflected the pallor of the moonlight. Their silky manes were thin and ink-colored, flowing across the canvases of their thoroughbred frames.

She stood motionless, half-transfixed and half-paralyzed, as one of the beasts moved slowly toward her. What did it even mean to see a herd of tetrine, instead of just one? What kind of omen could it be for one of them to approach her?

"What do you want?" The question slipped out of her mouth of its own accord, her voice halting and almost childlike, spoken instinctively in the highland dialect of the native tongue that she'd had to abandon when she'd gone to court at ten years old. She sometimes still dreamed in it, so perhaps it was appropriate. The tetrine paused, and Addilyn noted somewhere in the unfrozen back of her mind that it had two horns, not one.

The two of them simply stared at each other for a while, blinking, before Addilyn heard it in her mind: *"Lost fellow look bad help."*

She recoiled with a cry upon realizing that the thoughts floating to the edge of her consciousness weren't her own. The tetrine snorted and the presence in her mind suddenly withdrew, before gradually touching her consciousness again. Prepared for it this time, Addilyn was able to calm down and ascertain a vague sense that it meant her no harm. Its mind was cold and alien, unpleasant to encounter. But it occurred to her that her sentience must feel just as odd to the telepathic beast, and she thought it must have been in great need to try to communicate with her.

The tetrine seemed to be satisfied with her clear effort to relax, and after another moment a series of images began to flash through her head. They were unlike any she'd seen before, the colors blander and the faraway shapes blurrier through the tetrine's eyes, but she began to comprehend on a basic level what it was trying to show her.

She saw what looked like a human—a *man*—hooded and cloaked, coming into a clearing where a lone tetrine stood. He stumbled a little as if ill or weakened, and as he drew nearer to the tetrine, he raised his hands and incanted a spell that Addilyn didn't recognize. Instantly, a cloud of magic descended over the tetrine, seeming to lock it in place. She could feel the two-horned tetrine's terror through its memories of the event, which felt much less like human fear and much more like animalistic death throes. The loss of one individual struck the herd as though it was being chased by a deadly predator, although Addilyn was certain that no living animal preyed on the tetrine.

"Do you need my help?" Addilyn asked abruptly, in the high tongue this time, not trusting her clarity of thought enough to rely on telepathy. To her surprise, the tetrine gave no reply but simply turned and began walking back to its fellows.

"Why show me?" she went on, starting to feel a little panicked. "What do you want? What did that mean?" Tears of frustration blurred her vision, and when she blinked them away, the herd was gone.

By the Ancients, how was she going to explain this?

FOR THE REST OF the journey to Castleshire, which took another week and part of a second, Addilyn did her best to put the encounter out of her mind. She had no idea how to process what had happened and why. Part of her wanted to tell Eiyn, hoping that his holy orders might grant him some special insight into interpreting omens, but she didn't know him very well and even priests weren't to be trusted lightly. As it was, she spent the remainder of her time on the road in easy conversation with her associates, glad of the distraction provided by their company.

"I've never been outside of Eldwal before," Rasilyn, the younger of her two maids, said. "What's Castleshire like?"

Addilyn picked up on her meaning immediately. Of course, none of them had been to Castleshire before. Vermilion elves were rarely seen outside the borders of their ancestral home.

This was the opening salvo of Sa'el, a descendant of the conversational arts practiced by the upper classes that had been adapted by their servants into a kind of game. In its original form, it had been an exercise in the art of hospitality, built around elaborately complimenting a host in increasingly arcane ways. But this version tended to be more oriented around jokey attempts to sound knowledgeable on topics the speaker knew little about.

Some nobles of Addilyn's class would have taken it as mockery of a time-honored tradition, but Addilyn saw it for what it was—a simple and lighthearted diversion, intended for her benefit.

Apparently, she thought, with warm feelings toward her maid, *Rasilyn noticed my state of discomfort.*

"I hear it lies in the Aldredd Mountains, just off a deep lake," Eiyn put in, playing along a little clumsily. He was clearly unpracticed at the game, being a lower noble who'd spent most of his life among the clergy and not around servants. An easygoing sort, he seemed willing to give it a try.

"I hear it sits at the meeting of two generous rivers and that its spires shine like the sun," proclaimed Yala, the elder maiden.

"I hear its beauty steals the breath of princesses, and that its ruling body acts with a wisdom equaled only by that of the mighty Erud," Addilyn added, nearly ruining her round by laughing but just barely restraining herself. Her compatriots made a show of generously ignoring the slip-up.

"Is that any way for the ambassador's daughter to carry on the great art of Sa'el?" Rasilyn teased, turning around with a smile.

Addilyn bowed deeply and a little theatrically from her seat on the horse. "Most profoundly do I give apology to mine gracious host."

"That's enough, now," Yala said. "It's all in good fun, my lady, I know, but you oughtn't bow to us."

Addilyn grimaced slightly at that and then subsided, although she had to bite her lip to keep from grinning at Rasilyn, who was rolling her eyes behind Yala's back. She and her maidens had grown up together at her family home in the highlands, but Yala had always been far more conscientious about propriety than either Addilyn or Rasilyn, much to Yala's chagrin.

"Perhaps a short prayer to Nothos," Eiyn suggested earnestly, referring to the Ancient of Fortune, "to be sure that the appearance of disrespect doesn't taint the last steps of our journey."

Addilyn dearly wanted to refuse, exhausted as she was, but Eiyn had only been brought along in the first place to petition the Ancients. She didn't wish to offend Nothos by seeming ungrateful for his grace and good fortune.

"A beautiful idea," Addilyn replied instead. "Please do us the honor."

Eiyn smiled briefly at her and took a deep breath before beginning to sing in his pretty tenor. His voice was somewhat strained, from fatigue and the cold air, but it came through pure and clear over the sound of their horses' hooves on the dirt road.

Addilyn closed her eyes and listened to the melody of the prayer he'd chosen, which was so familiar she could have sung it backwards. It made her think of worshiping in the temple with her father as a little girl, the smell of scarlet mountain flowers filling the air and the sun rising outside, swaying a little on her feet from sleepiness but delighted to have the chance to show her devotion, knowing implicitly that her father was pleased with her. In her distraction, she was a little late to join in when the others began to sing the rote response, but she privately felt that Nothos wouldn't mind and sang along with all her heart anyway.

Just as their voices fell silent, the city finally came into view and Addilyn was unable to suppress an audible gasp.

Castleshire rose boldly in front of her, its towering spires glistening in the mild sunset of the autumn afternoon. She'd never seen its equal in size or beauty, as the capital dwarfed Eldwal by at least twentyfold. One hundred or more castles stared back at her, each unique in its design and each home to a different culture. At no time had she conceived the realm to be this big, this intimidating. And for all her studies and diplomatic practice, she now knew she had much to learn.

"Ah," Yala said lightly, "but it seems you were the victor after all, for the great city *does* steal the breath of princesses."

AS THEY ENTERED THE city, the party fell silent and observed as much as possible of their surroundings without appearing like a group of gawking tourists.

"Why do they shout so?" Rasilyn whispered to Addilyn, taking care to speak in their own language rather than Minsterian, the common language spoken across the whole of Warminster by nearly all races and cultures. "Are human ears deficient in some way?"

Addilyn looked at her reprovingly but only said, "They *are* rather loud."

All elves were blessed with sharper senses than humans, and thus they tended to be more easily disturbed than humans by noise, bright light, or confusing combinations of movement and color—all of which were present within the walls of the city.

"There's a tournament taking place today, my lady," Iolund, one of the guards, explained. "I doubt the city's atmosphere is always like this."

Rasilyn laughed at Addilyn. "The face you just made! Still such a warmonger. Just like every time one of our knights came to pay respects and you'd light up like a candle and badger him for stories until he begged for mercy."

"I'm no warmonger," Addilyn replied primly, trying to restrain her eagerness from reaching her face and aware that she was failing. "I simply have an appreciation for the noble art of combat."

"Don't throw such words around so lightly, Rasilyn," Yala advised. "Combat and war are two very different things."

Rasilyn rolled her eyes again, but Addilyn privately—and

perhaps a little self-servingly—felt that her other maiden had a point.

It wasn't long before the group reached the Vermilion embassy, where Addilyn's father, Dacre, served as ambassador. When they finally came to the stone doors graven with the royal insignia, Addilyn's exhaustion caught up to her all at once and she all but fell off her horse. The door attendant, a harried-looking little thing with spectacles and rather tragic-looking hair, rushed over.

"Lady Addilyn Elspeth?" she inquired, scrutinizing Addilyn like an illegibly written letter.

"As you see."

"You're the very image of your honored father," she said politely, "who, I'm sorry to inform you, isn't here. He asks you to meet with him at the Tournament of Colored Leaves."

"Thank you," Addilyn replied, concealing her mild exasperation. "I'll go on foot. While I'm meeting with him, the rest of my party will need to be quartered and given something to eat."

"You mustn't go alone, my lady," Yala said, sounding alarmed. "One such as yourself, in an unfamiliar city? We'll go with you." The rest of the party visibly wilted at this, if only slightly.

"I'll take Iolund or Mir with me," Addilyn conceded, and after a brief and silent communication between the two guards, Iolund came forward to accompany her.

They left Yala, Eiyn and Mir to rest and make sure the horses were seen to. The rest set off again shortly after, led by a young street urchin that the attendant paid to take them there. The boy, a smith's apprentice by his account, gave them a couple of curious glances but seemed otherwise unfazed by the arrival of an obviously noble-born and wealthy-looking foreigner.

After a somewhat confusing series of turns through the city's tumultuous streets, Addilyn passed at last through the gates of the festival. Her pace hastened as she pushed through the mass of partygoers, ignoring the sweaty merchants who were pitching everything from rum to rings. The crowd consisted of races from all over the realm, and not just Castleshire. Humans, elves, twergs, lardals, huldrefolk and others celebrated together, enjoying the safety of the city and the communal hope for a successful harvest.

She saw a line of flags waving over a more open area, the simple crimson banners of the Vermilion hanging over a grand tent that she knew must belong to her father. The central flag was marked with the heraldric crest of the Vermilion, a pattern with two vertical parallel lines, intersected diagonally by two thinner lines, the coat of arms of the Elspeth family. Bidding her companions wait outside, she took a breath and entered.

Her father wasn't in the tent, but someone else was.

A warrior was standing in the open area of the tent, her weapon flashing in her hands as she expertly went through a series of memorized drills, seemingly so focused on her practice that she failed to notice Addilyn's presence. Addilyn identified her as a Raven elf, short and dark-eyed where Addilyn was tall and fair, with a thin nose and jaw. Addilyn had no idea why this woman was here in place of her father, but she found herself entranced by the rhythmic movements of the drill and paused to admire the warrior's skill, despite her confusion.

It took another moment before the elf caught sight of her and quickly sheathed her sword, seeming taken aback. "My lady," she said with a bow, speaking clumsily in High Vermilion. "My apologies for my rudeness. Are you Princess Addilyn Elspeth?"

"I am," Addilyn replied with a smile, before switching to Ravenish, the language of the Raven elves. She guessed the warrior would be more comfortable with her own dialect. "But it appears you have me at a disadvantage, honored warrior. May I ask your name?"

The other hesitated briefly and then smiled back, seeming surprised at Addilyn's effort to accommodate her. "Jessamy Aberdeen, my lady," she replied, accompanying her introduction with another short bow. "I've been selected by your father to compete in this tournament to prove my worth."

"You certainly seem worthy to me," Addilyn complimented without thinking, and then she paused. "Prove your worth? For what purpose?"

Jessamy looked blank. "Why, to become your champion, of course," she replied, bluntly. For an instant, Addilyn wondered if she'd offended the other woman; she'd always found Raven elves hard to read compared to her own people. She had no opportunity to apologize, however, because another voice interrupted their conversation.

"I fear you've left my daughter speechless," Dacre Elspeth said from behind her. "The greatest and most cursed of rarities, for her voice is more beautiful than the songs of birds."

Addilyn whirled around, a huge smile coming over her face. "Father!"

"Hello, Addy," he said affectionately, and the two of them formally saluted each other in the proper style of highborn Vermilion before embracing.

Jessamy, watching the reunion, quickly bowed again and excused herself, citing her need to go and prepare for her next round in the tournament. Addilyn watched her leave the tent and caught a glimpse of Rasilyn's curious face outside before turning back to her father.

"Father, what did she mean, 'my champion'?"

"Just what she said, my dear," Dacre replied. His warm, red eyes, so like hers, twinkled. "But I suppose what you're really asking is *why* I decided to find a protector for you."

"Just so," Addilyn said, making a small face at his conversational fencing, which she knew was meant playfully but for which she was too tired.

He sighed, his expression turning more serious. "Well, I suppose it could be dismissed as a father's paranoia, my dear. You're of age, and sooner or later you'll end up taking my mantle as ambassador. Or, Melexis forbid, perhaps even inheriting the queenship, if something were to happen to both me and my sister."

Addilyn frowned at him, surprised. "You've never been worried about that before. I thought Coronelle Fia was going to outlive both of us, remember?"

Dacre smiled wanly. "Of course. I worry about you, that's all. I've felt of late that change is on the horizon, and I can't tell what its nature may be." He studied her, then reached out to smooth back her red hair. "I wished to be sure that whatever comes, you'll be looked after."

"Thank you, Father," she said after a long silence, her tone polite but a little stiff. She couldn't help feeling a mixture of affection at his concern and mild offense at the implied insult to her competence, but she knew he meant well and she didn't wish to appear ungrateful. His expression showed he'd picked up on her mixed feelings but was satisfied with her tacit agreement and didn't wish to pursue the matter further.

"Come," he said at length, "Jessamy's round will begin shortly, and I thought you'd enjoy watching her performance."

Dacre led the way out of the tent, passing her bowing attendants along with his personal guard, who all followed behind them at a discrete distance so as not to eavesdrop.

A fenced-off area had been set aside for the two of them, close enough to the tournament grounds to be able to see but far enough away that they wouldn't be hit by stray clumps of grass, mud, or blood. They settled in to watch as the proceedings began.

"Sir Danis of Castleshire," called the master of ceremonies, announcing Jessamy's opponent.

Danis was human, tall and wiry looking. He wielded a weapon known as a zweihander, a two-handed sword that lent itself to his frame and looked like it had seen a substantial amount of use. A moment or two later, Jessamy's name was called, and she strode out to meet him, her longsword shining brightly and looking small by comparison. The two combatants readied themselves, Jessamy appearing tense while the Castleshire native looked much more relaxed. Addilyn thought he might be trying to put her off her guard, but something told her that Jessamy wasn't one to be easily rattled.

"Father," Addilyn muttered, "on the topic of omens of change, there's something I need to tell you about."

Dacre glanced at her, startled, but as the combat on the field began, his gaze was quickly drawn back to the sudden movements of the two warriors.

"Yes?"

"On the journey to Castleshire..." She paused briefly. "There was an odd morning."

She winced a little as Sir Danis came close to drawing first blood, Jessamy narrowly avoiding a strike at her ribs.

"I woke up alone, very early, and everyone else was deeply asleep, as if in a trance."

Her father frowned, clearly feeling her retinue was somehow at fault for sleeping longer than they should have, but Addilyn cut him off before he could reply.

"It was magic," Addilyn said, "I'm sure of it, and you'll understand why when you hear what I have to say next."

"Very well," he conceded. "Go on."

Sir Danis had put some distance between himself and Jessamy, clearly meaning to rely on the longer reach of his weapon, but she successfully feinted to the side and closed the gap again to go for another strike. Addilyn was silent for a moment as she watched, but Sir Danis managed to dodge, and the action fell into another lull.

"I went outside my tent and toward the woods, away from the camp," she said. "I was following a noise that I kept hearing, the same one that woke me up. It sounded like horses, but these were no horses. They were tetrine."

From the corner of her eye, she saw him flinch. "Tetrine?" he said.

"Yes!" Addilyn shouted as Jessamy landed a strike, but the master of ceremonies denied her the win—incorrectly, in Addilyn's opinion. He motioned that the combat should continue. She glanced at her father, mildly abashed at his amused expression, and muttered, "Yes, it was. I'm sure of it."

"You said *they*," he replied with a questioning smile. "They're the rarest of creatures and yet you say you saw more than one?"

"There's something else," she added, looking back at Jessamy, who'd taken the unfair ruling in her stride and who looked to be sharpening her focus. "It spoke to me."

"Spoke?"

"Not *spoke*," she amended hurriedly. "Rather… communicated. Mind to mind."

She stopped for a moment, not sure how to proceed, and turned back to the melee. Jessamy circled her opponent, looking for an opening, and then lunged at Sir Danis and landed another clean—though shallow—strike. Before the master of ceremonies had the chance to make a ruling, Sir Danis bowed to her, obviously conceding the victory. Both Dacre and Addilyn began to clap loudly, soon followed by the rest of the onlookers, and Jessamy turned to salute the two of them with a slash of her sword followed by a deep bow.

"It seems you have a new champion, my daughter," Dacre commented, when the applause died down, his voice low. "And now, before we go and greet her, you'd better tell me everything you saw."

The two retreated to the friendly confines of the Vermilion tent to speak in private and await Jessamy's return. Dacre's deliberate pace concerned Addilyn, and his silence for the first few steps spoke volumes.

"Addy," Dacre started, gingerly, "I believe we should meet with Anselm Helenius, the great cryptid hunter. He hails from the human baronies of Warminster, near Thronehelm."

"What's he doing here, then?"

"The royals love to be regaled by his stories and to see his rare artifacts in person," Dacre replied. "Some here even offer silver cups full of gems and gold for certain trophies. He may be able to offer an interpretation of what you witnessed near Ravenwood. He knows the tetrine better than anyone in the realm."

Addilyn stared at her father, understanding and appreciating his concern for her and for what the portents might mean.

"What are you thinking about?" Dacre asked, faintly.

Addilyn stared at her father, their crimson gazes locking in a moment of silent lucidity. "I believe I might need a champion after all."

CHAPTER FOUR

"A Keeper shall keep no secrets."
—Edict of The Keepers of the Forbidden

DAEMUS HELD THE LANTERN high, his hands trembling in fear. The yellow flame flickered across the hard autumn ground, casting ominous shadows through the dark forest, their begging tendrils rolling out to him in a contemptuous invitation to enter.

Daemus felt the familiar grip of his prophetic nightmares taking control. He knew he was dreaming, but the ashen forest seemed real. The lump of fear in his throat swelled as his widened eyes searched desperately for the evil that surely lurked within. Yet all he could see were the deadened branches of the naked trees surrounding and taunting him.

The wind moaned through the hollow with the spectral voice of a haunting spirit while grey branches chattered together like nervous teeth in the tortuous melody of a *danse macabre*. His mind swirled incomprehensibly, trying to separate prophecy from beguiling dream, but terror raced through his mind in untimed explosions of panic. The young seer struggled to remain calm, his chilled breath escaping into the biting air in long wisps of mist.

"It's just a vision," he repeated to himself as he closed his eyes. "It's just a vision."

After a moment, he forced his eyes to open and took several involuntary steps forward, crunching through the dead leaves that spiraled at his feet. He didn't want to enter, but his feet moved anyway. They were numb—not from the cold, but from the abject dread of what awaited within.

The light from his lantern barely forced the retreat of the

foreboding darkness, the blackness waiting impatiently for the flame to die so that it could swallow him in its murky grip.

Daemus couldn't stop himself. His mind cried out to him to turn and run, but his body continued edging forward into the bowels of the forest. With a few more excruciating steps, he crossed the edge of the woods and found his lanternlight diminishing subtly, its radiance muted to but a few feet in front of him.

The ghostly constriction of the forest wrapped itself around his throat, making it hard to breathe. He looked up, hoping to find solace in the open night skies, but the horizon was obscured by a blackened canopy of twisted trees.

He shuddered through three more steps, then forced himself to take a few more. He reached a clearing in the woods, where he stumbled onto a broken path. The swaying lantern-light cast darting shadows along its clearing, crookedly curling between the husks of bowed timber.

Daemus stood silent. He waited, but nothing emerged.

As the young Keeper pulled himself together, he heard the unmistakable snapping of broken boughs underfoot. He knew he was no longer alone.

Before he could see it, the presence of evil groped at his shoulder. Gathering his courage, he turned toward the sound. An abomination of a creature stepped from the shadows a mere thirty paces from him. The horrific beast stood nearly twice his height, or so it seemed.

It rose on two crooked hind legs, reminiscent of a deformed goat. The monster possessed a naked grey torso of a once-human form, with corded muscles scarred with the wounds of a thousand battles. The creature's head took the form of a mutated bull skull with deer-like antlers protruding like wings from the bone, its gaping, eyeless sockets staring down the dark path at Daemus. It stood in silence, its gaze meeting that of the fledgling Keeper.

Daemus's jaw sank. He didn't want to move, but he knew he needed to. Pulses of adrenaline rushed through his veins as he watched the antlered man draw a wispy cold breath into its broken maw, a clue that this creature was somehow alive.

The two stared at each other, man against beast, for mere seconds, but they felt like minutes to Daemus. Then the creature snorted in anger, its breath forming a cone of mist. The massive fiend turned, its muscles rippling in the weakened flickers of the lanternlight.

Daemus could wait no longer. He had to move. Mustering energy from every fiber of his being, he ran for the clearing, dropping his lantern in his haste. The vessel cracked upon the hardened ground, setting off a brief flash of light that revealed the way out.

Daemus seized the moment, hoping that the light might blind the creature, and sprinted through the ensnaring arms of the forest, ignoring the cuts and scrapes he suffered as he stumbled through.

Glancing back, Daemus saw the creature snap to the hunt. Its first steps were those of a humanoid running on its cloven hooves, but after a short stretch, it fell to a stride on all fours, digging its claws into the ground. The abomination seemed undeterred, gaining on Daemus with every loping stride.

Daemus could hear the ghastly grunting of the creature as it clawed its way toward him. He looked ahead to the clearing just a few strides away, leading back from where his night-marish vision had started. Just one more anguished step and he'd be free…he hoped.

As the young Keeper crossed the treeline back into the moonlit field, he emerged violently from his prophetic vision—a vision like no other he'd ever had.

Falling to the ground from his bed as though in midstride, he could still feel the stings of the thorny branches that had cut through his cloak. His breathing raced, matching his heartbeat as his desperate eyes searched the confines of his lonely room for the antlered man.

Daemus swore he could still smell the odorous beast, his nostrils stinging from the creature's breath, a rank mixture of bile and copper.

As he gathered his senses and tried to recover, he noticed that the cuts weren't a manifestation of his imagination. The slashes from the trees had left open wounds across his face and arms, their marks swelling and lifting the healthy skin around them.

He sat for a moment, his breath calming, his wits gathering. A lone tear tracked slowly from the corner of his eye, mixing with his blood. He slumped to the floor. His hands balanced him, and he tucked his legs beneath his defeated body. He whimpered in silence, fighting back the urge to scream for help.

This wasn't a prophecy. Nor was it a vision. It was a warning. That was the last thought that passed through his mind before the darkness took him.

DAEMUS WOKE TO FIND himself in the cathedral's infirmary. It was a dingy place, hidden under one of the great spires in the Cathedral of the Watchful Eye. There was no natural light as there were no windows underground, and so Daemus didn't know if it was day or night. He was the only patient, surrounded by a host of deacons.

These attendants weren't Keepers but were instead attached to a different sect of priests that were known as the Divine

Protectorate of Erud. The deacons didn't have the Sight like Daemus and the other Keepers, and they were more a group of pious believers in Erudian law and edicts.

"Ah!" one of the deacons exclaimed. "You're awake!"

Daemus groaned and started to sit up in his bed, but he was quickly pushed back down into place.

"Wait," the deacon said. "First, drink some water."

Daemus accepted the proffered chalice gratefully and drank deeply, like a man who'd just wandered out of the desert.

"And how do you feel after your night terrors?"

"Exhausted." Daemus took a moment to gather his thoughts before gauging how much to tell his caregiver. "I had the strangest dream, but I feel much better now. I think I just need some air."

"Well, there's plenty of that, young man." He examined Daemus once again. "I suppose, if you're sure..."

"I'm sure," Daemus replied firmly. He picked himself up and swung his legs off the bed and onto the floor. Then he stood up and raced away from the infirmary before anyone had a change of heart and tried to stop him.

He had just enough time to swing by his chambers to collect his books before it was time to go to class. His roommate, Caspar, had already left, and Precept Radu had just started the day's lesson when Daemus poked his head sheepishly into the classroom.

"Late again, Low Keeper?" Radu teased. "Take your seat, please."

"Yes, Precept."

Precept Radu was a grizzled old man, pushing eighty in years but acting like a man half that age. He was middling in height for a human, with a lined countenance and a wisp of grey hair that blew aimlessly from side to side as he turned this way and that during his lessons. Daemus sometimes daydreamed of sneaking up on him and snipping it away, but he accepted it as part of his charm. The precept conducted lessons in the ways he'd learned over half a century ago, quick to embarrass pupils for careless answers and just as quick to wake sleeping students with a whack of his quarterstaff.

The day's lesson was a dull one, dedicated to the virtues of the arts of rhabdomancy, pyromancy, and horoscopy, and how the Low Keepers needed to learn each art in their quest for Erudian knowledge.

When Daemus had said he was tired, he'd meant it. His eyes wanted to close of their own accord, and his mind was too busy turning over his out-of-body experience to focus on the lesson, as quickly became apparent.

"Daemus," Precept Radu barked, interrupting him from his daydreams. "In which of the great tracking constellations can the figure of the Ancient of Death, Threnody, be found?"

"Uh…" he mumbled, stalling poorly for time. His mind was blank. He couldn't think of *any* of the constellations, never mind the one that represented the Ancient of Death.

"The answer is Memento Mori," the precept scolded, a brief annoyance flashing across his features. This subject was a passion of his, a passion he shared with the Great Keeper, who studied the stars from the top of the cathedral every night, scanning for clues from Erud in star charts by practicing the magics of astromancy. "The Ancient of Death has four sons. If all four ride together in this constellation, what does it mean?"

"I… I don't know, Precept," Daemus muttered, all too aware of the eyes of the room upon him.

"It means that an apocalyptic event is coming," Precept Radu replied. "You seem unusually distracted today, Daemus. I'd like you to stay behind after class."

Daemus was so lost in his thoughts that he didn't notice

that the lesson was over until the rest of the students had filtered out and Radu had placed a gentle hand on his shoulder.

"Now then, Low Keeper," the precept began, "something's troubling you. What is it?"

"It's..." Daemus began, faced again with the decision of just how much he ought to share. But Radu had always been a good teacher and a trusted advisor, so Daemus decided to go with the truth, or at least as much of the truth as he could wrap his head around. He told Radu about the visions that he'd been having and how their hangovers had followed him into the daytime, when the light of the sun ought to have dispelled the last vestiges of superstition.

"You can't hide from your visions," Radu said. "That's why you're here in the first place. You're here to learn how to interpret and control your oneiromancy. The Sight is a gift from Erud, and you should never hide the gift of knowledge from anyone, especially the Great Keeper."

"I know. And yet, I thought—"

"I know what you thought, son," Radu interrupted. "Remember, Daemus, that sometimes a Keeper's vision is recorded in *The Tome of Enlightenment*. The Tome is our living bible, our record of all of the knowledge bestowed upon us by Erud."

"Yes," Daemus agreed. "The Tome was a gift from Erud to the Keepers of the Forbidden. It was to be used for interpreting the visions that Erud grants. That's why we're called the Keepers. We're the Keepers of visions, the forbidden knowledge to those unworthy or incapable of its interpretation."

"Good." Radu smiled proudly at his young protégé. "Perhaps you've been listening in my lessons after all."

Then his face changed and Precept Radu looked serious again. He applied a little pressure to Daemus's shoulder and said, "As a Keeper of the Forbidden, you have a duty to share your visions. That's especially true when they're as potent as these night terrors that you've been having."

"I've never had visions like these before," Daemus confided. "Most of my visions are of things that come to pass almost immediately."

"Then perhaps Erud's wisdom has provided you with a different type of vision," Radu surmised. "As you grow and mature, you'll learn how to refine your abilities. Remember, Daemus, the wisdom of Erud comes to us from many sources and not just one. That's why we study the stars, the seasons, and the harvests. It's why we use dice, bones, and playing cards."

"I understand."

"If your visions were recorded in the Tome," Radu concluded, "the Great Keeper will see it anyway. Please return to your quarters and await further commands."

"And what will you do?"

"I'm sorry, Daemus," Radu said, "I'm duty bound to report this to Nasyr, the Great Keeper."

AS EVENING APPROACHED, DACRE and Addilyn left their tents and made their way through the streets of Castleshire. They quickly arrived at their destination, a tavern called the Brimming Flagon. It was one that Helenius had recommended, and of course, Helenius was late.

Dacre ordered some food and wine from a friendly barmaid and sipped his glass impatiently. Before long, they heard a commotion at the door as the great cryptid hunter strode in. Cheers from patrons and the bar alike greeted Anselm Helenius, and he returned their cheers by removing his cavalier hat and waving it in appreciation.

Addilyn could tell by the look in Dacre's eyes that this

was their man, and she watched Helenius scan the bar for her father before making his way toward them.

Helenius was a handsome, middle-aged human with a charismatic smile and thick black hair that matched the color of his hat. The gin blossoms on his cheeks suggested that this wasn't his first bar of the evening, and likely not his last. As he arrived at the table, he took a deep bow.

"A thousand apologies for my tardiness." Anselm snapped back to attention with a careless wink. "My previous engagement ran… long."

Dacre looked at the man, but before he could introduce Addilyn, Helenius had already reached for her hand and gently kissed it.

"You must be Princess Addilyn Elspeth," Helenius said. "Allow me to introduce myself. My name is—"

"Anselm Helenius," Addilyn interrupted. "I heard you arrive. It seems you have quite the following."

Helenius offered another respectful bow, pointedly agreeing with her. Then he placed his hat on a peg in the wall and sat down with them. Addilyn couldn't help noticing the snow-white plume decorating its brim.

Before she could ask, Helenius explained, "It's a feather from a rare bird called a caladrius. They're believed to have the power to steal sickness from the ill."

Addilyn smiled at the thought.

"The wealthy often hire me to capture them from the wild," Helenius boasted. "They like to keep them, just in case their powers are ever needed."

"Do they truly possess such abilities?" Addilyn asked, her voice tinged with an almost childlike wonder.

Helenius just smiled politely and didn't answer, turning the conversation back to Dacre and the real reason for their dinner.

"I'm curious, my lady," Helenius began. "Your father has told me of your encounter with a two-horned tetrine in the Dragon's Breath Mountains. I've never heard of such a beast. It must have been frightening."

"On the contrary," Addilyn replied, "the creature was rather gentle, as was the herd that followed her."

"Ah," Helenius murmured, his eyes narrowing at the thought of it. "How many were there? Twenty? Fifty? A hundred?"

"I couldn't tell," Addilyn replied. "Their numbers were camouflaged by the darkness, but there must have been at least two dozen or so."

"Hmm." There was something in the way he said it that spoke volumes about the hunter's disbelief. She scowled across the table at him.

"I have no reason to invent such an encounter," Addilyn blurted in a moment of disgust. "If there's one man in the entire realm who should believe the word of a Vermilion princess, it's the renowned cryptid hunter himself. But perhaps I was laboring under the misconception that a man who deals in the rare would take me at my word."

Helenius raised his hands to calm the elf and shot an awkward glance at Dacre, his benefactor.

"I meant no disrespect, my lady, but understand that I've spent my entire life dedicated to such animals. In no field, no bestiary, no song and no folk tale has it ever been mentioned that—"

"That a two-horned tetrine exists?"

"Well... yes," Helenius said, sitting back in his seat. "If you're correct and this creature does exist, your sighting may be the first to ever be recorded, at least until now. Not only that but you had a *conversation* with it."

Addilyn sat back in her chair, her smile gone. But then she noticed a sparkle in Helenius's eyes.

"But if you *have* seen her," Helenius added, "then what a find." He paused for dramatic effect, a move he was clearly fond of. "I'll help you to discover the truth of this matter. But for your own safety, understand that these creatures rarely bring welcome news. I'm glad that you've sought my advice."

"What will you do?" Addilyn asked.

"I have a friend here in Castleshire," Helenius said. "A wizard of sorts. He may be able to point us in the right direction. He's also close to some in Abacus who might have answers. With your father's support, I pledge to solve this mystery and to uncover what it means for you and the realm."

"When shall we meet again?" Dacre asked, unused to being left out of any conversation. "We travel to warn King Godwin at sunrise."

"Give me one cycle of the moon and you'll have your answers," Helenius said. "And if I need to travel to Abacus?"

Dacre read the man's tone and quickly produced a small purse with additional palmettes, a form of gold coins that were struck at the mint in King's Well. Helenius smiled.

"If you return to Castleshire and find me gone," the great hunter said, "look to the Boiling Beaker in Abacus. I stay with an alchemist there from time to time. He goes by the name of Jeric Tuttle."

The three stood from their table and clinked their glasses.

"To the discovery of new things," Helenius toasted.

"And to the protection of those we love," Dacre added.

CHAPTER FIVE

*"As silent as a graveyard, ye who walks
within Ghostwood truly walks alone."*
—Abbott Chytil of the Wendelin Abbey

RITTER WAS ALONE IN his room, killing time by pacing from one end to the other in the hope that it would encourage the dawn to come. When the pacing became too much for him, he paused to wash his face in the basin before glancing at his reflection in the mirror.

Sir Ritter had long, raven-colored hair just like his mother's, and his ears, not as pronounced as a true Raven elf's, still protruded pointedly through his sable hair. His coal-colored eyes, a gift of his mother's heritage, matched his pale gaze. The image he saw in the mirror reminded him that neither title nor deed could scrub away his ancestry. He was trollborn and had a mixed bloodline that he couldn't escape. Yet he was a Valkeneer of the Bridge, and his blood connected his human and elven families to the benefit of both realms.

There was a knock on the door. As it swung open, the candlelight from the room spilled out into the corridor, illuminating an apparition in white. It was Lady Amandaris Dakari, Ritter's mother. She wore casual garments, and her raven hair was pulled away from her elven face by a silver garland, revealing her half-smile. Even though she was older than her husband, she looked no older than her son Ritter, as elves of all kinds aged more slowly than humans.

"I heard that you avoided dinner," Amandaris said.

"It's good to see you again, Mother," Ritter said. "But you know as well as I do that I have an early departure in the morning."

"And I assume you've spent the entire evening pacing back and forth, alone in your quarters?" Amandaris smiled. "I won't have you leading an expedition if you haven't been eating. Here, I've brought you something."

She placed a small tray on Ritter's table, lifted the cover, and raised her eyes to catch her son's expression. Ritter walked over to look at it and whistled appreciatively.

"Einlauf soup." Ritter rubbed his hands together and flashed a greedy smile. "You know me all too well. Thank you."

"Eat up. You'll need your strength." Lady Amandaris watched her son for a moment, a look of intense concentration on her face, and then she walked over and sat down beside him. "What's on your mind, my son?"

"It's the princes," he replied, his sentences short and to the point and sputtered out between spoonfuls of the soup. "I'm worried about their safety in the wilds of Ravenwood. I know they've trained well and led many sweeps for trollborn intruders in Halifax, but this is much more dangerous than when we were at the academy. I'm not sure they should put themselves in harm's way."

"They're aware of the dangers they'll face on the road," Amandaris replied. "And my guess is the king wants them to quell this trouble themselves. It will be their first test and a laurel of their own if they succeed. Besides, you'll be there to guide them."

"Indeed," Ritter said, doing a poor job of disguising the gloom in his voice. He scraped up the last of the soup with a hunk of bread. "I'm glad that they came to us for help. Quite frankly, I'm honored. It's just…"

"Just what?"

"I knew them back in Halifax," Ritter continued. "I know what they're like. They'll be more of a burden than a helping hand. Yes, they're trained well in the art of the sword and shield, and they've fought on an open battlefield. But if we're hunting brigands who know how to work in Ravenwood, their inexperience in these types of campaigns may prove deadly to my troops."

"What would you have them do instead?" Lady Amandaris asked. "Remember, you knew them as boys, not as men."

"I'd leave them here for their own safety," Ritter said. "And I'd go out myself with the Longmarchers and Captain Shale."

Lady Amandaris laughed a little, trying to take some of the tension out of the room. "Son, you know the paths of Ravenwood as well as anyone, including my kinsfolk. For a young man, you possess the maturity of a man twice your age."

"You're blinded by your love for me," Ritter joked.

"Perhaps." Lady Amandaris paused for a moment as though trying to decide whether to say something. Ritter, engrossed by the hunk of soupy bread in his hands, barely noticed.

"I want you to come with me in the morning," she said at length. "I have to show you something that may help. We leave under the cover of darkness and return before your departure at dawn. We can sneak out of the keep and be back before anyone knows we're gone."

"That sounds unsettling." Ritter finished off the bread, pushed the bowl away from him, and grunted. "For what purpose?"

"Just meet me. You know the way?"

"Mother, can't you just—"

"Shh," Amandaris interrupted, pausing to look fondly at her son. Then she subtly changed the subject. "I wish you didn't hide your ears with that hair of yours."

"If I possess the maturity of a man twice my age, then why do you still mother me?"

Lady Amandaris smiled. "A mother's job is never done. Get some sleep, Ritter, then make use of the old tunnels to leave the castle. I'll meet you at the third hour of the pendulum clock, outside the gates on the other side of the bridge."

"Why can't we leave our own castle through the front doors?" Ritter asked.

"Trust me, this is the way it has to be." Amandaris rose, ending any debate.

"Fine," Ritter said. "It's as you wish. I'll meet you outside the gates as you requested. But first, may I ask a favor of my own?"

"You may."

Ritter grinned and pointed at the bowl. "Can you fetch me another bowl of soup?"

IT WAS STILL DARK when Storm woke Ritter by nuzzling against his cheek. The only light in his modest chamber drifted in from the moon and stars through the little window that looked out on the Bridge and Ravenwood beyond. It was a crisp, clear night.

Ritter had prepared his gear the night before, and it only took him a couple of minutes to dress himself and to don his lightweight armor. He covered his long black hair with a forest green cloak and strapped his sword to his belt before shouldering his quiver and picking up his bow.

His breath steamed up in front of him in the cold castle corridors. Ritter skulked from his room down a spiral stair-case at the back of the keep, looking around often to make sure that he hadn't been spotted. Convinced he was alone, he descended even deeper into the bowels of the castle and passed through a servant's corridor that was usually used for receiving supplies.

Ritter felt blindly along the ledge of the hallway until his fingers uncovered the outline of one of the old tunnels, a concealed passage that was known only to the Valkeneer family and their most trusted servants. He quickly but quietly removed the false door, which consisted of a small wooden panel covered with a skin of stone. He slipped nimbly into the secret passage, replaced the panel, and proceeded in a near crawl along the escape route.

Ritter cursed to himself. He'd remembered the tunnels as being wider than they were, the way they'd seemed when he and his sisters had used the labyrinth to play hide-and-seek. Occasionally, when the boredom grew too great, they'd used them to scare the wits out of unsuspecting castle staff.

Even in the darkness of the tunnel, Ritter's sharp eyes could pick up on the heat left behind by other recent footfalls. That meant his mother must have beaten him to it and used the same tunnel. He smiled and shook his head until his scalp scraped the top of the passageway, stopping him for a second. The castle was having the last laugh.

Finding his way outside, he carefully scaled the rocky terrace on the side of the castle, sticking close to the walls to remain undetected by the castle guards in the towers above.

His mother was waiting for him just outside the gates, as she'd promised. They greeted each other silently with the traditional Valkeneer shorthand known as Whispquick, the swift, unspoken sign language of the elves she'd taught her children when they were younger.

The path into the woods was overgrown and poorly lit, but Amandaris refused to illuminate their way until they were far enough from the castle for them to risk it. They held their silence until just before dawn, when they arrived at a mysterious reach of Ravenwood. The forest here was frozen in time, locked in the deathly grey of an unnatural petrification. The trees stood in stasis, never aging and yet never living. Their bark had an ashen hue, and the voice of the forest was mute.

Amandaris made her way quietly through the labyrinth of crooked trunks, leaving Ritter with the impression that she was familiar with the territory. After they reached the crest of a small hill, they came to a clearing, where a sunken pool of calm water rested.

"Sit down, Ritter," Amandaris said.

"What, here?"

"Yes." She motioned with her eyes and Ritter found an uncomfortable and fossilized tree stump on which to rest.

"Why have you brought me here?" Ritter asked. His mind wandered away from her as he absorbed the unsettling surroundings.

Amandaris paused for a moment with her back toward him. She stared into the distance.

"Before you were born," she said, her back still facing her son, "there was a great battle here. It was a magical battle, and the side effects of the conjured magic drew the natural energy from the soil and the roots of the trees. As you can see, it petrified this portion of the forest."

"I've never seen anything like it."

"From that day forward," his mother continued, "this copse of trees was called the Ashen Hollows, so named because of the color of the wood. Your cousins, the Raven elves, call it *Wealdaemon*. In the Ravenish tongue, that means 'Ghostwood,' which is the name that's used by the common folk of Valkeneer."

"That's the name I've heard." Ritter looked uneasily around at the petrified trees. "Are the tales true?"

"It depends which tales," Amandaris said. She sighed deeply and turned around to look at her son. "Powerful magic leaves a scar. They say that those who tarry too long in Ghostwood can hear the haunting echoes of the distant battle and are sometimes driven mad by it."

Ritter knew this from experience, as he himself had found feebleminded victims wandering in the woods during his Longmarcher sweeps. He'd escorted them to the stone confines of Wendelin Abbey, where Valkeneer's local abbots care for them.

"Why have you brought me to this horrible place?" Ritter asked, hoping to avoid hearing the voices of the dead.

"Close your eyes, Ritter."

"My eyes?"

"Yes, my son," she replied. "Close them."

Ritter complied.

"Now open your senses," Amandaris continued. "Reach out and feel the magic. If you concentrate hard enough, you can hear the distant voices of the ghosts speaking to us."

Ritter wasn't a sorcerer, unlike his mother, but her blood still flowed within him and he'd possessed a touch of magic from an early age. He did as she asked of him, feeling a little foolish as he did so.

"You have many of the same powers I do, my son," Amandaris said, her voice washing over Ritter like a bubbling mountain stream, refreshing him and helping him to focus his mind on the task at hand, despite the early hour. "That's why you have your special connection with Storm, and perhaps why Aerendaris attracts so many stray animals."

"Like Aliester," Ritter murmured. He shook his head dazedly and turned to look at his mother. "I felt... something. And I sense something, too. This isn't why you brought me here."

Amandaris grimaced and walked over to place a hand on her son's shoulder.

"I can't lie to you, Ritter," she said. "And nor would I want to. I brought you here because I have a gift for you."

"A gift?"

"Close your eyes again," Amandaris said.

Ritter complied and waited, listening to the rustling susurrus of movement. Half a minute passed.

"You can open them now."

Ritter opened his eyes and looked at the bow that his mother was holding out to him. She must have been hiding it beneath her cloak. He marveled at the weapon's beauty, drinking it in like a man dying of thirst. He knew that bow, as did all the Longmarchers. It was the Valkeneer family heirloom, a longbow hewn of ghostwood that his father had used in battle to protect Valkeneer and Warminster from the horrors of Ravenwood and the borderlands.

"You're giving me Silencer?" Ritter asked. The bow had earned its moniker. When an arrow was loosed from it, it projected no noise, a trait it may have inherited from the petrified wood itself. Others say that it earned its name by silencing the enemies of the land.

"Use it well, my son," Amandaris replied. "I know you've always longed to possess it."

"This gift is too much," Ritter said, shunting the bow in her direction. "I'm not ready for this, and nor do I deserve it."

"No," his mother replied, this time with a more forceful voice than Ritter was used to hearing from her. She rejected the bow and left him holding it out to her, like a war priest making an offering to Koss, the Ancient of War. "It's your time. You must take Silencer and bear it in battle. You must carry on the tradition of your father."

"I'm not worthy of such an honor."

"You are in my eyes." Amandaris retreated a few steps, her gaze lifting again as she spoke. "You're as ready as your father was when he fought in the Battle of the Bridge nearly twenty years ago. I fell in love with him in that battle. It made a hero of him, just as this mission will make a hero of you."

Ritter had heard tales of his father's exploits at the Battle of the Bridge for as long as he could remember. The battle itself had happened before he was born, had perhaps even been responsible for his conception. Many of the region's trollborn and humanoid tribes had banded together under the leadership of a half-giant king named Balthi the Brutal. When it became clear that they intended to attack the Bridge, Ritter's father had created an alliance with the Raven elves to stop the marauders and to maintain peace in the region. It was through this alliance that he'd met Amandaris.

The campaign culminated in a climactic last stand at the Bridge, where the castle's defenders tricked the tribesmen into filtering across the narrow bridge in near single file, gathering them into a vulnerable mass that was caught between the walls of the keep and the ambushing might of the Raven and Vermilion elves, who were perched amongst the branches of the trees and raining arrows down on their adversaries. Hertzog Valkeneer had fought most valiantly of all, and had used Silencer, the ghostwood bow, to slay Balthi, the half-giant. At the battle's denouement, his mighty body had been sent tumbling into the rapids below.

It was during this stressful time that Amandaris had fallen in love with Hertzog, and as tales of his battlefield exploits had spread, her heart had opened up to the young noble, especially at the feasts when he'd wooed her with his thoughtful words and his unfazed demeanor. Shortly after the Battle of the Bridge, Hertzog had asked the king coronel of the Raven elves for his daughter's hand in marriage.

"Yes," Amandaris said. "I can see from your eyes that you understand the significance of the gift you've been given. When your father and I were married, we sealed a union between our people. You, Ritter, are the fruit of that union.

You're a Valkeneer, and it's your familial honor and duty to carry this bow into battle."

She leaned forward and kissed him on the cheek, then added, "Make us proud, my son."

Ritter said nothing. He simply stared at the bow in the silence, appreciating its beauty as his mother watched the sunrise. Ritter hefted the bow, feeling the relic's reassuring weight in his hands. He held it up to his ears and then twanged the bowstring, seeing how silent it really was.

He wondered what stories he could possibly add to an artifact with such a rich history. And he had a feeling that he wouldn't have long to wait before he found out.

THE SUN HAD RISEN by the time Ritter and Amandaris returned to their quarters in the Bridge by the same secret passages that had served them earlier that night. They felt certain that they hadn't been missed.

Ritter washed his face and cleaned his boots to remove any trace of the forest, then headed out into the courtyard to meet the princes. They'd risen with the dawn and were ready to ride alongside the Longmarchers. To Ritter's surprise, the princes had forsaken their gaudy armor and instead donned studded leather, fashioned in the colors of Ravenwood. Their retinue had done the same, and Ritter had a difficult time telling them apart from the Longmarchers.

"Ah, Ritter," Montgomery said lazily, turning his attention away from the massing entourage. "Glad you could make it."

"Did you have to get permission to ride?" Everett added.

Ritter winced inwardly but gritted his teeth and bit his tongue. Decorum and decency demanded that he be respectful of the princes' titles, if not their abilities. As much as he would have liked to have openly scoffed at them, he chose the path he'd taken many times before at Halifax when dealing with those of high birth. He ignored them and turned to his family instead.

"May your arrows fly true," Hertzog waved, speaking on behalf of the family as a whole.

"Goodbye," Ritter said simply, making eye contact with his sisters first, followed by his father. "May Nothos, the Ancient of Good Fortune, watch over you in the coming days and weeks. Until we meet again."

CHAPTER SIX

"Crimson flags borne on horses of white,
see them ride, ye children of light."
—The Ballad of Eldwal

ADDILYN WAS DOING HER best to contain her nerves. Years of etiquette training had steeled them so that little emotion ever showed on her face without her allowing it, but anxiety still had the power to cloud her thoughts and push her into making errors. Now more than ever before in her life, it seemed as though mistakes were something that she and her people could ill afford.

She stirred from her thoughts when her wing of Vermilion rounded a hill and she stared at the human city of Thronehelm for the first time. Even from a distance, she needed to tilt her head to capture the full majesty of Castle Thronehelm, which crowned a bluff in the center of the city.

Addilyn rode at the front of the Vermilion wing, galloping alongside Dacre. Their delegation consisted of seventeen Vermilion, as was their tradition. She trailed just behind her two bannermen, positions given to the bravest of the Vermilion soldiers, whose crimson sigils waved proudly as they rode.

They crossed the threshold of the city under an ivory-colored arch, atop which stood a marble statue of the human mage, Warminster, his arms raised to the Hall of the Ancients above them. As they slowed their gallop, she took note of a group of marble shields that lay at his feet, each bearing the coat of arms of one of the baronies of their kingdom.

The stone walls of Castle Thronehelm, far more visibly weathered and worn than any structure in Eldwal, loomed in front of her. Addilyn half-expected to notice patches of repaired stonework like on the walls of Castleshire, but it occurred to her suddenly that perhaps no assailant had ever gotten so far as to lay siege to the castle walls. She closed her eyes briefly, trying again to steady herself, and reminded herself that King Godwin of Thronehelm wasn't an enemy to their people, and nor was he likely to become one.

"Calm yourself, daughter," her father warned from his place by her side. It appeared that he'd noticed her discomfort, and Addilyn chastized herself for being so unsubtle. "It won't do to show any weakness. Remember, we're here for a purpose beyond mere diplomacy."

"I know, Father," she replied, lowering her eyes and taking a deep breath. He was correct, of course. Instead of thinking about the court of nobles they were soon to meet, she tried focusing on her body, taking a tally of her senses as though marking items off a list. The ache in her feet and legs. The smell of the horses. The dull white glow of the overcast sky. It worked, a little. "Will they listen, do you think?" Addilyn asked, quietly.

"What's more important is that we listen to them," he said under his breath. "Eyes and ears. Pay attention to the spoken as well as the unspoken. If they don't have ears to hear what we have to say, it's their prerogative and it will potentially be their downfall, but this meeting is as significant for us as it is for them. How they respond will determine what we do."

Addilyn didn't know how to feel about that, though she nodded in acknowledgement of her father's advice. It had long been Vermilion thinking that the issues of other nations and other peoples weren't their direct concern. She understood why, of course. For such an ancient culture, they had limited resources and had suffered badly from their interference in world affairs in the distant past. But no one had ever been able to give her a satisfying answer whenever she pointed out that both in nature and in society, things tended to be interdependent. If the king and his court failed to believe them and make preparations for whatever was coming, she privately thought it likely that the Vermilion would end up suffering from that decision right alongside the humans.

Their entry into the castle passed in a blur, and before she knew it, she was in the throne room, standing next to her father before a group of richly dressed humans and bowing with a version of the customary Vermilion salute that was reserved for greeting foreigners. Her head tilted graciously to one side, her eyes never leaving those on the dais, and she bent subtly at the waist with her right arm raised in greeting.

Many of the humans were staring at them, rudely in her opinion, and a spiteful part of her brain told her that they weren't quite well-bred enough to realize what they were doing. Or perhaps they were just stupid and didn't recognize what their behavior communicated: ignorance. Quite a natural and understandable phenomenon in the privacy of one's own mind, but the greatest of sins when displayed publicly among her people.

"My most gracious greetings to you all," said the one in the middle, whom Addilyn identified as the king from the golden band around his head. He didn't rise from his seated position, but a brief glance at her father showed no sign of offense. Their own queen coronelle followed several rituals intended to show respect to her subjects from her position as a public servant, but perhaps humans conceptualized their relationship to monarchs differently. She suppressed an urge to judge this way of thinking, reminding herself that as a diplomat, she had to maintain at the very least the appearance of impartiality.

"I'm Dacre Elspeth, ambassador of the Vermilion," Dacre said, clearly intending on following Vermilion conventions of decorum to the letter, even if his opposite wasn't doing the same. "It's an honor to be in your presence, King, and may your reign continue until the stars fall from the sky,"

The king surprised Addilyn with a sudden and wry smile that appeared to be genuine. "No, Ambassador, the honor is ours," he said. "We'd like to know the purpose of your visit, but perhaps that can wait until further introductions have been made." He glanced at Addilyn, who knew herself to be visibly young for a personage of her station, with an expression of mild interest.

Dacre inclined his head. "Of course. Allow me to introduce Addilyn Elspeth, my heir and successor, present here as observer and interlocutor."

Addilyn bowed again, and added in turn, "And I introduce to you, King, Jessamy Aberdeen, my protector and champion, present here as observer." It was Vermilion convention to specify the social station of those present, as well as the capacity in which they were there. The highest-ranked individual was given the authority to speak unconditionally. Interlocutors would typically speak when spoken to, and observers were expected to remain silent due to their presence being in either an educational or a professional capacity, rather than a diplomatic one.

"Well met," the king said, the smile falling away into a more serious expression. "This is Amice, my queen," he added, gesturing to a gentle-eyed woman who appeared disinterested in the proceedings but who wore an expression of calm politeness. "Baron Dragich Von Lormarck of Foghaven Vale," he continued, pointing to a broad-shouldered man with enough battle scars on his face and hands to match the most experienced of soldiers. Baroness Cecily Maeglen of Queen's Chapel was next, a woman with the same light hair and fine features as the queen, and therefore probably a relative. Godwin finished with, "And Master Zendel Cray of Hunter's Manor," indicating a fleshy-looking man whose eyes darted nervously around the room as though he thought one of its spare and wavering shadows might contain an assassin.

Addilyn waited another instant, puzzled that he hadn't elaborated on their relative stations and their reasons for being there, but no further explanation came. She thought she remembered that baron was the rank just below viscount (certainly far below a king), but she wasn't sure about master.

As the introductions ended, the lower-ranking Vermilion and the servants—Yala, Rasilyn and Eiyn among them, none of them having been assigned a place in the forthcoming discussion— filed out of the room. Those of Godwin's people who hadn't been introduced began to follow them after a moment, recognizing that the conversation was important and not for their ears. One watery-eyed little man lingered at the exit, however, and at a nod from the king, he closed the door and remained inside.

Here, Addilyn knew, was where the real task of diplomacy began. The room was cold, and she stopped herself shifting her feet in search of warmth, registering reflexively that any display of discomfort could be seen as an affront to the king and queen's hospitality.

"So," said the king at length, his tone more informal. "Tell me, Vermilion, why have you come?"

Jessamy fidgeted visibly at this address, clearly put off by his lack of deference. Among other elves, Vermilion had the most honored station and were often seen not only as a higher caste but as some degree of holy. Addilyn, not wishing to test her bodyguard's patience, signaled for her to step away from the conversation. With a slight incline of her head that served as a minute bow, Jessamy did so.

Meanwhile, Dacre came straight to the point. "I have news of the tetrine."

Addilyn looked at him in surprise before she could stop herself, then lowered her gaze; she'd never heard him be so direct, except when speaking to her or another family member in private. No one else noticed her reaction, however, because the effect on the rest of the room was both visible and immediate. All the humans, even the queen, came abruptly to attention and stared at Dacre in utter disbelief and what looked almost like anger.

"What news can there be of legends?" Master Cray asked, his voice quiet. As he finished speaking, his eyes darted to Addilyn as if he'd already worked out why she was there. Addilyn met his gaze blankly, refusing to show any response.

"Legends, indeed," Dacre agreed. "But legend always has a root in truth, does it not?"

"Does it?" Baroness Maeglen muttered, still looking skeptical.

King Godwin raised a hand to silence her. Von Lormarck still hadn't spoken, instead staring intently between Dacre and Addilyn in much the same way that Cray had.

"So it may be said," the king replied. "Continue."

Addilyn stepped forward, and everyone but Dacre looked at her in surprise. "It's my account, and I'll give it," she said. Cray raised an eyebrow.

"Are we really to stand and listen to the fairy-stories of a child?" Von Lormarck asked in a resonant, accented bass. "How is this news?"

"Silence," the king said flatly, but his eyes flashed and Addilyn noticed that Von Lormarck was barely bothering to hide an expression of offense. "We'll hear her speak before passing judgment."

Addilyn inclined her head to him and took a deep breath. "I was traveling to meet my father with my party and stopped to make camp a little way from the road. I woke in the night to an odd noise, like the sound of many horses, but there was no one else on the road."

"If it was dark, how do you know there was no one on the road?" Von Lormarck interrupted, looking almost bored.

Addilyn didn't react at all, except to revise her explanation. "The sound wasn't coming from the road," she clarified. "It was coming from the woods in the opposite direction, on the other side of the camp. I noticed that my retinue was all still asleep but that our horses were awake and bowing toward the woods."

She paused briefly for effect, hoping they'd remember the tales they'd heard about tetrines and their servant-horses, the way she had.

"And then I saw the tetrine. A score of them at least, perhaps more—" Master Cray was trying to interrupt her now, but she didn't stop talking to listen, instead raising her voice. "—and one of them had two horns."

At that, the room descended into a contained chaos. The king was sitting silent, the queen looking at him and the three elves observing impassively, but all three of the other humans were loudly arguing and talking over each other, once or twice also jabbing their fingers rudely in Addilyn's direction.

"Crowley," the king said, and the nobles all fell silent at his voice. Addilyn realized after an instant that he was addressing the single human servant who'd remained in the room. "Fetch the First Keeper." He looked grave. Addilyn heard the door close behind her as the servant departed.

"Nonsense and superstition," Von Lormarck snarled.

"Be quiet, Baron," Queen Amice snapped, speaking for the first time. To Addilyn's relief, the baron listened and closed his mouth, although he still glared at the floor in obvious consternation.

After nearly ten minutes of tense silence, the servant returned, accompanied by a tall human man with flat black eyes and grey hair. The king's frown deepened; the servant looked shaken.

"The First Keeper is dead, sire," Crowley said in a thin, reedy voice. "I found him in his study, so I called for Baron Von Lormarck's Keeper to examine the body." He gestured to his companion.

Godwin was on his feet in an instant, and Addilyn reeled back a little at the suddenness of his movement.

"*What?*"

"It's true, sire," the other man added. "A shock, to be sure, but it appears to have been natural causes."

"What kind of natural causes?" Maeglen inquired. She was beginning to look a little ill.

"Apoplexy of the brain, by my reckoning," the Keeper said, stoically. No one questioned this judgment, aware as they all were that Keepers received medical training alongside their mastery of the Sight. "It would have been quick."

"Is there any possibility..." Cray began, then stopped for a long moment before continuing. Addilyn suddenly had a horrible feeling that she knew what he was going to say. "Is there any possibility that his abilities affected his brain? That perhaps he saw something that shocked him so much..."

There it was. She hadn't known how to interpret the tetrine sighting, and in truth she still didn't. But if it was true that a First Keeper had *died* from experiencing a similarly extreme omen at around the same time, it seemed impossible that the meaning hadn't been catastrophically bad. Addilyn had never even heard of such a thing happening, at least not in her lifetime.

"I can't say for certain." The Keeper hesitated and glanced at Von Lormarck, who hadn't spoken but who looked almost apoplectic himself. "But yes, it's a possibility."

"Guesswork serves no purpose now," Godwin said, sharply. "What's your name, Keeper?"

The man bowed. "Jhodever, my liege."

"Jhodever, have you seen anything of the tetrine? In recent weeks or months?"

Jhodever looked at Von Lormarck again, and then back to the king, shaking his head slowly. "No, sire. Erud has never provided me with any such vision. And perhaps fortunately so if my fellow's death is anything to judge by." Addilyn's eyebrows rose at the man's impertinence, but then again, he was probably right.

"We must send word to the Cathedral of the Watchful Eye," Godwin declared to no one in particular, "and ask for guidance."

"And a new First Keeper," his wife murmured, her expression pained and her eyes unfocused. "Samuels was a good man."

The king glanced at her, looking as though he shared her sorrow. "Until we hear from the cathedral, perhaps Baron Von Lormarck would be willing to lend his Keeper's services to the crown."

The baron, though still stone-faced, bowed low. "For my part, sire, I'd have you take him into your permanent service. In this moment, the crown has far more need of a Keeper than I do."

Although she'd privately decided that she didn't like the man, Addilyn found herself re-evaluating him. Vermilion didn't have Keepers, as their doctrines held the direct petitioning of Erud for knowledge to be a mild form of blasphemy, but Addilyn still understood what a major display of devotion and fealty this was for a human. Nobles tended to hold on to their Keepers for dear life, as the seers took years to train and often as long to replace if something went wrong. For all his undiplomatic behavior and harsh personality, Von Lormarck seemed genuinely loyal to the throne, if not to its current occupant.

Godwin appeared equally surprised. "Your generosity won't be forgotten, Baron, but that won't be necessary." He gestured to dismiss the room.

Addilyn felt a hand at her elbow, which she knew to be Jessamy's, and she allowed her protector to walk her out of the room with her father following a few steps behind.

In bed that night, she lay awake thinking of the dead man. How his eyes must have been wide in death, open to receive Erud's portents of the future. How Erud must have known, all-knowing as they were, that the man wouldn't survive his final vision. And why, when they might have both received the same omen, she'd been the one to live and he'd been the one to die.

CHAPTER SEVEN

"To see the heavens, you must climb to the heavens."
—Erudian Proverb

DAEMUS WAS STANDING IN his cloister with Caspar. A palpable but invisible remnant of his nightmare persisted, making the small chamber claustrophobic. The two of them had been trying to lighten the mood, joking around about Precept Radu, poking fun at the old teacher and his idiosyncratic approach to classroom discipline, when they were silenced by the arrival of a messenger.

"Daemus Alaric?" the messenger asked, consulting a document and trying to decipher the spidery handwriting that specified the addressee.

Daemus peered awkwardly at the messenger. "What is it?"

"I don't know," the messenger replied. "I'm not privy to the contents."

Daemus took the note from the man, and before either Daemus or Caspar had time to ask another question, he withdrew from the cloister and left them alone again.

The note was written on a stamped, faded scroll. The seal was nearly white, a similar color to Daemus's eyes, and depicted an open tome.

"That's the seal of the Great Keeper," Caspar gasped, his voice simultaneously awestruck and impressed. "Daemus, what have you done? The Great Keeper doesn't send letters to just anyone, especially in her own hand."

Caspar unintentionally stepped back from Daemus and the scroll.

"I'm not sure," Daemus replied, nervously tossing his unkempt hair from his face.

He swallowed hard and cracked the seal gently, apprehensively. He unraveled the parchment and read quickly through it before starting again at the beginning and taking it a little more slowly.

"Well?" Caspar asked.

Daemus swallowed again and explained, "I've been summoned to appear in front of the Great Keeper. I'm to meet her in the Cathedral of the Watchful Eye, in the observatory on the top floor."

"The observatory," Caspar whispered, dreamily. "I've never seen the observatory."

"I haven't even been past the second floor," Daemus replied. "Let alone all the way to the top."

"They say that you can see all of Solemnity from the observatory," Caspar said.

"I should hope so." Daemus stood and hid the scroll in the folds of his cloak. "Otherwise, why would you climb all thirty-six floors?"

"I could go with you if you'd like." Caspar was trying to play it cool, but he'd never been a good actor and Daemus knew him too well for a falsehood to slip past him.

Daemus smiled sadly at his friend but shook his head. "I'm sorry, Caspar. I know how much you long to see the observatory, but this letter can only mean one thing. Precept Radu told the Great Keeper of my dreams. I don't want my own ill fortune to pass on to you. No, no. It's better that you stay here."

"If you're sure."

Saying nothing more and with a heavy heart, he embraced his friend and then picked the letter back up again before slipping it into a pocket of his tunic. Then he sheepishly departed the cloister and began what felt like the longest walk of his young life.

As he descended the stairs, he wondered what punishment awaited him. Usually, it meant brushing and cleaning up after the stable of hippogryphs that the Knights of the Maelstrom kept as their steeds, a chore that left the unfortunate attendant smelling like dung for a week.

Hippogryphs were rare beasts that possessed the wings, head, and taloned foreclaws of a giant eagle and the hindparts of a powerful Vilchor plainshorse. They made an effective cavalry for the protectorate's knights, affording them a unique weapon that could both fly and charge into battle. The knights had maintained the unusual stable since the time of Erud's departure to the Hall of the Ancients. From what Daemus had been taught, the "gryphs" had gravitated to their order and the first Great Keeper, Quehm, had allowed their kind to stay in what would later become the village of Solemnity. *Majestic beasts, no doubt*, Daemus thought, *but smelly nonetheless.*

As Daemus dragged his unwilling feet across the campus, he saw members of each of the different sects—the Deacons, the Knights, the Disciples and the Keepers. All Keepers wore some form of white, though the Knights wore theirs on their armor and adorning their surcoats.

To Daemus, it seemed as though they were all looking at him, and what started out as insecurity quickly developed into full-blown paranoia. His mind was reeling with thoughts and questions that spiraled out of control. He was plagued with questions. *Does everyone know what happened? Why are they looking at me like that? Is it my mind playing tricks on me? And why was I summoned to see the Great Keeper?*

As far as Daemus knew, the Great Keeper had never sent for a Keeper of such a low rank. It just didn't happen. The very idea was laughable, like finding a Vermilion elf living in the slums of Thronehelm and eking out a living as a street performer. It seemed more likely that the sun would fall from the sky and do cartwheels as it ran naked along the street.

Daemus approached the cathedral, which stood tall in stark contrast to the great valley in which it sat. Its towering spire reached thirty-six stories into the heavens. He continued his shameful walk to the cathedral's entrance and in through its huge double doors. Slowly, one step after another, he climbed the cathedral's steep floors and made his way into the observatory. The cathedral had been gifted an elevator by the engineers of the scholar city of Abacus, but Daemus's robes marked him as being from a low level—far too low to use the contraption.

Daemus had long been looking forward to seeing the observatory, if only to see whether the tales were true. The stories said that it was filled with wondrous artifacts collected from across the realm. Some were magical, like their great scrying mirrors and their crystal balls. Others were new innovations that were designed to help the Keepers in the pursuit of Erudian knowledge, such as the astrolabes, star charts, and the one-of-a-kind telescope from the sages of Abacus, which was mounted in the observatory.

As he approached the entryway, he peered into the room, hoping that it lived up to the way he'd imagined it. To his amazement, it did and much more.

The sanctum stood open in front of the young Keeper, his wandering gaze immediately alighting upon a small dais in the heart of the octagonal room on which stood a white pedestal hewn from a large tree stump cut flat on its top. *The Tome of Enlightenment* lay atop the ancient trunk, its open pages glowing with the sacred scriptures of the sect. The only time that the light didn't emanate from the book was when the Great Keeper closed the Tome to better look for signs amongst the stars.

Daemus felt the warm radiance emanating from the Tome's light even from twenty paces. The relic's mere presence calmed Daemus and, for a brief moment, his anxiety abandoned him. Then he heard a soft voice pulling him away from the Tome and back to the matters at hand.

There were two figures waiting for him, and Daemus recognized them both immediately. The first was Amoss, the First Keeper of the Cathedral of the Watchful Eye, a man who appeared to be in his later years, with a wispy handlebar moustache and a trimmed goatee. His eyes were deep set and kind but marked by his advanced years. He wore the white surcoat of the Keepers, though it was trimmed in a gold that resembled the glow of the Tome.

Nasyr, the Great Keeper, stood but two feet from Amoss, whose gaze was nearly as unforgettable as the Tome. A little over five feet tall, she had the dark skin that was common amongst the people of the distant Phontu River Basin. Her hair was naturally straight and of a rich coffee color, her eyes deep hazel, an unnatural color for someone of her heritage. Daemus guessed that she was twice his age, or perhaps a little older. She too wore the white of the Keepers, but her robe was adorned with a graceful brooch in the shape of the seal of her station.

Finding it hard to ignore the *Tome*, Daemus followed her voice and slowly emerged into the observatory that he and Caspar had waxed poetic about just minutes ago. He stood at the apex of the cathedral, looking at the many stargazing instruments that were assembled under its dome.

When Daemus had first arrived in the observatory, First Keeper Amoss and Great Keeper Nasyr were both using a device that he'd heard of in classes and recognized from the illustrations in his textbooks. Now that he was standing at the base of the telescope, he realized that the pictures he'd seen in class paled in comparison to the instrument itself.

It stood angularly, supported by a wooden harness system, projecting nearly two stories to the opened ceiling. The giant apparatus was surrounded by other mechanical contraptions, not only to support it but also to move it from point to point in the night sky. The center of the mechanism was cylindrical, made of polished wood, and the width of at least four barrels.

"Ah, you must be Daemus," Great Keeper Nasyr said. "Your eyes give you away. I see that you received my summons. I expect you're wondering why you're here."

Daemus nodded and again scraped his hair from his face, though he said nothing, his voice momentarily deserting him.

"Precept Radu came to see me," she continued. "He told me about your powers of oneiromancy. He tells me that the accuracy of your dreams rivals that of our most trained seers. He also spoke of the nightmares you've been having. I've summoned you here to tell us what you've seen. This is important, Daemus. This isn't a time for silence, so please provide me with as many details as you can."

It was a request Daemus had been expecting but dreading. Every time he repeated his visions, it felt as though he was being dragged back into them and forced to relive every horrific second.

At first, the story came out of him in dribs and drabs, but the Great Keeper was kind and encouraging and after a while, Daemus grew in confidence, recounting his stories more fluently. He went into as much detail as he could, going back to those very first visions of over a month ago and telling the two powerful Keepers about the blind man that kept visiting him in his dreams.

"I thought the blind man was coming for me," Daemus concluded. "But now I realize that perhaps I was wrong. I don't think he was even aware of me until I screamed. I think he was reaching for something else."

"Like what?" First Keeper Amoss asked.

"I don't know," Daemus replied, apologetically. "Something behind me."

"What did the man do when he noticed you?"

"He laughed," Daemus said, shivering at the memory. "And then he said that he was glad I was finally coming for him. He knew my *name*, Great Keeper."

The Great Keeper turned away from Daemus and met the eyes of First Keeper Amoss. Though both stayed silent, an unspoken conversation passed between them. Then Nasyr turned back to look at Daemus.

"The man in your visions," the Great Keeper said. "We know of him. He was a former First Keeper of the Cathedral, a man named Graytorris. Surely you've heard of the tragedy of Graytorris, the fallen Keeper?"

"I'm afraid not, Great Keeper," Daemus said.

"What do they teach you in those lessons, boy?" Nasyr grumbled. "No, no, don't trouble yourself with an answer. There was a time when Graytorris was the First Keeper of the Cathedral. He was in line to one day become the Great Keeper. But then he made a fateful decision and violated one of the critical tenets of Erudian Law by trying to use *The Tome of Enlightenment* to see his own future. When he did, the Ancient of Knowledge punished him by taking his Sight."

Nasyr paused for effect. "You understand what I'm talking about, don't you, Daemus?"

"His physical sight or his Erudian Sight?"

"Both," the Great Keeper said, her expression grim. "That's why you saw him with bloodied rags covering his face. His eyes will bleed perpetually until the day he dies."

The Great Keeper paused for a moment, examining Daemus's face as though deciding whether to continue. She looked across at Amoss and caught his eye again, then quickly looked away.

"I came to find Graytorris on that fateful night in the observatory and scolded him for his hubris. Then I placed the Tome back on the altar as he rolled on the floor, howling in anguish with his hands over his eyes as though he was trying to stop the blood from flowing. I obeyed the will of Erud and excommunicated him for his sins. The Knights of the Maelstrom removed him from the cathedral and marched him through the courtyard below for all to see."

"A truly sad day," First Keeper Amoss murmured.

Daemus, meanwhile, watched the Great Keeper with rapt attention.

"The story doesn't finish there," she continued. "The next day, when I prayed and examined the Tome for guidance, I discovered that the life and story of Graytorris had been removed by Erud entirely, as though he never existed. Ever since that day, no member of our order has been able to scry upon him."

"What became of him?" Daemus asked.

"I wish I knew," the Great Keeper replied. Her voice was soft but sorrowful, forlorn and full of regret. "I dispatched the Knights of the Maelstrom, along with several Keepers and Disciples of the Watch. I hoped that Graytorris would retire gently, but knowing his temperament, I feared the worst. I was right to be worried. When they caught up with him not far from Solemnity, he worked his magic and escaped. The spell was successful, but it came at a cost. The magic transported Graytorris and the pursuing Keepers to a faraway forest, where they battled him. Many of the Protectorate's brothers and sisters were killed, and just when it looked like the battle had been won, Graytorris used a final spell that drained the nearby forest of its energy, petrifying the area around them. The spell's effects killed nearly all of our followers."

Nasyr paused for a moment to catch her breath before continuing, "One of the survivors was the captain of the Maelstrom Knights," she continued. "A man named Rhron Talamare. Rhron wasn't so lucky as to perish. Instead, he was cursed by the spell and transformed into the beast you know from your dreams. The one you described to Precept Radu as the Antlered Man. From what we know, Graytorris fled with the eyes of the cursed Rhron Talamare leading him away, disappearing into another portal and leaving no way for us to further pursue him. The only survivor of that great battle, the one who lived to tell the tale, was your precept, young Daemus. It was Radu."

Daemus stood in silence, absorbing the tale and starting to piece together the puzzle that was his dreams.

"But what does all this have to do with me?" Daemus asked.

The Great Keeper leaned toward him and placed a hand on his arm. "Daemus," she said, "your vision is the first time anyone has seen or heard from Graytorris since his excommunication nearly two decades ago, either in visions or in person."

She took her hand and turned away from him, staring distantly into the hearth. It was as though some mental barrier had risen between them.

"You shouldn't have withheld this information, Daemus," she said, plainly. "I can't even begin to explain how serious this is. As a Keeper, you're duty bound to share your visions, especially visions as potent and significant as these."

Daemus held his tongue for a few tense moments and then muttered the Keeper's edict. "A Keeper shall keep no secrets."

Nasyr raised her head from the fire and turned to Daemus,

repeating the verse with a grim tone. "That's correct, my son. A Keeper shall keep no secrets."

"I know, Great Keeper," Daemus said, "but I had no idea that—"

"Please, Daemus, stop talking," Nasyr ordered. "I'm sorry, but your actions have left me with no choice. I appreciate your candor tonight and thank you for eventually confiding in me. Unfortunately, my hands are tied. First Keeper Amoss agrees. Whether you knew it or not, you put the cathedral in danger. If Graytorris has returned, you've cost us a month in which we could have been searching for him or making provisions for his return. I don't doubt that you have a good heart, but by withholding these visions, you've shown yourself to be untrustworthy. Pack your bags and prepare to leave, Daemus. You have no home here anymore."

CHAPTER EIGHT

*"We who guard the Bridge hold the light
that guides from the dark of despair."*
—Longmarcher motto

FIRA'S EYES BURNED AS SHE blinked against the smoke. Her father's weight was heavy against her shoulder, and her small frame could barely support both him and the pack she carried for them. "Da," she whispered, not daring to speak any louder. "Da, come on, please. We've got to move. I can't carry you."

Her father, Silas, shuddered and took some more of his own weight onto his legs. "I'm sorry, Flower."

His voice was thin with pain, and Fira suppressed her growing panic, glancing at the arrow that still sprouted from his shoulder. He'd ordered her not to remove it and was keeping his hand pressed to the wound, but it was still bleeding through his fingers at an alarming rate. The two of them stumbled onwards, Fira focusing on placing one foot in front of the other and breathing in and out, trying not to cough as the fire spread into the woods. Knowing the bandits who'd burned their village to the ground could easily have followed them, she didn't dare to look back.

Silas was being too loud, the twelve-year-old thought, his shambling footsteps crackling through the leaves as his strength continued to wane. But there was nothing to be done about that; she wouldn't leave him.

"I'm thinking about Ma," she said in the same soft tone, barely audible over the noise of their passage. "How she would have fought them." Her mother had been a shepherdess and had been used to driving away wolves with a sling.

Silas gave a watery-sounding chuckle. "I know she would have killed at least t-two," he agreed, and then coughed. "She would never have let me forget it… once we got away."

Fira's vision blurred with tears. She wished her mother was there, helping her to bear her father's weight. She knew if it had been the three of them, they could have escaped much more quickly and quietly, instead of narrowly avoiding death. Although even her mother couldn't have saved all the townsfolk, who'd likely all died either facing the bandits or in the fires. Fira closed her eyes against the pain of her grief, then remembered to open them before she tripped over something and fell to the forest floor. There was no time for heartache.

The smoke was lessening now, and she began to feel they might be away from the danger. She didn't know how the fire had failed to spread deeper into the woods, but perhaps the bandits had brought a mage. There had been one man among them who'd stood out to her, his face pale and terrible with hatred, but she had no eye for magic.

"Da," she began, a little louder now as her fear ebbed, "do you think—"

Before she could finish speaking, Silas's weight slid from her shoulder and, though she scrambled to try to catch him, he crashed to the ground. The fear surged back, and Fira dropped the pack and fell to her knees, calling his name and shaking him, hoping she wasn't making his injury worse. After another horrible moment, his eyes flickered open. She noted in despair that his face was paler than she'd ever seen it, his skin waxen and sweating. He'd always been a thin and sad-faced man, but she'd never seen him look weak.

When he spoke, however, his voice was firm. "Fira," he said, "go."

"What?" she cried, and then she clapped her hands over

her mouth, whirling to look over her shoulder for bandits. None appeared.

"You have to go," he repeated. "I don't think I can make it any farther."

"No, no," the girl insisted, her dirty hands scrubbing at her eyes. "If I leave you, you'll die!" Her face had scrunched up and tears were running down her cheeks. "You'll die," she said again, thinking against reason that he didn't understand.

"Flower," Silas said, his voice now feeble, "whether I live or die is out of your control. If you stay right here with me, and we're both caught when the bandits come deeper into the forest, we'll both die."

Fira shook her head, and without words, she clung to his hand so tightly it turned white.

"I'll try to keep myself alive," he promised, "but you have to find help. Go." He flexed his hand against her grip, and with a weak push at her elbow whispered, "Now!"

Unable to stop sobbing, although she knew the noise could give her away, Fira picked herself up. She moved the pack nearer to her father, unwilling to force herself to take it, and then set off at a slow, bone-jarring, exhausted run.

The hours and miles passed in a blur. Without quite knowing how, Fira found herself sitting down and being handed a bowl of something. She ate, but she hardly tasted it. When she'd finished, she looked up into the faces of her rescuers, a group of traveling bards with kind smiles. Fira told them of her plight and passed some more hours in silence, trying to decide what to do as they went about their business. She couldn't ask a group of musicians, without a warrior among them, for help with bandits, but it was impossible to convince herself to leave her father to die.

It wasn't much longer before the answer to her unspoken

prayers arrived: a company of warriors led by three young men. The smallest of them, who had eyes older than his years, spoke briefly with the bards and then approached her.

"Hello, miss," he said, and she liked that he didn't stare or force a smile. "What's your name?"

She told him.

"Well, Fira Carling, we're seeking a group of bandits that have been troubling this area. Can you tell us anything?"

"They attacked our village just this morning," she said. "My father and I had just reached Emberlyn when they—" The corners of her mouth turned downwards. "Can you help my father? He's hurt bad, and he'll die if he doesn't get help. He made me leave him."

The young man's expression betrayed nothing. "How many were there?"

Fira's gaze fell to the ground as she forced herself to think. "I'm not sure. I think more than fifty, though we were too scared and too busy running away to take a count." She met the man's eyes. "I think they have a mage, too, but I'm not sure. They stopped the fire somehow, after it had already reached the woods."

His eyebrows drew together and he hummed in thought. "That's helpful to know. Thank you, Fira. Is there anything else about them that stood out to you?"

"One of 'em was tall and wore a cloak covered in stars," she remembered, her tone flat. "He was ugly. And he had a scar." She mimed its position on her own face.

"Veldrin Nightcloak," one of the other young men said loudly, and Fira jumped a little. "I'd bet my sword it's him. He's been a thorn in my family's side since I was a boy."

"Will you save my father?" Fira asked again, hearing a tremor in her own voice. "Please?"

There was a long silence. "We'll do what we can," the man who'd asked her the questions said at last. "For now, go and take refuge at the Bridge." He pulled an odd ring from his finger and handed it to her. Fira held it, knowing it to be much too large for one of her own small fingers. "Give that to one of my sisters, Lady Aerendaris or Lady Tishara. It's a signet ring and holds my family crest. When they see this, they'll look after you."

Without further fanfare, the company moved on, leaving Fira alone again with the group of musicians.

"Not to worry, dear," a grey-haired woman said. She'd introduced herself as their flautist, but Fira didn't remember her name. "We'll take you to the Bridge."

"It's out of our way," the boy with the drum argued, but the older woman shot him a glare and he fell silent.

"Thank you," Fira said in a quiet voice, taking a closer look at the ring as the bards readied themselves to begin traveling again. It was fashioned from silver and bore an image of what looked like two squat towers connected by a line. Gripping it in a closed fist like a talisman until it started to hurt her hand, Fira said a prayer for her father, the first of many that she'd make during her journey to the Bridge.

VELDRIN NIGHTCLOAK AND HIS brigands surrounded the ruins of what was once the village of Emberlyn. The familiar smell of carnage overwhelmed his senses, a mixture of smoky embers, the char of burnt horsehair and the distinct copper tang of blood.

To his right, a farmer's wagon lay on its side, its wheels spinning lazily in the air. To his left, another wagon had been grounded by a score of flaming arrows that had set its tarp ablaze and killed both its drivers and horses. In front of him, the village burned.

Veldrin flipped his greying ponytail over his shoulder and rubbed his bearded jaw. The sight was enough for even the dreaded Nightcloak to crack a smile. His bandits had killed the townsfolk and taken no prisoners, just as he'd ordered. They were pillaging their way through the remaining houses of Emberlyn, robbing them of any lingering treasures.

One of his men, a hatchet-faced human named Bassarab approached him. Bassarab sheathed his weapon in deference to the Nightcloak's suspicious nature.

"What are our orders, sir?" the man lisped through the gap in his teeth.

"Are there any survivors?" Veldrin asked, while wiping the blood from his sword on a dead man's tunic.

"No, sir," the man said. "Our men are the only ones alive."

"Our losses?"

"We lost three," Bassarab said. "The same number are injured."

"Acceptable losses." Veldrin met Bassarab's gaze. "And what of the merchant caravan?"

At the sound of a distant neigh, Veldrin and Bassarab both turned toward the commotion. Down the road, Veldrin could see the telltale haze of horses' hooves in the dust. The merchants they'd come for were making a run for it.

"Ride with haste and follow the fleeing merchants to the north. Cut them off when you can and bring them to me. If they resist, kill them. There shall be no escape."

CHAPTER NINE

"May Erud grant you wisdom on your journeys."
—Traditional Keeper farewell

DAEMUS DID SOMETHING THAT none of them had expected, him least of all. He fell to the floor and started crying.

Great Keeper Nasyr and First Keeper Amoss exchanged an uncomfortable look with each other, and then the Great Keeper smiled sadly and waved her hand in the air. Daemus looked up at her, confused, and then followed her gaze, which was fixed upon a spot somewhere behind him.

There was movement, and the three were joined near the giant telescope by a fourth man, who was dressed in the regal garments of Castleshire, his silken shirt dirty from the road. His cloak was adorned with a badge of the Alaric family crest, a coat of arms featuring the silhouette of a mountain peak against the sky with a fox at the foothills.

The stranger's familiar face rose to catch the tear-filled eyes of the Low Keeper. Daemus recognized him immediately, and not just because of the familial resemblance. He looked from the newcomer to Nasyr and then back to the stoic face of the figure, who returned his gaze. He pulled himself to his feet, his tears chased away out of sheer confusion, and embraced the man.

"Uncle Kester!" Daemus exclaimed. "What are you doing here? How did you travel so quickly from Castleshire?"

Daemus had other questions too, questions that he didn't dare vocalize. Questions like, "Is this really happening? Or is he an illusion, a spell cast by the Great Keeper herself to underscore her point?"

"Perhaps I can answer some of your questions," the Great Keeper said, and Daemus wondered for a crazy moment whether she could read his mind. "I sent for your uncle nearly a month ago as the road from Castleshire is long."

"But how?"

"I saw your misjudged actions written plain in the Great Tome," Nasyr explained. "I'd hoped that you'd come to me to ask for help, but instead you chose silence. Until today, I didn't realize the full extent of your concealment."

Daemus said nothing, his mind reeling as he tried to process this new information. It meant that the Great Keeper had summoned his uncle a month ago, knowing that she was going to expel him and yet waiting to see if he'd come forward, understanding that in the end he wouldn't. Erud was never wrong. Nasyr knew that, and so did Daemus. He never should have doubted her.

"Do you have anything else to say for yourself?" she asked. Daemus didn't.

"In that case," she said with a dispassionate glance, "good day, Daemus Alaric. May Erud grant you wisdom on your journeys."

Nasyr turned her back on Daemus and returned her attention to the telescope. Amoss walked the lad out of the observatory and back down the stairs as he held his head low and focused on his feet.

"FORGIVE ME FOR ASKING, Great Keeper," Kester said. "But what in the names of the Ancients was that all about?"

"Ah, Kester," she replied, lifting her head from the telescope's eyepiece and looking at him as though she'd forgotten he was there. "I suppose you saw through my little ruse."

"On the contrary." Kester gritted his teeth and took a few steps toward her. "I still don't understand why you called me here, and nor do I see why young Daemus has been sent down. If you saw his inaction in the Tome early enough to summon me, why didn't you begin the search for Graytorris immediately?"

"We did exactly that," the Great Keeper replied. "May I be frank with you, Kester?"

"Of course."

"Daemus's expulsion is for his own safety," she admitted. "From the moment he began to have his recent visions, he's been in danger here. I allowed you to hear the tale of Graytorris for a reason. I wanted you to understand the true extent of Daemus's oneiromancy so that you could better anticipate the danger he'll be in now that the fallen Keeper has revealed himself."

Kester looked troubled, perhaps unsurprisingly so, and what Nasyr said next did little to allay his worries.

"I didn't summon you here merely to collect your nephew," she told him. "It's imperative that we get Daemus to Castleshire as quickly as possible. Once there, he must meet with Disciple Delling of the Disciples of the Watch. I've sent word to him already, so he's expecting you. He'll help Daemus."

"I know of Disciple Delling." Kester scratched at his unshaven cheeks and took a moment to follow Nasyr's meaning. "He serves several members of the Caveat, the regent council of Castleshire."

He paused for a moment and looked into the Great Keeper's hazel eyes. They were cool, calm, and collected, but just a little sad. He saw no hint of deception there.

"If this is the task that befalls me, it seems that I have no choice," Kester huffed, a tinge of dissent evident in his tone. "I'll accompany my nephew to Castleshire, and we'll depart this very afternoon. But I have a question, Great Keeper."

"What is it?"

"Why is Daemus having these visions and not you?" Kester

asked, hoping to lay the blame for his nephew's misfortune at her feet. "Why not someone of your own immense power?"

Nasyr flinched visibly, as though some invisible gate-crasher had struck her. It took her a long time to answer, and when she did, she answered slowly, almost begrudgingly.

"Something is amiss," Nasyr lamented. "We Keepers are losing the power of the Sight, though not entirely. The pages of the Tome have been empty, at times. At others, the information we've gleaned from its hallowed pages has been riddled with inconsistencies and incoherencies. It's never the same from one day to another. And it lacks consistency of truth, the basic tenet inherent to our religion of knowledge."

"What does the Tome say today?" Kester asked.

"Today, the Tome is blank," Nasyr replied, her eyes distant and her tone desperate. "There are rumors amongst the pro-tectorate that Erud has deserted us. My visions have mostly ceased, and the same is true of First Keeper Amoss. But for some reason, Daemus still possesses the Sight. He can't control it yet, and he hasn't learned how to invoke and interpret the visions the great Erud provides."

Kester looked appraisingly at the Great Keeper and noticed for the first time that she was looking older and wearier, as though the months since their last meeting had aged her by a factor of ten.

"If your Sight is fading," Kester asked, "how did you know to send for me?"

"The Sight is *fading*," the Great Keeper emphasized, "but it hasn't abandoned us entirely. And you forget, I sent for you a month ago. Since then, the situation has deteriorated. For all intents and purposes, *The Tome of Enlightenment* has become…useless."

"So, what will you do?"

The Great Keeper sighed deeply and rearranged her robes, then paused for a moment to look to the heavens as though consulting them. Then she fixed Kester with a look he struggled to interpret.

"Let me worry about that," she said, eventually. "You should focus on getting Daemus to Castleshire."

"If your suspicions are correct and my nephew is in danger," Kester surmised, "perhaps we should travel in anonymity."

"I thought the same." Nasyr waved to a deacon who stood behind Kester in the doorway. "That's why I arranged to have your royal carriage replaced. The Alaric coat of arms is far too conspicuous. Instead, you'll travel in a plain, covered wagon. Keep away from the towns and the villages where you can. Deacon Burich here will show you to it."

"And what about the other Keepers?" Kester asked. "What about the precepts and my nephew's classmates?"

"Yes, we must cover your tracks," the Great Keeper agreed. "We'll tell them you took him south to Abacus and that you seek to consult the Athabasica to find a cure for his night terrors. It's plausible and will provide a diversion if there are any loose lips."

The two locked gazes in silence for a few awkward seconds, both unsure of what was to come. As Nasyr leaned forward into the lens of the gigantic spyglass, she ended the conversation sternly but politely.

"May Erud grant you wisdom on your journeys."

DAEMUS WAS IN HIS cloister, packing up his most essential belongings to the backdrop of Caspar's incessant handwringing and vexed murmurings. His classmate and closest friend was concerned about his imminent departure, and there was little the young man could do to allay his concerns.

"But I don't understand," Caspar was saying. "Why do you have to leave?"

"I just have to," Daemus replied. He wasn't sure how much he could tell his friend, but it almost didn't seem to matter. He didn't *want* to talk about his departure. His expulsion from Solemnity was still a fresh wound.

"But when will you be back?"

"I don't expect I'll be back for some time." Daemus pretended all was well as he sorted through his trunk. He was trying to narrow his worldly possessions down to a pile small enough—and lightweight enough—to carry on his back in a knapsack. "Here, Caspar. I've got something for you."

Daemus gave his classmate the belongings he had to leave behind, including his robes, cassocks, and clerical collars. It was a bittersweet moment for Daemus. He knew he had to leave them to prevent himself from being recognized, but he still felt an almost physical pain at having to leave his garments behind. They'd grown to be part of his identity.

He finished packing just as the sound of hoof beats on the sod signaled the arrival of his uncle. He lowered his bag to the floor and embraced his classmate.

"Goodbye, Caspar," he said, his expression forlorn.

"Goodbye, Daemus."

They broke their embrace, and Daemus picked his bag back up, then started walking to the door. There was a heavy tension in the air. Caspar started to say something, but he was interrupted by the opening of the door and the loud greeting that accompanied Kester Alaric into the cloister.

"Come now, Daemus," Kester called. "Time is of the essence. We must be off."

Daemus nodded and turned to take one last look at his cloister and his classmate, then followed Kester out of the halls and into the back of a waiting wagon. It was a rickety old thing that looked like it had seen its way to all four corners of Warminster and back. It was a world away from the more regal ride that Kester had arrived in, but at least it promised anonymity. It even came with a cover to ward off the elements and the prying eyes of other travelers.

As Kester took the reins and led the horses out of the courtyard, Daemus lay back in the wagon and let his thoughts drift away with the sound of the horses and his uncle's gentle encouragements. He felt like a failure, as though by being expelled from Solemnity, he was being forced to leave the only thing that gave his life any meaning. Worse, he was on the run and in hiding from a villain he knew only from his dreams.

He was confused and scared. The only solace during the long trip to Castleshire came from knowing that his uncle was at his side to protect him.

CHAPTER TEN

"The antidote for fifty enemies is but one true friend."
—Athabasica, the Poet

THERE WAS AN ODD atmosphere in Thronehelm on the day after their meeting with the king. Addilyn felt it as a series of downcast eyes, murmured rumors, fixed smiles and fidgeting hands. The people around her were calm, but with an undercurrent of concern; quiet, yet strained. The news she'd brought with her was being spread about in whispers, materializing as if by magic among the castle's cohort of servants despite the fact none of them had been in the room for the conversation in question. They were too socially adroit to appear openly worried, but not so much as to successfully banish the emotion altogether. Most of her own retinue had been sent home that morning, and part of her wondered how they would have reacted had they remained.

Addilyn found herself wandering the castle, alone except for Jessamy, burdened with a sense of ennui that she'd never experienced before leaving homeEldwal. The Keeper's death still weighed heavy on her mind, as did the hovering though nonsensical thought that it was somehow her fault, as if she'd been a catalyst and not just a harbinger. Jessamy watched her with dark eyes, clearly worried but aware that it wasn't her place to ask questions or to offer comfort unbidden. Ordinarily, Addilyn would have quickly divested her of that idea, but she was too weary.

She was making her way toward the stables with her body-guard, hoping to find some solace among the horses, when she encountered someone on her way back from a ride. It was a human girl, clearly a noble by her dress and manner of walking, who peered at her with interest. On a whim, Addilyn paused to look her over. The girl was smaller than she was, barely over five foot at a guess, and she was wide-eyed and rosy-cheeked with high-set brows and a winsome expression. Her hair was a color that Addilyn liked, brown but with flashes of red in the light, almost like bronze. She was disheveled and a little dirty, suggesting that she was more interested in fun than in propriety, which seemed like a good sign.

"Hello," Addilyn said cautiously. She started to salute the girl but faltered at her puzzled expression. The salute turned into an abortive wave of her hand. "Might I introduce myself? I'm Addilyn Elspeth, daughter of Dacre Elspeth, ambassador of the Vermilion."

The girl stared, her brows rising.

"It's an honor to be in your presence," Addilyn continued involuntarily, kicking herself mentally as she realized that the girl was totally unfamiliar with Vermilion social conventions. She probably sounded horribly over-formal, rather than courteous as she'd hoped.

After a moment, however, the girl smiled, a pretty, dimpled grin that lit up her face. The confusion in her eyes had cleared. "Oh, how fortuitous!" she replied, cheerfully. "If you're Princess Addilyn then you're the person my father asked me to find and make welcome. I've never met any Vermilion before, so you must forgive my ignorance. What pretty people you are! I love your hair. It's much redder than mine."

Addilyn flailed mentally for a moment, totally lost as to how to respond—imagine *admitting* ignorance outright in the middle of a conversation with a stranger! She fought the instinct to assume it was some kind of triple-veiled insult, eventually landing on a sincere, if slightly stiff, "Thank you."

"I'm Ember Fleury, by the way," the girl added. "My father

is Baron Dragich Von Lormarck, only I'm a bastardess, so I have my mother's name instead. I'm not ashamed, though, because she's wonderful." Her green eyes were bright.

Addilyn smiled wistfully back at her. "I haven't got a mother," she admitted with some hesitation. "Mine died many years ago. I only have my father." At her shoulder, she saw Jessamy glance at her and then lower her eyes. Her bodyguard seemed surprised at her openness; perhaps she even disapproved of it. *My propriety isn't her business,* Addilyn told herself. *Only my safety.*

"Oh, but I'm sure you must be very close," Ember replied, earnestly. "I love my mother dearly, but I sometimes wish I could be close to my father. I love him, too, of course... but he's not the most approachable of men." Her smile faded. "And I have siblings, you know, so he doesn't always notice me."

"Are you... close with them?" Addilyn tried, after a pause. The conversation had already tipped far beyond the boundaries of a typical Vermilion interaction, but the girl seemed easygoing and for some reason, Addilyn wanted to befriend her, so she did her best to push through her discomfort.

The bright smile returned. "Oh, yes. Well, most of them. I don't like Aarav much. He's my full brother. He used to be wretched to me when we were children, and he never really grew out of it. But my half-brothers, Emmerich and Donnar, were always kind, and they stopped him whenever they had the chance. Good, fine boys. Men now, really."

Ember beamed, looking proud.

"I'm younger than they are," she continued, "but we often joke that I'm like their mother. Their true mother died giving birth to them, so I'm the closest thing they have to one. So I took it upon myself to look after them. When they're not too busy looking after me, that is."

She laughed, and Addilyn felt oddly touched. Clearly, although she hadn't said it in so many words, this girl hadn't had an easy life. Yet here she was, smiling happily and talking about her circumstances with such ease to a total stranger.

"Let's be friends," Addilyn said, not caring that she was being clumsy and feeling a smile pull at her lips. "Please."

Ember giggled. "Don't be silly! We're already friends, there's no need to ask."

Ember might not have known it, but that was the best thing she could have said. Addilyn tried to ignore Jessamy, who was studiously avoiding looking at her, but she found herself switching back to formality and asking a question as though to justify the conversation. "What business does your father have at court?"

The other girl's lips quirked. "Me, actually. It's supposed to be a secret, but since you're new to court, it's all right to tell you. He's here to arrange my marriage into another one of the baronies, as I'm his only daughter. I don't know which one exactly, but I've seen him speaking to the baroness of Queen's Chapel, Cecily Maeglen."

Addilyn was familiar on an intellectual level with the idea of arranged marriages, but they still struck her as deeply strange.

"Really?" she asked, being careful with her tone to avoid seeming rude. "You're comfortable marrying someone chosen for you, even though you've never met them?"

"Oh, I've met them," Ember demurred, frowning a little. "I've met all the children of the noble families. Some of them didn't like me very much, and it's not as though I've spent much time with them, but we've all known each other since we were young. But now that you say it, I suppose you're right. I don't mind the idea of marrying someone for the sake of our barony, rather than just my own sake." She tapped her lips thoughtfully. "Besides, they say you grow to love the person you're with, and I'm told I have a loving disposition."

"We have no such practice," Addilyn confessed, "so my knowledge is only from books. But if you enter your marriage looking for happiness, I'm sure you'll find it."

"Yes, I'm sure I will," Ember replied, looking intently at her. Her tone was firm, and Addilyn wondered briefly if she'd been misreading the conversation and if her questions had made Ember feel attacked.

"I hope with my deepest heart that I haven't offended you," she said blandly, and the other girl's expression eased.

"Oh, no. We're friends now, remember. It's only that I worry he'll choose someone who doesn't like me, and I know I'd have to marry them anyway. It's nothing to do with you."

MUCH LATER IN THE day, Addilyn rendezvoused with her father, who'd spent several hours shut away in council with the king. When the two of them were together, they liked to talk about the day to make the most of not having to communicate via letters.

Dacre suggested a walk in the castle gardens and Addilyn eagerly agreed, paying no mind to her weariness from spending much of the day on her feet. The two of them strolled around for several minutes, commenting occasionally on the quality of the greenery—which was mediocre compared to the coronelle's much grander gardens at home, but interestingly varied—before a short silence fell.

"I made a friend today," Addilyn remarked, and her father glanced at her, looking pleased. "A very sweet girl. Ember Fleury, Baron Von Lormarck's daughter." She fell silent, a little conflicted as to whether she ought to bring up the other thing she wanted to mention.

He waited a moment, then prompted, "I sense you have more to say on the matter."

Addilyn felt her brow furrowing. "It's nothing of importance," she said, but then she went on anyway, aware that he wouldn't be satisfied with a deflection. "I felt as though we were talking at cross purposes. I know how to speak her language perfectly well, but I couldn't seem to say the right thing. We liked each other well enough, but… I don't understand why it was difficult."

She'd always had an easy time making friends, and it hurt to feel as though she'd lost her touch. She didn't say so, but she knew her father understood.

Dacre exhaled, his breath making a cloud of steam in the chilly, early evening air. "I wondered when I'd have this conversation with you. It's something every elf of our station learns eventually."

She glanced at him, surprised. She knew she was still a neophyte, still technically learning, but in the past few years it had seemed as though her father was coming to the limits of what he could teach her, and that experience would have to fill in the remaining gaps. Had he been holding something back?

"To be the most effective at what you do," he began, "and to best serve our people, your eyes must look outward and your ears must listen inward." He paused absently to pull up a weed.

"What does that mean?" she asked.

"It means that you must listen, first and foremost, to yourself and to the voice of your people," he said. "Understand what you see, but don't imitate. Reflect on what's before you, but don't change. We're called to transform ourselves constantly in the task of diplomacy, but too much transformation causes us to forget the needs and interests of our own people in favor of the needs of others." He looked at her, his scarlet eyes patient. "We don't have the luxury of true change. Rely on what you know, what you feel, and what you remember. The lights of the past, of what you were born to know and what you've been taught, will guide you."

She nodded, still frowning. If they'd had this conversation a few days ago, she might not have listened as readily. Now, though, she was beginning to understand that interacting with another culture directly, on a person-to-person level, was more complicated and difficult to navigate than she'd expected.

"What's left for me to learn, then?" she asked. "If I can't look to others, how can I grow?"

Dacre turned toward her and smiled. "Dear daughter," he said. She could hear his pride for her in his voice. "You can always look inward. Rather than looking to others for guidance, look to yourself. Learn to know your own soul and that of your people more deeply and more completely. That's how we all grow."

She saw the wisdom in that. Part of her still felt doubtful, but she trusted her father. "I understand," she said, twining her hands together. "How was your meeting with the king?"

He sighed at the question.

"He's concerned," Dacre said, and she intuited from his tone that he was understating things to save face for their host. "Rightfully so, of course. I think he's spent much of his reign simply responding to things as they occur, operating very much in the present, as opposed to the past or the future. It seems to have worked well for him thus far. I doubt he sees a clear path before him now, when the threat at hand is only a vague but serious omen."

"We don't have a clear path, either," Addilyn pointed out, her eyes on a patchy-looking little row of herbs.

"No," he agreed, "but being descendants of the great elven

Ancient, Melexis, we have divine knowledge. We're led by the hand and have no need of a path."

This was orthodox Vermilion doctrine, something Addilyn had been taught since she was a small child and had always accepted without thinking. She certainly didn't feel like she had any divine knowledge, though.

"So it's been said," she murmured vacantly. She missed Yala, who she knew would have been able to add some nuance to the rote phrase, something comforting and wise, or Rasilyn, who would probably have told a joke to make everything seem less grave. She even missed Eiyn a little, though she barely knew him; his earnest faith had always seemed to bolster her own.

"There's no shame in feeling uncertain about the future," her father said, interrupting her thoughts. She met his eyes as he continued. "All of us question, particularly when we're in the midst of an approaching storm that we can sense but not see. Use what's available to you. Listen to the words of the Ancients in your ear and trust your elders for guidance." He smiled. "You're my daughter, my greatest pride and treasure. I know that you'll do what's right, one way or another."

Addilyn smiled back, feeling a little better.

"Come," he said, "let's go and get some supper."

GHYRR RUGALIS, FILTHY WITH dust and sweat, had long lost track of the days he'd spent lingering in the open plains. It had to have been weeks, and he'd nearly run his horse ragged in his reluctance to rest for longer than hours at a time. It had always been a calm beast, purchased for its temperament, but even so it had at last started to show signs of mutiny. The nearest town, Sycamore Post, was several days away, and he had little time to spare. He knew a warm bed could wait.

He squinted; movement had appeared on the horizon. For

a split second, he thought it might be his sleep-deprived eyes playing tricks on him, so he blinked to be sure. Yes, there it was, a cloud of dust to the north, the tell-tale sign of a group of riders. It was soon joined by a second cloud, then a third to the east and west, all of them fast approaching his position. He slowed his horse to a canter and then drew to a stop. The grass and the wildflowers were tall enough to brush his steed's knees.

Scarcely daring to breathe, Ghyrr stroked the sweat-soaked neck of his horse, which was shifting uneasily beneath him. After a few more moments, he unsheathed his sword. If he knew anything about the trollborn clan that ruled those plains, it was a show of strength that would prove valuable in the delivery of his message.

The dust clouds grew closer and resolved themselves into just what he was expecting: three troops of mounted warriors, who were riding toward him as though charging into battle, which perhaps they were.

As they grew closer, he saw that they weren't horsemen after all. Instead, they rode horsehounds, dogs the size of horses that were renowned for being just as ferocious in battle as their riders. The fabled beasts stood a foot taller than their true equine cousins, possessing the forepaws of a wolf and the hind parts of a mastiff horse. Their head and jaws were of a blue Thalassian wolf, and their bodies were nearly fur covered and smelled like unaired laundry. And in the case of Clan Blood Axe, many of the horsehounds bore war paint and wild brandings.

The horsehounds bayed at an earsplitting volume as they encircled him, and Ghyrr's horse began to tremble. Within seconds, he was surrounded, with at least three dozen riders galloping in wild circles around him. They swung their swords and cried out in ululating war cries. In an instant, their stampede came to a stop.

The trollborn warriors all stared him, stone-faced, and began to hiss like vipers, a noise that made him twitch. At last, one of them drew forward, her horsehound growling.

"Aren't you afraid?" she asked Ghyrr, her expression unreadable beneath her war paint. In one hand, she held a cudgel that looked as though it could have knocked out her hound, huge as the beast was.

"I have no reason to fear," Ghyrr replied, despite his still trembling horse, which he patted with one hand.

"Do you know who we are?"

"Clan Blood Axe," Ghyrr said. "Lions of the Vilchor Highgrass. Who else would be bold enough to tame horse-hounds, or to hunt in the open fields in daylight?" This was flattery, but it was true enough that the trollborn would likely accept it without comment.

"Our fame precedes us," their leader commented, her sardonic tone suggesting that she had noticed his attempt to curry favor and was unimpressed. Her warriors caught her meaning and began rattling their weapons and allowing their horsehounds to bark.

Ghyrr, to his chagrin, flinched and had to stop himself covering his ears. The leader smiled, and after a moment held up her hand for silence.

"And yet you do not kneel?" she said. "You're not begging us to spare your life, feeble human though you are."

"I have no need to beg," Ghyrr snarled, projecting more boldness than he felt. "I carry a token." He reached down to a length of twine around his neck and pulled out a talisman that had been jangling against his chest for weeks, a symbol of a jackal's head carved into bone. With a sharp motion, he yanked at it, snapped it free, and tossed it at the trollborn leader, who caught it and scrutinized it closely. Her brows drew together, making her painted face appear even fiercer.

"The sigil of House Von Lormarck," the warrior said, looking at Ghyrr again. "Who are you, human? And what's your business here?"

"My name is Ghyrr Rugalis," he said. "And I'm here in search of Misael. I believe you can take me to him."

THE CLAN BLOOD AXE rabble regrouped into travel formation and led Rugalis to the outskirts of a nearby forest before dismounting from their horsehounds and entering the woods on foot.

Ghyrr had agreed to be blindfolded as they led him to their camp, aware that he was in no position to make demands of his hosts, particularly after they'd allowed him to leave his horse tied up near the treeline instead of feeding it to their horsehounds. He was, however, unable to talk himself out of resting a hand on his weapon the entire way there.

When the blindfold was removed, Ghyrr allowed himself to relax only slightly. Although he was glad to have use of his eyes, he was in even greater danger than he'd been out on the plains.

The camp was deep in a small, wooded area, which was rare on the vast highgrass. The camp was a heavily organized military outpost, and well-disguised from travelers. Despite himself, he was impressed.

Clan Blood Axe was made up of nearly a hundred trollborn marauders. Its members were the lowest of the low, bastard children of mixed races. To be trollborn meant to have the odds stacked against you from birth. That was why so many of them had been attracted to the gold and the violence Clan Blood Axe had to offer.

He was taken to a tent at the center of camp, plain and unadorned, but clearly the residence of their leader. The interior was dark, sparsely decorated and utilitarian, but Ghyrr noted with a prick of fear that the dirt floor was covered in stains of what looked like blood. A single figure sat within, carving at something with a hunting dirk.

The warrior Ghyrr had spoken to earlier drew forward to mutter in the man's ear before retreating, and for another several moments there was silence. Ghyrr, though exhausted and vibrating with nervous energy, knew better than to speak first.

"What business have you here, Ghyrr Rugalis?" Misael asked, his voice gruff but powerful with a little hint of madness hidden just beneath the surface. His eyes flicked up to Ghyrr's and then back down to his work.

Ghyrr collected himself before speaking. "My sovereign sends his greetings from afar."

Misael examined his carving. "In other words, your sovereign didn't have the bravery to show his face here."

Misael looked up at him for just an instant too long, and Ghyrr's blood ran cold at the simple gesture. The menace, perhaps even the madness, behind the chieftain's eyes was suddenly clear as day.

Ghyrr closed his mouth.

"Is it time for war?" the trollborn inquired after another moment, his tone deceptively calm.

"No," Ghyrr replied as neutrally as he could, "but the time grows nigh."

"If it's not yet time," Misael said, at last setting down his carving and dirk, "then why are you here?"

"I have come to give you a task." Ghyrr wondered if he'd lost his wits even as he spoke. What could have possessed the baron to ask this man for anything he didn't offer of his own volition? Despite himself, his loyalty moved his tongue.

"It's a simple thing. Something you and your people should have no trouble with."

"They aren't people," Misael interrupted with a laugh, "and neither am I! Don't be a fool, Rugalis. We're monsters. So they say of us, and so we say of ourselves."

"Your forces, then," Ghyrr continued, uneasy with the idea of where that thought might lead if he allowed Misael to follow it. "As I said, it's an easy task. You only need to find a boy, a young man, on the road from Solemnity and the Cathedral of the Watchful Eye. He's a stripling only, no threat to you."

Misael made an amused, skeptical expression. "Why should your lord and sovereign be threatened by him, then?"

"Not him. A… higher authority has made this request." Ghyrr's eye was caught by Misael's carving. It appeared to be a little figure, kneeling and wailing, its mouth wide open. He pressed his lips together, thinking inanely of his horse, which was still tied up at the edge of the woods.

"I assume you're not asking me to do this out of the goodness of my heart," Misael remarked, a hint of warning in his voice.

Ghyrr unclipped a pouch of unmarked gold palmettes from his belt and tossed it to Misael, who caught and opened it. The trollborn scoffed but put it aside without comment.

"And what of our pardons?"

"They'll be ready for you once your task is complete," Ghyrr assured him. *By the Ancients*, he thought, *I might get out of this with my life.* "When our sovereign reigns over Warminster, you'll be given free passage and granted land, and no man will call you outlaws. As long as you give us the boy—dead or alive."

CHAPTER ELEVEN

"From the silent bow, the arrow flies."
—Refrain from "the Ballad of Rillifane's Meander"

RITTER WOKE BEFORE THE dawn and was on his feet almost immediately. The sky was light enough to see by, and they needed to ride hard to keep pace with their quarry, Veldrin Nightcloak. Once the scouts returned, they'd be on the move again.

As it happened, Storm made it back to camp first, and after looping in a lazy circle around its perimeter, he swooped down and slowed to a controlled descent onto Ritter's outstretched falconhand. With his other arm, Ritter reached into a pouch on his horse's saddle and withdrew a chunk of leftover meat from the last hunt, then held it out for the bird to take. Storm snatched it happily from his hands and took flight again, circling round his head before coming back down to land on the low-hanging branches of a nearby tree. There, he hooked the meat to the branches with a gnarled claw and started pecking at it, stripping the flesh away from the bone.

Ritter closed his eyes and reached out with his mind until he could sense the falcon's familiar aura. They communicated silently, psychically, more in images than in words. The falcon showed Ritter what he'd discovered, the site of the brigands' latest ambush and the skirmish Fira Carling had told them about the night before. Ritter knew they were close, perhaps less than an hour's ride away.

The Black Cuffs and Longmarchers finished breaking camp and mounted their horses shortly afterward. Storm led the way, with the convoy following the war falcon to the north as the sun rose steadily in the sky. As they got closer and closer to the village of Emberlyn, the group slowed their horses to a trot and then a quiet canter, stopping as they arrived at the grisly scene.

The ruins of the village were surrounded on three sides by a horseshoe-shaped grove formed by the banks of Rillifane's Meander, the local river. The grove was home to a wild apple orchard whose fruits had fallen to the ground. The hooves of the brigands' horses had cracked the spoiling apples and blazed an obvious trail to Emberlyn.

The settlement looked to have been little more than a hamlet, only large enough to shelter twenty families. The villagers must have barely been scraping by. Ritter surveyed the burned dwellings, and his eyes narrowed. It had occurred to him before that Fira, poorly clothed and malnourished, didn't seem to have come from anywhere that would have made a tempting target for the Cloak.

Her neighbors, some of whom were now strewn across the ground like a spoiled child's pulled-apart and abandoned toys, didn't look any wealthier. Blood bathed everything, tinging the thick grass with its crimson hue. Biting back his anger at so much senseless death, Ritter said a quick prayer to speed their souls to rest.

He glanced back at the princes, who were covering their noses at the smell of burnt flesh that hung in the air, and his lips thinned in combined sympathy and chagrin.

"This is obscene," Wilcox remarked from his shoulder. "I can barely believe even the most hardened of outlaws would do something like this, and to such a poor village, no less."

Ritter sighed at De la Croix voicing his own thoughts. "Fan out," he ordered in Whispquick to his Longmarchers. "Look for survivors."

After a few tense minutes of investigation, Ritter identi-fied a trail leading north out of the confused mess of tracks that were scattered throughout the village. The departing trails were messy and overlapping, making it hard to track effectively. Clearly the Cloak knew how to hide his passage. Most brigands and trollborn tribes that Ritter had encountered had been little more than poorly trained highwaymen, armed only with basic weapons and the element of surprise, not experienced woodsmen. But tracks were still there for those with the eyes to read them. The bandits had scattered to the four winds to cover their own exits, and there was only one way to tell which trail was the real one amidst all the deception.

Ritter summoned Storm to his falconhand, then whispered to the great bird before releasing it again. He relaxed his physical body and slid to the eyes of his falcon. He hoped to examine the trail from the skies, offering a different perspective.

From the air, the battlefield looked different. The mess of tracks circled the camp, the tangled lines overlapping each other and wrapping together like a ball of string, but eventually, they all tallied and shared a single direction, where the riders had regrouped. The bandits had headed north, just like the girl said. And if the tracks were anything to go by, they were riding in number.

Ritter parted his mind from Storm and dismounted from his horse to get closer to the ground. Then he started searching for tracks, hoping to learn more of their adversaries from the type and size of the footprints and the discarded equipment. The most he could discern, though, was that the tracks were fresh, almost too fresh.

A subtle but familiar bird call caught his elven ears. When he turned, he noticed Marr summoning him to a burned hovel on the west side of the village. Walking to join him, Ritter saw the source of his concern and broke into a jog. Marr had found a survivor, a wounded man with an emaciated frame, his shoulder pierced by an arrow. Marr was in the middle of a prayer to the Ancient of Healing, and hand-signaled to Ritter that the man was alive but his condition was dire. As Ritter watched, the man's eyes fluttered open and met his own. Ritter knelt.

"Can you speak?" Ritter asked in a gentle voice, pitched low so as to not interrupt Marr's intercession with Ssolantress, the Ancient of Healing. The man only wheezed, eyes bleary, but his finger twitched in what Ritter thought might be a beckoning motion. He leaned in.

"Still," said the man, struggling to speak even that much. Ritter frowned at him, the hairs standing up on the back of his neck.

"Marr," Ritter said, and his companion fell silent, relying on his inner concentration to try to heal the man. Ritter waited another interminable few moments before the faintest of whispers met his ears at last.

"Still here."

Ritter forced himself to his feet, unslung his bow, and nocked an arrow. Marr signaled in Whispquick to the other Longmarchers, who silently drew their weapons. Only the princes looked caught off guard, drawing their swords a beat behind the rangers.

"What's going on?" Prince Everett asked, keeping his voice low.

Ritter put a finger to his lips and glanced at the treeline.

Prince Montgomery, a little quicker on the uptake than his brother, signaled for the Black Cuffs to create a perimeter, and Ritter motioned for the Longmarchers to do the same.

The Black Cuffs had not yet reached their positions when a shrill whistle pierced the air. Ritter threw himself to the ground as an arrow passed just above his head, burying itself in the mud up to the nock. From his other side, a hail of slingstones rained down on the princes' soldiers, slipping around the sides of their shields. One man went down after a direct hit, his helm insufficient to ward off the projectile; another Black Cuff was thrown from his panicking horse.

"Ambush!" Ritter cried. His mind raced as brigands emerged from hiding places along the treeline, from pits beneath piles of leaves and overturned carriages. A chaotic battle cry rang out and a line of brigands charged them from the rear, cutting off their only means of escape. In front of them, Rillifane's Meander frothed and churned, and to either side, the foothills of the Dragon's Breath Mountains rose into the sky, their steep scree slopes and treacherous banks cutting off any hope of escape. They were trapped, outnumbered, and stuck between the rocks and the harsh waves.

"Shield wall!" ordered Captain Shale, projecting his voice to carry over the din of battle. The king's men instinctively reacted to the command. They dismounted, drew together, and raised their shields. The Longmarchers, gaining a few seconds' advantage, selected their targets from behind the makeshift carapace and fired volleys of arrows in two staggering waves.

Ritter was in the thick of the first line of archers, wielding the ghostwood bow his mother had pressed into his hands. It was the first time he'd fired Silencer in battle, and he could feel its magical dweomer guiding his arms, his eyes, and his aim. He didn't know how, but the bow felt natural in his possession, as if it was an extension of his eyes and his thoughts. It had become nearly weightless in his hands. As he honed in on his approaching enemy, his bowstring drew back with barely any effort and he felt the ghostwood quicken his aim, adjusting his sight for him. It was if his thoughts passed through its petrified wood, reacting to his will faster than he could himself.

His first arrow leapt from the bowstring, flying true and silent, and struck the first brigand in the chest. It pierced through his padded armor, felling the man. His second shot lamed a second attacker, cutting through his leather armor at the knee.

But volleys didn't stop the advance. As the bandits crashed into the shield wall, the sound of screeching metal and the shouting of men rang through the air. After seconds of chaos, Captain Shale and the princes gathered themselves and responded to the frontal assault with a flanking maneuver, one that Ritter recognized from his own training at Halifax.

Shale waded into the teeth of the ambush, swinging his shield viciously through the air, connecting with an approaching bandit's face and sending him buckling to the ground. The captain pirouetted away from the stunned man and dropped a second with an arc of his sword.

Taking advantage of the opening created by Shale, Everett and Joferian rushed forward to mimic his maneuver, using their shields to hem small groups of bandits together in a swinging gate gambit that they'd learned at Halifax. At the academy, Ritter recalled, it had been moderately effective. In the field, it was deadly. They lunged past Shale with their men in tow, tearing a hole through the brigands' advance.

Even with his mind occupied with battle, Ritter ordered Storm to stay out of the way. The bird's eyes were useful to him, but he couldn't bear the thought of his companion being hurt. Turning back to the battle, he loosed a third arrow from Silencer, slipping it through the defenses of an onrushing bandit to lodge in the man's skull. He fell dead only feet from Ritter. They were closing in.

Ritter blinked, shook himself, and took stock of his own position. The Black Cuffs and the princes were able warriors, thank the Ancients, but he knew there was more to be done. His eyes tracked over what he could see of the treeline from his position. There had still been no sign of either the bandits' leader or their supposed mage, which struck him as a bad sign, despite the tide of the battle turning his way.

Slinging Silencer onto his back, Ritter scaled one of the few small huts in the village that hadn't been burned. He was taking a risk by putting himself in this position, as he'd make for an easy target if he was noticed, but on the other hand, it gave him a commanding view of the battle.

Ritter watched the king's knights advance, as a couple more brigands fell under their blades while more Black Cuffs spilled into the breach created by Shale, Joferian and Everett. They started to attack the bandits from both sides, bringing the advance to a sudden stop.

One of the knights, Warwick, led a second group of three through the breach and repeated the move. He was backed by Wilcox de la Croix of the Longmarchers, who'd forsaken his bow and waded into the melee with his flamberge, a two-handed sword with a curved blade, mimicking the flickering of a flame. He swung in a wide arc around the fence of shields that Warwick had created and quickly dispatched two more brigands.

Wilcox cried out for Shale's group to reposition, but the crafty myrmidon had already done so, advancing through the hole to meet a second wave of bandits with his sergeants, Padar and Ross-Colmar. The three were veterans of many battles and moved to stem the brigands' advance.

Satisfied that Shale and the princes were in control, Ritter turned his attention back to considering how to root out the mage when a horn from the treeline sounded and another wave of brigands advanced, this time led by two massive figures. They were smaller than the mountain ogres that Ritter knew from Ravenwood, but they were too broad and thick to be human. The two creatures waved their weapons above their heads and shouted an unintelligible command. The second wave of bandits followed them, flowing from the orchard and charging at the knights and Longmarchers.

Ritter's lips thinned as the charge neared Shale's position. The two ogrish trollborn stomped their way past several knights, creating a breach in the Black Cuffs' shield wall and allowing half a dozen bandits to follow them through to cut off Montgomery and Everett. Ritter's immediate impulse was to shoot one of the massive trollborn attackers, but doing so would have revealed his position. It was a risk he couldn't take with the Cloak and the possibility of a mage weighing on his mind. For the moment, the Black Cuffs and their leaders would have to fend for themselves.

Relegated to watching from afar, he noticed that Montgomery, in the absence of Shale, was commanding the left flank of the shield wall. The firstborn prince ordered his men to lurch forward at the point of his raised sword, creating space for the Longmarchers to fire a volley into the nearing wave of brigands.

The rangers fired in near unison, their arrows whistling through the air and cutting into the brigands' ranks. Rushing bodies fell dead in the field, some falling at the feet of the Black Cuff phalanx. Ritter welled with pride. His men had saved at least one prince. But then he saw Montgomery catch the point of a blade, a brigand's sword making it past the shield wall and piercing through a gap in the prince's armor near his shoulder. For a second, Ritter feared the worst, but then he saw Montgomery spin away from the stumbling bandit. The man's momentum carried him forward, and he fell flat on the ground at Montgomery's feet. The prince showed no mercy.

Ritter breathed a sigh of relief but seconds later, one of the hidden threats he was waiting on revealed itself. Veldrin

Nightcloak, identifiable by his garish, spangled coat, drew out of the trees on horseback and charged the battlefield, bellowing something to his remaining reserves.

Ritter nocked and sighted an arrow, feeling the connection with Silencer surge into his hands. Frustration prickled at the back of his neck as the Cloak made for the princes. The Cloak had found accidental cover behind the remaining shield wall. Ritter's shot would have to wait.

For all his showiness, the Nightcloak was an able swordsman, dispatching several hard-faced Black Cuffs that fell in his path as he waded into the thick of the battle. He spurred his horse forward and called for his trollborn champions.

"Arakk! Goth!" he cried, loudly enough for Ritter's keen elven ears to hear him. Then the Cloak pointed his sword at Shale. "That one," he bellowed. "Kill that one!"

But Captain Shale didn't stand alone. He'd been joined by Montgomery, Everett, Joferian, and Talath, and the five allies worked with all the precision of a war machine from Abacus. Their movements were rapid and precise, their tactics from a common playbook.

One of the ogrish warriors leapt at Shale, his sword lancing forward as it shone in the sunlight. Shale's shield deflected the blow to the left. The captain spun away from the trollborn and slashed at his legs, catching him off guard. The blade sliced across the back of his exposed calves and he fell to his knees with a blood-curdling roar.

The trollborn rushed to stand, but the wounds had cut deep and he collapsed back to his knees. His shield warded Shale off for a second as the melee paused, but the trollborn's greatest advantage—his size—had been taken away. Shale charged him head on, slamming his shield into the trollborn's face.

The trollborn pushed forward, but Shale clearly anticipated

the move and used his momentum to spin again, this time sinking his trained blade deep into the ribs of the trollborn enemy.

The half-ogre roared in pain and dropped his sword, then collapsed slowly to the ground. Shale stepped up and delivered a coup de grâce, striking a fierce blow to the trollborn's exposed throat that sent his blood spurting through the air, and then he kicked his fallen foe's weapon away. He celebrated for a second or two while he caught his breath, and then the enemy was on him again. The second trollborn lumbered toward him.

Ritter waited impatiently, sighting his arrow and keeping his eyes on the bandit leader. His line of fire was too close to allies to let loose, but time was slipping away. The Cloak moved too quickly to be an easy target, weaving his horse expertly through the throng of bodies, closer and closer to the princes. He was twenty yards away from them, then fifteen, then ten.

A Longmarcher stepped in and thrust a barbed spear at him, but in a move Ritter had never thought he'd see in a real battle, the Nightcloak changed the hand that held his sword and used the momentum of the horse to rip the spear from the man's hands. As the horse clipped the Longmarcher, the ranger fell and the Cloak rolled his steed over him.

Meanwhile, the charging trollborn and the second wave of brigands had exploited the hole in the Black Cuff's defenses and rushed through the breach with a dozen brigands pressing in behind their champions.

The move cut Montgomery and Everett off from the rest of their comrades, and they appeared to be facing down half a dozen bandits on their own. Ritter had no choice. He had to fire.

His arrows flew across the battlefield in silence, one finding the back of a bandit. When the second attacker turned to see what had killed his ally, the other arrow sliced through the man's jaw, stopping only when it lodged in his shoulder.

The princes stood back-to-back, and the surprised bandits froze for long enough to allow the princes to attack. Montgomery's sword struck first, slapping the stunned brigand's club away and slashing back across his exposed neck. Everett stepped forward and spun, startling one of the assailants with his speed before he chopped down, nearly severing the man's leg. Then they were reinforced by Sergeant Padar, who leapt onto the backs of two more, tackling both men to the ground before finishing them off.

Ritter had no time to smile. He changed his position on the roof in case anyone had seen him or the flight of his arrows. It appeared that Nothos had blessed him. Luck was on his side. He nocked an arrow and waited, peering into the scene of the battle once more.

He trained his eyes on the Cloak, who was now nearly upon the princes. To Ritter, it appeared that the man was taunting the brothers, visibly toying with them, swinging his sword in frenetic circles and spitting in the air. But it was clear that the young princes, for all their academy-drilled skills, were far outmatched.

Veldrin Nightcloak approached from their left, giving himself an advantage against right-handed swordsmen, and it was Everett Thorhauer who was first in his sights. The Cloak leered at his opponent and lifted his blade into the air.

Ritter exhaled and loosed his arrow. Silencer fired soundlessly, the arrow finding its mark, tearing through Veldrin's armor.

There was a sudden flash of startled confusion in Veldrin's eyes. His sword paused in its descent and his shield hand went limp and slipped off the horse's reins. The man's face turned down to look at the bloody flights of Ritter's arrow sticking from his chest. He floundered for a moment and then fell backwards off his horse at the feet of the two princes.

Allowing himself a moment of satisfaction as the remaining Black Cuffs and Longmarchers sent up a weak cheer, Ritter scanned the battlefield again. One of the part-ogres looked to have been felled, and Talath, Joferian and Shale were moving to attack the second while he was distracted by the Nightcloak's death.

The ogrish beast howled in defiance, barging through his own men to get to Shale. His axe was high in the air, and he bellowed a war cry in some unintelligible language. The captain had just enough time to raise his shield before the blow landed. There was a sound like a thunderclap, the resounding din of metal on metal, and Shale's shield collapsed in on itself. Shale was a heavy man to begin with and his armor added to the total, but he was still thrown back by the impact.

Shale unsheathed a vicious-looking dagger with a blade sharp enough to slice through bone. As the momentum bore him backward, he slipped the dagger into his hand and swiped up at his opponent's skull. Slow as he was, the trollborn reacted just in time to dodge a killing blow, but Shale's blade slashed against his lower jaw, gouging out a chunk of his lip and shearing off his tusk.

The trollborn howled in pain and horror, grasping at his bloodied face. He swung wildly around, elbowing the viscounts in the process. Joferian and Talath pointed their swords at Shale to signal their maneuver, and the three men surrounded the trollborn, feinting and parrying as he fended them off with his great axe. To one side, Padar and the injured Sergeant Ross-Colmar occupied the remaining brigands so that the other three could focus on the half-ogre.

Joferian advanced alone, drawing the trollborn's attention and quickly raising his shield to catch the oncoming blow of his double-bladed axe while Talath and Shale cut at his legs. The huge creature moaned and collapsed, nearly crushing Joferian, who rolled away at the last moment.

With their commander and champions gone, the bandits were fighting with increased desperation. But the Battle of Rillifane's Meander wasn't over.

A GLINT IN THE CORNER of his eye made Ritter turn, but he saw nothing. Then came the shrill whistle of an incoming projectile and a black-feathered arrow traced a path through the air and found its mark: the small, inch-high eyehole on the left side of Shale's helmet. As the great knight fell to one knee, another arrow pierced the air and buried itself in Shale's neck, finding the seam between his breastplate and helmet. He fell to his other knee and stayed there for a moment. Blood gushed in claret fountains from his wounds and then Captain Leowin Shale fell forward on to his face and moved no more.

A chill went up Ritter's spine, his body stilling as though paralyzed. He'd seen men die before, but this was a captain— *his* captain, his mentor. Ritter hadn't known the brigands had been hiding a sniper in the treeline, and gauging by the shot, they were talented. He should have focused on finding the hidden threats instead of chasing the most obvious targets. He could have stopped it. Shale had a wife, he remembered in anguish. After another moment, Ritter took several deep breaths, trying to collect himself and suppress his panic and distress. There was no time for grief.

The air seemed to thicken, and Ritter shifted uneasily as he realized that a sparkling hale of magic was descending over the battlefield. Here, at last, was the mage. The bandits cheered at the appearance of their final, most pressing advantage.

A pale-faced, green-cloaked man emerged from the trees, his hands raised and his lips moving in a muttered spell. Before his incantation could finish its effects, Ritter saw Wilcox raise his bow and fire off an arrow in the mage's direction, but the arrow changed course before it reached its target and went wide.

The mage's spell dropped onto the battlefield, falling like a flashing green cloud on the princes and viscounts, freezing them in place. At that, the remaining brigands rallied, lurching forward in a single wedge formation and focusing their attack on the royals.

As they tried to wade through the ranks of the Black Cuffs and Longmarchers, Ritter closed his eyes and breathed. If he allowed himself to panic, he knew his aim would falter. He took two precious seconds for himself before he opened them again, sighted his arrow, and fired. Noiselessly, the arrow cut through the mage's protections and struck him in the shoulder.

The man cried out in surprise, his hands flying to the wound. Blood stained his green cloak, turning it near black. Ritter drew another arrow, nocked, and shot. The second arrow pierced the mage's hand, which rested over his heart. With a harsh cry, the mage fell.

The battlefield, which had almost fallen silent, descended into chaos. Freed from their paralysis, the princes and viscounts sprang into action, commanding the Black Cuffs and Longmarchers back into formation to counterattack. Montgomery and Everett were still outnumbered two to one, staving off the stubborn advances of the brigands' swords and flails. De la Croix made his way toward the princes, followed closely by Rufus Crag. Crag's daggers were quickly bloodied as he dashed in from the side, allowing de la Croix to launch his considerable frame at two bandits, knocking them to the ground.

The bandits fell into a chaotic rabble and broke ranks. They started to flee in different directions while the knights and the Longmarchers resaddled themselves and started to run the fleeing brigands down. Montgomery and Everett Thorhauer led the pursuit.

"Take them alive!" Montgomery bellowed.

From the looks of things, Ritter doubted it would be long before they claimed a decisive victory. His mind, however, was elsewhere. His head pirouetted like a trollborn dancer in a sleazy tavern, and at the same time he barked a psychic order at Storm, who was still circling high above the battlefield. Ritter's trollborn eyes saw a lot and Storm's falcon eyes saw even more, but the battlefield was too chaotic and the enemy sniper was too well-hidden. All Ritter had was a direction, and even that was a guess.

But it was better than nothing, and so while his Longmarchers pursued the fleeing bandits and his healers treated the wounded, Ritter struck off at an angle toward where he thought the arrow had come from.

Storm found a small trail that suggested some movement, and Ritter followed the falcon's vision to the sniper's abandoned perch. There was no sign of the assassin, but it was clearly the spot where they'd been standing. Some of the grass had been trodden down and two black arrows were dug tip first into the ground, ready to be plucked, notched, and fired.

Ritter pulled the two arrows from the ground and took a moment to calm down from the battle. He'd done his duty, ridding the realm of the Nightcloak while ensuring the princes and viscounts were safe. But many were dead and more were injured, and the Black Cuffs had lost their leader to the mysterious marksman.

Ritter gathered the sniper's arrows, breathing deeply to slow his heartbeat as he allowed the fever of battle to fade. As

Ritter took account of the losses, he suddenly remembered the injured man whose warning had saved their lives from a deadly ambush. In a flash, he rushed to find him.

"WHO IS THIS MAN?" Montgomery asked, watching in fascination as Marr pulled herbs and unguents from a small leather satchel and started stemming and cleaning the man's wounds. As the group's healer, Marr was a valuable asset to the Longmarchers, and his hybrid approach of first aid and divine intervention was enough to see the majority of them through their injuries.

"Silas Carling," Marr said for him. "It's the girl's father."

Ritter looked to Marr, who drew his lips into a doubtful line and subtly shook his head. Ritter knew the man's time was limited, and so he bent down to cradle his head and to lean in close.

"Mm—my daughter?" the dying man asked, struggling to speak and tripping over his words.

"She's safe," Ritter replied, offering Silas some peace. "She's on her way to the Bridge."

Silas's voice failed him, but he managed a relieved smile.

"She'll be cared for by my family until our return," Ritter confirmed.

"The Bridge?" Silas mumbled, his bloody hand weakly finding Ritter's. "Thank you."

Silas paused for a moment to drink some of the water that Marr proffered.

"Please, take care of her."

"You have my word," Ritter said. "I'll treat her as a Valkeneer."

Silas replied with a tearful nod and the mixed emotions of a dying man. Ritter felt the strength in the man's hand diminish as his eyes glazed. With a gurgle and a whimper, he let go in Ritter's arms.

"Priest," Montgomery said solemnly to Marr. "The Lament to Threnody, the Ancient of the Dead, for the fallen."

"Of course," Marr replied as Ritter lowered Silas's body peacefully to the ground.

Marr stood over the man and led the group in prayer. The Black Cuffs and Longmarchers gathered around the corpses of Silas, Shale and their other fallen allies, then sang the Lament to Threnody.

Threnody, the Ancient of Death,
it is to you whom we lament.
To the Hall of Ancients with our friends,
we watch your dark ascent.
Turn then, most feared visitor,
from this veil of tears.
Where they, our friends, shall rest,
and forever hold no fears.

THE MOOD AT CAMP was subdued that evening, understandably so. Another of the Black Cuffs had passed away from his wounds, and two more were feverish and delirious. Marr had treated the wounded as best as he could, including the injured prisoners, but there was only so much his battle medicine could do. Their fate was in the hands of the Ancients.

Everett and Montgomery had thanked Ritter and the Longmarchers for playing their part in the battle, and Ritter for raising the alarm and dispatching the Nightcloak. They'd also taken the cloak that had given Veldrin his name, and they planned to present it to their father as a trophy.

It was a long, black woodsman's cloak that made the wearer almost invisible, especially in the dark. It looked like a tapestry of a starry night, a deep grey that turned into a pitch black when the night rolled around. It was patterned with silvery stars that seemed to blend naturally with the material, as though they were integral to the very fabric. Those who possessed the ability could see that it was surrounded by a faint hale of magic.

Ritter, meanwhile, had been busy examining the arrows. Even to the most novice eyes, it was clear they weren't normal projectiles. The arrows in Shale's body matched the two he'd found from the sniper's hideout, but their scouts had spotted no sign of their owner. Each had been crafted with care, and the shafts had been marked with the sniper's signature, a delicately carved black rose. There were vicious barbs on the ends so that they'd cause even more damage when they were removed, and they'd cut through the metal of Shale's visor like a hot knife through butter. They were beautiful but deadly, designed for nothing but malice.

The fact that the archer had left two of the arrows behind suggested he'd left in a hurry. Ritter must have only just missed him.

While the rest of the brigade mourned their dead and treated their wounds, Ritter was deep in thought, trying to wrap his head around the problem of the bandits. This wasn't a run-of-the-mill raiding party. This was something different, the likes of which he'd never seen before.

He was interrupted in his musings by the approach of footsteps and a hand at his elbow. Everett and Montgomery had spotted him lurking away from the campfire and had wandered over with a goblet of ale. They handed it to him, and he accepted it gratefully, then drank greedily from the cup.

"What are you thinking about, Ritter?" Everett asked. "The dead?"

"Yes and no," Ritter replied. "I've been thinking about the sniper. Who was he and why was he here?"

"You know bandits," Montgomery snorted carelessly. "Probably some desperate trollborn trying to make his name."

"No." Ritter shook his head, ignoring the prince's inadvertent insult. He held out one of the arrows so the prince could see it. "This isn't the work of just any fletcher. What brigand would have weapons such as these?"

"You worry too much, Ritter."

"I wonder."

From the firepit, the sound of a sad song rose as the men drowned their sorrows with harsh spirits and banded together to mourn the dead. Til Aarron of the Longmarchers, an amateur bard, pulled out a rough-looking flute carved from bone and composed a song to commemorate the battle. He called it "The Ballad of Rillifane's Meander" and sang it to the Longmarchers and Black Cuffs by the light of the fire.

From Castle Bridge, the thirty ride,
The knights of Queen's Chapel go side by side.
Their swords and spears are held up high,
From the silent bow, the arrow flies.
The Cuffs of black and Cloaks of night,
They clash and charge with trollborn might.
The battle sounds before the dawn,
The 'fane's Meander, red anon.
From walls of shields the sunlight shines,
The brave knights fall to hold the line.
The knights of Queen's Chapel, with heads held high,
From the silent bow, the arrow flies.

"Come, Ritter," Montgomery said, turning to glance at their comrades around the fire. "Your fears may yet prove to be groundless. In the meantime, we have a victory to celebrate. It was dearly bought, but it was a victory nonetheless. We'll take Shale and the other dead back to the city for honorable burials. They died as they lived, as heroes."

But Ritter wasn't in the mood to celebrate.

"Two shots, one piercing the helmet of a knight, is rare." Rittter shook his head again in disbelief, nearly ignoring the princes. "But for a shot to pierce the eye slit at that range is almost unheard of. I'm not sure that I could make those shots, and nor could any of my men. So, who was this archer? I'm telling you these are no normal bandits."

"Forget it, Ritter."

"And another thing," he continued, oblivious to the weary looks the two princes were sharing between one another. "How did they know we were coming?"

But the royals wouldn't be drawn into speculation, and Ritter soon dismissed them with a nod so that he could return to his thoughts. Around the fire, the Black Cuffs and the Longmarchers were still singing, although it would have to come to an end soon enough. They'd also rounded up the prisoners, the dead, and the injured and loaded them into the backs of the few wagons they'd been able to salvage.

They planned to ride at dawn.

CHAPTER TWELVE

"Never trust a trollborn."
—Overheard in the Dagger's Sheath Tavern

FOR DAEMUS AND KESTER, the journey back to Castleshire was a lonely one. Silence was pervasive, and paranoia weighed heavily on the two travelers. Every passerby was a potential threat, and so Kester had ordered Daemus to stay inside the carriage throughout the hours of daylight. Even in the evenings, when he let the boy out to stretch his legs, see the stars and feel the wind on his skin, he was hesitant.

For the most part, the trip was uneventful. Kester and Daemus stood in front of the sundial at the town square in Sycamore Post, dressed in commoners' robes and wearing hoods over their faces, ostensibly to ward off the sun but equally to cast their features into shadow to make them harder to remember.

"Let's make this quick." Kester jumped down from the carriage and turned to Daemus. "Meet me back at this spot in an hour. Purchase only the provisions on the list that I gave you and do nothing to call attention to yourself."

"Understood." Daemus checked over the list, still unsettled by the journey and the secrecy that seemed to surround it. "And what are you going to do?"

"I need to visit the smithy." Kester pointed to their rickety cart. "I'm worried about one of the bands on the wagon's wheels."

Kester nodded at Daemus and struck off in the direction of the blacksmiths, leaving Daemus to head toward the market. Sycamore Post catered to travelers and pilgrims alike. Home to several hundred permanent inhabitants, each window had a different sign beneath it. No building was wasted, and the trading post bustled with inns, blacksmiths, general stores and brothels. It was already late afternoon and the vendors in the open-air market had started packing their wares away into their carts. Daemus had stocked up on the basics, and his shoulder sack was packed with fruits and bread. He was perusing a string of dried fish when the Sight came upon him.

He had warning, but not much of it. Panic rose in his chest as he backed away from the stall and tried to find some space. He'd only ever had visions during his sleep. This was something different.

Daemus stared blindly ahead, his white eyes aglow with his vision but blind to the real world. In his mind, the hustle and bustle of the trading post had disappeared to be replaced by the now-familiar pool of placid water. The white robes of a Keeper levitated above it, and though there was no physical form inside of them, they were holding a great book in the air in front of the empty cowl.

It was a ponderous tome, shaped in the form of an upside-down triangle. *The Tome of Enlightenment* was no ordinary book. It opened from top to bottom so that when the covers were spread, it looked like a diamond. It was bound from some mysterious, well-oiled material and was chalk-white in color. The cover was blank except for two unremovable marks. The first was a sunset orange stain that moved magically throughout the grimoire from page to page, never dissipating and resisting all attempts to clean or remove it. The second was a faint thumb-print on the lower flap. Legend had it that it was the fingerprint of Erud, though there was no way to know for sure.

The water in the pool beneath the empty robe had changed, running rancid with scum and blood, feces, bile and other putrescence. The stench of it was unbelievable, an assault on his senses. As Daemus recovered from the vision, he bent over and retched, sending his lunch tumbling to the street. He fell to the ground himself shortly afterward.

THE NEXT THING DAEMUS felt was the strong arm of his uncle around his back, hoisting him up to his feet and half-walking, half-dragging him away from the marketplace. Daemus was woozy, like one of the punch-drunk boxers in the traveling carnivals, and he barely remembered the journey back through the crowds of milling people and into the covered wagon. As soon as the doors had been closed behind him, Kester was behind the reins in the driving seat and heading out of town as fast as the horses could take them. The wheel still hadn't been repaired, and it made angry clunking sounds as it sank into ruts and bounced over stones.

They rode at pace, as though the hounds of hell were behind them, and Daemus had no way of knowing how much time had passed before the wagon eventually slowed to a stop. There was a triple knock at the door, one that Kester was using to signal when the coast was clear, and then the boy's uncle was climbing in through the door and settling in beside him in the back of the wagon.

"That was too close for comfort," Kester said. "What happened?"

Daemus tried to answer, but his speech was slurred and incoherent, as though he was deep in his cups. Kester pressed a flask of water into his hands and Daemus drank deeply from it, then composed himself as best as he could before he spoke.

"That was a first." His voice was weak and crackled when he spoke. "Until now, I've only ever had visions in my sleep."

"What did you see?"

"I saw the robes of a Keeper." Daemus shuddered at the

thought of it. "And *The Tome of Enlightenment*. I saw the spring run red with blood."

A shadow passed across Kester's face. This was troubling news. "Get some rest, Daemus."

The boy didn't need telling twice. Exhaustion had him in its grip, and he was semi-comatose at best to begin with. Kester laid a blanket over his nephew and kept a watchful eye on him as he mumbled and murmured his way into unconsciousness.

KESTER STEPPED CAUTIOUSLY BACK out of the cart. He was worried and was sure it showed in the way he scanned the road for pursuers. Daemus's spectacle in the market wouldn't have gone unnoticed. If anyone was on their trail, they'd find plenty of news in the inns of the trading post. Everyone had seen the boy and his telltale eyes. Their anonymity had been blown.

Climbing back into the saddle and pushing the horses ever onward, Kester was deep in his own thoughts, though not so deep that he wasn't keeping at least one eye on the horizon.

If we're being followed, Kester thought, *what if we're caught? And if we're caught by someone—or worse, something—how can I defend Daemus on my own?*

And then he had an idea.

WHEN DAEMUS AWOKE IN the back of the covered wagon, he had no way of knowing where he was or how much time had passed. He opened the hatch to look outside, and the bright, snow-covered forest of fir trees did little to help him, though the shadows told him that sunset was rapidly approaching. He could see a crystal lake from the other window, and with both hatches open, a cold air blew in and chilled him to the bone. He could tell that they'd traveled a good distance and wondered how long he'd been out. Surely for much longer than a couple of hours.

Kester must have detected movement from within. He slowed the horse to a stop in a burned-out grove that had been the victim of a lightning strike. The trees surrounding it offered decent protection from the road, and he'd been riding all day. It was as good a place as any for them to make camp for the night.

Wordlessly and without a sound, he lit a fire with his tinderbox. Daemus only felt strong enough to venture forth once the wood was crackling and a slain rabbit was roasting on a spit. When he stepped out into the flickering firelight, Kester greeted him with a nod and gestured for him to sit down.

"How long have I been unconscious?" Daemus asked, by way of greeting.

"Tomorrow would have been your fourth day," Kester replied. "I'm glad to see you're feeling stronger. You've been unconscious for most of the journey."

"By the Ancients." Daemus rubbed his eyes, his head sinking back into his hands. "Nothos must have watched over me. I've never had a vision like that. It was more like a seizure than anything else."

"You made quite the scene." Kester took a moment and turned the roasting rabbit. "We had to press on as quickly as we could."

"Where are we?"

"We took a diversion," Kester told him. "I couldn't be sure we weren't being followed. I thought it would help us to lose any trackers."

"And where are we going?"

"We're heading into a small village known as the Hearth," Kester explained. "The mountains at the edge of Loch Keefe. We're going to meet a friend who can help us."

"What makes you think we're being followed?"

Kester stirred the embers and threw another log on the fire before replying. "I have no way of knowing either way," he confided. "I've seen few folks on the road and none have approached, but I still felt the need to divert the tracks of anyone who might be following us. But we need to stop soon."

"Why?"

"We need new transportation," Kester said. "This cart won't bear us much farther, especially with the wheels in the state they're in. Besides, we could do with some allies to help us to reach Castleshire safely."

"Who did you have in mind?"

"I thought we'd seek out Faux Dauldon," Kester replied. "She's one of the few people who we have cause to trust."

"I thought all of the Dauldons had been executed," Daemus said, remembering the grisly spectacle from his childhood.

"Not all of them," Kester said. "One of the family line remains."

"But *who*?" Daemus asked, his eyes alight with excitement and almost as bright as they were when he went into his trances.

"Her name is Faux," Kester replied, pronouncing the word so it sounded as though he was talking about the foxes that made the fields their homes and that gorged themselves silly on the wild rabbits. "She owes me a favor or two. If anyone can help us, it's her."

CHAPTER THIRTEEN

"Behold, before you, the draughts of the Ancients.
The draught of mead from the Well of Ssolantress.
The draught of ale from the Mountains of Koss. The
draught of wine from the vineyards of Nothos. The
draught of cider from the forests of Melexis. The
draught of nectar from the Chapel of the Queen."
—Warminsterian Marriage Vows

EMBER FLEURY WAS WOKEN by a rap at the door. For a couple of seconds, she looked around uncertainly, confused by the unfamiliar surroundings of her bridal suite in Thronehelm. She'd slept poorly, kept awake by the excitement and the apprehension.

The door opened and swung inward, and she tensed in her bed for a moment before she saw who it was. It was Aarav, her brother, and her uncle, Lothar, already dressed in their finest robes for the occasion. She knew why they were there. Tradition meant that they had to collect and protect her on her big day. It was a touching gesture, but she was too full of wine from the night before to appreciate it.

"Rise and shine, sister," Aarav teased. His voice bounced around Ember's skull like the tolling of a funeral bell and when he walked over to the window and threw the ornate curtains open, the light spilled in and lit a fire behind her eyes. "Looks like someone can't hold her drink."

"Aye." Lothar laughed. "And there'll be plenty more wine before the day is done. Come, Ember, it's time to meet your future husband. You're to marry a hero who's returning from defeating the bandits that have been threatening Foghaven Vale."

"Who is he?"

"Can't tell you that. It'd ruin the surprise."

"Then tell me this instead," Ember said. "Is he old or young? Ugly or handsome? Rich or poor? Weak or powerful? And where am I to live?"

Ember coughed and cleared her throat, and then she rose from her bed in her nightgown and quaffed the water that a considerate servant had left on her nightstand. She rang the bell, trying not to wince at the piercing sound it made.

"Wait outside," she said, keeping her sentences short because every word seemed to cost her. "I'll dress with haste and join you as soon as I can."

Her maidservants arrived shortly afterward, and Aarav and Lothar were ushered out into the castle corridor, where they continued to talk with Ember as her servants dressed her. They'd brought buckets of warm water to wash her hair and her face in the basin. Once that was done, they pulled out a comb made from pig bones and dragged it through the tresses of her hair, ironing out the knots and styling it into something more befitting a woman on the day of her betrothal.

"I learned something from our Vermilion visitors last night," Ember said, projecting her voice a little so it would reach the men in the corridor. The wash and the water had helped to make her feel a little more human, but she still winced at how loud her voice seemed in the relative silence of her bedchamber.

"Oh, aye?" Arrav replied. "And what might that be?"

"The elves don't arrange marriages," Ember explained. "They're free to choose their own spouses."

From the other side of the doorway, Ember could hear the muted sound of Lothar and Aarav trying not to laugh at the idea. She could imagine them there, pressing their hands over their mouths, their eyes rolling wildly in their heads as they shared a mischievous look with each other. She knew what they thought, and she also knew that they had a job to do. Tradition decreed it.

"Let's have less of that," Lothar said, injecting a little sternness in his voice, though not enough for it to hide the underlying mirth. "You have a duty. Let's not entertain such attempts to dodge your responsibilities. You're no longer a little girl."

"But I—"

"Enough," Lothar barked.

A terse silence descended, during which Ember's handmaids continued to dress her for the wedding. She was donning a regal-looking gown in the colors of her kingdom. As a jackal of Foghaven Vale, that meant black and burned orange. The outfit was rounded off by a brooch in the shape of the Silver Trident of Deadwaters Fork, a trinket she wore in honor of her mother and her mother's people.

"Lothar?" she called. "Are you still there?"

But she was greeted by only silence.

When her handmaids were satisfied with the state of her outfit, she took one last look at herself in the expensive, full-length mirror, smiled nervously, and then departed for the common room to meet her future husband.

A JUBILANT BUT SOMBER MOOD hung over the Black Cuffs and the Longmarchers. The dead and the injured in the carts cast a shadow over the long ride home, and many of the Longmarchers were dismayed to find themselves heading farther away from the Bridge. It wasn't that they didn't want to be in the field. They just wanted to be in the fields around their home instead of taking on an unexpected and potentially unnecessary trip to Thronehelm.

Ritter had tried to convince Montgomery to let him and his men return to the Bridge, but the young prince scoffed at the idea. He was still bathing in the glory of his first major battle, and nothing Ritter said was enough to change his mind.

"You're the man of the hour," Montgomery insisted. "The hero of the battle. Your bard sang songs of your deeds. You're sure to be rewarded by the king for your service."

"I don't need a reward." To Ritter, it mattered little. More comfortable knee-deep in mud than in silk, he willingly adopted the life of a woodsman over that of a royal. The idea of celebrating the battle in court was disturbing.

In truth, Ritter's thoughts were on neither the battle nor the procession and the feast that likely awaited him and his men when they reached their destination. He was thinking about the girl, Fira Carling, and wondering whether she'd made it to the safety of his family.

It took two days of hard travel for the group to reach the gates of the castle. At the sight of the high walls, a cheer went up from the Longmarchers and the Black Cuffs alike. The journey had taken its toll on them and the bodies in the backs of the carts had started to smell.

Montgomery rode proudly at the head of the procession, and the iron portcullis was quickly raised once the guardsmen saw who it was. To Ritter's and the Longmarchers' disdain, he'd called a brief halt to the convoy so he could dress himself for the occasion. He rode up to the gates with the Nightcloak's head on a pike and with his infamous cloak trailing from the shaft like an unholy banner. His brother and cousins rode behind him, followed by the Longmarchers and then the Black Cuffs at the rear, bringing in the dead and the wounded. Captain Shale was carried on the shields of a half-dozen knights, the Black Cuffs affording him one final honor as they bore him toward his final resting place.

When the procession reached the castle, it split into two, with most of the Black Cuffs moving on to the barracks while the princes, the Maeglens, Ritter and the Longmarchers entered the court. It was a busy day with many dignitaries in attendance. Trumpets sounded throughout the city as the beat of marching drums rolled down from the nearby mountains.

In front of the court, Montgomery took the fore and told the story of their great victory, glorifying the battle in a way that would have made even the most experienced of bards green with envy. In Montgomery's tale, the allied Black Cuffs and Longmarchers were outnumbered a dozen to one, and it had been his own courageous bravery and inspired leadership that had sealed the victory. He talked animatedly and at length, and the rest of the court hung on to every word as though they feared to miss a single syllable.

Ritter, who'd been ushered to one side of the great room with the rest of his Longmarchers, nudged Wilcox de la Croix in the ribs and murmured, "See how the prince embellishes the battle. I wonder if he understands quite how close it really was."

De la Croix and the nearby Longmarchers nodded in agreement, but they wisely remained silent. It wasn't the time for truth.

Montgomery finished his story by praising Ritter's bowmanship, and then he did something unusual by breaking protocol and inviting the Longmarchers to speak to his father. One by one, they lined up before Godwin's raised dais and shook the king's hand, exchanging a few pleasantries and dredging up what little etiquette they remembered in an attempt to remain diplomatic. They didn't need reminding that they were there as representatives of the Bridge.

Ritter was the last to speak to the king. While they spoke, the king's oldest son told the story of the battle, reminding the court that it was Ritter's arrow that had killed the Nightcloak and turned the tide of the battle.

"Thank you for your service to the kingdom," Godwin said, shaking Ritter's hand and beaming delightedly at the hero of the battle. "I see that the legend of Silencer continues to grow proudly in the hands of its new owner. I remember it served your father well. May I see it?"

"Of course, sire," Ritter replied, unslinging the bow from his back and handing it over. King Godwin examined it closely for a moment and then stood up from his throne. The court around them fell into silence.

"I've seen this bow in battle," the king announced to the heaving court of gawking nobles. "It's named Silencer for a reason. The bow and its projectiles make no sound, and in the hands of a skilled archer, it silences the enemies of Warminster for good."

All eyes were on King Godwin, who seemed to thrive in the role of storyteller, just like his son.

"I recall the days when I fought alongside your father, Ritter," he began. "We defended the Bridge against Balthi the Brutal."

Ritter nodded to the king, affirming the story. He hadn't been born at the time, but the history between the Thorhauers and the Valkeneers went back several generations. Before King Godwin had inherited the throne, Ritter's grandfather had defended Godwin's father from a trollborn ambush. The progenitor of the family's fabled archery prowess, Ruthor Valkeneer had killed eleven trollborn with as many arrows, saving the king's life in the process. In return, King Gideon Thorhauer had gifted Ruthor Valkeneer with the Bridge.

"And now," Godwin concluded, "it seems as though this fine bow has fallen to the latest of the Valkeneer heroes to build on its legend."

"You honor me too much, Your Majesty."

"Not at all," the king replied. "As my beloved son won't stop reminding us, you slew the Nightcloak. A fine kill from a fine bow. May it be the first of many such kills in the service of the land."

Ritter's face flushed. He'd killed the Nightcloak because he'd had to, because it was his duty, but he was in no mood to celebrate the death of any man at his hands, even such a rogue as Veldrin Nightcloak. And besides, the king was embarrassing him, intentionally or not. The public accolades, the flattering words and the colorful stories had been traded in open court for everyone to hear.

"I'd like to make you an offer, young man," King Godwin announced. "In the spirit of the continued partnership between our families. My father gave your grandfather eleven hundred gold palmettes, eleven knights, and eleven horses. I'd like to give you the same in acknowledgement of your bravery and heroism."

Ritter froze, a chill passing down his spine. He looked around the room at the expectant faces and started to feel dizzy. It was stuffy in the room and difficult to breathe. He was unaccustomed to flattery, and nor was he comfortable being the spectacle of any gathering.

"With respect, Your Majesty," Ritter said, delicately, "I must decline your offer."

"What?" King Godwin boomed, his sonorous voice echoing around the room and disturbing the dust on the ancient rafters. "Is this how you reward generosity?"

"I admire your generosity, sire," Ritter replied. "And I'd like to see it applied for the good of the people. Keep your men and deploy them to protect the borders. As for the palmettes, I humbly request that you divide it between the families of those who were slain by the bandits."

"Hmm," the king murmured. He nodded at Ritter and turned to look at his men.

For a moment, time stood still in the audience chamber. There was electricity in the air. Then King Godwin laughed, a deep, booming sound befitting his huge frame. It dispelled the tension and quickly spread to the rest of the court.

"I'm impressed," Godwin said, clapping Ritter on the back with a meaty hand. "You have integrity, young man, just like your father. And you command an admirable loyalty of your men. I'll do as you say and distribute the palmettes amongst the people."

At this decree, the laughter evolved into a round of applause that shook the rafters amidst cries of "excellent decision, Your Majesty" and "very wise, sire." Ritter noted cynically that the king's hangers-on had forgotten it had been his suggestion. But amidst the applause, which continued to thunder for several minutes, the king took Ritter aside and whispered something into his ear.

"I don't believe this is over, Ritter," he murmured. "I give you my word that the gold will be distributed. But in return, I want to ask something of you. Accept the help of my knights and horses. Put them to use in the defense of your realm and remain on the lookout for a resurgence amongst the bandits."

Ritter nodded at him and said, "Thank you, sire. I see the wisdom in your proposal. On behalf of Valkeneer, I'll gladly accept your offer. The Bridge can always use the help, especially from men as skilled and as disciplined as yours."

The two men clasped hands with one another to seal the deal, and the gesture seemed to mark the end of business for the day.

"We'll celebrate my son's victory," King Godwin declared. "I'm calling for a great masquerade to be thrown in honor of the sacrifices made by the dead and the heroic deeds of the living."

Ritter and the Longmarchers looked at each other silently, unspoken thoughts passing between them. They belonged in the field, not prancing around to the music of minstrels as noblemen gorged themselves on fine meats and wines.

And as the man of the hour, Ritter bore the worst of it. While his men could at least take some time to themselves to catch a breath of air or to talk to one another, Ritter found himself being passed between an endless procession of noblemen, each of them keen to strike alliances with him now that he was so clearly in King Godwin's favor.

RITTER'S APPEARANCE AT COURT HADN'T gone unnoticed by the Elspeths. When she was sure she could pass comment without being overheard, Addilyn leaned toward Dacre and asked her father what he knew of Sir Ritter Valkeneer.

"I've heard little of him or his family," Dacre replied, carefully. "Our history tells of the Battle of the Bridge, as a wing of the Vermilion fought there, but I know little else of his kin. I've heard rumors of a low-born noble family on the borderlands."

THE ELSPETHS WEREN'T THE only ones with their eyes on the young Valkeneer. Ember Fleury was watching him too, her eager young eyes tracking his every move. She was keen to see what this stranger was like, especially because it seemed clear to her that Sir Ritter Valkeneer was the man she was to marry. She smiled contentedly to herself and turned away from the court.

And then her hopes and dreams were dashed when her uncle Lothar grabbed her forcefully by the shoulder and said, "Come, Ember. Let us leave this spectacle. It's time to meet privately with your father and your newly betrothed."

EMBER, AARAV AND LOTHAR Von Lormarck made their way briskly away from the crowd and down a corridor to a royal chamber. Joferian Maeglen, Viscount of Queen's Chapel, was there, fresh from his battle against the Nightcloak, along with Baroness Cecily Maeglen, Talath Maeglen and Master Zendel Cray. A servant stood by with a jug of wine, topping up their glasses when they ran low.

Donnar and Emmerich were there, too. The two Von Lormarck twins were the spitting image of their father, Dragich. They stood well over six feet tall and were all bulk and muscle, with dark hair and rough features. Donnar was the firstborn and was a hair taller than Emmerich, but most people struggled to tell them apart, except for Ember.

Aarav was their half-brother, the thirdborn son to Dragich Von Lormarck in a union with Lady Isabeau Fleury. He had little of the familial resemblance and was thin, with an almost elven quality to his build and posture. He suffered from extreme alopecia, perhaps from a blood disease, and so he had no hair and no eyebrows. He was a feared warrior who'd been spearheading his father's wars against the twergs, the mountain and cave-dwelling folk from the Dragon's Breaths. They were shorter than humans but stout and hearty, with wild manes and tails that nearly met the ground. They were miners, jewelers, craftsmen and, most of all, warriors.

"Well, here he is," Lothar said. "One of the true heroes of the hour. Ember Fleury, allow me to introduce you to your betrothed, Viscount Joferian Maeglen of Queen's Chapel."

Joferian looked nervously at Ember, and she looked anxiously back at him. Then he broke out in a smile and strode over to introduce himself, kissing her hand politely before bowing to her as she curtsied.

"May your union cement the alliance between our great houses," Lothar said. "And may the Von Lormarcks and the Maeglens share destinies for many generations to come."

From half a step behind her, Aarav leaned in and murmured, "Joferian is also a bastard and the second-born, but he's been recognized as a true Maeglen by his father and the king. When you marry, you'll become a Maeglen by name and title."

"This marriage will be gainful to both sides," Lothar continued. "The Maeglens' lands in Queen's Chapel have been pillaged by the Cloak just as much as our own lands of Foghaven Vale. With this marriage, perhaps the rebuilding can begin in earnest. However, we still need to ask King Godwin for his blessing before the marriage can take place. And what better time is there to ask him?"

The servant was dispatched to request the presence of the royals, who used the summons as the signal to dismiss the court to begin preparations for the masquerade. When King Godwin and Queen Amice entered the chamber, the gathered nobles bowed low before Lothar summarized the discussion so far and asked Godwin for his approval.

The king chortled softly to himself and stroked his chin with a calloused hand. "I give my consent to this union," he decreed. "Let us announce it at the masquerade tonight."

Joferian and Ember shared a nervous but content look, and with the approval of the king and the Von Lormarcks, the two new lovers took each other's hands and started to converse in hushed voices as Godwin and Lothar talked business and hatched plans. Before discussions grew too in-depth, the king called a halt to proceedings and declared that they'd reconvene later to finalize the details. Before he left, he took Joferian and Ember aside for a private word of advice of his own.

"I know a little of arrangements such as these," the king said. "They're not easy, and the two of you will need to work at this marriage if it's to work. Joferian, you're the man of the castle and, as its head, you're entitled to… absolutely nothing."

Joferian and Ember snickered as a wry smile appeared on King Godwin's usually stoic face.

"Ember is your future baroness," he continued. "As long as you treat her as your queen, all will be well. But remember, while the men play their games in public, it's the baroness who rules the home in private. So, here's my advice to you, Lady Ember. Watch Queen Amice. Watch Baroness Cecily. Watch your mother, Lady Isabeau. Let them be your beacons."

PRIVATELY, WHEN THE KING and queen had a rare moment of solitude together, Godwin said, "This marriage of the two bastards is a little extreme."

"Aye," Amice replied. "And razor thin."

"Perhaps their union will calm the tensions between our family and the Von Lormarcks and help to bring them back into the fold," King Godwin said.

"We'll see," his queen replied.

WHEN THEY WERE FINALLY left alone, the conversation between Ember and Joferian was a little stilted, which was to be expected. The two were young and unskilled in the art of love, and it showed in the conversation, at least to begin with.

Ember found Joferian attractive. Both he and his brother, Talath, were handsome in their own ways. Privately, she'd worried that she'd be married off to a pauper knight of considerable age. Joferian was young, tall, and possessed a shock of strawberry blond hair that reminded her of the color of their wine.

But then Joferian started talking about his homeland, and that quickly caught Ember's attention, an interest of hers beyond the physical. Before long, she was hanging on to his every word as he waxed poetic about the beauty of Queen's Chapel.

And Ember, for her part, returned the favor, regaling him with tales of Deadwaters Fork and Foghaven Vale.

"The Fork lies in the sultry murk of the Borlach River," Ember explained. "It was named for the two rivers that carve the peninsula from the mainland. The peasants say the Deadwaters move so slowly that time itself stands still on the surface. At times, it looks like a polished mirror, reflecting images and light at odd patterns and angles. Even at night, through the humid fog, the lagoons still shine with the reflection of the starlight. The town itself is on the bayou, spreading from meander to meander."

"It sounds stunning," Joferian replied, looking into her eyes.

"It truly is," Ember said. "I hope we can see it together sometime."

"Let us drink a toast to it," Joferian replied, uncorking a bottle of the rare Queen's Nectar, a draught created by the master vintners from the chapel's orchards and vineyards. The unique brew was famous throughout the realm, but only the richest of the nobled gentry could afford to drink it. "You know, they say that the Queen's Nectar is a powerful aphrodisiac."

"Is that so?" Ember replied. She flashed a youthful smile at her betrothed and then took a huge swig from the bottle. "Truth be told, I could use the courage. I must confess that I'd been worrying about this match. I was worried that you wouldn't accept me as a bastardess."

"But I'm a bastard, too," Joferian said. "In fact, I'd been worrying about the same thing."

"Did you know your mother?" Ember asked. "Your true mother?"

Joferian shook his head and said, "Alas, no. My father had a distant affair in Castleshire, and I was the result of it. After I was born, I was taken back to Queen's Chapel. The Lady Cecily Maeglan adopted me as her own and has always been fair to me, treating me like a true son."

"And you know nothing of her?"

"Only that she was said to be a traitor and that she was condemned to death not long after my birth," Joferian said sadly. "But enough of that, for my tale is a sorry one. I know your father, but what of your mother?"

"My mother is Lady Isabeau Fleury," Ember said. "She raised my brother Aarav and I, but Aarav left for Foghaven Vale at the age of ten. I followed him when I was thirteen. I wish she could be here for the ceremony, but I'm not even sure if my father sent word in time to reach her. I'm sure that if he had, she'd be here. In fact, I've only just learned of our family's intent to marry me."

Joferian nodded in silent understanding and reached gently for her hand. He could sense regret in her voice, a regret that he could neither help nor soothe.

The two youngsters talked all evening and late into the night until the sun peeked over the horizon. It was only then, when the dawn's early light filtered through the castle's windows, that the two realized how late it was.

"Apologies, my lady," Joferian said, kissing her hand respectfully as he led her through the castle to her chambers. "I didn't mean to keep you up all night. If I'm honest, I woke up this morning fearing that today would be the worst day of my life. As the Fates would have it, it may well have been the best. May I kiss you?"

Ember said nothing in answer. Instead, she grabbed his face in her hands and pressed her lips to his.

CHAPTER FOURTEEN

"No road is too long for the company of a good friend."
—Longmarcher saying

DAEMUS AND KESTER WERE still on the road, maintaining a low profile in their covered wagon and traversing as much distance as they could without driving either themselves or their horses to the point of exhaustion.

It was close to evening when they arrived at the Hearth, a small town on the banks of Loch Keefe, its lifegiving waters responsible for the founding of the settlement in the first place. At the heart of the Hearth was an old ratskeller which served as both a trading post and an inn, making it the center of community gossip. It was the ratskeller that Kester made a beeline for, with Daemus in tow, wearing a hood and scarf to cover his face.

If he'd been hoping to make a low-profile entrance, he was disappointed. Almost as soon as the two of them entered the ratskeller, which was already starting to fill up as the night approached, a cry went up from one of the punters and Kester found himself being greeted like an old friend, which he was.

The first person to see him was Faux Dauldon, a young, comely woman with red hair and fair eyes. Kester hadn't seen her in years and couldn't help smiling in the presence of his friend, despite both their circumstances.

She'd spent the majority of her life roaming from town to town and making her living as a rogue of sorts. Dauldon was accompanied by some usual familiar faces, including her huldrefolk accomplice Blue Conney and his war dog, Jericho. Huldrefolk were half the size of humans, and Conney's tribe, the Springheels, were a vicious, ill-tempered subrace of huldrefolk berserkers that possessed the ability to leap great distances both forward and backward, as well as being able to jump twice their own height from a standing start. Conney had a face tattoo, like many of his kind, which resembled a blue mask around his forehead and eyes. Jericho came from a long line of hounds that had been bred for war, herding, and even as steeds for his people.

Faux's half-brother, Marquiss, was also in tow, the Dale elf blood from his mother's side making itself known in his mint green hair and the subtle tint of his skin. Born out of wedlock, he'd been a faithful companion and confidante for Faux ever since her exile. He was the group's troublemaker, less disciplined than Faux but fiercely loyal.

Their party was rounded off by Arjun Ezekyle, the long-time captain of the Dauldon family who'd served as Faux's protector since an early age. He was Faux's rock and a surrogate father of sorts, but was originally from Abacus. A freed slave himself, he'd been trained at the High Aldin, the scholar city's legendary military academy. He was blond with moppish hair that fell across his face and obscured his blue eyes, and he was known for the ferocity and speed with which he fought. No one, not even Arjun himself, knew how old he was.

They were also joined by two other mercenaries that Kester didn't know but who looked like a good fit for the motley band of adventurers.

"It's good to see you again, Kester," Faux said, taking him by the shoulder and leading him over to their dimly lit table in the corner of the ratskeller. "The Ancients know that I wouldn't be alive today without you."

"I only did what any honest man would have done."

"Aye," Faux said in her broguish accent. "And there are precious few of those around."

"And what of your companions?" Kester asked, gesturing to the two mercenaries. "Are they honest men?"

"Of course not." Faux nearly laughed. "They're rogues. They'd have to be, to travel with me. Their names are Chernovog and Burgess. Chernovog has worked with me before. Burgess used to be a guardsman for House Dauldon before the fall and has followed us these recent years out of loyalty to my father and Arjun."

"If they travel with you, my lady, I'm sure they can be trusted."

"So, what brings you here, Kester?" she asked. "And why are you so far away from Castleshire?"

"Is there anywhere more private?" Kester scanned the bar, looking for prying eyes. "The tale I have to tell isn't for just anyone's ears."

"My party has a room out back," Faux said. "Let me take you there."

Kester nodded at Daemus, and the young lad took a seat in the corner and introduced himself to Faux's companions. Then Kester followed Arjun and Faux into the rear of the ratskeller.

BEFORE DAEMUS KNEW IT, the drinks were flowing and tongues were wagging. As the outsider, he bore the brunt of the jokes, and he was sober and they weren't, at least to begin with. But before long, Blue Conney had called for more ale and pressed a flagon of it into Daemus's hands.

"Drink it down, lad," Conney said. "In one, if you can."

"I don't—"

"Drink it!" Conney repeated, and then his companions started slapping the table with their hands and taking up the chant until Daemus, feeling the peer pressure, gave in and tried his best to quaff the ale. He got halfway through and then almost vomited, which set his new friends off again as a howl of uproarious laughter passed around the table.

"Attaboy." Conney feigned an effort to mop up the spill with his cloak. "Come, finish up and we'll get you another."

THE RATSKELLER RENTED OUT its back rooms to weary travelers, and as such they were sparse and relatively low on amenities. Still, Faux and Arjun did their best to make Kester feel welcome."

"Please, take a seat," Faux gestured. "And help yourself to meat and mead."

"Thank you." Kester sat. "The journey has been a long one."

"So, what brings you here?"

"The boy," Kester said. "He's my nephew, Daemus. Allow me to be frank with you. The two of us are in great danger. I'm under strict instructions from the Great Keeper to return him to Castleshire as quickly as possible. Once there, we need to find Disciple Delling from the cathedral, who's waiting for us. I was hoping that you could help me."

"Ha!" Faux laughed, her red hair cascading across her shoulders as she threw her head back. Then she took another look at Kester and her demeanor changed. "By the Ancients, you're serious."

"I am," Kester replied. He took a pause before proceeding. "And I know what that could mean for you as the last Dauldon."

"Aye," Faux said, softening slightly and adopting a faraway look as she glanced into the past. "I've lived in exile for nearly a decade, running and escaping from one town to the next. And you'd have me walk into the belly of the beast?"

"I can give you a purse of laurels and palmettes."

"I don't need your gold," Faux snapped, looking offended at the mere suggestion. "No amount of gold could tempt me to return to certain death."

Kester sighed and thought for a moment, gesturing for

Arjun to pour another drink and taking a deep swig from it while he formulated his words.

"I was hoping it wouldn't come to this," he said, eventually. "But the truth is, Faux, I have no one else to turn to. Perhaps you've forgotten that you owe me a favor. Perhaps you've forgotten that I risked much to save your life, smuggling you out of Castleshire at great peril. And perhaps you've forgotten the promise you made to return the favor if such an opportunity presented itself. This is such an opportunity."

Now it was Faux's turn to sigh and to drink.

"You have a point," she conceded, begrudgingly. "How much silver do you have?"

"Not much," Kester admitted. "But all I have is yours."

"You understand, Kester," Faux motioned, holding out her hand and taking his leather purse from him, "I'll give you my time for free. I can't ask the same of my comrades."

"If my laurels buy their help, I'll happily give it."

"And they'll happily take it," Faux replied, laughing to herself. "I'm doing this for you, Kester. For you and the boy. He's about the same age I was when you smuggled me out of Castleshire. But you must see the irony. You smuggled me out of the city. Why, now, must we smuggle someone in? Why not just walk through the gates if he's an Alaric?"

Now it was Kester's turn to laugh, though his laughter was less comely and a little hoarse from the time they'd spent on the road.

"It had crossed my mind that there's a certain poetry that it should be you, of all people, to help me." Kester grimaced. "If only it were as simple as riding in through the gates and announcing our presence. Alas, I've been warned of the need for secrecy by Great Keeper Nasyr. There are many pairs of spying eyes and a thousand differing agendas throughout Castleshire. That task won't be easy."

"I'll say," Arjun grumbled, but he did so good-naturedly. "I'll go and fetch the lads. If we're to do this, they should be here while we hatch our plans."

Faux nodded at Arjun, and the swarthy rogue winked at her and left the room to rescue Daemus from his companions. Kester watched him leave and closed the door behind him before opening up his traveling bag.

"I have something for you," Kester said, withdrawing a leather scroll case with the Dauldon seal emblazoned across it, a chevron with a clover just beneath the gable in a light green color. He handed it over and Faux opened it, withdrawing several well-preserved scrolls covered in the spidery handwriting of a Warminsterian scribe.

"What is it?"

"It's the Dauldon patents of nobility," Kester explained. "I've held on to them these past years in the knowledge that one day, the Ancients would bring us back together. Now that you're a woman, the time is right to return them."

"But House Dauldon is no more," Faux replied. "I have no need of them."

"Not yet," Kester said, smiling softly at her in the same way he occasionally looked at Daemus. "The years have changed you, and it's likely that no one will recognize you. That will serve us well, at least for now, but a time may come when you need to prove your name and your lineage. If such a time comes, these will help you."

"I hope that you're right." Faux paused for a moment and turned her back on him to examine the patents before rolling the scrolls up and returning them to their carrying case. "I'm tired of running."

"If you help me and my nephew, I'm certain that the Caveat will look kindly upon your cause," Kester told her. "I'll fight to my dying breath to see that you get clemency for a crime you didn't commit."

"Unless Castleshire is much changed, I doubt they're ready for my return."

"Castleshire is the same as ever," Kester mused. "What do you remember of the city?"

"Just its beauty," Faux replied, no doubt thinking of its high walls, its talented sculptors and stonemasons. "But perhaps time is playing tricks with my memory."

"Castleshire is beautiful," Kester asserted, "though you may find it a little smaller than you remember, now that you're fully grown. But the city itself isn't the problem. Only politics could turn such a beautiful city so ugly."

"And what news of Jaxtyn Faircloth?"

Kester laughed at this, and Faux's cheeks flushed as she turned her head to one side to try to hide it.

"You haven't forgotten your childhood sweetheart, I see," Kester replied. "Jaxtyn is now a man, and before you ask, he's an eligible bachelor."

"I'll drink to that," Faux replied.

THE PARTY REUNITED IN the main room of the ratskeller and spent the rest of the evening drinking heavily and hatching plans for the return to Castleshire. Daemus and Kester hadn't eaten properly for several days, and so they feasted on platters of breads and cold meats while the rest of Faux's companions proceeded into deeper and deeper states of inebriation. Kester was an old hand at the taverns, and he had no problem holding his wine with the rest of them. But Daemus didn't have the same constitution, and he was soon slurring his words and spilling his cups on himself.

Arjun and Kester were old friends, and they celebrated

their reunion with the telling of old stories, including the tale of how they'd smuggled Faux out of Castleshire by hiring Captain Eruduel Morley to take her away by boat. Faux listened on politely, though she'd been there herself and heard the story more times than she cared to remember, while Daemus slouched in the corner with his hood over his eyes, being teased mercilessly but good-naturedly by Blue Conney and the others.

"Come on, Your Majesty," Conney was saying, sarcasm dripping from his words like poison from the blade of an assassin. "Let's see if a Keeper can outdrink a scoundrel."

Daemus said something indistinct and flinched a little as another full cup was pushed over to him. Then he turned to Marquiss, hoping he'd have a little mercy on him, and said, "Ish he alwaysh like thish? I'm s…shtruggling to keep theesh drinksh down."

"You get used to it," Marquiss teased. He paused for a moment, thought about it a little, and then added, "Well, eventually. He's a softie at heart, although you wouldn't want to cross him on the battlefield."

"Aye." Conney laughed. "Be thankful we're on the same side. Drink up, boy. My dog has more of a taste for beer than you do."

"Ish that sho?" Daemus slurred. An idea took him, and he tried to subtly empty his flagon into the dog's mouth, but he had a drunk's dexterity and he couldn't carry it off. When Blue Conney's sharp eyes saw the movement, he slapped Daemus with a heavy hand on a muscular arm and sent him tumbling to the floor, his ale spilling all over his robes.

"That drink is for you, boy," Conney growled. "Jericho has a nose for ale but not the stomach. If he shits the bed tonight, I'll make sure you have a taste of it."

"Leave him alone, Conney," Faux called out as she and the others made their return. "He wasn't brought here for you to torment."

As the moon rose higher in the sky and the other patrons started to stumble home, the Dauldon table grew louder and more animated. After a while, a serving girl, a diminutive human dressed in little better than rags, drew the short straw and was sent over to ask them to keep the noise down and finish their brews. Grumbling about it but acquiescing, the party retired to the back room, where Daemus immediately fell asleep. Faux followed suit shortly afterward, signaling the end of the evening.

BEFORE THEY TURNED IN for the night, Arjun and Kester poured out a final drink and went to sit on the stoop outside the ratskeller, sharing a pipe and another tale or two. Kester was the more morose of the two, and it showed in his face and the way he was only half paying attention to the conversation.

"What troubles you, old friend?" Arjun asked.

"It's nothing."

"Kester, I've known you for many years," Arjun pried, looking his friend in the eye. "I can tell when there's something troubling you. What is it?"

Kester sighed and reached over to take the pipe back. He seemed to be silently weighing something up. Then he arrived at a decision and told Arjun about what Great Keeper Nasyr had said to him in the observatory. They drank and smoked as they talked, and the moon had shifted in the sky by the time they finished.

"We have to get Daemus to Castleshire at all costs," Kester concluded. "No price is too high. This is more important than we are. If it costs us our lives, so be it."

"You ask a lot of us, Kester," Arjun replied.

"Aye," Kester said. "I wasn't sure if Faux would help us."

"She learned from a great noble." Arjun took his turn on the pipe and inhaled deeply. "You should be proud of the woman she's grown into. It wouldn't have been possible without you. She owes you, Kester. She was always going to help you, just like you helped her. I just hope you're not leading her into danger."

A rat scuttled along the dirt path away from the front of the ratskeller and over to a waiting human. Kester, distracted by the movement, looked up to see a man who was wearing brown leather armor with a green cape clasped together by a brooch in the form of a dull green shield with an emerald embedded into it.

The man pushed himself up from the treestump he was sitting on and approached the two men outside the ratskeller. "I hope you don't mind me butting in," he said. "My rat friend and I overheard your conversation about your traveling companion, Daemus. I may be able to help you."

Despite the drinks, the two men reacted quickly, and Kester was on his feet with his sword in his hand in seconds, a look of deep concern and consternation plastered across his face.

"Who sent you?" he growled, holding the point of his sword out at the stranger, who appeared unarmed.

"No one." The man lifted his empty hands. "Allow me to introduce myself. My name is Lachlan Barrett and I'm a druid of the Emerald Shield. I've been following your trail since Sycamore Post."

"Why?"

"I have my reasons," Barrett replied. "Lower your weapon, please. I'm on your side. I wanted to deliver a warning."

"What warning?" Kester asked, still holding his sword out, though his arm was starting to tremble from the alcohol.

"I'm not the only one who's following you," Barrett confided. "Misael, the chieftain of Clan Blood Axe, has his spies out. They're coming for you." The man looked around to the open night sky. "The Emerald Shield communes with nature, and I've tasked the birds, the trees, and the wind with keeping watch on the trollborn tribes to help travelers such as you. I can help you to reach safety."

Arjun and Kester exchanged an uneasy look. They weren't sure whether to trust Lachlan and his magic, but there was something in the way he spoke that made him seem reliable. And besides, he had information. Slowly, almost reluctantly, Kester lowered his sword, although he kept it close at hand, just in case he needed it.

"Who are Clan Blood Axe?" Arjun asked.

"They're the worst of the worst," Barrett said. "The lowest of the low. A clan of trollborn degenerates riding horse-hounds, fell crossbreeds that maraud the plains of the Vilchor Highgrass. Their steeds cover broken ground like no other creature. If Clan Blood Axe is on your trail, they'll catch up with you. You can't run, and you can't hide."

"How do they know of us?"

"I'm not sure," Lachlan admitted. "Yet my rat friend and I saw your display at Sycamore Post, and so did one of Misael's trollborn spies. There must be a bounty on the Keeper's head."

"Then what would you suggest?" Kester replied. He was warming to the stranger, and he resheathed his sword and made do with keeping his hand on the pommel, an old habit from his years in the field.

"You fight," the druid replied. "But not alone."

"And who will fight with us? You?"

Barrett shook his head. "I can't help you there, but I know who can. You must travel the plains toward the Eternal Forest, where the Dale elves will take you in and rally to your cause."

"The Dale elves?"

"Aye," Barrett said. "I see one of your group is part Keldarin. The one you call Marquiss."

"Keldarin?" Kester asked.

"It's the elven name for their kind," Lachlan replied. "You must seek them out. When you arrive, ask for Coronel Adulth Briar. If you tell them I sent you, they'll help you."

"And why should they help us?"

"The enemy of an enemy is a friend," Barrett said. "Remember that, Kester. The Keldarin and their Circle of Swords seek to keep the trollborn in check. Go to them. Speak to Adulth and say that Lachlan and the Emerald Shield sent you."

Kester and Arjun exchanged a glance. There was a tenseness and a wariness there. Though neither man spoke, a silent conversation passed between them. Arjun's eyes were full of caution.

"It's too dangerous," Kester said. "I can't risk taking Daemus there, but I have a plan. Thank you for your help, Lachlan Barrett. I'm sure we'll meet again."

Barrett nodded at the two men, whistled a farewell to his rodent friend and struck off away from the ratskeller. Kester and Arjun watched him go.

"Arjun, I don't want to scare Daemus," Kester said, breaking the short silence. "I'll leave first thing in the morning and ride with as much haste as I can muster. I'll take the covered wagon as a diversion in the hope that our pursuers will follow my trail and not yours."

"Are you sure?" Arjun asked, an air of doubt in his voice.

"Tell Daemus that I'll see him in Castleshire," Kester replied.

"And will he?"

Kester hugged the man but didn't answer.

IN THE MORNING, WHEN the sun was yet to rise in the sky and everyone else was asleep, Kester stole silently into the sleeping quarters and woke Faux by shaking her shoulders while holding one hand over her mouth to prevent her from crying out. The young woman tensed up immediately at his touch and one hand flew to the side of her bed, where her knife was stashed beneath the mattress. She dragged it out, but then stopped herself when a moonbeam filtered in from behind a cloud and through the window, illuminating Kester's face. At the same time, he whispered something urgently and Faux froze, then relaxed herself in his grip. He nodded at her and then left the room, meeting her on the stoop outside the ratskeller five minutes later once she'd donned some clothes and a weapon, just in case.

"What's wrong, Kester?" Faux asked.

"I wanted to speak to you before I leave," Kester said.

"You're *leaving?*"

"I have to," he replied, before briefly summarizing the events of the night before. Faux listened in silence, her brain whirring into life as the fresh air woke her up.

"If you're going to find the Keldarin," she said, once he was finished, "then where does that leave me?"

"I need you to take Daemus and press on for Castleshire," Kester said. "I suggest traveling via Forecastle and posing as servants. You won't be able to enter the city through the main gates. You can't afford to be recognized or to compromise your true identity until the time is right."

"And when will the time be right?"

"You'll know," Kester said. "And besides, young Daemus

travels in anonymity, too. For now, the two of you must remain in the shadows. Once you arrive in Forecastle, seek out Ellissio with House Alaric. In your scroll case, you'll find a newer document sealed with the mark of House Alaric. Deliver the scroll and have him follow my instructions."

"Understood," Faux replied. "And what then?"

"The Great Keeper told me to take Daemus to Castleshire," Kester said. "But she didn't say *where* in the city to take him. She said that a man named Disciple Delling will make contact. Deliver Daemus to Delling and then make your escape from the city. Accomplish that and we're even."

"You make it sound so easy," Faux complained.

"One more thing," Kester said. "I need you to deliver a message to my brother and sister. Keep it secret, even from the rest of your party. No one must know."

"What's the message?"

"I can't tell you here," Kester murmured, lowering his voice and looking around for fear of being overheard. "I'll have the message sealed in a scroll necklace for you to wear. I'll give it to you before I leave. Do you know where to find them?"

"I can find anyone."

She stood up and hugged Kester, then turned to make her way back to the ratskeller. She paused and looked back over her shoulder. "Good luck. May Nothos watch over you."

FAUX DAULDON CRAWLED BACK into her cot in the ratskeller, her mind too disturbed by Kester's departure to fall back to sleep. She thought back to her childhood and wondered what her life might have looked like if things had worked out differently.

The Dauldon family was one of the founding families of Castleshire, known for being great statesmen, merchants and warriors of justice. They'd been part of Castleshire's inner circle for generations, but that had all changed when her family had been caught selling the waters of a poisonous river that the locals called the Venom of the Abyss. It was used to make deadly poisons that were odorless and tasteless but could kill a whole village if even just a goblet of the stuff was introduced to the well. In concentrated form, coating a blade with it could guarantee death for even the hardiest of enemies. When diluted, it was rumored to cause disease and to hasten aging. Its possession and sale were punishable by death, but that didn't stop it from being sold on the sizeable black market in the backstreets of Saracen. The venom had already been blamed for several prominent deaths in Castleshire alone and the nobles were under a lot of pressure to locate a culprit. Once the Dauldons were accused, not even their nobility could save them.

Most vividly of all, to Faux at least, was the echoing sound of Iron Jack, the fabled Gavel of the Caveat. As was tradition, at the end of the trial, the Regent of Castleshire clapped the magical warhammer against a mighty shield bearing the city's coat of arms. In Castleshire, the Caveat was judge, jury, and executioner. It was said that those sentenced would forever hear that noise in their ears whenever they thought about their crimes until their sentencing—and their penance—was complete.

Faux heard the sonorous clang of metal on metal every night when she went to sleep and every morning when she woke up.

CHAPTER FIFTEEN

"The whispers of ancient trees are a cure for a lonely heart."
—Melexis, the Ancient of elves

"SO, WHAT ARE WE to do now?" Wilcox asked, breaking the short silence. The man looked unkempt and out of place, and it wasn't helped by the fact that his rangy seven-foot frame was folded awkwardly into a chair that was much too short for him. "Just sit here and take orders from the king's men? We're no heirloom royal bodyguards, to be forever lounging about at court and getting soft."

It was the day after their return to Thronehelm, and Ritter was sitting with his men in an antechamber just off his guest room, which was near to the king's own quarters. The Longmarchers, quartered closer to the royal guard, had been spoiled nearly as much as he'd been with enormous quantities of food. But Ritter could tell they were still unhappy at being forced to travel to Thronehelm instead of returning home to the Bridge. The atmosphere in the room was restless.

Ritter glanced at him, then looked meaningfully at the slightly open door and Wilcox closed his mouth. He valued Wilcox's straightforwardness and incisive judgment and felt it made him an excellent second, but Ritter had occasionally suffered for his lieutenant's lack of tact. He usually made an effort to rein it in, even when he privately agreed.

Rufus snorted from his place in the corner. "Tell them you hate them a little louder, Wilcox, I don't think every single fish in the Thalassian Sea quite heard you."

"Stuff it, Crag," Wilcox replied. "I know you all noticed too." He kept his voice low, to Ritter's relief.

"Are you two finished?" Ritter asked after another moment,

raising his eyebrows, and the room fell silent. "All right. Wilcox, Rufus, you're both staying here at Thronehelm with me." He ignored Rufus's quiet scoff of disappointment, knowing it to be an expression of simple frustration rather than insubordination. "Marr and Til, you'll go home to the Bridge with the king's troops, and I'll also need you to deliver a message to my parents."

"What message?" Marr asked, his eyes attentive.

"I'd like them to give Fira Carling enough of the king's palmettes to give her a new start," Ritter told him, folding his hands over his knees. "She's been orphaned and we must afford her shelter. Phrase the request in whatever way you see fit; you've always been more persuasive than I have. Just make sure she's taken care of, please."

Marr inclined his head in assent.

"But won't your father—" Til started, looking concerned, but Ritter cut him off.

"She's of our people," he pointed out, "and her father saved many of us by warning of the brigand ambush. She's lost everything. It's only right."

"It was the king's mistake," Wilcox muttered, though his tone was without acrimony.

"No, it wasn't," Ritter replied. "The bandits were on our land, terrorizing our people and acting under our noses."

"Not only *our* land," his lieutenant pointed out, his lips thinning. "If the issue was solely the responsibility and purview of Valkeneer, the king wouldn't have bothered to help at all."

"Enough," Ritter growled, growing impatient. "It doesn't matter, do you understand? They need to be taken care of, one way or another. It's our responsibility to look after them. Throwing blame around will accomplish nothing."

Wilcox looked as though he still disagreed, but he didn't voice it further. Ritter didn't blame him; most natives of the

Bridge had neutral to negative opinions of the Thronehelm royals. Historically, they'd received little from the crown in the way of either help or hindrance, but Ritter's family had personal ties to the Thorhauers, and he didn't have the luxury of showing any resentment toward the king. It could damage their relationship and cause Valkeneer to fall out of favor.

He dismissed his men shortly afterwards, but only moments after he'd finally found himself alone, a light knock came at the door. Ritter turned to see a small, mousy-looking man, whom he thought he remembered being the king's personal attendant, hovering anxiously out in the hall.

"What is it?" Ritter asked, trying to sound more civil than he felt. Privately, he knew it wouldn't be much longer before he suffocated under the castle's stifling atmosphere, but he also knew the man wouldn't disturb him unless it was for a good reason.

"I apologize for interrupting your thoughts, my lord," the butler said with a smooth and practiced bow. Ritter twitched at the honorific, suppressing the urge to snap at the man to call him Ritter. The butler shrank back slightly, seeming to notice his agitation, and Ritter made a conscious effort to ease his expression.

"It's no trouble," he lied. "What can I do for the king… and what's your name?"

The servant inclined his head. "Meeks Crowley, my lord, if it please you," he said. "His majesty the king asked me to turn away any individuals of insufficient station who wished to meet with you today, but there are two requests I couldn't decline on your behalf in good conscience."

Ritter's breath evened out at this. It spoke well of the king to have thought of his guests' comfort, and it was astute of him to have observed that Ritter was unadept at navigating the court and would want to be left alone. He didn't like the idea of being pulled into more politics, and he dearly wished for what seemed like the hundredth time that he and the Longmarchers had been allowed to go home, instead of being dragged back to Thronehelm by the princes. Nevertheless, he nodded to Meeks and gave a signal for the man to continue speaking.

"Ambassador Dacre Elspeth sends his regards," Meeks said, blinking his pale eyes, "and asks that you put aside a moment to speak with him at the king's masquerade ball."

That sounded simple enough. Ritter had no idea who the ambassador was or where he hailed from, but he had no objection to learning more. He didn't like parties much, but at least it was better than a formal meeting where he'd be trapped in a room with someone who wanted something from him.

"Fine," Ritter agreed. "And the other?"

Meeks shifted his weight, looking vaguely nervous again. "Baron Von Lormarck has asked to speak to you today, sir," he said at length. "He wouldn't tell me why or what he wished to discuss, only that it was important."

Ritter drew back, flinching a little. The Valkeneers and the Von Lormarcks had been on poor terms for the better part of Ritter's life, and the relationship had once or twice nearly escalated into a full-on blood feud. "Dragich Von Lormarck?" he repeated, stunned, although he knew what the answer would be. Ritter had no idea why an ambassador he'd never heard of would want to speak with him, but the notion that the reigning patriarch of the Von Lormarck clan would want to interact with him made him actively suspicious.

"Yes, my lord," Meeks said.

Ritter blew out his breath and considered it for a moment. "Is there any way I can avoid speaking to him without getting myself into trouble?" he asked, his voice low.

The butler hesitated and then answered quietly, "I don't know, my lord. It's possible that you could give some excuse that he'd believe, but the baron isn't a patient man. If he wants a meeting, he'll do everything within his power to get one while you're here at court."

"Very well," he said. Feeling that he might as well get it over with, he added, "I'll meet with him presently."

The butler, who looked appropriately sympathetic, bowed, promised to fetch him again within the hour, and left.

Impulsively, Ritter collected Storm and took the falcon outside. He knew that he might be missed if he didn't return in time, but he felt he had to get out of the castle so he could collect his thoughts or else he'd end up hysterical before meeting Von Lormarck.

Almost as soon as the two of them were outside, with Ritter's telepathic permission, Storm took to the skies. Ritter jogged beneath him, not trying to keep up but happy to feel the dirt under his feet and the fresh, cool air on his face, as well as the whispering of trees around him instead of the murmuring of courtiers. He slowed and paused, however, when Storm began to descend, and a few moments later the falcon sent him a projection of an image. Someone else was in the woods.

As soon as he followed the bond and found his bird, he saw that she was an elf. Storm didn't seem to understand the differences between the various classes of elves, much less that Ritter was trollborn and not a full-blooded elf, but he couldn't begrudge his war falcon for trying to find him a friend. The young woman looked to be one of the Vermilion, the highest class of elves, but she had an easy, unaffected air that made him want to try speaking to her. Perhaps she was a servant or one of the ambassador's retinue.

"Hello," Ritter said in Minsterian, as he knew nothing of the Vermilion tongue. "Nice woods." He cringed at his misformed statement; social grace had never been his strongest suit. She took his awkwardness in stride, however.

"They are," the woman agreed in a musical voice. The

two of them stood smiling for a moment, scrutinizing each other, before she appeared to make a decision and continued speaking. "We don't really have woods like this at home. Not this thick, at least." She looked around. "One wonders what little creatures might be wandering around out of sight with all this greenery everywhere."

Ritter smiled a little at the comment. "Does the thought disturb you?" he asked.

"It doesn't," the Vermilion replied, a little defensively. Then she seemed to reconsider her statement. "Not very much, anyway. I've heard of a few animals that I'd prefer to stay away from me."

"There are some unpleasant things out in the wilderness," Ritter agreed, "that much is true. They're only animals, though, and they only behave the way animals behave. The trick is to learn their habits, the ways they think, and then they're not as hard to predict. And less frightening, I think."

"Is that so?" the woman asked, looking suddenly rather somber, her gaze distant. Ritter half-expected her to react to what he'd said about being frightened, but she surprised him by ignoring his unintentional rudeness altogether. "I suppose it must be," she continued, but it almost seemed as though she was talking to herself. "But I think some things might be frightening regardless of how hard you try to understand them."

"Are you all right?" Ritter asked, attempting to gentle his tone. He tried not to compare it to the voice he used to calm his horse. The thought dissipated when he realized that the answer to his question was probably "no."

"Oh, I am, of course," she said. "I'm so sorry. Here I am speaking nonsense to you, and I haven't even asked your name."

"It's Ritter," he offered. "And yours?"

"Addilyn," she said, with a smile that didn't quite reach her eyes. It looked as though something was troubling her, but he had no idea how to help. A part of him wondered why he wanted to help her at all. He normally avoided strangers like the plague, and sometimes he even struggled to open up to his friends. People were much more work than animals, plants or weapons. Somehow, though, she was easy to talk to in a way that surprised him. It reminded him of his bond with Storm, as if he understood her meaning before she spoke.

"I don't think I heard any nonsense," he tried, in answer to her earlier self-deprecation, and he was rewarded with a brighter look in her eyes, though the smile had disappeared.

"You're a very generous spirit, Ritter."

"So, if you don't mind me asking, what are you doing out here by yourself?" he asked. Addilyn pouted as if in thought and leaned against the trunk of a nearby tree.

"Well, if I'm being honest," she said, "I wanted to get away for a little while. I suppose I don't really feel at home here. And, of course, I'm a guest." Her eyes flicked to Ritter's, checking if he understood her. Apparently satisfied, she went on. "What I mean is that I... still don't feel I quite understand things here. People." Her red lips drew themselves into a line. "It's as though everything I say is slightly wrong. I understand that things have to be this way, but it's difficult for me." Her face flushed, and she seemed embarrassed by the surge of honesty, which pulled at Ritter's heart.

"I think I know what you mean," he said. "I feel the same. It's much easier at home, but here..." He shook his head. "It's as though everyone is reading from the same book, one that I'm not allowed to see."

"And they try so hard to be friendly," Addilyn added, with an expression of relief. "It only makes me feel..."

"Worse," Ritter finished the thought, and grimaced. "Exactly." To his own profound surprise, he found himself asking, "What's your home like?"

Addilyn smiled. "Our great city is called Eldwal," she said. "It's beautiful. Huge towers carved out of red stone, broad and open streets, and flowers everywhere. But I didn't grow up there." She paused, her bright eyes unfocusing in memory. "My family home was more remote, up in the mountains. I loved it at court, but I never stopped wanting to return there." Her smile had turned wistful. It suddenly occurred to him that when she spoke about court, she didn't sound like a servant.

"I know what you mean," he said. "It feels wrong if I'm not out in the wilderness."

Addilyn nodded. "There's something about it, isn't there?" she agreed, softly. "It's like everything comes more easily. Magic. Laughter. Love." Her eyes flicked downward. "I don't quite know why I'm talking to you like this, as if we're friends. Or why I just said that."

"Well, if you're uncomfortable, we needn't continue," Ritter said, his brow furrowing. He was concerned that she seemed distressed.

"I didn't say that," she replied mildly, and he felt his frown ease. "I'm surprised, that's all."

"You said something about studying magic," he put in at length, wondering if she was a court mage, a handmaiden or perhaps a lady-in-waiting.

Addilyn nodded again. "I've been doing it since I was a little girl. It comes easily to the women of my bloodline, although I know I still have much to learn."

Ritter smiled at this and considered remarking on her modesty, but he didn't wish to embarrass her or put her on the spot. "My mother used to perform illusions for me and my sisters when we were young," he said. "She doesn't do it much anymore, because she claims the gift has mostly gone."

Addilyn hummed. "I've heard that can happen, if one moves into a different kind of lifestyle than one had before." She looked at her hands. "Something about the body sensing that magic isn't needed any longer, or that it's become a crutch. But I've never seen it myself. We're not a people who tend to go through significant life changes, as a rule." After another moment, she twisted a hand in the air in a sharp and abrupt motion, and two glittering scarlet butterflies burst forth. Ritter marveled at them, grinning. His mother had always liked to make flowers, and he thought the two would have made a pretty scene together.

"My form is rather bad," Addilyn commented, her lips quirking into a rueful half-smile. "I used to do these for the coronelle, and I'd always see my tutor glaring at me out of the corner of my eye. It's meant to be more like this." She demonstrated another gesture, smoother and more graceful, which produced nothing but a brief shimmer in the air.

"I like your version better," Ritter argued. "It's more decisive."

She laughed again and opened her mouth to reply, but they both paused at the sound of a voice calling Ritter's name. Ritter grimaced: it was Meeks.

"I've been out here longer than I intended," he confessed, "and now I think I may have missed an appointment."

Addilyn's expression was back to calm professionalism, although her eyes were warm. "Well, you'd better go and make your apologies, then," she said. "I'm sure I'll see you again sometime soon."

Ritter bowed to her, feeling Storm fly off ahead of him through their bond. "I hope so."

With a final smile, he turned and made his way back to the castle. He didn't like that he'd broken his word, but then he hadn't wanted to meet with the baron, and it was difficult to regret the decision given how the rest of the evening had gone. Surely, if Von Lormarck had a good reason to speak to him, he'd be patient for a few moments longer.

CHAPTER SIXTEEN

"Horsehounds possess the speed of the flightiest of racehorses and the vicious bite of the meanest of stray dogs. If you should find yourself being hunted by a horsehound, don't bother running. Make peace with your Ancients instead and then prepare to meet them."
—A Warminster Bestiary (Fourth Edition)

DAEMUS STIRRED SOFTLY IN his sleep, stretched out in his cot, and slowly opened his eyes. He felt terrible, as though someone had dragged his brains through his nose and stuffed his skull with sawdust. There was a harsh metallic taste in his mouth and his body ached for two things: to relieve itself and to rehydrate. He could remember little of the night before.

A lonely ray of sunlight filtered in through the window, and with it came a chill breeze followed by the crack of a whip and the sound of wheels on mud. Normally, Daemus wouldn't have been able to tell the sound of one wagon from another, but this was different. He'd spent days on end listening to those wheels as they bore him away from the Cathedral of the Watchful Eye.

He was on his feet in an instant, surprised and relieved to find himself fully clothed, though barefoot. He raced out of the room and into the street outside the ratskeller. The sleepy little village was just starting to wake up, and the early morning traders were setting up stalls and bringing out their wares. Daemus's eyes darted around as he sought his uncle, but at first there was nothing. Then he saw a cloud of dust in the distance, and he didn't need the eyes of a Vermilion to tell what he was looking at.

"Uncle Kester!" he bellowed. He took a couple steps forward and then broke into a run, bellowing his uncle's name as he chased after his trail. "Uncle Kester! Don't leave without me!"

"Silence, child!" This came from Arjun, who had the advantage of height and a longer stride.

Daemus wasn't sure how or why Arjun had found him so quickly. He bucked against his arms, and then a hairy palm was thrust against his mouth to silence him. Daemus surprised himself by clamping his jaws down, then received a cuff against the side of his head as a reward for his efforts.

"Be quiet!" Arjun hissed. "For both our sakes. Your uncle is trying to save your life. You were being followed."

"I don't understand. Why can't—?"

"Not here," Arjun said. "We have much to discuss, but let's discuss it in private."

Back in the ratskeller, Arjun told Daemus what he could of the events of the night before, relating them in a hushed voice in a shady corner of the main room.

"I don't understand," Daemus said. "Why did Uncle Kester have to leave?"

"He's diverting the enemy's attention," Arjun replied. "He aims to lead them away from our group. We need to make good on the time that he's bought for us and get out of town before we're spotted."

"But he took the wagon."

"Aye," Arjun said, patiently. "It's the wagon that they'll be searching for. Don't worry, young Daemus. I've arranged a horse for you."

The group didn't stop for breakfast, but they did load their packs with meats, breads, and cheeses so that they could eat on the move. As they rode out of town, Daemus couldn't help turning back to look at the path his uncle had taken, but his cart had long since passed over the horizon.

They rode toward their destination in silence for an hour

or so, and then stopped for a rest to give Daemus a chance to stretch his legs. He wasn't used to riding, and it showed in his posture in the saddle.

"Better make this quick," Faux said, her impatience showing through her strained smile and the way she kept scanning the horizon as though she had some nervous tick. "We don't have time to keep stopping. Every minute we spend at the roadside is a minute our adversaries can use to their advantage."

"I'm sorry." Daemus stretched through the pains in his back. "I'm not much of a rider."

"I've noticed," Faux said.

"Could you teach me?" Daemus asked. "You look like you were born in the saddle. Where did you learn to ride?"

Faux smiled at him, but she didn't answer. Instead, she nodded at Arjun, who brought over an armful of wood and metal and handed them over. Daemus found himself holding a small but brutal-looking mace and a lightweight hand crossbow, as well as a quarrel of arrows. He examined the weapons closely and then looked at Faux. He didn't have to vocalize his question because it was written all over his face.

"I hope you'll never need them," Faux said. "But the day may come when you thank me, especially if Kester—" She paused for a moment, a frown passing over her face.

"What is it?"

"It's nothing," Faux said, although her face showed that she didn't believe it. She opened her mouth, closed it, and then opened it again. "I suppose I can tell you now. Your uncle asked me to deliver a message for him in the utmost secrecy. He was to give it to me before he left, but he didn't. Let's hope it's not important."

"If my uncle forgot to give it to you, I'm sure it wasn't," Daemus replied. "But you're trying to distract me. What am

I supposed to do with these?"

"Wield them."

"But I'm not trained to use them," Daemus protested.

"Perhaps I can help with that," Arjun said. He patted Daemus on the shoulder. "Come on, lad. I'll train you on the journey, but we have no time to dwell at present."

As the party climbed back into the saddles, Faux rode up behind Daemus and tossed him a blanket.

"For the saddle sores," she explained. "Don't worry, we'll make a warrior of you yet. I know of no greater combatant than Arjun and I'd hate to find myself opposing him on the battlefield. He was trained at the High Aldin in Abacus."

"Then I'll be learning from a true master," Daemus replied, thinking back to his lessons and the stories the Keepers had told. He was so deep in thought that he didn't notice Blue Conney right up alongside them, a playful grin on his face that gave Daemus flashbacks to the night before, when the rogue had pressed cup after cup of ale into his hands. Suddenly, he felt as though he might throw up.

"Better learn to use those things quickly, lad," Conney needled. "There are wolves in these parts. Coyotes, too. Wild horsehounds, if we're unlucky."

"Wolves?"

"Oh, be quiet, Blue," Faux said. "Can't you see you're scaring him?"

Blue Conney grumbled something inaudible and spurred his war dog forward. Daemus looked across at Faux, who'd settled into her own saddle, and said, "He's joking, right?"

Faux spurred her own horse forward and called to Daemus over her shoulder. "We'd better get moving. We've got a long journey ahead of us."

KESTER WAS EXHAUSTED, FIGHTING against sleep so he could stay on the move. He'd already pushed his rickety wagon and the beaten horses to their limits. They'd been on the road for three days and three nights, barely stopping to rest, and yet his pursuers had followed him. Their speed and their stamina were beyond belief, almost superhuman. He'd started out with at least a half day's lead, and yet now he could see their standards on the horizon, their infernal war drums echoing in his ears, even from the distance.

Boom! Boom! Ba-boom!

He whipped his horses again and bellowed some encouragement, knowing that at any moment they could give up on him and collapse to the ground. In the great plains of the Vilchor Highgrass, there was nowhere to run and nowhere to hide. He was out in the open, an unmistakable target in the open expanse, and his cart and horses were carving great divots into the ground. He had but one hope, and even that was a long shot. If he could hold them off until they reached the Emerald Dales, as the druid had suggested the night before, perhaps he could still escape them.

Boom! Boom! Ba-boom!

Kester rode on, risking a look over his shoulder at the clan. They were still too far away for him to make out their numbers, but if the cloud was anything to go by, there were a lot of them. And those damned drums kept beating.

He wasn't far from the Eternal Forest and its relative safety, but his horses had started to froth at the mouth, and he knew from experience that they were close to collapse.

"How are they still gaining on me?" Kester murmured, half-delirious and unaware that he was even talking. "Why don't their horses tire as mine do?"

He reached a small turn in the road and used the

camouflage of a nearby hillock to his advantage. It gave him one last roll of the dice.

Hopping quickly from his seat at the front of the cart, he cut a lone horse loose with a swift swipe of his blade and then flicked his whip again. The remaining horses bolted, taking the now riderless cart with them as they dashed madly into the distance. There was little life left in the horses, and if they tried to pull away from each other instead of working as a team then the cart would stall and the game would be up. All he could hope for was that the hill and the remaining energy of his horses would be enough to deceive them.

Boom! Boom! Ba-boom! Boom! Boom! Ba-boom!

Kester held his breath and waited, hidden on the rear side of the hill. The quiet thunder of the distant pursuers grew, their rumbling roaring ever closer. Within seconds, the riders began to pass by.

Up close and personal, he could make out an imposing man in spined armor and bone-colored battlepaint. He wore the scalps of his enemies around his neck and rode at the head of nearly a hundred trollborn mercenaries. It had to be Misael, the man Lachlan had spoken of.

The riders were astride large, maned dogs the size of adult horses. The creatures bore their riders with ease, and Kester was astonished by their speed and endurance. Suddenly, he had an answer to the mystery of how they'd kept on his tail for so long. Whatever the creatures were, they moved with an uncanny ease. If he'd stayed on the wagon, they would have caught him within the hour. He recalled the druid, Lachlan Barrett, calling them horsehounds, and now he knew why.

Kester waited in silence as the procession continued inexorably past him and rode toward the horizon. Each slow second was a torturous nightmare, and he expected a cry to go up at any moment and for him to be dragged out and fed to the vicious steeds. He didn't dare move an inch until long after they'd vanished over the horizon and he could no longer hear the sound of their war drums.

As tired as his lone remaining horse, Kester cursed to himself, spat on the ground, and then climbed back into the saddle. He closed his eyes and kissed the holy symbol of the Ancient Nothos that he wore around his neck. It was a lucky charm, a relic of his younger days when he'd spent most of his time carousing and gambling away the family fortune. He kissed the symbol a second time and then recited the holy words.

"Nothos, father of good fates, I pray to thee," Kester said. "Return my nephew, who's as a son to me, to his home safely. Shield him from harm and vulturous eyes. Bestow him with good fortune in exchange for my own."

Then he spurred the horse onward and rode west to the Dales and the safety of the Keldarin before his pursuers realized their mistake.

ONLY HALF A DAY HAD passed, and the sound of the war drums had returned. Kester's horse wasn't just on its last legs; it was only still moving because of its momentum. He'd long ago given up on whipping the poor creature because it looked as though one more blow might finish it off. But he couldn't afford to let it rest either, so he tried to give the dying beast some solace by whispering to it in Melexian, the universal language of the elven races. He hoped the mystical dialect would coax it to keep on running, using a few words he'd picked up from a trollborn traveler in a tavern somewhere.

It was well-known by the realm's scholars that Melexian words had power, but all the words in the world wouldn't have been enough to keep the doomed horse going. Eventually, inevitably, the horse fell to its knees and then collapsed to the ground for good.

Boom! Boom! Ba-boom!

Kester rolled out of the saddle and hit the ground running, barely pausing to look behind him. His steed was convulsing in a heap, whinnying hoarsely with its limbs spasming in its final death throes. Less than half a mile away, he could see the individual outlines of his pursuers on their horsehounds.

But he was just a couple hundred yards away from the line of the trees, and he was closing the distance at a rapid pace. His eyes were heavy, his mind clouded. His limbs were stiff from being in the saddle for so long, but they also rejoiced when he finally unleashed them to flee across the unsteady ground toward the trees.

The great forest on the horizon had started out as a mass of green that had slowly resolved into a line of individual trees. Kester had passed the forest on dozens of occasions, but he'd never truly appreciated their beauty. Or perhaps it was just relief that was coursing through him. With a bit of luck, the forest would become a protective wall of green between him and his unrelenting trollborn hunters.

Had Lachlan Barrett warned the Keldarin of his coming? Were the rangers of Lachlan's Emerald Shield hiding in the treeline? Would his pursuers be brave enough to cross into the forest?

He ran as though the hounds of hell were at his heels, which they were. The barking of the horsehounds echoed out across the plains and rang in Kester's ears like the screams of dying men on a battlefield. He ran at full pelt, shedding anything he could drop to lighten his load. He was carried by desperation and blind terror, his eyes flush with tears, his pulse racing in his veins. But the barks and drums were getting closer, ever closer.

Kester could hear his heart beating in his head, and his legs had felt like two swinging lead pendulums until they'd started aching and then gone numb. His eyes darted around, searching for some sign of salvation. Where were the elves? Where was the Emerald Shield?

His fears took hold of him, and he risked a glance behind him as he reached the outskirts of the forest. It was a fateful decision, and one that cost him. His foot looped around the intertwined branches of a rogue conifer, and he went stumbling to the ground less than thirty yards away from the first trees.

So close, he thought. *And yet so far.*

He tried to push himself up from the ground but only made it as far as his hands and knees before his exhausted body hit the wall and he collapsed back down again. In that moment, he knew he was as good as dead.

Lying there in the tall grass, his body twisted and unresponsive, he reached out for the Ancients in his mind and accepted the inevitable, murmuring the words of a short prayer. Within moments, the horsehounds had him surrounded, the riders hollering and screeching as their steeds tossed their heads back and howled at the heavens. They were celebrating their victory, and they weren't subtle about it.

For Kester, the most awful thing of all was the sound of the beasts' infernal breathing as their trollborn riders wheeled their steeds around in circles. There was something unnatural about them. The war cries, the drums and the rustling metal was terrifying, of course, but it somehow wasn't as bad. Perhaps it was because it was designed to intimidate, and Kester was intimidated enough.

And besides, the only thing that was important was that with his own life, perhaps he'd bought his nephew enough time to distance himself from their relentless pursuers. It was a steep price to pay, but it was one he would have happily paid ten times over.

Kester was still lying where he fell, his body too worn for him to move and his mind racing to make up for it. From behind him, he heard the telltale jingles of an armored man getting out of the stirrups. Cursing, he shifted position slightly and turned to look at the monstrous figure of a huge trollborn painted in the tribal, scarlet war colors of Clan Blood Axe. Kester watched the man carefully, waiting for his doom to approach him but maintaining a sense of calm and serenity. His death might be painful, especially if he was torn apart by the jaws of the horsehounds, but he could take some solace in the fact that he'd forfeited his life to give young Daemus a chance. The fate of the entire realm might have depended upon his actions of that day.

"You must be Misael," Kester said, his voice calm and measured as he addressed the behemoth in front of him. "I've been warned that you've been hunting me."

The trollborn slowly raised his wicked battleaxe, which was adorned with feathers and still stained with the blood of his last kill. He leered at the beaten man, exposing his sharp teeth.

"Where's the Keeper?" he asked in a throaty, guttural voice.

Kester grunted in acknowledgement, but he didn't answer the question. Instead, he started murmuring to himself as he addressed a prayer to Threnody, the Ancient of Death.

Misael smiled again, and it was the last thing Kester saw. The trollborn wasted no time on negotiation or torture and simply swung his axe through the air. When he raised it again, it was bathed in the fresh blood of Lord Kester Alaric.

AS THE MARAUDERS WHOOPED and banged the hilts of their weapons against their shields and their armored chests,

Misael took a closer look at his vanquished quarry, searching through Kester's bag and pockets for any hint or clue as to his ward's destination. Kester had jettisoned almost everything he carried in his flight for the forest. At first glance, it seemed as though there was nothing there to learn from.

But Misael had keen eyes. When he got down in the tall grass and the blood, he saw something. A small scroll necklace had tumbled from Kester's neck at the moment of the fatal blow and almost been buried in the muck. Misael examined the scroll necklace, opened the scroll, and read it.

"To Sir Ranaulf Alaric and Lady Mercia Alaric," he read. "I must keep this message brief for time is of the essence. Daemus is traveling to you with a longtime friend of mine from the High Aldin. I'll explain more once I'm able to join you. Take care of him, as I know you will. He's in grave danger."

Misael stared at the scroll for a moment and then tossed it to the ground, along with the chain it had been carried in. Then he spat in the dirt and covered the parchment with a layer of mud and blood.

"The fool forgot about the message around his neck," Misael murmured.

"So, what happens next?" one of his lackies growled. She was a pock-faced trollborn woman who'd risen to the rank of second-in-command by demonstrating an unparalleled ferocity on the battlefield and a certain inventive cruelty that stood out even amongst the clan.

"I know where the Keeper is headed," Misael replied. "We must follow the trail, and with haste. We need to make up for lost time and hunt down that accursed child before he reaches Castleshire."

Then he slung his axe across his back, still fresh with Kester's blood, before climbing back into the saddle and turning to address his clan. His horsehound reared up on its hind legs, and Misael raised a fist into the air in a combined salute and demand for attention.

"Trollborn!" he shouted. "We've clashed with royalty today. My blade is stained with the blood of an Alaric, the blood of a privileged member of the gentry, those rich men with no souls, with their soft hands and their perfumed hair, hiding behind their high walls amidst their wealth."

The clan listened to his insults, hanging on to his every word and occasionally parroting them or emphasizing them by banging their weapons against their shields again. As he spoke, Misael's eyes roamed across his marauders, catching the eyes of each of his riders in turn before ranging on to the next one.

"I have good news for you," Misael continued. "Our hunt is not yet over. We're off to chase down another noble, and more Alaric blood will be spilled before the full moon rises.

"So, tell me, riders. Who is it that rules the plains of Warminster? Is it King Godwin on his unearned throne?"

"No!" the riders chanted.

"And what about the Great Keeper in her tower of learning?"

"No!"

"Then tell me!" Misael roared. "I ask you again! Who is it that rules the plains of Warminster?"

"Blood Axe!" the riders shouted back at him, their voices joining the clanking of their weapons and armor and the barking and yipping of their steeds. "Blood Axe! Blood Axe! Blood Axe!"

"Soon, we ride," Misael decreed, ushering his horsehound closer to the crumpled heap that represented the physical remains of Kester Alaric. "But first, we feed our mounts. Strip him of his clothes and give him to the hounds. Let us leave no evidence that he was ever here."

CHAPTER SEVENTEEN

"The kingdom can't be without its jackals."
—Baron Kainus Von Lormarck

RITTER CAME TO REGRET his decision to avoid Von Lormarck the moment he returned to Castle Thronehelm, as the king's attendant Meeks rushed him through the corridors, apparently more worried about his own standing with the baron than Ritter's. Unable to come up with another escape route, Ritter reluctantly acquiesced and made as much haste as he could to ready himself before Meeks all but dragged him to one of the smaller chambers off the throne room.

Before Ritter knew it, he was standing in the open doorway and looking at a tall, broad-shouldered man whom he presumed to be Baron Von Lormarck. He didn't look happy. Ritter mentally chastized himself for the error.

"Sir Ritter of Valkeneer," Meeks proclaimed, before bowing himself out of the room. Ritter tried not to resent the man for fleeing so obviously. Then again, he didn't envy any servant who had to be around a Von Lormarck for any length of time.

"I'm pleased to make your acquaintance," the baron said flatly, his dark eyes scanning a mosaic map of the realm on the wall.

"Likewise," Ritter replied politely, trying not to stare. The man was commonly held to be a hard but fair ruler and had interfered little with the affairs of the Bridge since inheriting his father's title, but Ritter had been raised on stories of the Von Lormarcks' crimes against his family and even against their own people. In truth, he could discern little in the baron's manner that indicated he was any better than the rest of his kin. His face and hands were scarred, the indicators of a dedicated swordsman who rarely fled from a fight, so at least it could be said that he wasn't a coward.

"You're wondering why I asked to meet with you," Von Lormarck began without further preamble, speaking at a metered pace.

Ritter inclined his head in assent. The ensuing silence must have lasted nearly a minute before the baron spoke again.

"It shames me to say this." Von Lormarck's heavy brows had lowered into a frown. "It's difficult for me. I'd be grateful for your patience."

Von Lormarck paused to look around the room and then back at Ritter. Then he walked around behind him and whistled softly to himself.

"That's quite a bow, Sir Ritter," Von Lormarck said. "With wood such as that, it can only be Silencer. I've heard tales. May I take a closer look?"

"I'd prefer to keep my bow across my back," Ritter said.

"As you wish," Von Lormarck replied. "Though 'tis a pity. It's a fine weapon, much like my own."

At this, he unsheathed his two swords and placed them on the table.

"This is Malice," he said, as he laid the first one down. "And this is Woe."

"Fine names for fine blades," Ritter said, and he meant it. The dual weapons had clearly been crafted by master blacksmiths, and their edges looked sharp enough to slice through a butterfly's wings if it flew too close.

It was hard to tell whether Baron Dragich Von Lormarck was trying to threaten him. At the very least, it was an attempt at intimidation.

Von Lormarck must have seen the look of hesitation in Ritter's face. He smiled grimly and said, "I like to keep my blades close at hand, but they have no use for diplomacy. And, yes, perhaps I can't help showing them off. But you'll forgive me for my pride."

"They say it comes before a fall," Ritter murmured. He was nearing the end of his patience and had to bite his tongue to stop him from saying anything further. The baron appeared to be sincere, and it wasn't like Ritter to make such harsh judgments before getting to know a person. He could at least hear the baron out. "Yes?"

"I wish to apologize," the baron said at last, "for the... actions committed by my people against yours."

Ritter blinked, caught in a strange limbo between pleasant surprise and suspicion. "What?"

"There's much bad blood between our two families," Von Lormarck explained, as if Ritter didn't already know. "We have a history of strife, bitterness, misunderstanding, and unnecessary bloodshed. I'm extending a personal apology, as well as my wish to make reparations to the people of the Bridge."

His slow speech ought to have made his words easier to understand, but Ritter still found himself struggling to register or believe what the man was saying.

"Reparations?" he repeated when the baron's point had finally sunk in.

Von Lormarck appeared not to notice Ritter's lack of enthusiasm and continued speaking in his startlingly deep voice at the same glacial pace. "I heard of your fine work in service to the crown," he said. "With all of his other duties, the king sometimes pays less attention than he might to the defense of the borderlands, namely your home and mine."

"No man is perfect," Ritter trotted out blankly, somewhat thrown by the change in subject.

"Indeed," Von Lormarck agreed. "Every monarch needs

competent, hardworking servants of the crown who can see what they can't and act in their stead. I've been impressed by your ability to do so."

"I wasn't the only agent of the crown involved in the matter," Ritter said, beginning to grow uneasy. "I couldn't have done any of it alone. In any case, there's nothing magnificent about leaving enemies of the crown on the loose."

Von Lormarck looked at him. "You failed to account for all the parties involved?"

"No," Ritter amended, suddenly reluctant to share his discoveries of the vanishing sniper and the arrows marked with the black rose. "Not exactly. I only feel that these events haven't yet concluded."

The baron's mouth quirked, and one of the larger scars on his cheek danced sideways with the movement. Something in his face seemed to have eased. "You're a perfectionist," he declared, his tone full of mock pity. "Too hard on yourself, like many clever men I've met in my lifetime. Eh?"

He plainly meant it as a friendly half-joke, but Ritter, still uncomfortable, watched him and made no reply.

"The work you've done has made you an asset to the crown, and the bandits are gone," he continued. "That ought to be enough, don't you think?"

Ritter said nothing.

"I'll provide a number of my own men to assist with the defense of the Bridge," Von Lormarck said, "in addition to paying monetary reparations to the Valkeneer family."

"Gold from your war with the twergs?" It popped out of Ritter's mouth before he could stop it, and the other man's eyes narrowed.

"What does it matter where it comes from? By rights, it's now your gold."

Blood money.

Ritter didn't say it aloud, but a bitter taste lingered in his mouth, nevertheless. He couldn't possibly accept such a gift, particularly if it came with strings attached, which the baron hadn't said but also hadn't explicitly denied.

"I must consult with my father," Ritter stated, making an effort to even his tone.

Von Lormarck waved a massive hand, beginning to look frustrated. "Surely, sir, you have the authority to accept a simple gift on your family's behalf? An end to the long years of enmity between our good houses?"

Ritter's suspicion deepened. "I regret to say otherwise," he answered through gritted teeth, and managed a barely civil, "Good day," before turning out of the room.

He didn't know what he'd expected, but it felt as though the meeting couldn't have gone any worse. Ritter half-ran back to his chambers, already composing a letter to his mother and father in his head. If he hurried, he'd have time to write it and send it on its way before preparing for the evening's festivities.

ADDILYN GLANCED AT HER reflection in the mirror, then at that of her bodyguard, who stood by the wall, looking at the floor. She'd been fiddling with her hair and face paint for nearly an hour, putting off the final step, which was to lace up the heavy gown she'd naïvely chosen to bring with her when she'd been packing at home. She had, of course, assumed that her handmaidens would be staying with her, and that she'd have no trouble getting dressed, but now that she was in a room with only her bodyguard for company, Addilyn was beginning to regret her overenthusiastic indulgence in the more high-maintenance side of her wardrobe. Steeling herself, she reached for the laces. After struggling with them for a few minutes, she'd managed to do them up about a third of the way, but at length she reluctantly forced herself to give up.

"Would you help me with this, please?" Addilyn asked Jessamy quietly, once again finding herself dearly missing Yala and Rasilyn. She'd accepted help from them when preparing for special occasions and had usually helped them in turn if they were allowed to attend along with her, but she felt that her bodyguard wouldn't be comfortable letting her charge braid her hair or straighten her clothes for her. Even if she had, helping her with her clothes was simply not Jessamy's job. The whole situation made her uneasy, but she was short on time and wouldn't be able to get ready fast enough without the other woman's help.

Silently, Jessamy came forward and began lacing the gown.

"Thank you," Addilyn said, remembering this time to use Jessamy's preferred Raven dialect instead of High Vermilion.

"It's no trouble," Jessamy replied. "Are you looking forward to the masquerade, or is it just another boring social function?"

Surprised by the frankness of the question, Addilyn took a moment to consider her answer. *Raven elves,* she thought. *Always straight to the point.*

"I don't know," she replied, honestly. "I normally like parties and being around people, but I'm not sure if it will be like it is at home. There are one or two people I'm looking forward to seeing again, at least."

"The Von Lormarck girl?" Jessamy asked. Addilyn had difficulty reading her tone but sensed that Jessamy was trying to be friendly.

"Yes, Ember Fleury, the baron's bastardess." Addilyn cringed slightly at the memory of her awkward first meeting with the girl, but she'd liked her and would be glad to speak to her again.

"I'm sure it'll be good for you to spend some time with a friend," Jessamy agreed, and added with a smile that Addilyn could hear in her voice, "even if it's a human."

Addilyn laughed at that. "I'm sorry to ask you to do this," she said, surprising herself. "I worry that it's beneath you." She hadn't felt that way when it was Yala or Rasilyn attending her, but the three of them were close friends and constantly blurred the lines of class and station.

Jessamy exhaled softly behind her. "It's no trouble," the warrior answered, blithely. "My mother used to do it for me, and I'd sometimes do it for my sisters when they were growing up. There's no shame in needing help, even if it's with something simple."

Addilyn hadn't thought of it that way before. Distracted by the tidbit of personal information, she changed the subject. "You have sisters?"

"Three," Jessamy said, sounding fond. "They're all much younger than I am. I started pursuing my training a year or so after the youngest was born, so I don't know her very well, except what she was like as a baby." She scoffed lightly, but Addilyn could still hear a smile. "She was very fussy."

"Perhaps one day you can tease her about it," Addilyn remarked with a grin, and Jessamy's hands stilled for a moment before she resumed her work.

"I don't know how soon that will be," she said. "I can't return home until my oath is fulfilled or you release me from service."

"Oh, forgive me. I wasn't thinking," Addilyn murmured, embarrassed. She knew Jessamy wasn't asking to be released. Among elves, it was seen as a great shame for a young warrior to be discharged from service before their time under oath was properly completed. It seemed obvious now that Jessamy wouldn't wish to be reminded of her inability to see her family, though.

"It's all right," Jessamy replied. "I was very happy to win this position. It's not easy being away from them for so long, but I know my family speak of me and love me even though not all of them know me. I'll see them again, in this world or the next, Threnody willing." She sounded, to Addilyn's ears, untroubled by the notion.

"Indeed," Addilyn said, faintly. "I thank you for your service, and for your ear. Your sacrifice doesn't go unnoticed." When Jessamy finished the laces and lightly patted her on the shoulder, Addilyn turned around. "I suppose I have two new elven friends, now," she finished with a smile.

Jessamy smiled back. "Two?" she inquired, sounding puzzled, and Addilyn's heart sank.

"Have I misread things? I'm sorry," she began, but Jessamy waved a hand at her.

"No, no," Jessamy said. "Who's the other one? I didn't hear you mention meeting another elf." Addilyn bit her lip, realizing she'd have to confess to lying to escape Jessamy's eyes the previous afternoon.

"Do you remember when I said I wanted to spend some time practicing my magic, and that I'd stay where you left me with the castle guards outside the Keeper's solar?"

Jessamy rolled her eyes. "Let me guess," she said. "You didn't. Well, see if I let you out of my sight again."

"You have my deepest apologies," Addilyn said, earnestly. "But anyway, I was out in the woods, and I met a friend. A Raven elf, I think, like you. His name is Ritter."

On hearing the name, Jessamy's eyebrows lowered. "Ritter Valkeneer?" she asked. Her tone was suddenly flat. "Is that who you mean?"

"There can't be more than one Ritter running around the castle," Addilyn replied, stung by her bodyguard's cold response to what she'd thought was happy news.

"My lady, Ritter Valkeneer isn't a Raven elf. He's a trollborn,"

Jessamy told her, and her scowl deepened at Addilyn's answering blank stare.

"Trollborn," she repeated, as if Addilyn hadn't heard her. The word meant nothing to Addilyn; her best guess was that it was some kind of slang term that didn't exist in Vermilion. She wasn't about to admit ignorance in front of Jessamy, however, particularly not now. She waited for the other woman to elaborate.

"He's a half-breed," Jessamy explained at last, now looking more pitying than upset.

Addilyn looked down, blanking her features to avoid showing her genuine distress. She'd never met a trollborn before, but she knew what Jessamy was trying to remind her of: Vermilion convention barely allowed members of the royal family to fraternize with the lower castes of elves. Keeping a friendship with a trollborn, even one with some elven blood, would be tantamount to political suicide and could potentially even create negative consequences for the reigning coronelle, her aunt. Her duty was immediately clear, and that was to cut all ties with Ritter and pretend they'd never met. The thought of doing that to the first person she'd easily befriended since leaving home, someone who'd been kind to her, was painful.

"I'm sorry, my lady," Jessamy said.

"There are times when I wish Melexis had never existed. That there was no 'holy' caste of elves, or at least that I wasn't a part of it."

The atmosphere in the room had changed in the blink of an eye, and Addilyn could tell that Jessamy was shocked by her blasphemy, though she didn't say a word. In silence, Addilyn finished her hair and put the final touches on her face. Her bodyguard stood behind her, a wordless presence who almost seemed to exist only in the mirror.

CHAPTER EIGHTEEN

*"The worst of sanctuaries is neither the dark
recesses of a cave nor the lonesome hollows of
a forest. It's the desolation of your own mind."*
—Anthraxus of the Monastery of Blight

THE MAN WITH THE bloodied blindfold was riding through the night on the back of his pale horse, looking like a harbinger of the apocalypse. He was alone in the Killean Desolates, which was normally an easy way for someone to consign themselves to the grave. But this man, Graytorris, was different. He feared nothing, including death, as death would be a merciful relief from his accursed existence.

The Killean Desolates, on the far eastern reaches of Foghaven Vale, were mostly uninhabited because of their harsh conditions. It was a windswept, arid plain filled with cracked ground, little water and even less wildlife and game. A foul-smelling river cut a deep canyon into the parched landscape, which was pocked with dangerous crags and caves. They were held by outlaws, humanoids, trollborn rogues, and other scoundrels who were on the run from the law and the long-reaching arm of Castle Thronehelm and scraped a living through in-fighting and plundering the wares of anyone foolish enough to venture through the Desolates.

His horse slowed as he approached Spine Castle, a small, ruined tower in the middle of nowhere. The windstorms were picking up and the dust whipped around in great tornadoes. The air crackled with electricity and thunder rumbled in the distance. A bolt of lightning arced across the sky and earthed itself in the arid ground.

There was no risk of an opportunistic hustler trying to

steal his horse, and so he left it to graze in the dust as he made his way into the crumbling stronghold. The man with the bloodied blindfold, Graytorris, had been given permission to move freely by the one man who could claim the Desolates. His troops guarded the borders and performed a double role. They kept the raiding trollborn tribes out of Warminster and they kept Warminsterians from following Graytorris. Not that any of them were foolish enough to follow him into the Desolates.

Spine Castle was a twisted spire of three stories that seemed to somehow defy gravity with its top-heavy design and its large spire. It looked like a treehouse built out of stone... or the head at the top of a spine. The spire was shaped into a conical roof with a flat top that lay exposed to the vicious elements. Graytorris's living quarters were two floors below in a converted lighthouse of sorts, a relic of earlier days when watchmen had lit lanterns to guide lost travelers to relative safety.

He started to climb the spire, placing one booted foot ahead of another as he ascended the crumbling stonework. At the top, he pushed his way through an imposing set of oak doors and into his study. It was a bleak chamber, save for two distinct features. A large mirror hung along the far wall, reflecting back on a pedestal desk and a raised stool. A leatherbound diary and a red-feathered quill rested in the center of the desk, plucked from the tail of a Killean vulture.

"*Plectrum scribae*," he murmured in the conjurer's tongue, a variant of the Minsterian tongue that incorporated many of the old words and ways. "*Pulsat eburno.*"

As he spoke, the quill lifted into the air on its own before floating over to the tome and touching down on the pages. It needed no ink. Graytorris wrote in blood, the blood from his cursed eyes, and it flowed from the quill as soon as it touched the vellum.

"For years, he has come for me, yet I see him but once," the quill wrote, the script sloppy and shaky as though written by a trembling hand. "My dead eyes aflame with his visage, one I cannot unsee. Do the sands pass through my hourglass or his? A tempest of wind splits the sky, yet I endure it. A flash of lightning rents the clouds, yet I cannot see it. But I hear the growl of his distant thunder. He erodes my strength by existing within this ethereal border of sleep. I always enjoy killing thee, Daemus Alaric."

The madman paused for a moment, consumed with introspection and reflection. The quill levitated in the air beside him, awaiting its next instruction, but none came.

"Seek," Graytorris whispered, using the Minsterian tongue.

The quill fell to the desk and Graytorris turned his back on it, walking instead over toward the window. His blind eyes showed him nothing of the view across the Desolates, but some other secret, more magical sense told him that the Antlered Man was emerging from the shadows in the courtyard below him, waiting to be commanded.

The horrific beast stood at nearly ten feet tall on its crooked, goat-like hind legs, possessing the naked and grey torso of a near-giant. He had burly, corded muscles and bore the scars of innumerable battles. His head resembled a mutated cattle skull, with twisted antlers protruding like wings from the bone, and gaping sockets of darkness where its eyes should have been.

It was an abomination.

The Antlered Man inclined his head slightly to acknowledge the order and then turned, in a stoic silence, to depart. His first steps were those of a humanoid running on two legs, but after a short stretch, the beast fell to all fours, digging its claws into the ground and leaving scars—not prints—on the surface.

As stoic and inscrutable as the creature he commanded,

Graytorris turned to look at a large mirror on the wall, one that his eyeless face couldn't perceive.

Called Traumefang, the mirror at Spine Castle was one half of a pair. Its partner, Dromofangare, hung in the inner sanctum of the Cathedral of the Watchful Eye. The two portal mirrors could be used for scrying, and those who knew their names could even travel between them.

"*Cathedralis speculo petunt,*" he murmured. "*Scry et aperta via.*"

The smooth surface of the mirror began to change, and a building appeared in the glass: The Cathedral of the Watchful Eye. Graytorris couldn't see it through his blinded eyes, but he didn't need to. His wooden face broke and dissipated into a smile the likes of which are known only by those at the frayed ends of sanity.

The mirror's glow increased, and Graytorris's smile grew wider as he felt the magical portal open in front of him. He leaned forward, the floor of the observatory mere inches from his face. And then, out of the darkness, there came an echo of the pillar of light rising from its observatory that had first blinded him all those years ago.

The Fallen Keeper had returned.

ON THE OTHER SIDE of Warminster, Daemus was in a spirited but one-way training session with Arjun, who was teaching the boy to wield his mace and crossbow. Both weapons were designed to be easy for beginners to use, but Daemus had poor hand-eye coordination and the physical dexterity of a three-legged horse on its way to the knackers.

Arjun was taking it easy on the boy, fighting left-handed and remaining on the defensive, allowing Daemus to charge him instead of throwing himself at the boy as he would have done if they'd been facing one another across a battlefield.

"Come on, boy," Conney chuckled. He was watching proceedings idly while resting a pipe between his lips and blowing lazy smoke rings into the cool evening air. "Put your back into it."

"I'm trying," Daemus muttered, his brow furrowed in concentration as his mace carved up the air again. Arjun stepped effortlessly aside and flicked his blade up, catching it on one of the weapon's spikes. With a twist of his wrist, he sent it clattering to the ground.

"Too easy," Arjun said, picking up the mace and holding it out to his protégé. "Here, try again. One last round of sparring and then it's time for target practice. Now pay close attention. I want you to watch the way my hands move when I—"

As quickly and abruptly as an assassin in the night, Daemus lost control of his body, his limbs taking on a life of their own and his eyes glazing over and plunging him into darkness. Arjun watched on in concern as the boy froze, staring sightlessly down at the heavy mace he was holding. Then Daemus slumped to his knees and Arjun raced at him, but Conney got there first and slowed his fall, lowering him to the ground.

"Daemus?" Arjun shouted. "Can you hear me?"

"It's no use," Conney said, something approaching awe creeping into his voice. "There's no doubt about it, Arjun. The young man has the Sight."

"Aye," Faux said, removing her cloak and bundling it beneath Daemus's head. He'd gone into convulsions, so she tilted his head to one side to make sure that he didn't swallow his tongue. "Or perhaps it's a curse. Look at him, for Ssolantress's sake. He doesn't control the visions. The visions control him."

WHILE DAEMUS'S EYES WERE LIT up with the golden glow of his Erudian Sight, his mind was several hundred leagues away on the borders of the Emerald Dales. He was watching the hunt from above, bellowing his uncle's name as Kester Alaric fled on foot for the treeline. He wasn't even aware that he was screaming, and it seemed as though Kester wasn't aware of it either, for he didn't react to the sound. He was too busy looking ahead to safety or back to his pursuers to waste a moment looking up to the heavens.

Daemus watched on in horror as his uncle fell at the hands of the monstrous trollborn, and as he watched, he realized something. This wasn't like his other visions, like a series of cryptic clues that pointed to some truth his Ancient wanted to reveal to him. This was as if he was really there. He could feel the sunlight on his arms and smell the vile hides and the foul breath of the horsehounds. He felt close enough to reach out and touch them.

Daemus saw the axe fall. In that moment, as it swept through the air, it was as though he and his uncle were one. Daemus dropped to his knees and his hands flew up to his neck, groping for the fatal wound that wasn't there.

And then he was back with his comrades, his cheeks flushed and tears welled up in his eyes. He felt sick to his stomach, but he also felt relieved because Faux had wrapped her arms around him and was whispering comforting words into his ear. It was small consolation, but it was consolation, nonetheless.

"What did you see?" Faux asked.

"I saw…" Daemus began, but then the tears took him again and he paused to take in a deep gulp of fresh air and to wipe his face. "I saw Uncle Kester. I… I saw him die."

Slowly, and interrupted often by the great sobs that were tearing him apart, he recounted what he'd seen in his visions, culminating in a thorough description of their leader.

"I recognize this man," Faux said, when Daemus had calmed down enough for them to continue their conversation. "From what you've said of him, it can only be one person."

"Misael," Arjun supplied.

"Aye," Faux said. Noting the look of confusion on their young ward's face, she added, "Clan Blood Axe is a group of merciless trollborn known for their brutality and the efficiency with which they hunt their prey and pillage caravans and outposts. And worse, those mounts that you described... they're called horsehounds, and they can ride faster, harder, and longer than any other creature in the realm. If Clan Blood Axe is on our trail, we're in trouble."

"Uncle Kester was many leagues away," Daemus argued.

"Then at best we have a head start," Marquiss grumbled, spitting a wad of phlegm into the grass and reaching instinctively for the blade at his waist as though he expected riders to show up on the horizon at any moment.

"If Kester talked before they killed him, they'll be relentless in their pursuit of us," Faux said. "He was loyal to us, of course, but the clan has ways of making people talk."

"It didn't look as though they had much time for talking," Daemus replied, the hint of a sob creeping into his voice again. "Praise the Ancients for small mercies. My uncle died quickly."

"Then that's something," Faux said. "Let us hope there'll be time to avenge Kester's death in the future. For now, though, his life has bought us some time, and we must make use of it."

DAEMUS AND HIS FELLOW travelers were pushing on for Castleshire, fearing their pursuers were still hot on their tail. They'd been traveling for four days, and their spirits were low.

"Not far to go now," Faux said, injecting a false sense of optimism into her voice as they passed through the outskirts of yet another nameless hamlet.

"I wish I'd had more visions," Daemus lamented. "I've seen nothing since... since Uncle Kester fell. Perhaps my interpretation was untrue. After all, I'm just a novice. Maybe Uncle Kester just—"

"Your uncle's dead, boy," Marquiss said. "I'm sorry. The sooner we face facts, the safer we'll be. We can't afford to waste our time with—"

"Diplomatic as ever, Marquiss," Faux interrupted, shooting her brother an inscrutable glance before turning to look at Daemus. "Your Uncle Kester has gotten out of stickier situations in the past and is the veteran of a dozen campaigns. He knows how to protect himself and you should take some solace from that."

"But he was outnumbered."

"Aye," Faux replied. "But he's been outnumbered before and lived to tell the tale. Have your visions ever been wrong?"

"I don't know," Daemus admitted. "I'm still learning to control the Sight. But the Great Keeper told me that visions are never set in stone. They're gifts from Erud, and it falls to us to interpret the visions and to discern the meaning of the clues that we've been given."

"I'll admit that I know little of the ways of the Keepers," Faux said.

The party continued their slow trek in silence for a couple of moments before she added, "Have you ever tried to use the Sight more aggressively?"

"What do you mean?"

"I mean what I say," Faux replied. "Have you ever tried to summon the Sight instead of waiting for Erud to deliver it? And have you ever tried to control its direction?"

Daemus shook his head.

"I usually try to suppress the visions," he said. "The truth is, they scare me."

"If you're worried about your uncle," Faux said, "perhaps you should try."

He thought about it for a moment and then nodded his assent as the travelers settled their horses and dismounted. Blue Conney wandered off behind a tree to relieve himself with his war dog in tow, while Marquiss lay down with his pack beneath his head and stared up at the sky. Daemus settled down in the long grass and steadied his breathing, while Arjun and Faux watched him.

Daemus closed his eyes, and when he opened them up again, the world had changed. He was standing in a stadium of sorts with a lush, green infield of manicured grass. Off to one side, a teenage Faux Dauldon rode a stallion with a snow-white coat, and a young man was a dozen yards behind her on a chestnut mare. Daemus had never met the man, but something in his head told him the name and he whispered it aloud in his trance.

"Jaxtyn Faircloth," he murmured.

Jaxtyn was about the same age as Faux, a strikingly handsome young lad already showing signs of the man he'd become. He was well-groomed and athletically built with dark hair and blue eyes. Daemus had never met Jaxtyn, but his visions imparted their own special wisdom.

Daemus's eyes, glazed and aglow, repeated the same words over and over "You'll see Jaxtyn again. You'll see Jaxtyn again. You'll see Jaxtyn again."

His voice slowed and his breathing steadied. Slowly, his eyes returned to normal.

"What happened?" Faux asked.

"I saw him," Daemus replied, his voice measured but tinged with a hint of excitement. This vision had been unlike his others. It held no terror for him. He'd been able to control it. "Jaxtyn Faircloth. Who is he?"

"He…" Faux began, her face flushing. "He was someone I knew a long time ago. Before I left Castleshire."

"Aye," Arjun teased. "You knew him, all right."

"Closely," Marquiss added.

"That's enough," Faux said, turning away so that her companions couldn't see her face. There was a note of hurt in her voice, an old wound that would never heal and was best left unpicked.

"I'm sorry," Daemus said, averting his eyes from her and staring instead at the ground. "I didn't mean to spy on your past if that's what I did. I believe it's a sign from Erud, a confirmation that you'll soon see him again."

"If you've seen their reunion," Arjun murmured, "this must mean that we'll successfully make it to Castleshire."

"I can't fault your logic," Daemus replied. "I just hope that I haven't misinterpreted the Sight."

"Only time will tell." This came from Marquiss, who was leaning against a tree and clearly itching to get back on the move.

"Still, we can ride with hope," Faux said.

AS THE GROUP TOOK turns to watch over the open stretch, Daemus descended once more into the Sight. He fell asleep beneath the stars and had dark, disturbing dreams about a fearsome trollborn mounted on a horsehound, barking orders as scores of his minions reared up on their mounts.

Still asleep, drenched with a cold sweat and rocking from side to side as though trying to throw off an invisible assailant, he murmured, "Misael. Misael. Misael. The two shall meet tomorrow on the hill. The two shall meet in an old fort, left abandoned and built from necessity. The two shall meet and blood shall flow."

And then, just as suddenly as he'd started, the unnatural glow disappeared from Daemus's eyes and he drifted slowly into full consciousness, this time remaining calm. The Sight was becoming a little easier to master.

"What did you see?" Arjun asked. The warrior had been keeping watch and was the first at Daemus's side as the others were roused by the commotion.

"I saw a fort atop a blood-stained hill," the boy replied. "It was under siege by dozens of trollborn on the backs of horsehounds."

"That can only be one place," Arjun said, the others listening in with mounting fascination. "Homm Hill."

"Homm Hill?"

Arjun nodded and gestured for the others to sit. They were all awake by then, some of them reluctantly, and so the party gathered round to listen. While he talked, he kept an eye on the horizon to scout for potential threats.

"There was a skirmish there," Arjun said. "Let me see, almost a dozen years ago. Two combatting armies clashed until a river of blood was shed. The garrison in the fort consisted of warriors of the High Aldin, stationed there to protect travelers moving between Castleshire, Abacus, Aldredd, Aerendash and the other towns on the western end of the Vilchor Highgrass."

"What can you tell me of the High Aldin?" Daemus said. "Faux mentioned it before, but I've only heard tales."

"The military academy in Abacus," Chernovog supplied, in response to Daemus's evident confusion. "They're known for their use of new technologies for the purpose of warfare. They know the secrets to making fire rain from the sky."

"And who were their opponents?" Daemus asked, leaning forward as though to better absorb the story through proximity alone.

"Mercenaries," Arjun replied. "An army of them led by a trollborn general named Dragomir Jair who united the clans of the Highgrass. They said he was half-human and half-dragon. Jair was the ultimate trollborn, spewing acid and fire and soaring above the plains."

"And was it true?"

Arjun shrugged and then shook his head.

"I never saw any evidence of it. Either way, he was a fearsome ruler. He knew that the key to opening up the Highgrass under a single ruler was to destroy the last remaining fort on the plains."

"Fort Homm," Daemus said.

"Correct," Arjun replied. "The High Aldin soldiers were outnumbered, but they held the high ground. They began to dig trenches and tunnels in some places, then deployed what war machines they had along the lines, wherever gave them the best vantage points over the hill."

"So, what happened?" Daemus asked.

"Jair attacked the fort with his combined forces," the grizzled warrior explained, pausing momentarily to rekindle his pipe. "They were a hodgepodge of mercenary trollborn clans, a force of over one thousand versus the sixty-man garrison of the High Aldin. The outmatched army on Homm Hill held off the attackers for nearly two days and the fortress held, but at the cost of hundreds of trollborn lives. The historians don't call it the Battle of Homm Hill. They call it the Battle of Blood Ridge."

"Tell the boy how it ended, Arjun," Blue Conney grunted.

"Aye, I was getting to that," Arjun said. His face took on a somber, thoughtful expression. "Jair's lieutenant was a fearsome trollborn warrior named Misael. Jair trusted him unconditionally, but Misael betrayed him. He accepted a bribe from the High Aldin to turn on the other trollborn after the fighting reached a stalemate. Misael took the gold and killed Dragomir with his mighty battleaxe... or so the legend goes."

"How do you know all this?" Daemus asked.

Arjun chuckled, as did their companions. He took a moment to relight his pipe on an ember from the fire while Faux swept the perimeter, and then he continued, "I was part of the army that held the fort, fighting for the High Aldin. Who do you think gave Misael his gold?"

As he spoke, he fell back into a thousand-yard stare, as though he'd been cast back into the fortress by the memories. Daemus nudged the man gently by the arm, his eyes begging him to continue his story.

"If you fought there," Daemus said, "then you must surely remember the hill and its fort."

"Aye," Arjun replied. "If the fortifications haven't fallen into ruin, there's a chance we can use it to our advantage. If we can force a confrontation with Misael at Homm Hill instead of in the field, we might just have a chance."

"You have a point," Faux said, returning from her sweep. "Misael never made it into the fort and likely knows little of the defenses, save for what he experienced outside."

"It may be our only chance," Arjun concluded.

From the edge of the group, where he'd been keeping watch, Blue Conney swore and spat into the dirt.

"What's wrong?" Daemus asked.

"There'll be no sleep for us tonight, son," Conney said, stowing his belongings and preparing to mount Jericho. "We'd better start moving."

CHAPTER NINETEEN

*"On the open seas, his enemies quake
at the approaching sails of Doom's Wake."*
—WARMINSTERIAN SONG

MEEKS CROWLEY HUSTLED FROM station to station, charged with the evening's splendor. The colors of autumn flooded the great hall, which was hung with tasteful tapestries and bedecked with flower arrangements. Aromas of baked bread and delectable desserts wafted from the kitchens and throughout the keep's halls.

Preparations for the masquerade at Castle Thronehelm were well underway and the buzz was spreading far and wide. All the royals and dignitaries of the seven baronies had been invited, and all of them were expected to attend, celebrating not only Warminster's victory over the brigands but also a betrothal between two important houses.

The Von Lormarcks had already arrived, as had the Thessalys from the barony of Gloucester. They'd ridden into Castle Thronehelm alongside the military procession from Halifax Military Academy, which had brought the Faxerian, Lucien Blacwin, to the halls. And most recently, the delegation from Saracen, led by Sasha Scarlett of the Guild of the Copper Wing, had just entered the gates.

"What can we expect, Chantrant Tresser?" Meeks asked of the king's personal vintner.

"You'll have eighteen barrels of the Queen's Nectar," Tresser replied. "Handpicked by me, of course. We'll also feature a variety of seasonal ciders and ale, as well as charcuterie from Hunter's Manor and Gloucester. Only the finest for our honored guests."

"Thank you, Tresser," Crowley said, twirling his moustache in anticipation. "Your taste is impeccable, as ever."

She curtsied and he bowed, then moved onto his next task. He headed over to the stage, which was still being assembled.

"You there," Crowley said, approaching a group of bards who were tuning their instruments. "Are the Jesters Three ready for their performance?"

"All is well," the troupe's lead singer replied as they stood to greet their benefactor. "We're excited to perform for such a grand audience. Thank you for the opportunity."

"Of course," Crowley said. "Let me show you where you'll play."

He escorted the musicians around the hall and back, talking to the bards as he went.

"This is the royal table," Crowley explained. "You may perform beneath the dais, but no closer. Here's where the other noble families will sit. This, too, is off limits, save for the floor in front them."

"Of course."

"And here's your payment," Crowley added, handing a small purse of laurels to them. "Half the silver up front, half after, as agreed."

"Thank you," the troupe replied in near unison, a habit picked up from a thousand nights of close harmonies.

"You may call the princes on stage for your ballad," Crowley said. "I won't tell them of the honor so that their surprise will be genuine. I'm sure that Montgomery, in particular, will revel in the moment of glory. Now, back to tuning your instruments."

THE AFTERNOON PASSED QUICKLY, and the castle brimmed with excitement and anticipation as the hour of the masquerade drew nearer. The great hourglass clock that hung in the halls of Castle Thronehelm showed that it was well into the evening as nobles began to arrive from all four points of the compass. A pleasant susurrus rose over the hall as the guests mingled and made conversation, awaiting the arrival of the Thorhauers.

The great hall was filled with the sigils of the seven baronies and beyond, their costumes and masks matching their family colors. Ritter stood with Wilcox de la Croix and Rufus Crag, absorbing the scene from a far corner. They'd arrived on time, which meant they were early for a social call such as this, but they spent their time wisely, helping themselves to the food and wine.

"You should shoot brigand kings more often," de la Croix quipped. "I could get used to this pampering."

He filled his mouth with warm bread and Ritter noticed he was chewing like a Longmarcher, not a noble. He looked at Rufus and the two of them laughed.

"You look great in silk," Rufus said with a wry smile.

De la Croix always looked awkward in anything that wasn't made from studded leather. He was nearly seven feet tall and looked naked without his flamberge.

"That's enough of that," de la Croix retorted. "One more word out of you and I'll tell the guards to remove your trollborn—"

Trumpets blared, interrupting the inevitable exchange of vulgarities and signaling the arrival of the royal family. The Thorhauers emerged from the long corridor at the back of the chamber, leading a procession of the other barons into the great hall to the sound of rapturous applause.

The Thorhauers dressed in rich purple with white and gold trim, highlighting the white shield on their coat of arms and the purple helmet in its crest. Foghaven Vale followed next, with the Von Lormarcks in their standard black and burned orange, prominently displaying their jackal brooches. Master Cray was the only representative from Hunter's Manor, and he sauntered into the hall dressed in deep plum and mustard, his robes embroidered with the silhouette of a running stag.

Ritter looked on, hoping he'd never be part of such a spectacle. He felt a nudge at his elbow from de la Croix.

"Why aren't you up there?" the Longmarcher teased.

Ritter cracked an awkward smile and turned back to watch the rest of the arrivals. The last to enter were the guests of the king and queen, the Vermilion delegates from Eldwal. The high elves entered in a subdued fashion. The ambassador wore a white suit of decorative armor and a matching cape, along with a crimson mask that covered half his face. His daughter floated in beside him, her crimson mask mirroring her father's, but with a feminine touch. It was like something out of a dream, but a dream Ritter recognized.

Ritter blinked when he saw Addilyn, the mage woman he'd met in the woods, whom he'd thought of a few times since and had been hoping to meet again. Now it all fit together. She wasn't just a mage; she was a princess of Eldwal.

He raised a hand to wave at her, smiling under his mask. She clearly saw him, because she made eye contact briefly, but after a brief hesitation she turned away without a response.

Ritter dropped his hand in unhappy surprise. His first thought was that he'd offended her somehow, the second that she hadn't recognized him with his mask, but he discarded both; he'd seen the look of recognition in her eye, and she'd been friendly enough the day before that he doubted her feelings had changed so quickly.

With a flash of bitterness that he quickly tamped down, a third and more likely possibility registered, which was that she hadn't known he was trollborn but had somehow found out after their first meeting. That would at least explain the cold shoulder. He was used to outsiders who weren't from the Bridge reacting with discomfort around him or quietly ending the acquaintance when they noticed his ears. He always tried his best not to let it bother him.

This time, though, it was difficult to not feel betrayed. He'd been charmed by Addilyn and thought that she'd felt the same. Making friends had never come easily to Ritter, and so he felt the loss of one keenly. Addilyn hadn't exactly been his friend, but she'd been the beginning of one.

"Don't stare at the sun for too long," Rufus said, pulling Ritter back out of his trance.

Ritter's face flushed. He felt exposed, as though his companions had observed something private, which he supposed they had. He shuffled uncomfortably.

"Cat got your tongue?" de la Croix teased.

Rufus Crag and Wilcox de la Croix burst into silent hysterics, but Ritter, for once, had no response.

AS THE NIGHT MOVED along, the wine flowed by the barrel and Admiral Valerick LaBrecque of Seabrooke arrived in the gilded archway. He stood for a few moments, surveying the sea of nobles that rolled like gentle waves in front of the grand staircase. Always fashionably late, LaBrecque made his usual entrance and descended into the crowd.

Hearts raced, heads turned, and women swooned. The peacock of a man strolled confidently across the ballroom, flirting with the ladies of court on his way to greet the king and queen.

For a man in his early thirties, LaBrecque had accomplished more than most did in an entire lifetime. He didn't hide behind his station, and he'd learned to conquer the seas from an early age. His seamanship and pedigree had helped him to rise straight to the top, until the king had entrusted him with Warminster's navy.

LaBrecque wore no costume, only his usual tailored leather and cavalier hat with a plume in the deep blue color of his noble house.

"Ah, LaBrecque, the Seawolf of the Firth of Fury, you've made it," the king flattered him as he approached. "Where's your mask?"

"I didn't want to hide this gift to the women of your court, sire," the Seawolf said with a smile. The two laughed, and Godwin waved for him to climb the dais and join him.

"Your entrance was as spectacular as ever, Admiral," Amice said.

LaBrecque bowed and tipped his hat to his queen.

"Come," Godwin said. "We have much to discuss in private."

The two walked down from the dais and proceeded down a side hall and into the king's study.

"I've brought a gift for you, Your Majesty," LaBrecque said, before Godwin could begin. "It's a powder from the city of Abacus."

"I'm intrigued," the king replied. "What does it do?"

LaBrecque handed over a small pouch of the material and Godwin loosened the purse strings to find a fine, silvery powder.

"It's called silver flake," LaBrecque explained. "It was created by the scholars in Abacus. The substance, when used properly, will help your smithies make stronger seals and welds."

LaBrecque tossed a pinch of the powder into the hearth, igniting the flakes, which flashed brilliantly. The three averted their gaze from the burst for a few seconds until the hearth's flames returned to normal.

"Amazing," the king said. "But I felt no heat?"

"Aye," LaBrecque said, rasing his finger to confirm the

king's perception. "Abacus uses it in many ways, including for improved armor and weapons."

The king smiled and patted LaBrecque on the back. "Who makes such a product?"

"The damned tinker lardals in Abacus," LaBrecque replied. Lardals were smaller, thinner versions of twergs, distant cousins it was thought, who had a talent for mixing discovery with magic. "The twergs mine it and the lardals learned how to infuse it with their magics somehow. My ship is laden with sacks of it, sire, as a gift to you from the Barony of Seabrooke."

"You're a worthy subject," Godwin said. "Crowley, have it unloaded and taken to my smithies in the morning. I can't thank you enough, LaBrecque."

"And which is your ship, sir?" Crowley asked.

"*The Doom's Wake*."

"Of course," Crowley said. He smiled obsequiously and moved to refill their goblets.

"That will be all, Crowley," Godwin said, dismissing him with a condescending wave.

Meeks bowed low to them both and crept out of the study. Then the king grabbed the decanter of Queen's Nectar and poured out two glasses.

"Have a seat," Godwin said, turning to stoke the fire.

"What troubles you, sire?"

"This masquerade is a ruse."

"A ruse, sire?" LaBrecque replied, his face contorted with confusion.

"It's false," Godwin said. "My sons killed the Cloak, no doubt. And yes, the bastard son of Baroness Maeglen and Von Lormarck's bastardess are to announce their betrothal this evening. But I see little to celebrate."

"Sire?"

"I have suspicions, Valerick," Godwin said, finally turning to face him. "I'm unconvinced that this recent spate of incidents is over or, for that matter, coincidental."

LaBrecque let the gravity of Godwin's comments settle and then nodded in agreement. "You think there's more to come?" he asked.

"Aye," Godwin replied. "But from where?"

"I've heard the Vermilion are here… and stories of a tetrine sighting," the admiral said. "That can't be good…"

Godwin took a deep breath. He leaned on the oak table and took a sip of wine before answering.

"They shine like a beacon of trouble," he said. "I ask that you stay as my guest in Thronehelm for a while. There may be a need for you and your mariners, and I don't want you on the high seas somewhere unreachable."

"I'm at your service, my liege," LaBrecque said. "And you're in luck. I've sailed into Thronehelm on my fastest ship. Shall I send word to Seabrooke? I can have the fleet here in days, and with them will be three thousand mariners at your command."

"Not yet," the king said. "Such activities alert enemies."

"And who are our enemies?"

"If only I knew," the king replied.

"Ah," LaBrecque answered. "And thus, the masquerade?"

But the king said nothing. He just smiled at his young admiral as they clinked their goblets together.

RITTER WAS STANDING BY himself in a corner of the great hall, subconsciously tapping his foot to an old Sylvan waltz and wondering why he was still there. Wilcox and Rufus had left him to hunt for more ale, but he wasn't drinking anymore. His high spirits gone, Ritter was beginning to regret coming to the masquerade. The pleasant fog of the alcohol was subsiding into a low, cold weight in his stomach that left him feeling ill.

The crowd in front of him flowed back and forth through the halls and the bards strummed their lutes and played ballads for the royals. They, too, were in costume, and the beat of their drums kept the tempo for a dance floor that ebbed and flowed with a tide of enthusiastic nobles.

"Good evening, my lord," Meeks Crowley said politely, his manner professional as usual. "May I have the pleasure of introducing to you Ambassador Dacre Elspeth of Eldwal, and his daughter Addilyn Elspeth?"

Ritter flinched, wondering how the three of them had managed to sneak up on him so effectively. Ritter couldn't help looking at Addilyn first, yet she wasn't returning his gaze, her elaborate mask hiding her expression as she averted her eyes to the floor. Ignoring their obvious discomfort, her father started to speak. Meeks, ever the coward, moved off as soon as the conversation began.

"It's my honor to meet you, Sir Ritter." Ambassador Elspeth greeted him with a small nod. "I wish to congratulate you on your fine leadership at Rillifane's Meander."

Ritter hid his annoyance. This was exactly what he'd feared would happen at the ball, and it had come up just when he'd been about to leave.

"Everyone seems to know what I did, even those who weren't there," he blurted thoughtlessly, regretting it as it passed his lips. He realized just how rude the comment sounded, but Ambassador Elspeth seemed to share his daughter's talent for pretending away awkwardness and only smiled politely.

"I'm sure," he agreed, his expression turning somber. "The tale always far exceeds the reality, and it never includes the names of the dead, only the victors. Perhaps we'd all benefit from remembering that the cost of war doesn't extend only to the glamorous deaths of heroes. Yet we wanted to thank you, Sir Ritter, for vanquishing the Nightcloak and his men."

Ritter shuffled stiffly, thinking of the faces of Silas Carling and his orphaned daughter, Fira. He regretted his ill feeling toward the ambassador, realizing that the man had meant to ask after his well-being and not just to cluelessly congratulate him.

"You exaggerate my importance, Ambassador," Ritter replied after a moment. "It was a victory for the princes."

"Come, now." Dacre paused, throwing an arm around Ritter's shoulders. "We saw the king showering you with accolades yesterday. And it's right to thank you for what you and your Longmarchers won for us."

"And what was that, ambassador?"

"Time," the Vermilion replied earnestly, looking deep into Ritter's eyes. The single word held unexpected conviction. As Ritter contemplated the ambassador's meaning, he felt Dacre's hand grip him at the elbow. "I think my daughter wishes to dance," the ambassador commented, glancing between the two of them with a shrewd expression. Addilyn flinched slightly but made no other response. "Would you be so kind as to accompany her?"

Ritter turned to Addilyn, who was rigid but who nodded to him slightly, and took her hand. "Of course," he said.

With a nod to the ambassador, the two of them moved out toward the dancers.

There was a short, uncomfortable silence as they found each other's hands and began dancing. "My lady," Ritter began, looking across at Addilyn, "I'll do my best, but I'm not much of a dancer. I know little of our own dances, let alone those of the elves."

"I'm so sorry," Addilyn began, neatly ignoring Ritter's attempt to deflect from the matter between them. Ritter, thinking she was going to tell him they couldn't be friends, almost interrupted her, but instead he closed his mouth. He had no control over what she was feeling or what she'd say, and nor could he control what would happen after she spoke her piece. "I shouldn't have been so rude to you," she said instead.

"It's all right," Ritter replied, instantly relieved. "Are you well? Did something happen?"

"No," she said, looking down as though embarrassed, although her expression barely changed. "It's only that I really shouldn't have listened. You're my friend." Another wave of calm happiness hit him with her words, though it was tempered when he processed the rest of what she'd said.

"Someone told you that I'm trollborn," he guessed, keeping his tone even.

"It doesn't matter to me any more than it does to you," Addilyn said, fastening her gaze on his. "Truly. And I don't mean to make excuses, but I'm the ambassador's daughter, and we're of the royal family…" She was speaking quickly now, obviously wishing to explain herself and perhaps expecting him to interrupt her. "It's considered taboo for us to be publicly close to anyone outside of our own kind, even full-blooded elves from the other castes."

Ritter was stung by this, despite her obvious guilt and distress, and the undertone of defensiveness to her words wasn't helping. It wasn't as though he'd asked to be born a trollborn, but if he was being honest, something deep within him was proud of his dual heritage and he hated the implication that it was some kind of flaw. Pressing his lips together to contain a hasty retort, he took a breath and waited for her to continue.

"Our traditions and *prejudices* aren't your fault," she said, seeming to have some difficulty with the word as though it was occurring to her for the first time. "And they aren't fair."

She looked up at him again, her expression intent, and he suddenly realized that her eyes were beautiful. "I don't think I want to follow our traditions anymore. And I'd like to be friends, Ritter." After a brief hesitation, she reached up and pulled off her mask.

Part of him still wasn't sure if he wanted to be close with someone who didn't understand about him being trollborn. He wondered at the leap he'd already made in his mind to think of her as a friend. But he felt she'd listen if he talked to her about it, and there was a bigger part of him that just wanted to know her. "I'd like to be friends, too."

She grinned at him, and the unrestrained expression in her normally composed face was startlingly radiant. "Oh, good!" she said. "Thank you."

After another moment, she leaned into his hands. Ritter tripped over his feet in surprise, but she caught him so elegantly that she made it look like part of the dance. She didn't even laugh at his clumsiness.

Ritter caught Rufus's eyes across the room, and he flushed when his friend waggled his eyebrows and elbowed Wilcox next to him. He knew that they were probably getting the wrong idea. But then, he reflected with some pleasure, it wasn't as though the wrong idea would be so bad.

"Were you injured in the battle?" Addilyn asked.

"I was lucky to escape injury," Ritter replied, solemnly. "Many soldiers died that morning." Most of his Longmarchers would have basked in the chance to tell stories of war, but Ritter saw no glory in battle. He only saw desperation and death. Ritter took a long, slow breath. "I know the venture was a success, but it feels wrong to claim victory and status for myself when it came at the cost of others' lives."

"I'm sorry," she said earnestly, the corners of her mouth

turning down. "I can't say that I fully understand. I've never been in a real battle, but… I still feel that I know what you mean."

Something in that sounded loaded, like a few other comments she'd made over the course of their brief acquaintance, and he wondered what she was thinking.

"Tell me about your home," she said, deftly changing the subject. Perhaps she'd noticed that he didn't want to talk about the battle. Ritter's countenance improved and he smiled.

"My family hails from a small town called Valkeneer," he explained. "It sits on the border of Ravenwood, at the foothills of the Dragon's Breath Mountains."

"I'm familiar with the tales of the Battle of the Bridge," she replied, much to his surprise. "A Vermilion wing rode to give aid and battled alongside your kin."

"Aye." Ritter smiled. "I wasn't born to see it, but my father and mother both speak highly of the Vermilion support. Your people helped to win the battle."

They both smiled, finding some level of common ground, even if it was before their time.

"The Bridge is my ancestral home," he began again, "and it rests atop a windswept mountain. It overlooks the crystal lakes and the blue waters of the Gossamer River, which rushes below the castle. In the early mornings, when all is quiet, you can hear the river from a distance, whispering you awake. The tip of the castle is at such an elevation that sometimes the clouds break upon the peaks and surround the town, which is how the Dragon's Breath Mountains got their name. The locals once thought that the clouds could only come from the nostrils of the mythical beasts. In the winter, the snow gathers in pillows on the firs of Ravenwood. It's my favorite time to be in the woods. Its purity and beauty are unequaled."

"It sounds captivating," Addilyn said. "You must miss it."

"Yes," he said with a smile, "but I needed to heed the call of the king and Baroness Maeglen."

"When do you return?"

"I don't know, my princess," he replied. "That's for the king to decide. But I worry for someone we rescued on the hunt for the Cloak."

"What happened?"

"We came upon a village that the Cloak had ambushed. A young girl had escaped. I sent her back to the Bridge to the safety of my family."

"How old was the girl?"

"Her name is Fira," Ritter said. "And I really don't know. Ten? Twelve, perhaps? I don't think she knows, either."

"So, your family will take her in?"

"Aye," Ritter said. "It's our duty to ensure that all who travel our lands are safe, regardless of their station."

Ritter could sense that the story had affected Addilyn, but he couldn't discern if it was endearment or if he'd offended her. He hurried to change the subject.

"I've heard of your people," Ritter said, "but I've never seen a Vermilion up close."

"Now that you have, what do you think?"

He was mulling this thought over when he noticed a flashily dressed, unmasked nobleman leaving the ballroom with the king. Ritter didn't recognize him, but he had the bearing of a military man, probably an academy graduate, a decade or so ahead of Ritter and the princes.

"Look," Ritter murmured, flicking his eyes toward the front of the room. "The king is leaving. I wonder what could be so important that he'd step away from his own party."

Addilyn followed his glance and was silent for a moment. "I don't know for sure," she replied, "but it might have something to do with why we're here. Things are happening, Ritter. I don't know if they're good or bad, but they're big. The king knows it too, I think."

He looked at her in surprise; there was that weight in her words again. Then he smiled. "Was prognostication part of your magical training?"

She didn't play along. "Only Keepers can do that, but I can still see what's right in front of me. There's a storm coming. I'm sure you must sense it too."

That sobered his mood. For some reason, he found himself thinking of the sniper with the black rose arrows. His gaze returned to her eyes, and he nodded silently in agreement. Then their conversation was abruptly interrupted.

"Welcome, one and all," the master of ceremonies announced theatrically from the front of the stage, raising his hands to the ceiling. "My ladies, my lords, the king and queen welcome you to a celebration of victory and love."

As he spoke, he gestured first in the direction of the princes and then to Joferian and Ember, who were sharing the dance floor.

"We, we, the Jesters Three, present you with a gift," the bard continued. "'Tis a gift of song, a ballad we've composed to memorialize the fall of the Nightcloak at the hands of our valiant princes. Prince Montgomery, Prince Everett, may we invite you to join us on the stage as we honor you with our song?"

Ritter and Addilyn clapped, and he watched the two princes walk toward the stage, knowing that Montgomery enjoyed the spotlight while Everett was more reserved. The bards readied their instruments and the massed crowd swayed gently across the great hall, showing their respect for the coming spectacle. With the minstrels in place, the lyrist plucked away at the opening notes of the ballad. The flautist began to whistle and then the singer picked up the vocal line.

From the Bridge, in the autumn dawn they rode,
A trail of hooves and blood, their destiny showed.
The Cloak in the shadows, arrows in the air,
As the princes fought bravely through their snare...

"What do you think?" Addilyn asked as the ballad progressed.

"I'm just glad my name isn't mentioned," Ritter replied.

AMBASSADOR ELSPETH WAS ENJOYING the festivities, along with perhaps a little too much of the Queen's Nectar. The wine just kept flowing and he'd lost count of his tally several goblets ago. His wise eyes monitored the queen, just as she was intently watching her sons as they were showered with accolades. He used the opportunity to steal her husband's seat on the dais, hoping to gain her ear.

"Ambassador, sitting in the king's throne may be unwise," Amice said gently, stopping the Vermilion from making a huge breach in royal etiquette.

"Apologies, Your Majesty," Dacre stammered, forgetting himself.

"A pleasant song," the queen said, as he sidled over to her. "Don't you agree?"

"Aye, Your Grace," Dacre replied. "By all accounts, they've earned their place in Thorhauer lore."

The two tapped their wine glasses together in a subtle toast, then turned back to the dancing throng in front of them. Dacre waited for the right moment to weigh in, but he didn't want to interrupt the queen's joy at her sons' success. It would have to wait until the music died.

Queen Amice rose to her feet and motioned to a jester who stood next to the dais. "My dear jester," she called over the noise, "why are you not your jovial self? Should it not be the Jesters Four?"

"I'm sorry, Your Majesty," the jester said, bowing to Dacre and the queen. He then nimbly leapt onto the dais and sauntered over to Amice. She nodded at him and awaited his performance.

Dacre took another sip of the Queen's Nectar and motioned to a servant to refill his glass. In all his years, he'd never tasted such a forbidden fruit. The nectar lived up to its reputation in every way. He turned his glossy eyes back to Amice and the matter at hand.

The musicians' lofty ballad reached a crescendo. As the music ended, it was replaced by a jubilant round of applause that filled the chamber. With a dramatic gesture, the jester shed his colorful cloak and stole the show, revealing a hidden sword. For a moment, Dacre's mind played tricks on him, his foggy thoughts struggling to keep up with what was happening. But then the glint of steel forced him from his stupor.

"Guards!" he exclaimed. "Protect the queen!"

But his voice was lost amidst the applause. He tossed his goblet to the floor and drew his own sword in the same fluid motion, rushing to her defense.

Amice spilled her wine, trying to slide her heavy throne away as the rest of the royal table gasped in horror. A mere second later, the flashing blade was in the jester's hands.

Dacre lunged, thrusting his weapon to block the jester, but the jester's sword was meant for him. His steel swung to defend a blow to the queen that never arrived. Instead, he felt the deep bite of the jester's blade as it carved into his torso.

He tried to back away from its sting, but the jester thrust it deeper, twisting the blade before recovering it. Dacre grabbed at the wound and felt the warmth of his blood spilling to the floor, where it mixed with his wine.

"Guards!" the queen screamed, but its hollow ring meant nothing to him. His mind flustered as his legs gave way. He watched helplessly as the queen reached for him, her eyes staring at the wound he feared to look at himself. Then his arms fell to his side and his blade dropped harmlessly to the floor.

Dacre stared ahead at his assailant, watching him slowly remove his mask, revealing himself as a Bone elf. The assassin leapt over the table and landed squarely on Dacre, crushing his ribs. The Vermilion squealed in pain as his breath escaped him.

The Bone elf leaned over the fallen ambassador and dug a knee into his chest. "I've waited years for this day," he growled to the flailing Vermilion. "I've dreamed of my steel tasting your dying flesh. Your daughter is next. May you live long enough to witness the end of your line."

With a flash of his hand, the jester produced a black rose from his costume and dropped it on Dacre's chest. Dacre didn't understand, but he was also helpless to stop it.

He could only watch on in terror.

ADDILYN SCREAMED IN HORROR from across the ballroom, watching from afar as the jester attacked her father. Around her, the oblivious crowd was dancing to the minstrels' song. In a sudden burst of activity, Addilyn left Ritter's side and barreled her way through the mob of bodies in front of her.

"Father!" she screamed, her voice tremulous and piercing, rising above the sound of the song and the festivities. For a brief instant, she wondered where the castle guards were, but then she saw a couple of them making their way toward the death jester, their swords drawn and vengeance plastered across their faces. There was a quick dance of steel and before Addilyn knew it, both men had fallen to his blade.

She could sense Ritter trailing her, and her peripheral vision settled on the two princes as they watched the grim spectacle from their perches at the side of the stage. Ritter was calling her name and shouting something, but she couldn't hear it and she didn't care. Only one thing mattered.

She had to get to her father.

AS MONTGOMERY BOLTED ACROSS the stage at the assassin, the bards—who moments earlier had been singing his praises—drew hidden daggers from their puffy sleeves and stepped forward to block him. Unarmed, Montgomery paused his approach and parried a leaping attack from the lyricist, who'd revealed a hidden garotte made from lyre strings.

"Everett!" he yelled. "To me!"

The singer had joined the melee too, and it was only his Halifax training that stopped Montgomery from falling to the swipe of a dagger at his midsection. The blade sliced clean through his ruffled vest, but the edge missed its mark and caught nothing but air. With a quick flick, Monty brushed the dagger aside and countered with a punch that caught the jester in the face. The blow knocked him from the stage, and he was swallowed by the panicked crowd.

The second bard arced his garotte over Monty's head and tugged violently at the prince's throat.

Monty guessed at the move, the only one the assailant had left, and slid his forearm between the devilish coil and his neck. The wire cut into his forearm, but it was better than tearing at his exposed throat. Instinctively, Monty twisted, turning on his attacker and rendering the weapon ineffectual.

Montgomery caught him with a swift headbutt, sending the second assailant to the floor, dazed and bloodied. Seizing the moment of freedom, Montgomery jumped from the stage and waded through the advancing castle guards to get to his mother.

While Montgomery was taking on the lyrist and the singer, Everett was in a fierce melee with the third and final musician, the percussionist. The drummer produced a hidden weapon, tearing it from the drum's cylinder and spinning it about his head like a bola.

Everett raised his hands to block the swings of the improvised implement, ducking under the spinning rope and dodging its metal head.

Unarmed, the young prince waited for the assassin's next lunge and then skillfully escaped in a feinting parry, his hand grabbing the rope as it spun by. It wrapped itself around Everett's arm and he tugged violently at it, sending the bard tumbling over his drum set and toward the floor. Everett dropped a knee into the assassin's back, collapsing the man face-first into the floorboards while he wrestled the rope from his grasp.

The man grunted feebly as his face smashed into the stage, but Everett wasn't finished. He completed the kill with the man's own weapon, driving its metal head into the base of his skull and twisting it until the musician stopped moving.

ADDILYN RUSHED BLINDLY TO her father's aid and fought her way through the wave of fleeing gentry. Pandemonium seized the hall as other hidden threats emerged amongst the panicking crowd. Castle guards rushed forward to confront a dozen would-be assassins while nobles scrambled for the exits. She spotted a fallen guard and pulled a bloodied dagger from his back.

"*Cantomar repudium domovoi!*" Addilyn raged, launching a spell at the unsuspecting jester. She felt the swell of magic in her fingertips, and she directed the energy away from her as she ran. A golden ray leapt from her hands and gripped the king's throne within its hale. With a twist of her wrist, the spell thrusted the throne against the assassin, knocking him to the floor. Knowing she had only seconds to act, Addilyn deftly leapt the table and landed beside her adversary.

At first glance, Addilyn thought he was just another one of the imposter bards that had attacked the princes. As she neared him, however, she got a closer look and could clearly see the imposing features of a Bone elf, the daylight brethren of the Shadow elves. With ashen hair and black eyes, Bone elves were bred to withstand the sunlight and live as war proxies in the daytime world for their despotic cousins. Her father had warned her about their existence and even told her stories of skirmishes with their kind when she was a girl, but this was the first time she'd seen one face to face. She shuddered.

Her father's eyes were upon her, and she met them for a second as she closed ranks with the false jester. They stood there for a moment, measuring each other's defenses. Addilyn knew that her opponent had the reach, his longsword against her dagger, but she had a trick or two up her sleeves and fury burning in her heart, so she waded in regardless.

In a whirlwind, Addilyn's blade met the Bone elf's longsword, once in a twisted parry and then again in consecutive slashes. The elf wasn't strong, but his moves were faster than Addilyn's. He stepped back and dipped his blade for another slash, then turned quickly with a blind thrust. Addilyn kicked her legs back in a desperate attempt to dodge, barely escaping his attack. It worked, but it left her vulnerable to his next tactic. The Bone elf quickly lifted his longsword into her wrist, cutting her along the way.

Addilyn dropped the dagger in pain and grabbed at the gash in her forearm. Blood seeped through her clenched fingers, and she looked at him helplessly, waiting for the killing blow.

The Bone elf's face lit up in anticipation, and with his sword raised, he swung it with a passion she didn't understand.

She closed her eyes as the blade fell.

Instead of the pain of deadly steel, Addilyn heard the clang of metal inches from her face. She dared to open an eye and saw Ritter and his extended sword, somehow diving in and blocking the vicious blow. She glanced at him and then back at the Bone elf, all three of them surprised that the desperate move had worked. Ritter's sword was not his own and it was already tainted with blood, perhaps from another encounter on his way to her. But there was no time to dwell on it, and Addilyn wasted little, grabbing the fallen dagger with her unwounded hand. She scrambled to her feet and saw Queen Amice trying to staunch Dacre's wounds while the other nobles scrambled for cover.

Once she was back in the fight, Addilyn quickly saw that Ritter was outmatched. The young trollborn had engaged the Bone elf with a quick flurry of parries, but the jester's mastery of the sword was evident. With a smile, the jester chuckled at Ritter's feeble attempts to defend himself.

"You're not as skilled with the sword as you are with a bow," he taunted. "Are you, trollborn?"

Addilyn paused for a moment, unsure how the two knew each other, but then she launched into action, using the distraction to slash at the Bone elf's leg. She cut through his costume and drew a line of blood across his thigh. Then the assassin jumped backward, knocking her blade aside.

The three looked at one another for a split second, long enough for a shrill whistle to cut above the chaos in the chamber.

Jessamy Aberdeen had made her way to the front of the melee, her sword drawn and a look of cold fury in her eyes. With a glare that could have pierced through armor, the Raven elf challenged the jester, calling him to her with a flick of her sword.

The Bone elf smiled at the challenge and turned away from Addilyn, who felt Ritter's arms around her shoulders as he lifted her away from the coming melee. But she didn't look at him, her eyes falling instead on her wounded father laying but a few feet away.

The test of their swords rang in her ears as Jessamy and the jester met in a fierce and equal flurry of steel, their blades meeting at impossible speeds only to stalemate seconds later. The two combatants broke apart and looked at one another, appreciating each other's skill.

In a fit of rage, Addilyn threw her dagger at the Bone elf, but his uncanny awareness allowed him to deflect the attempt with a slice of his sword. Still, there was a flash of fear in his eyes. He was outnumbered and the fight was turning against him.

"I'll see you soon, Vermilion," he cried above the noise of the crowd. He stepped back from the fracas and leapt over the downed table. Jessamy followed in relentless pursuit and darted after him, swinging at him and missing him by a hair.

"Are you okay?" Ritter asked. His voice was hurried, and he worked while he talked to investigate the wound and to make sure it wasn't deep. He grabbed some loose napery from the table to bind the wound. Addilyn, meanwhile, was tugging at his shoulder, pulling him to attend to her injured father. Dacre was conscious, but neither he nor Queen Amice was able to stave off the bleeding.

"I need a healer!" Addilyn called in vain.

She and Ritter lifted Dacre from the stone floor to carry him to the king's study. As they made the door, they nearly ran into LaBrecque and the king, who were returning to check on the commotion.

"My wife!" Godwin shouted in a panic, seeing Amice

trailing the bloody Vermilion in her own soaked dress. "Are you okay, my love?"

"Yes," Amice replied, her voice shaking. "It was the jester… an assassin."

"And the boys?"

"We're here, Father," Montgomery said, the two princes emerging from the mob right on cue.

"But Lord Dacre has been wounded," Everett added.

"Aye," Ritter growled, his voice rising above the hubbub, "and he's bleeding out in our arms. Make way, make way!"

The throng parted and Ritter and Addilyn carried Dacre along the corridor and into the king's study. Moments later, First Keeper Jhodever hustled his way in to attend to the ambassador.

"My lady," Jhodever said, reaching for Addilyn's blood-stained hands. "You must let me examine his wounds."

Addilyn backed away, but only by inches. Jhodever stepped forward, maintaining the pressure as best as he could while examining the damage to Dacre's body. After a couple of seconds, he raised his eyes and signaled the grim reality with a shake of his head.

"Mortal," he said.

"No!" Addilyn screamed, her desperation magnified by the harsh echoes bouncing back off the castle's stone walls. "No!"

Ritter reached for her, but she shook him off, choosing instead to go to her father. Dacre looked up at his daughter as she embraced him, resignation etched into his face.

"I'm not in pain," Dacre whispered, weakly.

"This can't be happening," she wailed, her tears mixed with confusion.

While they talked, Jhodever continued to buy them precious seconds as he feverishly worked to stop the bleeding as best he could.

"Addy," Dacre mumbled, "my bag."

"No, father!" Addilyn whispered. "Hold my hand."

The two continued to embrace each other and to converse in a low stream of high Melexian while Ritter and the princes stepped outside to give them some privacy. The king and queen remained behind, but they shuffled to the side of the room, embracing each other, and whispering in their own low monotone while Addilyn and Jhodever remained at Dacre's side.

Addilyn wiped her tears away on her bloodied gown and looked down at Dacre, who was all but limp. A knowing grin crept across his face as death drew nearer.

"You're now Ambassador Elspeth," he murmured, as Addilyn shook her head in defiance. "Carry the crimson banner high."

He pointed to his bag again, which had fallen from his robes during their hasty entrance. The gesture clearly cost him, and Addilyn wondered what could possibly be so important. Finally conceding, she leaned back and emptied its contents on the table. Several Vermilion scrolls tumbled out, along with his signet ring and royal seal.

"They're yours now," he whispered, too weak to even reach for them. "You're not safe here. The assassin will come for you."

"Father, stay with me," Addilyn replied, still fighting futilely against her tears.

"Find Helenius," Dacre said, his voice barely even audible. "Stop what's to come."

Something in Dacre's eyes started to fade, and his body shuddered and then settled down with an eerie stillness. His lips moved one final time as he expelled his final breath of air.

"*Insoro kaste fortudo,*" he whispered, his last message of love to his daughter.

CHAPTER TWENTY

"The wisest warriors often warn
It's always darkest before the dawn."
—WARMINSTERIAN SAYING

DAEMUS WATCHED BLUE CONNEY return on dogback from trailing the group, scouting the horizon for the tell-tale signs of Clan Blood Axe.

"They're coming," Conney said, not bothering to dismount Jericho when he arrived at their impromptu camp. "We have half a day on them at most."

Faux stared wordlessly at Arjun and then turned to look at Daemus. His vision had come to pass.

"How many?" Arjun queried.

"The whole damned clan," Blue replied, "including the horsehounds."

"We're only an hour from Homm Hill." Arjun sounded resolute. "The Fates have decided for us. It's there that we'll make our stand."

"*Our stand?*" Marquiss repeated incredulously, pointing to the distant dust clouds of the approaching marauders. "Seven of us against that?"

"Eight, if you count Jericho," Conney said. "Which I do."

"We're all going to die," Marquiss spat.

"Not necessarily." Arjun looked over his shoulder in the direction of Blood Ridge. "If we make it to the fort, we have a chance. The trollborn are too fast and will catch up with us if we remain in the open. If we fight in the plains, it's a battle we can't win. At least the fort gives us an advantage. And besides, I know that old fort well."

"We can't defeat the clan in the Highgrass." Marquiss shook

his head, pointing again. "But we can't defeat them at Blood Ridge, either. All we can do is postpone the inevitable."

"We'll see about that," Arjun replied.

Daemus sighed aloud. He knew it was the Sight that had showed him this, but he couldn't help feeling responsible.

Blue Conney strolled over to him and clapped him on the back with a rough hand as he tried to lighten the mood. "Seems like you're a Keeper after all," the springheel said. "You're gonna have to teach me that trick, lad."

Daemus looked down at him from his horse, but his worried frown didn't change.

Faux pushed her horse forward and the group stepped up the pace, making for the old fort with as much haste as the animals could muster. The horses were tired and made the last leg of the trek at half speed. An hour of silent introspection passed between them, broken only when they saw Homm Hill on the horizon.

Homm Hill rose in defiance of the vast grasslands, a mound of white stone at its base capped with a green plateau. The ruins slouched at the center of the bluff, their battle-weary walls darkened by time and endless winds. At the foot of the mound, jutting rocks broke from the hill and created a natural labyrinth, making a cavalry approach near impossible.

"Arjun," Faux said, "are you all right?"

Arjun didn't respond. The group stood solemnly beside him until he broke the silence.

"Blood Ridge will claim more ghosts before our work here is done," he said.

"Has anyone got the key?" Blue Conney asked.

His joke fell on deaf ears.

"No keys needed," Arjun replied. He took the lead, carefully guiding his horse up the craggy rocks and along an old goat path toward the summit. The others followed.

The fortress lay in ruins. A hulking portcullis rested between two sulking towers at the face of the stronghold, aged in place and petrified with rust. Parts of the outer walls crumbled with decay, but most of the formidable defenses were still in place.

"We have much to do and little time," Arjun said, as he led them around the ruins.

"What do we need to do?" Conney asked.

"We'll need to look for weaknesses in the remaining defenses," Arjun explained.

After their quick inspection, he dismounted from his horse and walked to the edge of the hill. The rest of the party joined him and from the crest, they surveyed the sprawling Vilchor Highgrass. To the northeast, they could see the hazy soot of Clan Blood Axe wafting above the plains, barely two hours away at a full gallop.

"Sixty of us held this fort against a thousand," Arjun said, as though the Battle of Blood Ridge had happened yesterday. "We fought for two long days. This fort is rough, but it'll even the odds. We'll have cover while they'll be forced to climb the rocks. We must look to the arsenal inside, along with the remaining war machines. We must see what we can repair before they arrive."

"How do we enter?" Faux asked.

"There are many secret entrances," Arjun explained. "There are also tunnels that Blue and Jericho can use to surprise our enemies. Blue, you'll be able to maneuver where the enemy can't, but we'll first have to see what needs to be cleared. I'm sure there have been collapses."

"Aye." Blue petted Jericho's flank. "Those bastards won't know what hit 'em."

"Chernovog and I will look at the battlements and war machines." Burgess pointed to the slouching walls. "We'll refortify what we can."

"Good," Arjun said.

"What about me?" Daemus asked. "What can I do to help?"

Arjun threw his arm around Daemus's shoulder. "Daemus, whatever happens to us, you must survive. Always remain behind the walls and learn to navigate the tunnels with Blue. They may be your only escape if things go poorly. I want you to stay clear when the battle starts. Shadow Faux, but don't—"

"I can't just stand around while you fight," Daemus protested. "You're fighting for me, and if I'm to survive then you should put me to use. You showed me how to use this, didn't you?"

He hefted the mace they'd been training with and gestured to the hand crossbow holstered on his hip. Arjun nodded.

"Very well," he said. "Daemus, you'll fight alongside Faux and Marquiss. They'll rain arrows down from the parapets and the catwalks. You'll take on the bigger targets."

"Why?" Daemus asked. "Do you think I'm ready?"

"No, lad," Arjun replied, chuckling to himself, and tousling the boy's hair. "I just don't want you to miss."

ARJUN LED THE GROUP to the rear of the fort and quickly found what he was looking for. The escape tunnel, barely large enough for a human to sneak through, opened easily as Arjun muscled his way into the musty hatchway. Encroaching grass and soil camouflaged the entrance from the naked eye, but Arjun knew exactly where he was heading. He lit his lantern and led the group into the shaft.

The tunnel's buttresses still held the ceiling and walls in place, and the group cleared debris as they made their way underground and into the fort. The tunnel ran straight and was meant for a quick exit and not for combat. The ceiling was barely four feet from the ground, making it impossible to swing a sword or even to stand upright.

They emerged into a flooded cellar which held several inches of putrid water that had leeched its way down over the years.

"The stairs are here," Arjun said, leading the group carefully up them to a closed door. He tried the handle and the door opened without a fight. The lanternlight spilled through the doorway and as they emerged one by one, they found themselves in a small war room.

"This was the last line of defense," Arjun said, pacing around the room and conjuring up memories for himself. "If we were forced back here, our only escape was through that tunnel. We should leave the horses at the rear in case we need to make a quick getaway."

"What's through here?" Daemus asked, holding his nose as he approached one of the doors.

"You don't want to go that way," Arjun said. "That smell is coming from the food stores. Whatever's left has been there for a decade."

Daemus scowled at the smell and walked toward a different door. As he pried it open, sunlight flooded the chamber, cascading from a short staircase that led to a collapsed archway.

"What's this?" he asked.

Arjun grinned and said, "That, my friend, is the courtyard."

ARJUN EMERGED INTO THE heart of Fort Homm and scanned the battlements from the inside. Ballistae were stationed in each of the forward towers, while the back of the courtyard housed several stale catapults that needed a quick refit.

"Burgess, Chernovog," Arjun said, "I want you to take the ballistae. Marquiss, you and I will work on the catapults."

"I've never seen a catapult before," Marquiss said.

"Then we're lucky you're a quick learner," Arjun replied. "Blue, let me show you the tunnels. I want you to learn them so you can navigate your way around. Take Daemus with you. He can help clear the rubble. But before you do, I have an ugly chore for you and Daemus. Fetch some of the rotten supplies. I have an idea that might just work."

"Yer gonna smear maggots on the doors?" the springheel asked.

"Something like that." Arjun grinned.

"And what of me?" Faux asked.

Arjun pointed to a building at the rear of the fort.

"That's the old arsenal. If Nothos is with us, we'll find usable weapons and supplies."

A few hours passed as they readied their defenses as best they could. Even with Arjun's help, Burgess could only get two ballistae in working order. He'd man one and Chernovog would man the other.

Arjun and Marquiss readied the catapults, but with no real stones to hurl, they filled the buckets with rusty swords and broken spears from the armory. One was even loaded with a special surprise from Arjun. They'd have to do.

Faux and Daemus discovered nearly a dozen longbows and crossbows, most of them still in working order, and they placed them along the battlements and catwalks so they could grab them on the move as needed. Daemus had also helped Conney to clear the tunnel systems and to set snares and traps for unwary enemies.

"When we were here, we fought from every tower and parapet," Arjun explained. The group sat huddled atop the towers at the front gate. "We defended Blood Ridge from every angle. Be patient, mark your targets, and we can do the same. We can win this fight. We *will* win this fight."

The group listened intently to the old captain of House Dauldon, letting him take them back to when he was a young soldier from the High Aldin. Blue sharpened his daggers on his whetstone while Faux checked her bowstring.

"The walls were slick with blood," Arjun said. "The stones were so bathed in it that it looked like the Ancient of War himself had been born here."

The group fell silent for a moment and all heads turned to Arjun.

"I can still smell the boiling oil we poured from the towers," he continued. "Our archers would light their arrows and burn those caught below. The fires sometimes kept a wall from assault for a time, but the screams…"

Faux put her hand on the captain's shoulder.

"Anoki and I sometimes fought alone, back-to-back at the gates and in the tunnels. There were just so many of them."

"Who's Anoki?" Daemus asked.

"She was…" Arjun began, before stopping for a moment of introspection. "She was a soldier like me. A better swordswoman, no doubt. Quick as a jackalope and smart enough to have figured our way out of here. She saved my life. She saved all who remained."

Arjun's story was interrupted by a horn carrying its awful groan across the winds of the plains to the top of Homm Hill. Their eyes captured each other's gazes for a moment before Arjun broke the silence.

Boom! Boom! Ba-boom!

"It's meant to intimidate," he said, calmly. "Don't let it."

"It's time," Faux said. "Get to your battle stations."

THE DUST OF ONE hundred horsehounds spread across the base of Homm Hill, their riders staring at the aging gates of the abandoned fortress. Misael dismounted and walked ahead of the horde. With a powerful swing, he planted the feathered flag of Clan Blood Axe into the ground as his followers cheered and hollered, the bloodlust high and the adrenaline rising. The flag, tattered by the winds of the plains and the bustle of a dozen battles, featured the faded symbol of a bloody battleaxe.

Misael's keen eyes surveyed Blood Ridge. Fort Homm looked abandoned to the untrained eye, but Misael knew better. Appearances could be deceiving.

"We know you're there," he shouted, his powerful voice echoing off the imposing rocks. "We can smell your fear."

"Ah-ooh!"

The clan cried it out as one, banging their weapons rhythmically against their shields as their mounts sounded off with howls and growls like a pack of wolves on the path of a rabbit.

Misael surveyed his troops with approval and then lifted his fearsome battleaxe. The chants behind him ceased as quickly as they'd started.

Misael tilted his head back and drew a protracted breath into his trollborn nose. He smiled at the result.

"Is that you I smell, Arjun Ezekyle?" he shouted. The taunt in his voice was obvious. Misael waited a few seconds, hoping for a response that never came, before he spoke again. "Your woman isn't here to protect you this time, Ezekyle."

The silence continued. It was a heavy, oppressive kind of silence, the kind that hung heavy in the air like when the great crowds gathered in the courtyard of Castle Thronehelm to honor the dead on the anniversary of the Battle of the Bridge. Even twenty years on, there was power in that silence.

But here, the silence was also tinged with an unspoken, underlying threat, as well as the panting of five score impatient horsehounds.

"I don't want to kill you, Ezekyle," Misael yelled. "Give us the boy or we'll take him by force."

A few moments of silence passed between predator and prey. Then Misael saw a trapdoor open at the base of the fortress. A human figure stepped through to face its aggressor, and Misael saw the familiar but aged face of Arjun Ezekyle looking down at him. Misael smiled and waited for Arjun to surrender.

He was disappointed.

Arjun drew his sword, a blade that Misael knew far too well. Arjun had taken it from the High Aldin when he'd left their service. Unlike the ruggedly forged swords of Clan Blood Axe, Arjun's shining katana had been crafted by the master smithies of Abacus. Misael could see its keen red edge glinting in the sun, even from a distance. It was a weapon that would be the envy of any swordsman.

It was Misael's turn to stand in silence as Arjun surveyed the trollborn from his vantage point on the edge of Fort Homm. Arjun took his katana and patiently scored a line on the ground with the edge of his sword. Then he turned slowly, never taking his gaze off the trollborn, and disappeared back into the fortress.

Misael cracked a half-smile and growled to himself at the gesture. He promised himself that Arjun's sword would be his when the battle was over. But first, the battle must begin. He threw back his head and howled an order.

He signaled the charge with the drop of his axe, a cruel weapon that seemed to slice the very air in two. The horsehounds and their trollborn riders alike howled in a cacophony of battle cries as they surged ahead.

As they rode, there was a flurry of movement on the battlements as Blood Ridge's defenders worked to bolster the fort's defenses. Even above the noise of his riders, Misael could hear the familiar aching and groaning of an old war machine, perhaps a catapult or a ballista. For a ruined fortress, it seemed to be surprisingly well-equipped.

"Shields!" he yelled, but while his trollborn moved swiftly to obey his orders, they weren't quick enough. The first volley came from the ballistae on the near parapet. Giant arrows designed to cripple machines of war leapt from their rusty casings and pierced through the charging phalanx of mercenaries, scattering their ranks. Their war cries turned into howls of pain and surprise.

Misael couldn't hear the war machines reloading over the thundering hooves of his horsehounds, but he could make out the defenders' helmets. Then another familiar sound roared over their charge. Catapults inside the fort had loosed a payload of rusting swords, broken spears and improvised projectiles, and the metal rained down across the trollborn ranks. A dozen riders and steeds fell to it.

"How?" Misael growled, but he continued to charge ahead.

Then a second volley from the catapults launched high in the air, its payload spreading like a swarm of bees as it ranged closer and closer.

"Shields!" Misael yelled again as the objects descended.

The sounds of glass shards and tin vials shattering on the ground rose above even the cavalry charge, spraying up into the approaching horde. One cannister exploded in front of him and he saw rotten food and decayed pig flesh flying out of it.

The spoiled foodstuffs knocked a few riders from their

steeds, but the shower of moldering lard and ruined preserves also confused the horsehounds. His cavalry charge turned into a feeding frenzy for their mounts, horsehound fighting horsehound for the rotting flesh that had fallen from the heavens. Some riders were bucked from their steeds while others struggled to regroup and continue the charge. Some of the larger horsehounds killed lesser ones in the frenzy.

"Attack!" Misael commanded, wondering what other surprises Arjun had in store for the clan. "Forward!"

Another ballista shot tore into his lines, knocking several more riders and their steeds to the ground. They were close enough to the base of the hill that the war machines, however deadly, couldn't fire straight down and were rendered useless. He'd earned the cover of Homm Hill, but the hill was steep with a single road funneling them to the old gates. Another price to pay in flesh, not gold.

But despite the carnage, the clan had weathered the storm of the first attack and reached the crest of the hill and the fort's outer walls. Their numbers had thinned, but they still outnumbered the defenders seven to one, not counting their steeds.

From the outside, the remains of Fort Homm looked like a bundle of weatherworn wood, buttressed with improvised stone walls. But as several of the clan's riders dismounted at what looked like a weakened gate, they found it was bolstered by something substantial on the other side of the door.

The clan scrambled to find an alternative entrance, but Misael recognized their plight too late. They'd ridden into an ambush.

"Circle the fort!" he shouted. "Leave the gate!"

A shower of arrows penetrated their ranks. Their steeds howled with rage and anguish, and some went to ground, losing their riders.

The survivors quickly dismounted and sought shelter against the crooked walls, their mounts pressing in beside them or bounding off across the plains, away from the deadly volleys.

"No!" Misael commanded. "Keep riding!"

A second and then a third barrage kept the trollborn pinned against the wall, while from somewhere above them, the defenders let fly with crossbow bolts, rocks, and spear thrusts from hidden murder holes. Misael looked up and caught a glimpse of his quarry, the Alaric boy, and then he was gone again, and a fresh rain of death was crashing against his shield.

The horde was taking terrible losses, but Misael thought he saw an opportunity. It seemed that the defenders were throwing all their might at this one side of the fort, which left only one logical course of action.

With a quick hoot and a swing of his axe, Misael signaled an order to abandon the western wall and to ride with haste for the east. But before the trollborn could make the turn, the springheel emerged from a trap door, revealing a hidden tunnel in the side of Fort Homm. He was mounted on the back of a war dog, and Misael instantly recognized him as Blue Conney, a threat he'd been warned about. Conney's berserker rages were infamous, and Misael was about to experience one first-hand. Nearly blind with battle rage, the warrior showed no mercy, splitting the trollborn columns in a suicide run.

Misael stared in awe as the blue-faced berserker rushed between and under his men and their steeds, guiding his dog with his legs while stinging and slashing at the trollborn mounts with toothed daggers. The berserker screamed in a high-pitched wail as his arms stroked back and forth, cutting deep into the flesh of the horsehounds, causing mass panic and disorder in their once-organized ranks. As quickly as he'd appeared, Blue Conney disappeared into another tunnel at the front of the fort, with nary a sword swing in his direction.

By now, Misael's ranks had been halved, but they still outnumbered the defenders and the trollborn were undeterred. Misael quickly dismounted and urged his remaining warriors to use their torches as weapons, setting the old wood aflame. While the walls burned, the trollborn axes and hammers bashed a hole that was large enough for them to enter. They fought through flames and emerged from the hole undaunted, but in single file. The fire had also helped the defenders, setting light to some of their hide armors.

Their success was short-lived. With a resounding thud, a larger section of the outer wall collapsed under the crushing blows of Misael's battleaxe, and he barked another order as the trollborn horde rushed forward.

Misael himself dismounted and approached the fiery wall. He could hear the sound of steel clanging on the other side of the burning fort and knew the defenders had moved to counter their attack.

The familiar voice of Arjun Ezekyle came from beyond the wall. "Watch the breach!"

Misael gritted his teeth and swung his mighty axe into the flames, watching pieces of wood crack under his blow.

"I'm here, Ezekyle!" he yelled. "I'll have your head and your sword before the sun sets!"

His marauders, bolstered by his goading, whooped and kicked at the wood, making a second hole for them to enter. Misael waved his clan on, filtering in one by one through the breach. They were met by two defenders, each covering a single hole. But more importantly, he saw Ezekyle rushing to their aid.

He swung his axe one more time and knocked a larger section of the wall to the ground. His troops cheered and charged into the flames. Arjun slashed at one of the trollborn as they sprinted toward him with a small fire growing on their back. Arjun's blade cut swiftly, and the marauder fell to the ground, dead and burning. Again and again, Arjun faced down the intruders as they slid through a growing number of breaches. Two of Arjun's defenders jumped in to help and they were able to keep the first few waves at bay.

With a resounding thud, a large section of the outer wall collapsed under the crushing blows of Misael's battleaxe, and he barked another order as the trollborn horde rushed forward. One of Arjun's men raced over to stop the advance and killed two of the clansmen, but Misael moved into the gap and met the man, pitting steel against steel. The soldier was quick, and Misael could tell that Ezekyle had trained him well, but he was no match for his strength and prowess.

The two crossed weapons again, and Misael's blow nearly knocked the man off his feet. His knees buckled and Misael seized the advantage, raising his boot and kicking the unbalanced defender to the ground. The man raised his sword to deflect the inevitable swing, but Misael's axe powered through the defense and buried itself in his chest.

A second defender rushed to help his fallen friend, a look of horror plastered across his face. He waded through two of Misael's mercenaries to reach the dying man, his blade sending trollborn blood tumbling to the ground. Misael turned to face the onrushing veteran and, with a quick flurry of axe against sword, used the back of his weapon to pin the blade to the ground. He could see that the man knew what was coming, but he was also helpless to stop it. Misael spun his battleaxe and lifted it high, then swung it through the air to land a blow to the side of the defender's head, cracking his helmet and his skull with a single impact.

His body fell limp at Misael's feet.

THE TIDE OF THE battle was turning away from them, and Faux Dauldon was the first to notice. Glancing to her right, where Daemus was perched defensively behind a block of fallen granite, she barked, "Go! Go now!"

It was time for Daemus to desert his friends and escape through the hidden trenches, exactly as they'd planned. But Daemus wasn't ready. He wiped tears from his eyes, the same tears that had been flowing since the start of the battle, and shouted, "No! I won't leave you!"

"You have to!" Faux bellowed. "Now! Before it's too late!"

She watched as Daemus started to descend the wall, heading south toward the hidden horses at the far side of Homm Hill. With any luck, he could escape the fortress and make a run for it while the unsuspecting trollborn were occupied with the assault.

She knew it was his only chance.

Despite the thrill of adrenaline coursing through her veins, despite the clamor of the battle and the smell of blood in the air, she felt a sense of relief. If nothing else, the boy would be safe.

Faux shouted an order at Marquiss and refocused on the melee, turning around to unleash arrows on Misael's position, thinning his ranks and bringing the fight closer to an even keel.

DAEMUS HIT THE GROUND running and fled along the tunnel. He could hear his friends screaming and had just seen Chernovog and Burgess die. Terror gripped him and adrenaline pumped through his veins.

"Get to the horses," he told himself.

He ran through the tunnels, bouncing off the wooden buttresses as he stumbled through the unfamiliar labyrinth.

Splinters cut into his arm after the first collision and then his shin caught a tricky brace at his feet, sending him stumbling to the ground.

His heart raced and he gasped for breath. He tried to stand, struggling to keep his wits. As he pulled himself to his feet, he started off again, blind to his own pain. His feet kept moving toward the horses, but his head was guiding him elsewhere. He couldn't abandon his friends. He couldn't let them die for him.

He stopped for a moment in the darkened trenches and dropped his crossbow. Then he brandished the mace that Arjun had given him. He looked at the mace intently, his white eyes focusing on its head. It was too clean. He knew that it wasn't what Faux or his Uncle Kester wanted, but he couldn't leave.

Throwing caution to the wind, Daemus darted deeper into the tunnel system and disappeared down one of the passageways, running toward the battle. Fear morphed into fury and the young Keeper charged to help his friends.

MISAEL LOCKED GAZES WITH Arjun from across the burning battlefield, growling and pointing his bloodied axe at him. "Ezekyle!" he shouted. "I gave you a chance and you spurned it. Now it's time for you to taste the steel of my battleaxe."

"Come at me, if you think yourself worthy." Arjun waved him on with his sword.

The two started at one another across the carnage-strewn courtyard. Then they approached each other cautiously, their weapons held at the ready, but before they had a chance to meet, Blue Conney surfaced again, riding Jericho into the middle of the fray.

The springheel launched himself from his saddle, clotheslining one trollborn and slitting his throat in the same motion before landing on the back of a second, jamming his twin daggers in and out of the defenseless mercenary until he fell to the ground in a bloody heap. At the same time, the war dog broadsided a different trollborn and knocked him to the ground while snapping with his deadly jaws at another. His vicious claws ripped into the first downed soldier while his teeth tore into the other. Two more mercenaries were out of the fight.

Then two warriors, a green-haired Keldarin and red-haired human woman arrived at the scene, dropping their bows and drawing their swords, prepared to fight and die in one final, desperate stand. They fought back-to-back while surrounded by the last line of trollborn.

As they fought, Arjun and Misael finally met and slowly circled one another, looking for weaknesses in each other's defenses. The remaining trollborn saw the spectacle that was about to unfold and slowly halted their attack, pulling back to watch their chieftain battle the master swordsman from the High Aldin.

Faux, Marquiss and Blue lowered their weapons too, taking advantage of the lull to sieze a respite. The battle all but paused as attackers and defenders alike turned to watch the two great warriors facing each other down. Then sword met axe in a dance of death.

Arjun and Misael squared off, but it was obvious from the start that the hulking trollborn's strength gave him an early advantage.

"It's over, Ezekyle," Misael said, as the two embraced in a close melee. "You should have surrendered the child."

"Never!" Arjun replied, pushing himself forcefully away from the engagement. He ducked as Misael spun ferociously, his axe flailing harmlessly above Arjun's head.

Misael shifted his momentum and swung low at Arjun's knees, but he surprised the leaning trollborn by leaping high above the blade. Then he returned the favor with a lightning quick slash that skimmed harmlessly off Misael's hide armor.

The two warriors broke apart and then faced off once more. Misael lunged forward and Arjun had to give up ground, the back of his boots scraping dangerously close to a trench and leaving little room for error.

The two exchanged blows again and Misael's overwhelming strength wore on Arjun, his blocks and parries growing weary.

Misael could smell victory. His every swing was blocked, but he was also knocking his opponent from side to side. And then it happened. Arjun stepped too close to the trench's edge and slipped, falling backward into the ditch. Before he could recover, Misael leapt on top of him, his weight pinning the prone master to the dirt.

Faux jumped at the bulging trollborn with her longsword in a desperate attempt to stave off the fatal attack, but Misael saw her coming and grabbed her by the throat with one hand in midair. He tensed and flexed his powerful muscles and tossed her into the pit with Arjun. As the two lay, crumpled on top of one another, powerless to stop the trollborn, he raised his axe for the coup de grâce. Behind him, his horde rattled their weapons against their shields, whooping and hollering as their mounts howled with anticipation. The sound echoed around the courtyard and rose above the crackling of the burning fort.

His axe rose high, poised to fall on Faux and Arjun. But with his arms raised to attack, the massive marauder had exposed his midsection to Daemus, who was emerging at a sprint through the underground tunnel system. His deadly mace was already cocked in a half-swing. Misael saw Daemus at the last moment, far too late to block the mace. The blow hit home, crushing the trollborn's rib cage.

The break was pronounced and violent. Misael's ribs snapped with a sound like logs popping on a fire, and several broken bones protruded from his chest and abdomen. He doubled over, racked with excruciating pain, grabbing at his gaping wound as his great and bloody axe fell harmlessly to the ground behind him.

Daemus stood above the fallen mercenary, who was now on his knees. Misael found himself face-to-face with his prey, as he watched the boy slowly raise his mace for the killing blow.

"I misjudged you, boy," Misael growled, still fighting the inevitable.

"Yes," Daemus said. "You did."

The young Keeper smiled, though there was no humor in the situation. Then he calmly and resolutely switched his grip on the mace and moved in for the kill.

"This is for my uncle," he said.

Then he swung the instrument of death through the air and smashed the head of the mace into Misael's face.

The last thing he saw was the vicious lump of spiked metal gliding through the air at him.

MISAEL'S BODY SNAPPED BACK FROM the blow, hitting the ground hard and spewing out trollborn blood, adding to the stains on Blood Ridge.

Murmuring in disbelief, Daemus heard the trollborn gurgling something about dying at the hands of a boy. It didn't matter to Daemus, who smiled with satisfaction as he watched Misael draw his final breath. The remains of Clan Blood Axe stood in reverent silence, staring at their leader lying dead in a trench.

"What's going on?" Daemus mumbled, but neither Faux nor Arjun could answer. He helped them to their feet as one of the remaining trollborn stepped to within five paces of the pit, her cudgel lowered. She stared at the gruesome corpse of Misael and wiped her own blood from her face.

Daemus refused to provoke her and kept his mace at his side. The three watched as she raised her free hand, signaling to the horde. She turned to meet Daemus's eyes, and he returned the stare, unsure what else to do.

"His axe is yours," the trollborn said in a voice made of gravel. She turned to the clan and waved her cudgel in a circle. Slowly but surely, the remaining trollborn followed her lead and walked away from the battle. Daemus and the others watched on in amazement as their enemy left, the fight lost. The remnants of the once-feared horde mounted their steeds and departed in muted defeat, gathering their flag but abandoning the dead and wounded.

"Come," Arjun said. "Let's leave this place before they change their minds."

"No need," Daemus replied. His body was there but his eyes were miles away. The voice he spoke with was not his own. "They're defeated, but the survivors are now hers."

He paused and then added, "We'll meet her again."

Then his eyes returned to him. Arjun and Faux stared unnervingly at him, and Daemus realized that his Sight had manifested itself.

Marquiss and Blue made their way to the trench and helped them to climb out.

"Chernovog," Blue said, his voice dipped in sorrow. "Burgess."

It was all the springheel could muster. Daemus saw his rough exterior melt for a second, but his eyes held no tears. Marquiss knelt and put an arm around his friend, and the two shared a moment of prayer and reverence to Koss in honor of their allies.

"I'm sorry," Daemus said, his eyes wet with tears. "They died because of me."

"They died because it was their time," Blue replied.

CHAPTER TWENTY-ONE

"To die in battle is to die honorably. To die at feast is to die dishonored."
—Soldier motto

THE BODIES OF DEAD guards and would-be assassins littered the floor in front of Jessamy as she chased the Bone elf from the drawing room and up a spiral staircase. She didn't know where they were heading, but she knew she had her prey cornered. The only ways out were through her or off the parapet.

She rounded a bend in the stairs and found the jester waiting for her, giving him the high ground.

"There's no escape," Jessamy growled, inching closer to the Bone elf.

The jester smiled and baited her on with a wave of his sword. Their steel clashed once again and the flurry ended in a stalemate, but that was fine with Jessamy. She just kept on edging him up the stairs toward the parapet, where the fight would be more balanced. She lunged at his feet, but the jester nimbly parried his foe, climbing the stairs backward to keep his deadly opponent in check.

They came together for another round, and then again, and then the jester had his back to the door of the tower and the tip of Jessamy's sword at his front.

"This is where it ends," Jessamy said, steadying herself on the thin spiral stairs. "There's nowhere left to run, wretch."

The Bone elf stabbed down, only to be knocked aside by Jessamy's quick reaction. Then the door to the tower opened from the other side. A small, winged creature, no more than the size of a toddler, fluttered just outside the door.

The Bone elf grunted and signaled to Jessamy to ascend,

giving her room to emerge unharmed. Jessamy wasn't sure if it was honor or hubris, but it didn't matter. She seized the opportunity and welcomed the chance to engage him on an even footing.

The assassin lunged at her, allowing Jessamy to riposte, counterattacking and striking him high on his arm. The jester cringed in pain and quickly switched to defense, gathering himself for the next round of attacks. Jessamy could tell his arm was injured by the angle at which he held his sword. He couldn't lift it higher than his chest.

With one eye on the winged creature, she lashed out in a flurry, attacking to her left, sensing weakness and trying to use his lameness to her advantage. But the Bone elf blocked the first swing and switched hands with his blade in the same fluid movement. It was a move that Jessamy hadn't seen before, and one she'd never forget.

He took two steps back, spinning the sword in his new hand. As he did so, the creature began an incantation, a ritual that Jessamy was intimately familiar with as the champion for a spell-caster. She swiped at the beast, hoping to disrupt its casting, but it was too little too late and the spell flew from his hands. To her surprise, it wasn't aimed at her, but at her opponent.

For a moment, Jessamy saw the jester's feet swell in a hale of green magic. Then the man leapt from the battlements, empowered by whatever powers the fluttering creature had evoked. Jessamy rushed to the parapet and looked down into the courtyard below, watching her enemy land safely under the power of the spell before quickly disappearing into the panicked crowd. He'd escaped the wrath of her sword this time. It wouldn't happen again.

She turned back to watch his dreadful accomplice staring back at her from his perch on the nearby battlement. She took one step toward it and raised her sword, but the fiend stretched its bat-like wings and flew off into the night sky.

Discouraged by their cowardice, Jessamy rushed down the stairs to find her ward, her sword still in her hand.

WHILE JESSAMY WAS ON the battlements, Ritter and the princes were returning to the great hall. The princes had made quick work of the bards, but there were more assassins hidden amongst the ranks, dressed as servants and even guests.

Ritter turned to look at Baron Dragich Von Lormarck, who was wielding Malice and Woe and fighting alongside his three sons and his brother, Lothar. They were finishing off the remainder of the assailants, their swords stained with the blood of their enemies, but the Von Lormarcks appeared no worse for wear.

Von Lormarck was standing on the same stage that the bards had occupied minutes earlier, looking out at what was left of the noble crowd. Many of them had scattered, leaving the room only half full, excluding the spilled tables and dead bodies.

"Where's the damned king?" Von Lormarck barked, pointing at Montgomery and Everett with his sword.

"Lower your weapon, Baron," Sir Anson Valion, the king's new captain of the guard, cried. "It's over."

As the two men passed veiled threats back and forth, Ritter noticed something strange in the pool of Dacre's blood. He took a few steps away from the princes and bent down to pick up a black rose, which was now stained crimson.

He stood slowly, engrossed in his discovery. Around him, the Von Lormarcks and the Thorhauers had lost their tempers, their raised voices mingling together in a perverted echo of obscenities.

"I said, 'Where's the damned king?'" Von Lormarck shouted, pointing his sword at Montgomery again. "Is he cowering in his study? He should be out here defending his castle and his nobles."

"I'm here," Godwin bellowed as he re-emerged with LaBrecque. "I was tending to my wife, who was a target, and to Ambassador Elspeth, who has unfortunately been slain."

Ritter turned to watch the spectacle, realizing that no one had seen him retrieve the bloody flower. He still held a dead guard's sword in one hand and the rose in his other, but the conflict before him was too charged to interrupt.

"This is out of control, Godwin," Von Lormarck said. "I came here tonight to celebrate a victory for our land and to welcome a new son into our home. But instead of a celebration, a tragedy has befallen our realm. You claim that your wife was the target, and yet it was members of my own family who were almost killed. The Von Lormarcks have bled enough for the Thorhaueurs."

"Silence!" Godwin barked. "Hold your tongue before you say something you'll regret."

Ritter watched the Von Lormarck faction slide closer together near the stage, joined by the Thessaly family, which was wearing the coat of arms from Gloucester. None of them lowered their weapons. Montgomery moved to Ritter's left and grabbed a sword from a dead guard. Everett did the same.

Ritter caught the gaze of the two princes and stepped to their side, showing Von Lormarck that he, too, was with Godwin.

"We came here to celebrate a hollow victory, my fellow nobles," Von Lormarck said, addressing the remaining crowd. "Yet whatever plagues this kingdom remains unresolved, as we were persuaded to believe it would be with the Nightcloak's death. Our king has let us down for the last time. This union of baronies remains imperfect and should be no more. We barons must protect ourselves, as the Thorhauers can't protect this realm. The king can't even protect his own castle."

"You, sir, are guilty of treason!" Godwin roared. "Your seditious words will see you to your grave."

"How dare you threaten me, Thorhauer?" Dragich hissed. "It's Von Lormarck steel that's been bloodied here, while you were off crying with your bride. Foghaven Vale has borne the brunt of Warminster's weaknesses, paying with the lives of its citizens and soldiers, for far too long. If matters don't change, my family can support this union no longer. We'll be forced to secede and to focus on protecting our own barony."

"Those are rash words, Baron," Godwin said, but before he could continue, he was interrupted by Sasha Scarlett of Saracen and the Guild of the Copper Wing.

"My king," she said, "I fear that Baron Von Lormarck has a point. I, too, was a near victim of tonight's assault. I'm sorry, my lord, but the needs of the merchant city of Saracen and my own people must come first. I have to return home to protect them. Too many of my merchant caravans have disappeared in recent months, falling victim to the Nightcloak's assaults, and too many of my guild sisters and brothers haven't returned home. How can you protect the roads when tonight has shown that you no longer control your own castle?"

Scarlett turned to leave, and she was followed from the hall by the leaders of the other guilds.

Ritter, meanwhile, said nothing, watching the drama unfolding in front of him and waiting for the shouting to cease. The remaining nobles stared on in shock while King Godwin glared at Von Lormarck.

"Captain Valion," Godwin said, a calm returning to his voice. "Arrest the Von Lormarcks. I smell treachery afoot."

The Von Lormarcks stopped briefly to count the odds, their swords against those of the castle's guard. They stood down when Dragich lowered his swords.

Ritter saw Jhodever sneak onto the dais from the study and whisper something to Godwin. Ritter's elven ears could hear more than most, and Jhodever's murmuring carried over to him across the hall.

"My king, let the man go," Jhodever argued. "He needs to calm down. A public arrest will only embolden him."

The standoff continued for a few seconds more before Godwin relented, signaling to his guards to lower their swords.

Von Lormarck stared at Godwin, saying nothing. Then he slowly signaled for his family to gather and leave. Jhodever stepped away from the king and bowed to him.

As they departed, Von Lormarck beckoned to his step-daughter, Ember. She'd been sticking close to Joferian, whose sword was bloody from protecting her during the melee.

Ritter felt for them. Ember was a Von Lormarck, if only a bastardess. Joferian was a Maeglan. They were being pulled in two different directions by politics. Ritter knew Joferian was no enemy to her, but new lines had been drawn around the happy couple, dividing the two houses. The couple held each other's gaze as long as they could, until Ember disappeared.

"Dragich," the king said. "We've all seen things tonight that can't be undone. But can't you see? Whoever's behind this is trying to destroy Warminster. Don't let them win. Take the night and return in the morning. I want all seven baronies to accompany me for a discussion to better understand tonight's events. I hope you'll return to join the discussions when the hourglass clock reaches its meridian."

THE BABBLE OF NOISE in Castle Thronehelm's great hall was quieting down. Captain Valion and his castle guards were escorting the remaining nobles away, detaining some for questioning and directing others to their quarters. Eventually, a hush fell over the hall, only interrupted by the sounds of servants cleaning and removing the bodies.

Ritter stood in the main hall, observing Valion. The captain had already started his investigation, somberly commanding the guards to take the bodies of the assassins away for the priests and wizards of Thunder Cove to examine.

"Your Majesty," Valion said, bowing smartly to Godwin. "We've found no coins on the bards, and no clues as to where they come from. But I have some suspicions about how they arrived here. Let me speak to the housekeepers and the butlery before evidence is destroyed."

Godwin looked sullenly at his captain but shook his head, denying the request.

"But Your Majesty, how—?"

"In private, Captain," Godwin growled, not looking at Valion but instead staring back into his study, where Addilyn and Amice were still huddled. "Not in front of the ambassador or the queen. They've both suffered enough for one night. Have the priests use their magic. I won't have my hall tainted by this violence any longer."

"Sire," Valion said, bowing respectfully.

"Captain," Ritter offered, "I think I've found a clue."

He held the black rose out, its stalk sullied by Dacre's blood. Valion, Godwin, and the two princes approached Ritter, and Ritter handed the rose over to the captain of the guard.

"It matches the arrows we found at the ambush," Ritter said. "The markings are undeniable."

"What's this?" Godwin asked. "Where did you find this?"

Ritter pointed to the floor where Dacre had fallen. Everyone started talking at once, but their incomprehensible babble about the rose was interrupted by the return of Jessamy

Aberdeen. She trudged into the hall, her sword still drawn and bloodied, and headed straight for the study.

"Jessamy, wh—" Ritter managed.

"He escaped my blade," she growled. "He and his little… minion."

"How?" Valion asked.

"His creature cast some kind of spell on him," Jessamy explained. "He was able to leap from the tower and to land unscathed on the ground below. I tried to pursue him, but I lost him in the crowd."

"A creature?" the king growled.

"Yes, Your Majesty," Jessamy said. "A creature the size of a human child helped him to escape. It had wings like a bat and the tail of a lizard, and it knows the ways of magic. It must have been the Bone elf's plan all along: to kill the ambassador and run to the tower. Others would run to the gate. His escape would be unopposed and go unnoticed."

"Your sword is stained black," Ritter said. "Is it the assassin's blood?"

"Aye," she said. "I injured his arm in the melee and the bastard bleeds this color, but it was only a flesh wound. If you'll excuse me, Sir Ritter, I must attend to my lady."

She turned and disappeared through the study doors. The others followed, as did Ritter, wanting Addilyn to know about the black rose.

ADDILYN WAS INCONSOLABLE, THOUGH Jessamy was doing her best. There was a distinct possibility that she'd never feel anything again. She watched the proceedings in front of her, guards and servants and officials coming and going, with a numb, disinterested detachment that she'd never felt before. She had no desires anymore, no wishes and no hopes.

Ritter was standing in front of her with a worried look on his face. In the back of her mind, she registered that an hour ago she'd dearly wanted to be friends with him. It was hard to even imagine now. To her, the room was filled with an assemblage of shapes, without personhood, familiarity, or even meaning. Ritter might as well be a puppet animated by her own mind.

"Addilyn," he said, then continued in a language she knew she spoke but had no desire to translate. At her total lack of response, his worried expression intensified. Looking at it was unpleasant, so she allowed her gaze to drift away from him.

"My lady," a voice said in accented High Vermilion, and Addilyn's eyes flicked instinctively to the speaker. It was Jessamy, her supposed champion. A fine job she'd done, protecting Addilyn's shell of a body and allowing her heart to be destroyed. Distantly, Addilyn recognized that she was being unfair, but she couldn't bring herself to answer the bitter thought with something kinder.

"What?" Addilyn spat.

"It's time for you to sit down," Jessamy said with a firm tone.

Addilyn considered being shocked or angry that her bodyguard would have the gall to order her around after failing so abjectly in her duties, but then she thought better of it and simply sat down where she was on the floor without a reply. It felt as though she'd been on her feet for days. How long had it really been since her father... her father...

"Did you kill him?" Addilyn asked Jessamy in High Vermilion, knowing the truth of the matter from hearing the discussion in the halls.

At that moment she hated Jessamy, so it seemed she could feel things after all, although the hatred felt far away, as though it existed in a splinter of herself that had remained frozen in time in those final few minutes with her father. Jessamy looked back at her calmly and then sat down beside her.

"My lady, I failed you," Jessamy said, dropping slowly to both knees and removing her sword from her back. She laid it on the floor at Addilyn's feet. "I was your champion, and I served you as best I could, but it wasn't enough. I fear that I've lost the right to serve you. I shall return home in shame."

She bowed her head, waiting to be dismissed. Addilyn looked down at the young warrior and knelt, leveling herself with the Raven elf.

She knew that Jessamy meant every word. Taking a second to regain some semblance of composure, she gently took Jessamy's chin and raised it. "I trust you with my life," Addilyn confided, even if her words were half-hearted.

"But your father?"

"He wasn't your ward," Addilyn insisted. "I am."

"I knew him but a short while," Jessamy said. "But in that time, I grew to love him. He was an honorable man. One who treated me as an equal."

"That was his way," Addilyn reflected. "It was an ideal that he shared for all of us. We all bleed the same, regardless of our race or station. That's why he sought you for the tourney. He knew you'd beat the best, and you proved him correct."

"What of the Bone elf?"

Addilyn smiled and said, "Were you supposed to jump to your death from the tower to follow him? We have magic too, and now that we know who our enemy is, we'll know how to defeat him next time. You'll have a chance to even the score. Now pick up your sword, champion. Your duty to me is not yet over."

Jessamy stood and slung her sword without comment, then reached out and embraced Addilyn.

The feeling of being held came as a shock. Addilyn breathed slowly and methodically, but it wasn't long before she found herself sobbing quietly into the other woman's shoulder. Her father, the greatest comfort and cornerstone of her life—who'd smiled gently at her over breakfast and sung next to her in temple, who'd taught her the names of the mountain flowers and elaborately praised her work even when she failed, who'd joked with her through wordless glances and listened to her half-formed opinions on politics and read to her through nights of fever when she was too ill to sleep—would never put his arms around her again. What was anything without him?

More time passed before Addilyn, remembering her surroundings, finally got a hold of herself. She drew a steady breath and leaned back.

The queen sat beside them, staring at the broken body of the Vermilion ambassador. "Why didn't he come for me?" the queen wondered aloud, looking to Godwin for answers. "He stood inches from me and yet chose to kill the ambassador."

"I think I know, Your Grace," Ritter said, gently placing the black rose on the table next to Dacre's body. "We found this where he was slain."

Amice looked confused, and Addilyn's eyes drifted from her father to Ritter and then to the rose.

"What's the meaning of the rose?" the queen asked.

"It means that the jester fought with the brigands but a few days ago," Montgomery answered, taking a step toward his mother. "The arrows that killed Shale had the same rose design on their shafts. Clearly he survived that battle and found his way here tonight."

"Mere coincidence," Valion replied. "How would he have time to remove a rose in the heat of battle? It must have fallen from the table or been dropped as people retreated."

"He knew me," Ritter said. "He was there when we killed the Cloak."

"How do you know?"

"He confronted Ritter when we fought him in the hall," Addilyn said. "I heard him mock him."

"LaBrecque?" the king said, staring at the rose.

"Sire?"

"I need you to take your ship and sail immediately for Castleshire," Godwin decreed. "Take Master Cray and find Disciple Delling of the Disciples of the Watch. He's from Hunter's Manor and a loyal subject of the crown. He'll listen to Cray. Tell him we need help from the Cathedral of the Watchful Eye. With Samuels gone, we're crippled without their help, and I'm not sure I trust Von Lormarck's Keeper. In truth, I don't know who to trust, but Delling's loyalty is beyond question."

"Of course, Your Majesty," LaBrecque replied. "Consider it done."

"I'll sail with you," Addilyn said, boldly. "I must find Anselm Helenius. He may have information on the tetrine. I'll not let my father's death be in vain."

"I assure you, Princess," Godwin replied, "his death will be avenged. But if you seek Anselm Helenius, I can have him recalled. He's a subject of mine, and a loyal one at that. If I send a summons, he'll answer it."

"I've met him before," Addilyn said, "but I need to meet him again. I can't wait for him to receive word from you and to travel to Thronehelm. I must leave for Castleshire at once."

"In that case," Godwin said, "it would be an honor for you to travel with the admiral under the flags of Thronehelm."

Addilyn nodded at the king.

"Valion," Godwin continued, "I won't allow this 'Black Rose' to escape unpunished. Search the castle grounds and beyond, leaving no stone unturned and no attic or cellar unchecked. I want this Bone elf fettered and shackled and brought before me. Sons, you'll protect the new ambassador on her journey. Thronehelm must earn back what's been taken. Sir Ritter and your cousins will accompany you. Nothos brought good fortune to your first expedition. Perhaps he'll do the same on your second."

"Your Majesty," Ritter said, "I'd be honored to join the expedition, but if the bandits and the Black Rose are truly linked, the problems in Ravenwood may just be the start. I fear the worst for House Valkeneer."

"You have my commitment to protect the Bridge in your absence, Sir Ritter," Godwin replied. "It's an important stretch of land for this kingdom, especially if Von Lormarck doesn't return to the fold. I won't let anything happen to your home. I'll dismiss your remaining Longmarchers so they can return to the Bridge to fortify it. Their services will be better deployed in Ravenwood than on a ship."

"Thank you, sire," Ritter said. "I'll alert my lieutenants of your decision."

IT WAS NEAR DAWN as Ember watched her father sitting impatiently, waiting in their carriage several miles from Castle Thronehelm. The carriage had pulled away from the road and up a long trail that emptied into a secluded clearing in the nearby trees. At night, it was hidden from passersby, offering a private meeting point.

Ember didn't understand why they'd stopped, but she didn't care to ask. She was lost in her own emotions and desired no small talk, save perhaps for some pity from her father. None was forthcoming.

Donnar, Emmerich and Aarav sat just outside the carriage door, watching the road for curious travelers. Ember sat sullenly across from Dragich, contemplating the events of the day. The sun was only a few hours from rising, but she hadn't considered sleeping. It was the first time she'd witnessed true combat, and the beauty of her betrothal announcement had been marred by its turmoil.

"What are you brooding about?" Dragich asked.

"I've never seen blood spilled before, Father."

"Get used to it, girl," Dragich said. "You'll see plenty more."

Ember sat pensively, listening to Von Lormarck's words. Her brothers had all faced the horrors of combat, but it wasn't in her nature to suffer such violence. A few moments of silence passed between them and then she heard her brothers whispering to someone outside.

"Is that him?" Dragich asked, nearly jumping from his seat and out of the carriage door. Ember leaned forward in her seat and the bloody jester himself appeared in front of her. He was still in his costume, which was torn and stained. Her eyes widened and she nearly gasped, sitting back in the shadows to avoid his gaze.

"Ah, Incanus Dru'Waith," Dragich said, sarcastically. "The Black Rose, the Terror of Thronehelm. And I see you've brought Skullam, your imp. The damned creature makes me shudder. And what are you wearing? Take off those silly rags. Or do you prefer being a fool?"

Incanus slid out of the torn garb, revealing the leather armor underneath. His thigh and upper arm were dressed in bloody bandages, but he seemed immune to the discomfort.

Ember noticed with a shock of recognition that Dru'Waith was a Bone elf. His skin was an ashen, ivory color and his hair was a greyish-white. His eyes were dark and almond-shaped, and he was a little taller than other elves, standing only an inch or two smaller than a human. Skullam, his imp, was about a third of his size with skin that was mottled and putrid, the color of a bloated corpse. He had a smooth, hairless head and a long, spiked tail like a third appendage, as well as four bony fingers on each hand, sharpened teeth, and goatish legs with claws at the end.

"How dare you ruin the plan?" Dragich spat in a muted voice of contempt. "The royals were the target, not the Vermilion. You stood inches from the queen and brought me the wrong pound of flesh."

Ember shuddered in fear. She struggled to believe her father's words. Tears welled in her eyes, but she didn't dare make a sound. Not from fear of the man he called the Black Rose, but from fear of Dragich's temper.

She was also battling with her own inner turmoil. She had eyes and ears, as well as a mind that was shrewd enough to put the pieces together. Dragich had made it perfectly clear that he was behind the attempt on the royals… and so where did that leave her? And more to the point, where did it leave the Barony of Foghaven Vale and Warminster itself?

"I don't care about your personal wars," Von Lormarck continued. "I told you that you'll have a chance to collect the skulls of the Vermilion once you've taken care of my targets. Thus far, you've gathered the skulls of an old captain and a drunk ambassador, and at great cost to Foghaven Vale. You've brought me no skulls of my own."

Incanus remained silent.

"If you want to keep killing Vermilion, you need to kill for me first," Dragich said, wagging his finger in the Bone elf's face. "There are more battles to fight, but we must start the war first. You had the queen dead to rights and failed to finish the job. Your bards failed to kill the princes. My sons and I had to clean up the mess you left. You caught your own assassins off guard. They were supposed to attack the princes first. You signed their death warrants when you disregarded the plan. And let's not forget the abject failure of the Nightcloak raids. That operation cost us both time and laurels."

While Von Lormarck talked, Incanus just stood there, letting the scolding wash over him. Ember watched them surreptitiously with doubt clouding her eyes.

"If I may, my liege," Skullam said, in a raspy voice. "All is not lost."

"What do you mean, imp?" Dragich replied, pacing back and forth in front of Incanus.

"I returned to the scene as you asked, under a spell that rendered me invisible to the eye," Skullam explained. "I spied on the king and his people. They're sending Admiral LaBrecque to retrieve a man named Disciple Delling from Castleshire."

"What's your point?" Dragich growled. "If he's not a Keeper, what good is this man to the Thorhauers?"

"LaBrecque sails for Castleshire this morning," Skullam said. "He's accompanied by the princes and the Vermilion princess. She seeks a cryptid hunter to learn more about the tetrine. I didn't learn his name. Perhaps we could attack them on the seas?"

The group fell silent for a moment. Ember leaned forward, hoping to catch a whisper, but there was silence as Dragich pondered the new information before turning to the assassin again.

"You've missed twice now, Dru'Waith," he said. "You won't fail me a third time. You're no longer in charge of yourself. Your imp has been more useful to our cause than you have."

The two locked gazes like tigers watching their prey. Neither relented. Ember couldn't tell which of the two looked the thirstiest for royal and Vermilion blood.

"Donnar?" Dragich said.

"My lord?"

"Where's Morley?" he asked. "Is he far out to sea?"

"He's just outside Thronehelm Harbor, in the Firth of Fury," Donnar replied. "He awaits your instructions."

"Good," Dragich muttered, a smile slipping across his face. "A man who can follow instructions. Incanus, pursue LaBrecque on the high seas and stop the Vermilion and the princes from reaching Castleshire. You'll be under the command of Captain Morley. He sails the *Phantom*, one of the vessels we purchased from the High Aldin. Have your imp fly to them and make them aware of our plans. Morley is from Castleshire and knows the seas between here and there better than any seaman, especially that strutting imbecile Valerick LaBrecque."

Incanus nodded in the direction of Skullam, and the group watched him mutter an incantation and turn invisible before flying off to find the *Phantom*.

Ember shuddered as his feathery wings beat against the air. If it was possible to know a man by the company he kept, that meant her father wasn't the man she'd thought he was. Even supposing he was right, and that there was some truth to his late-night rantings about the Thorhauers that were as regular as his bladder when he was in his cups, it felt like her father was going about things the wrong way. Sometimes a realm needed a savior, but those saviors rarely communed with murderers and rogues.

"My war wizard Kryslexx will ensure that there are no more gaffes," Von Lormarck continued. "He'll meet you on the *Phantom*. You'll sail under no flags or banners. It's time for you to redeem yourself."

Ember listened incredulously to the one-sided conversation. Her mind raced as she thought of running to Castle Thronehelm to tell King Godwin what she'd heard, but to betray her own family? Her own lineage? What could she do?

Dragich took a deep breath and then, folding a conciliatory arm around Incanus, continued, "We'll move ahead with our secession in the morning. The Thessaly family of Gloucester will declare for Foghaven Vale, as I'm still close to my first wife's family. They want to be free of the Thorhauers too. When the merchant guilds of Saracen cut off their winter foodstuffs and Gloucester closes her doors to Thronehelm, Godwin will starve as we attack. We'll win this coming war and overthrow the Thorhauer regime."

"What about the Moor Bog?" Incanus asked, speaking for the first time. "Without me here and with the Cloak dead, how will you communicate with them?"

"Let me worry about that," Dragich replied. "You worry about catching the princes and bringing me their heads. With Godwin's line dead and his kingdom in shambles, the true ruler of Warminster will emerge."

Ember watched as Incanus silently departed the scene, sticking to the woods. Von Lormarck and the others climbed back into the carriage, and their driver hustled them back on the road to Foghaven Vale.

Ember sat staring at her father, trying to hide her tears. Perhaps she'd finally lost her innocence. She felt like she was staring at a monster, and not at the man she knew. Fearful of reprisals, she sat in extended silence and wiped the tears from her face.

After a few minutes, Dragich cut into the tension between them. He skipped to the meaty part, as was his nature.

"I'm doing this for the benefit of the realm," he said to her, a tinge of arrogance dripping from his tongue.

"Why hide it from me until now?" she snapped. "I am and always have been an obedient daughter, no different than your sons. They knew. Why not me?"

"The king could have my head for this," Dragich replied. "The fewer people that knew, the better. And besides, you know now."

"Was my marriage to Joferian part of your plot?" she asked.

"Of course, girl," he replied disdainfully, staring straight into her eyes. "A marriage to a Maeglen will help us to secure an alliance after the war. You were always a pawn on this chess-board. Now we wait for the king to make his move."

CHAPTER TWENTY-TWO

"For a scavenger of the Highgrass, the
patience of a vulture is a virtue."
—Waharan the Collector of Caste Knoh

MYRKUS BENT OVER TO pick through the trollborn's corpse. His caste of scavengers had fallen upon a treasure trove that night. The nomads of the Vilchor Highgrass had found over seventy bodies to plunder, scattered on the bloody hill at the foot of the old fort, untouched—yet—by human or crow. That fact alone told Myrkus that the battle was recent, its age counted in hours and not days. The blood was still fresh and the bodies of the trollborn and their horsehounds were unaffected by rigor mortis.

"Found much?" Horegard whispered to Myrkus, covering the light from his hooded lantern to keep out the prying eyes of rival castes. "This is a year's bounty in one night. I can't wait to trade it at Sycamore Post."

"I've found plenty of swords and spears," Myrkus said. "Plus armor and the occasional pouch."

"Any survivors?" Horegard asked.

"Not anymore," Myrkus said, both men muting their chuckles beneath their weatherworn scarves.

The scavengers picked efficiently through the dead for several hours, silently loading the loot onto their rickety carts. With a dozen nomads in total, Caste Nedelyn ransacked the grisly battlefield to perfection, gathering more than their own fair share of the spoils.

"The Ancients favor us," Horegard remarked. "Never have I seen such a—"

Horegard was interrupted by the stirring of horses. He

and Myrkus quickly closed their hooded lanterns, as did the rest of the clan. A few seconds passed, and as their eyes grew used to the starlight, the horses stirred again.

"Myrkus, do you—"

"Shh," Myrkus interrupted, putting a finger to his lips with one hand and covering Horegard's talkative mouth with the other. Both men crouched in the high grass, hoping whatever had stirred the horses would pass.

The seconds wore on, the tension growing, and then one of the horse teams reared up, riding off and dragging the carts—and the caste's newfound treasure—with them. Before Myrkus or Horegard could react, a second team of horses followed the first.

Both men slowly readjusted in the high grass, rolling over on their stomachs and coming to their knees to peek above the grass line. They weren't prepared for what they saw.

A four-legged beast came rambling from the flatland beneath them, tearing its way through the high grass toward their caste.

The scavengers knew they were no match for the ghastly cryptid that had found them.

The Antlered Man fell upon the unsuspecting grav-erobbers with the sharp violence reserved for the cruelest of animals. He waded ferociously into their ranks, and the coppery tang of blood was soon omnipresent in the air. The gruesome slaughter was devoid of emotion or mercy. Limbs were torn from torsos, heads slapped clean from necks with brutal swings of the cryptid's arms. Bodies were gored apart by his skeletal antlers.

Myrkus grabbed Horegard and dragged him down, pressing them against the ground and using the high grass as cover. They could hear the unanswered cries for help from below, but they were powerless to stop the slaughter. They could only hope that the creature wouldn't find them.

The two men, petrified with fear, stayed low and looked at each other. They listened to the sounds of their dying friends until there was silence again. A minute passed, then two.

The silence was broken when the creature inhaled deeply through its skeletal maw. As it exhaled, its hideous call echoed through the Vilchor Highgrass.

"Clawk, clawk, clawk."

The creature gargled like a dying rooster, tilting its head to the moonlight and dropping back down to all fours.

"Clawk, clawk, clawk."

Then the Antlered Man stopped, its supernatural senses detecting the scent of its prey. It moved through the ranks of the freshly dead, tracking the scent up Homm Hill and disappearing into the broken walls of the smoldering fortress.

Myrkus tapped Horegard and pointed at the road, a good quarter mile from them. In the starlight, the two could see the silhouettes of the horses that had abandoned the tribe when the Antlered Man arrived.

"This is our chance," Myrkus whispered. "While it's in the old fort."

"No, no!" Horegard begged. "It passed us. It's looking for something else."

"I'm going," Markus replied. "With or without you."

Horegard tugged on his arm, but Myrkus pulled away and ran for the horses in a partial crouch. He didn't look back.

INSIDE FORT HOMM, THE dreaded beast continued his search, sniffing and pecking through the trollborn remains. Then the Antlered Man caught the scent of the blood he was hunting for.

Stepping into the ditch that contained Misael's corpse, the

creature scoured the ground and grabbed a torn cloak. He lifted it to his osseous maw and inhaled the pungent odor of blood. The scent stayed with the cryptid, allowing him to pick up the trail. The smell of human sweat—the blood and flesh and the unmistakable odor of their horses—blazed a perfect pathway. The creature, frenzied with the scent of his quarry, loped through the ruins and began his long hunt to find them.

SEVERAL DAYS HAD COME and gone, and Daemus's weary party was riding at a more deliberate pace with the immediate threat of Clan Blood Axe behind them. They stopped more frequently to rest and to tend to their wounds. The Vilchor Highgrass wasn't the place to forage or find shelter, but Arjun and Faux always seemed to find somewhere to lie low.

Daemus watched them closely, learning as much as he could. He'd spent most of his life in cities and inside buildings. Over the last few weeks, it felt as though he'd spent more time outside than he had in his entire life. Eventually, the high plains gave way to trees and forests, a sight for sore eyes.

"We're a couple of days' ride from Castleshire," Marquiss observed. "The forest will provide shade from the southern sun and plenty of food and water. Have you ever hunted before?"

"I've seen it done," Daemus replied, turning to Marquiss. "Mostly fox hunts in the Alldred Mountains, but I was always too young to ride."

"Now, lad," Blue Conney said, "I've seen yer ridin' skills, and I'm not sure the fox would have lost."

"I'd bet on the fox," Marquiss quipped.

The group chuckled together and even Daemus had a laugh at his own expense. It was the first time in a long time that they'd felt comfortable enough to share laughter.

That evening, they rested just inside the treeline, finding a safe place to hole up for the night beneath the eaves of an imposing elm tree. When morning came, the party rode until noon, when they could finally see the Shirian Valley in the distance.

"Can't be more than half a day's travel to Forecastle from here," Faux said, an exhausted smile passing across her face.

"I thought we were going to Castleshire," Conney said.

"Forecastle is a worker city just a few miles south of Castleshire," Faux explained. "It's home to the servants and the workers of the city and the Shirian Valley. If we're to seek Ellissio, the man Kester told us to find, we'll find him in Forecastle. He'll help us to sneak into the city. Ellissio is a servant of the Alaric family and he lives in the Alaric compound."

She took out the scroll Kester had given her back at the ratskeller. Blue nodded in agreement.

"Don't worry, Blue," Arjun said with a smile, "Forecastle is more your type. It's full of taverns, beer and trollborn wenches."

Conney placed his hand over his heart and looked to the sky. "My kind of town for sure," he said.

BY EARLY EVENING, THE group had arrived at the unguarded gates of Forecastle to find a bustling town of commoners that teemed with worker homes for the servants of Castleshire's nobility. As they rode quietly into the city proper, they passed many small stores and several bustling marketplaces.

Daemus was on the verge of collapse. His body wasn't used to the physical exertion of riding, let alone combat. Faux wasn't much better. With little to distinguish the taverns apart, they decided to stop off at the first one they saw. They found an inn not far from the entrance to the city. An aged sign above the entrance proclaimed it as the Halo.

The group entered the inn, and Faux and Arjun approached

the barkeep to make the necessary arrangements. Daemus's mouth watered at the smells wafting in from the kitchen.

"Ah, warm beer," Blue Conney said, cracking a smile and rubbing his awaiting gullet.

"Welcome to the Halo," the man said. "Let me guess. You're looking for rest, room and rum?" The barkeep was in his later years, plump from ale and decades behind the bar.

Faux cracked a smile and nodded in agreement. The inn-keeper reached below the bar and produced a key.

"We're all out of private rooms," he said. "But you can stay in the common room."

"Any chance we can get the room to ourselves for an extra sheaf or two?" Arjun asked, referring to the copper coins in his pouch.

The man looked them over.

"Yes, for a few sheaves more," he said. "And I can arrange for a healer to visit you from the Temple of Ssolantress. They don't ask many questions, and you folks look like you don't want to give any answers. The common room is all yours. I'll have food and drinks sent up."

Arjun slid the barkeep the additional sheaves, and the man pointed to a door behind him, revealing a stairwell. Faux and Arjun both nodded at the same time, then waved for their friends to follow them up the stairs.

The common room was designed to hold twenty visitors, and so for the five exhausted travelers, it was as palatial as any mansion in Castleshire. The room was dark, intentionally so, and it smelled of sweat and feet, but they didn't care. They spent the next few hours eating, bathing and, in Daemus's case, trying to sleep. The combination of a full belly, a hot bath and saddle aches had caught up with him. Blue Conney followed soon after and started snoring the moment his head hit a pillow.

Soon after they finished their meals, there was a gentle rapping at the door. Daemus moved to get up, but Faux beat him to the door and opened it. A young healer from the Temple of Ssolantress stood in the threshold. He recognized Ssolantress's follower from afar, as they were easy to find and hard to forget. Their bright blue capes and equally blue hair, eyes and lips made them immediately identifiable. In this case, the young healer's colors stood starkly against the dark greys and browns of the aging inn.

"Good evening, my lady," the hooded priestess said, pleasantly. "Gigerold, the barkeep, sent for me. He said you were in need of Ssolantress' blessings."

"Please, come in," Faux said, stepping away from the door to make room.

The priestess looked around, surveying the wayward group of travelers and starting toward Arjun first. His wounds were manifold. Faux reached for a pouch of coins, but the priestess raised her hand to stop her.

"I require no payment," she said. "And I come here with no judgement. I'm only here to help. A servant of Ssolantress tells no tales. You may tell me the nature of your injuries so I can better treat them, but the story will never leave my lips. I ask only that you offer a prayer to Ssolantress, the Ancient of Healing, the next time you pass her temple."

"I'll offer the prayers," Faux said, handing the pouch to her anyway. "One for each of us, plus two for those who didn't make it this far. But please, keep the palmettes so that you can replenish your supplies when you're done. I expect you'll need it."

The woman nodded and accepted the small payment before kneeling next to Arjun to attend to his wounds.

"What's your name, priestess?" Arjun asked.

"My name is Katja Seitenwind," she replied.

She worked gently. When she finished and turned to walk away, he smiled. He hadn't felt a moment of pain.

"Thank you, Katja," Arjun said, and the young woman returned his gratitude with a smile.

"Here," she replied, handing him a reddish-black root. "Chew on this. It'll help with the pain and stop the wound from festering."

"What is it?" Arjun asked.

"It's called slippery elm bark," she said. "It's used to heal wounds, among other things."

Arjun slipped the root between his teeth and started chewing.

"It'll taste bittersweet to begin with, but it'll mellow over time," she said. She smiled again and picked up her things before moving to help Faux.

The slight rustling and conversation had stopped Daemus from finding sleep.

"Faux, I'm trying to—" he muttered, but he stopped midsentence when he saw the apparition of beauty who was kneeling between the two of them. His eyes locked with hers for a second and then his face flushed. He stammered to catch himself but couldn't say a word.

The healer lowered her cowl, revealing her comely visage, which held the mark of her priestess. The mark was small, but it glowed softly with the blue healing hale that was common to her divinity. It took the form of a pair of servant hands cupped inside a triangle, which itself was inscribed within a circle. It appeared to be tattooed beneath her skin.

Faux coughed theatrically and said, "This is Katja Seitenwind from the Temple of Ssolantress."

"Hello," the healer said.

Daemus said nothing. Faux smiled apologetically and said, "Katja, this is Daemus Alaric."

"Alaric?" Katja repeated. "Of the Castleshire Alarics?"

Daemus nodded, continuing to stare at the young woman, his mind finally catching up with his heart. "Yes," he managed. The young woman smiled, and Daemus smiled back.

Katja continued to visit the travelers one-by-one, dressing wounds and occasionally conjuring magic to help them to heal faster. Daemus watched from afar, trying not to make his affection known.

Arjun shot Daemus a wink when Katja's attention was elsewhere and the others smiled, save for Blue Conney, who snored through the entire ordeal.

Then she came to Daemus. As she opened her satchel, Faux tapped Arjun on the arm and said, "We have work to do."

They rose from their cots. Marquiss didn't need a signal from Faux and the three left Katja and Daemus alone, save for the snoring springheel at the other end of the room.

THE TRIO RE-EMERGED IN the bar and saw that business had picked up as the evening had given way to night. Faux made her way back to Gigerold and asked, "Where can we find the Alaric compound?"

Gigerold turned toward them, glass and dirty towel in hand, and leaned over the edge of the bar to make it harder for spying ears to hear. "Go toward the town square," he said. "Then take Auddinger's Alley. Their compound is a few blocks from there."

Faux thanked Gigerold and flipped him a copper sheaf for his help. He let it clank on the bar while Marquiss took a seat.

"Not goin' with yer friends?" Gigerold asked.

"Nah," Marquiss remarked. "They don't need my elven ears there. They'll be better off without me."

Both men returned to their duties, Gigerold drawing an ale and Marquiss drinking it.

"Have only a few, brother," Faux reminded him. "And keep an eye on the others."

Marquiss lifted his glass, nodding in agreement.

WITH THE OTHERS GONE, Katja approached Daemus and kneeled next to him.

"Where are you injured?" she asked.

"I'm unhurt, for the most part," Daemus said. "My wounds are more inside than out. We lost friends on our way here. I'm not sure you have a potion for that."

Katja smiled, sensing Daemus's hidden meaning, then pulled a small flask from her bag and held it in front of him. He took it and uncorked it, sniffing its contents. The potent draught had a bracing aroma, one that caught his nostrils off-guard, and he cringed at the smell. Katja giggled.

"What is it?" he managed, handing the flask back to her.

"It's alcohol," she replied. "Some of my patients drink it to numb the wounds I can't reach."

They both laughed at the thought, and Daemus begrudgingly took a swig, scowling at the taste.

"It tastes no better than it smells," he said. Then he bashfully lifted his tunic, exposing his bruised ribs. She reached out gently to touch the contusion, and Daemus winced for effect. They hurt, but not nearly that bad. He was hoping for some sympathy.

"I fell," he said.

"In battle?" she asked.

"No," he said, his face flushing. "I fell from my steed."

To his surprise, she didn't laugh. Instead, she reached into her bag and produced a small jar containing an equally odorous unguent. Daemus flinched as she applied it, but the cream helped to numb the bruises. His eyes burned a little from some ingredient in the ointment, but when she helped him back into his tunic, the smell and irritation abated.

"Thank you," he said, happy to be close to her.

"Shall I look at your eyes next?" she offered.

"Why?" he asked, awkwardly. "I'm not blind. I get asked often, but I can see."

"I know you can see," Katja replied, her eyes never leaving his. "I just wondered why a man of House Alaric couldn't find his way home and chose instead to sleep at an inn but a few miles from Castleshire."

Daemus smiled at her calling him a man, but he was also afraid of the direction the conversation was taking. If she said anything to the wrong person, his return could be jeopardized.

"I'm sorry for how I reacted," he said. "In truth, I was born blind, or so I'm told. A mage visited me when I was a baby and brought sight to me. However, my eye color never changed."

Katja said nothing, which surprised him, and after a moment of silence he continued, "I'm returning from the Cathedral of the Watchful Eye," he said. "My arrival here is... complicated."

Katja adjusted herself so they could sit shoulder to shoulder against the wall, but she said nothing. Daemus wasn't sure what she was doing, but he didn't mind her sitting so close to him. Then he realized she was waiting for him to speak. He struggled for a minute, not wanting to talk about his return, but then he acquiesced and chose to trust her intentions.

"I was a Keeper of the Forbidden," he started cautiously, trying to gauge her reaction. "But I violated an important edict and was expelled. I'm returning home in shame."

He paused for a second to watch her. She responded by

reaching out to hold his hand. Her warm touch gave him comfort at first, then faith that she'd keep his secrets.

"But why stop here?" Katja asked. "Why not complete your journey home?"

"That, too, is complicated," Daemus replied. "You met Faux this evening. She helped me to fight my way back to Castleshire, but she's banished and can't re-enter the city. If she's caught helping me, she'll face dire consequences."

"Can't your family save her?"

"Perhaps," Daemus said. "But for now, we have to sneak back in until I can assure her safety. That's why she left tonight."

"Why would you have to fight your way home?"

"That's an even longer story," Daemus replied. "One I fear would take all night."

"I have time for you, Daemus," Katja said. "I don't mind listening. Pray tell, what *is* a Keeper of the Forbidden?"

"We're a sect of prophets," Daemus said, breaking into a half-smile and looking at his feet. "We receive messages from our Ancient and interpret their meanings. Erud, the Ancient of Knowledge, calls on but a few, imbuing them with the Erudian Sight. They often become Keepers."

"It sounds like we have much in common," Katja replied. "The Blue Lady brings us wisdom so we may treat wounds to both the body and the soul."

"Don't you tire of helping others?"

"Ssolantress is the Ancient of purity and health," she said. "We, like you, are called to serve. Our needs are washed away when we ascend."

"Ascend?"

"As adepts, we train until our our matron or patron believes we're ready," Katja explained. "That's when we make a pilgrimage to our lady's most sacred place, the Crystal Well.

It was the last place she stood in the realm before departing for the Hall of the Ancients. If we're worthy, we're shown the Well, and once we bathe, we ascend into our new forms."

Katja pointed gently to her blue hair, blue eyes and blue lips. Then her finger slid over to her cheek, where the symbol of Ssolantress flickered in blue underneath her skin as she rubbed it.

Daemus heard every word, but he barely took them in. He was too enthralled by the magic flowing freely from her.

"Where's the Crystal Well?" Daemus asked, innocently. "Can it heal all?"

"It reveals itself only to a priest or priestess who calls upon it," Katja replied. "The Crystal Well is deep in the Silvercroft Mountains, far from Castleshire."

"The Silvercrofts?" Daemus asked. "They're the ancestral home of the Alaric family, though I've never seen them. Until recently, I'd seen little save for the road between Castleshire and the cathedral."

"You'll see the mountains soon, Daemus," Katja replied.

Daemus knew he could trade stories with Katja all night, but curiosity about the Crystal Well was burning at the back of his mind. She'd said something that had sparked some long-lost memory, but it eluded him.

"Tell me more of the Crystal Well," Daemus said.

"It's in a valley at the edge of the mountains," Katja said. "Its waters are still and clear. When I first saw it, it reminded me of a mirror."

Daemus's stomach wrenched as he understood what he was missing. In his visions, Graytorris was striding across the surface of a placid lake against the backdrop of a distant mountain range. Could this be what his oneiromancy had revealed to him? Without noticing it, his hand tightened involuntarily around Katja's.

"What is it?" she asked.

"My visions," he said. "I fear they intersect with the Crystal Well."

"Pardon?"

"A Keeper shall keep no secrets," Daemus said, more to himself than to Katja.

Katja looked at him intently.

"I had a series of recurring nightmares," Daemus confided. "Portents that I should have reported to the Great Keeper. Instead, I chose not to. Those nightmares were a warning from Erud about a fallen Keeper named Graytorris. The dreams showed me his return, a clear sign of ill omen. I fear it may somehow involve your Crystal Well."

"How?"

"Every night, I saw Graytorris reappear from a distant mountain range," Daemus said. "He walked across a lake of still water, much like the one you've described. It's no accident that we met this evening. I believe the Great Keeper meant for us to find one another and for Erud to reveal the meanings of my visions. As the Great Keeper would say, our paths are star-crossed."

"Why would this man seek the Crystal Well?"

"In my dreams, he pollutes the waters with blood and bile," Daemus said. "I don't know why. The Great Keeper believed him to be dead, but my visions revealed that he's returned. I'm unsure of his purposes, but he must be stopped. I'll visit the First Keeper of Castleshire, a mountain twerg named Aliferis Makai that I know from childhood. He initiated me into the Keepers. He and his ancient wisdom will help me."

"I have no doubt that the Blue Lady will protect her waters," Katja said. Her calming voice and demeanor were all that stopped Daemus from overreacting. "He can't find the well on his own. A priest or priestess of Ssolantress must reveal it to him. What else does he do in your visions?"

"He reaches for me," Daemus replied. "Or at least, that's what I thought. In my last vision, I learned that he was reaching for something behind me, though I don't know what. He speaks my name as if we know each other, but we've never met."

"All will be well, Daemus," Katja said. "The Ancients shall protect us. Have faith."

With that, Katja traced a finger in the air, inscribing a subtle figure of the Blue Lady. It pulsed with a calming blue light for a second or two. Daemus started succumbing to the effects of her healing spell, one that had been emanating slowly from her hand. He hadn't noticed it until now. Sliding into a peaceful sleep, he no longer felt the aches and pains. He felt only her hand in his.

WHILE DAEMUS SLEPT, THE Antlered Man appeared outside of Forecastle, hidden by the treelines of the Shirian Valley. Unerring in his tracking, the cryptid had gained several days of travel on his prey. He stood in the growing shadows of the woods on his goat-like hindquarters, staring into the lights of Forecastle below.

The cursed figure's eyes surveyed the gates from afar. Even at this distance, he could smell the flesh of oblivious humans wandering in and out of Forecastle's main entrance. His sharp ears captured the noise of laughter, shouting, and even the neighing of horses and other livestock. He'd tracked his target this far but had lost them in the hustle and bustle of the small town. Even with his powerful nose, too many scents would cause him to lose their trail. He knew they were below. That was enough.

Sitting against a tree, the Antlered Man reached into a bloody satchel at his side, his eyes never leaving the town.

He pulled a severed arm from the sack and began to gnaw upon it. The flesh had belonged to the hapless scavengers that he'd slain several nights before.

The cracking of teeth on bone continued as he chewed upon the carrion until nothing remained. His hunger sated momentarily, he leaned against the tree and waited for his quarry to reemerge.

CHAPTER TWENTY-THREE

"Sometimes the best outcome is a stalemate."
—Warminster, the Mage

IT WAS STILL DARK when Ritter updated Wilcox de la Croix and Rufus Crag on the king's commands. The two had been at the masquerade but relegated to mere spectators in the far corner of the room. They'd stayed through the early hours of the night to check on Ritter's condition and that of the princess.

"Safe travels," Ritter said, hugging them earnestly, not knowing when he'd see them—or his homeland—again.

"We'll tell your parents of your deeds and the king's decision," de la Croix replied. "May Nothos bless your travels. Rufus and I will keep Marr in line, don't worry."

"And we'll stop Til from writing any more songs about you," Rufus added with his crooked smile.

"He's a bard who thinks himself a Longmarcher," Ritter joked, "but we know the truth. Tell Driscoll to watch the eastern reaches. If Von Lormarck leaves the union, the road to the Bridge will be the only way to get food for the winter. Guildmistress Scarlett broke off trade with Thronehelm last night at the masquerade. Without their food, Warminster will struggle to feed its people if the winter is long. The eastern road from the Bridge may be the only way to Saracen, and Von Lormarck knows it."

"Consider it done," Wilcox said.

DAWN HAD COME TO Thronehelm, and the morning rays found Addilyn and Jessamy preparing to depart. Addilyn hadn't slept, her mind racing with disjointed memories of the night before. The evening had started with a dance and ended with a tragedy. Nary a word passed between her and Jessamy for several hours; then came a knock at Addilyn's door, which Jessamy opened. A herald stepped into the room and bowed with a deep flourish before introducing their visitor.

"My ladies," he said, "I have the honor of presenting to you King Godwin Thorhauer, the rightful ruler of Warminster."

Addilyn and Jessamy curtsied as the king came in, but he waved impatiently for them to dispense with the formalities and to take a seat.

"I apologize to intrude upon your private chambers, my lady," Godwin said, addressing Addilyn but looking at Jessamy. "Although of course, I'm glad to see that your champion is by your side to protect you."

"It's a pleasure to welcome you, my lord," Addilyn said. "To what do I owe this honor?"

Godwin nodded at his heralds, who melted back into the corridor with his personal guard. He closed the door, leaving the three of them alone, and then lowered himself gracefully into a seat.

"I have questions for you," he said. "Questions about the tetrine and Anselm Helenius. Tell me, was Helenius as they say he is?"

"He's all that and more," Addilyn replied. "He's handsome and charismatic. He has a tale for every situation but with Helenius, it's hard to know the truth from the legend. I knew his name from *The Ballad of Eldwal*, where it's said that he rode a tetrine. You must judge its veracity for yourself."

"So, what did he share with you about the tetrine?"

"Not much, I'm afraid, Your Majesty," Addilyn said. She nodded at Jessamy, who interpreted the hint and relaxed her posture, taking a seat opposite the king as Addilyn sat on the end of her bed.

"There must be something."

"Helenius said he'd never heard of a two-horned tetrine," Addilyn replied. "They've never been recorded in the field, in folk songs or in bestiaries. At first, I fear he struggled to believe me, but I won him over through my sincerity. He asked if I'd been afraid, but the creature was rather gentle, albeit panicked, as was the herd that followed her."

"Ah," Godwin murmured, his eyes narrowing at the thought of it.

"Helenius told me that the tetrine rarely bring good news," Addilyn added.

"My new Keeper, Jhodever, tells me the same," Godwin replied. "He said that the tetrine haven't been seen for years, not even in their homelands in the south, near Deadwaters Fork. Where did it happen?"

"It was at night," Addilyn said. "Not far from the peaks of the Dragon's Breath Mountains. The tetrine emerged from Ravenwood amidst the crackle of a magical hale. We elves call such a magical presence *whyrr*."

"They're southern beasts, from what I know. It's unheard of for them to roam the Dragon's Breath Mountains this far north," King Godwin said, half to himself. "What did Helenius agree to do?"

"My father paid him well to investigate," Addilyn replied. "Though I have an inkling that he would have done it anyway, just to satisfy his curiosity. Last I heard, he planned to visit a wizard in Castleshire to learn more, but we left for Thronehelm the following day and I haven't heard from him since. He was to send word once he'd sought his answers."

She paused for a moment to consider her next words. "Your Majesty," she began. "There was one other aspect to my encounter that I've refrained from mentioning. I was tentative before, as many who heard my story were quick to doubt me. Yet I have no reason to lie."

"Go on," Godwin prompted.

Addilyn paused for a moment to gather her thoughts, then said, "The creatures were looking for a missing stallion, and that's when the great mare spoke to me. I saw what she wanted me to see for a time."

"What did it show you?" the king asked, his eyes looking away from her and focusing instead on some distant figment of his own imagination.

"Fear," Addilyn replied.

THE CASTLE, STILL AWAKE from the tragedy hours before, was full of hustle and bustle. The servants were directing a morbid cleanup of the great hall. The chore was conducted with a muted reserve, one that Thronehelm's stone walls were unaccustomed to. King Godwin had left Addilyn's chambers after satisfying his curiosity about the tetrine, but neither of them had managed any sleep. Nobody had.

Addilyn and Jessamy emerged from her chamber to find Verrigo Releante, her Knight Hobelar, waiting for her.

Releante was the eldest of her wing, the leader of her father's light cavalry for nearly two centuries. But none would know it by his youthful, elven appearance. The quiet sage of their group, Releante rarely spoke first, but that day was different.

"My princess," he said, bowing to her.

"Releante," Addilyn replied in acknowledgement as she continued past him and down the hall.

He kept pace with the two women, and they soon found themselves at the center of attention as they made their way through the great hall. Addilyn couldn't help turning to see the spot where her father had been slain, but the specter of his death had been cleaned. In her mind's eye, she still saw the collapsed table, the turned chair, and the puddle of blood he'd left behind.

She lowered her head and trudged on, all too aware of the servants' eyes following them across the room. The trio arrived in the courtyard, where the Vermilion stood at attention. Her father's thin alabaster coffin sat at the head of the procession. Dacre's horse waited behind the coffin, saddled but without its rider. Her retinue—Eiyn, Rasilyn and Yala—watched on from their spot to one side of the procession.

Eiyn, the priest of the wing, stepped to Addilyn's side as he bent to touch the coffin. Eiyn placed one hand on the princess's shoulder and the other on the lid of the coffin. Then he began to pray aloud to their Ancient, Melexis.

Innuan serenitus trevitae
Melexis, joquato veresist
Opange, Ssolantress, Medige

Eiyn's humble prayer gently lifted the coffin and it levitated at the rear of their guard. Following their custom, Addilyn draped the crimson flag of the Vermilion over the casket, which was floating just high enough to keep it off the ground. She touched it lovingly one last time and closed her eyes in introspection.

"Thank you, Eiyn," Addilyn said. "Knight Hobelar, take my father back to Eldwal, where he'll rest forevermore. Ensure that the Queen Coronelle knows what happened and that I intend to avenge him and solve the mystery of the tetrine."

She handed him a scroll that she'd sealed herself as the new ambassador, using the stamp on the signet ring she'd inherited from her father the night before.

"Princess, you're the only heir to the throne," Releante said. "Are you sure it's wise to continue alone?"

"I'm not alone," Addilyn said, nodding first to Jessamy and then to the Thorhauer contingent, who were watching from a distant balcony. "Travel well, Knight Hobelar, and may Melexis go with you."

"And may Melexis go with you too, Princess," Releante said, bowing to her from the saddle. Then he turned to join his wing at the front of the procession and raised his lance, which bore a small crimson banner.

Addilyn and Jessamy watched from the courtyard as the Vermilion who'd arrived in high spirits left Thronehelm in quietude and despair.

FROM THE BALCONY, HIGH above the courtyard, Ritter watched the procession with the Thorhauers and the Maeglens, who'd gathered to send the Vermilion off.

"The tragedy of the masquerade reflects poorly on both Warminster and the Thorhauer family," Godwin said to the gathered nobles. "We'll struggle to reassemble the pieces of last night's affair."

"The Von Lormarcks rode home last night, against your orders," Amice said.

"As did the Thessalys," Baroness Maeglen added.

Godwin took a deep breath and lowered his eyes to the courtyard, watching the Vermilion wing depart. Then he turned to the group, his tired face reflecting his concern.

"I'll take care of the conclave of barons," Godwin said, his voice devoid of its usual command. He turned to his sons and nephews. "LaBrecque will take you to Castleshire with all the haste the four winds can muster. Master Cray, bring Disciple Delling home. And Princes Montgomery and Everett, tell the regency of this tragedy. They should hear this grim news from a Thorhauer. You must also ensure the princess's safety. It falls to us to right this wrong."

Ritter needed no instruction and didn't mind not being addressed directly. He closed his eyes and connected with Storm. The war falcon had been staking out *Doom's Wake*, watching LaBrecque and his crew as they prepared to shove off, and awaited Ritter at the docks.

As they broke from their small huddle, King Godwin and Queen Amice hugged each of the princes and viscounts, saying their goodbyes. Ritter and Cray stepped away for a moment to allow them some privacy.

"Are you a gambling man, Valkeneer?" Cray asked, as they both leaned against the parapet.

"It depends upon the game," Ritter replied.

"Good answer," Cray said, smiling and pushing his hair from his face.

"Why do you ask?"

"The king just threw some heavy dice," Cray murmured. "The future of Warminster hangs in the balance and he sends his sons and his admiral away to Castleshire while Von Lormarck and Thessaly ride from the union."

"They'll be needed to sway the regency to take action," Ritter said. "It's not just the union that's at stake here. We must deliver word of the tetrine and the assassination. Much is afoot. The king sees fit to send his sons over a legate to underscore its importance."

"You have much to learn of politics, my friend," Cray said, chuckling and turning his head toward Ritter. "Castleshire is famous for talk, not action. Diplomats play games and much time will be wasted on the floor of the Caveat with speeches and fancy words. I doubt we'll return to Thronehelm to find peace. By the Ancients, the Jackals have awaited this moment for generations. One doesn't ignore a king unless the die has already been cast. And to kill a king..."

Ritter listened to Cray's ominous words with mounting concern. Warminster had many enemies, but was Von Lormarck bold enough to be behind them all?

"A laurel for your thoughts?" Cray said, flipping the silver coin to Ritter and stirring him from his contemplation.

"Von Lormarck?" Ritter muttered quietly, not believing his lips had dared to make such an accusation.

Cray sighed and turned to look at the horizon. "Ah… It may be too obvious."

They descended into silence once again, and then the mood changed when Addilyn and Jessamy returned from their goodbyes and appeared on the parapet.

"We're ready, good King," Addilyn said.

"May your Ancients go with you," Godwin and Amice replied in near unison.

The queen reached over to hug the princess and they shared a pointed look that hinted of their shared trauma the night before.

"And may yours go with you," Addilyn replied.

THE TRAVELERS LEFT THE parapets and rode from the castle gates to board *Doom's Wake* for their weeklong trek by sea. LaBrecque greeted the contingent on the planks.

"Good morning, Princess," the admiral said, taking her hand to help her aboard. "Welcome to my home on the seas."

"Thank you, Admiral," Addilyn said, as the others boarded behind her.

"You've had a long night and we have an even longer journey in front of us," LaBrecque said. "Please, use my quarters and try to get some rest. Call for me if I'm needed."

Addilyn accepted with a melancholy nod. She knew that sleep was unlikely to come, but the privacy of his quarters was a welcome gesture.

As the sun crept over the horizon, *Doom's Wake* sailed out of Thronehelm's harbor into the Firth of Fury and set out along her charted course to Castleshire.

KING GODWIN WAITED ALONE on the balcony to watch the future of his realm sail away from him. Queen Amice and Baroness Cecily had both departed the parapet for warmer climes, and the rest of their gathering had sailed with LaBrecque.

"Meeks," Godwin said, his commanding voice returning to him.

"Yes, Your Majesty?" Crowley replied. He made his way obsequiously onto the balcony.

"What of the conclave?"

"Your Majesty, five of the seven baronies remain in the castle," Meeks said. "They'll be ready at the meridian, as you commanded."

"Have we heard from Von Lormarck?"

"Nay, Your Majesty," Meeks replied. "It's unclear whether he or Baron Thessaly will send a representative to the conclave."

"Summon my royal war wizards and battle priests from Thunder Cove," Godwin commanded. "I need them here."

"It will be done, Your Majesty," Meeks affirmed, as he turned to leave to follow his commands.

"I'm not finished, Crowley," Godwin said.

"Sire?"

"Find out who was responsible for last night," he said. "They must be punished."

"Your Majesty," Meeks said, his head bowed low. "I fear that I was responsible, for it was I who hired the bards. We're collecting information and carrying out searches of the town and castle. The investigation is still ongoing, sire. I expect Captain Valion to return before the conclave."

Godwin tilted his head in acknowledgement, his hands folded and his back to Meeks. He continued his thousand-yard stare across the city. He could sense Meeks standing behind him, awaiting his punishment, and Godwin tormented him for a few seconds more. Then he sent Crowley on his way with a dismissive wave of his hand, not bothering to turn.

"Thank you for your mercy, sire," Meeks mumbled, slinking away from the balcony.

But Godwin remained behind, contemplating the coming conclave and the events of the night before. He stood alone and watched the sunrise on the distant horizon. It was the first day during his time as king that he'd felt powerless and alone. He didn't think much of his chances of restoring Warminster to how it had stood only twelve short hours ago.

The Vermilion had left. Saracen had suspended trade. Von Lormarck had publicly mocked him and threatened secession, which almost assured that the Thessalys of Gloucester would follow. His Keeper was dead, and he'd just sent his two inexperienced but capable sons to a distant city steeped in politics, treachery, and intrigue, full of opportunists who smelled vulnerability all the way from Thronehelm to the gates of Castleshire.

He was alone and his kingdom was on the brink of civil war.

CAPTAIN ERUDUEL MORLEY AND Boatswain Macabre watched from the harbor atop the decks of their ship, the *Phantom*. They'd sailed inconspicuously into the harbor the night before on the orders of their sovereign, Baron Von Lormarck. As the two watched *Doom's Wake* disappear into the Firth of Fury, Skullam appeared at their feet.

"I have to know, Macabre," Morley joked, while looking at the imp. "Is this your little brother?"

Macabre was a trollborn that Morley had known for years, but the resemblance to Skullam was unmistakeable. Both were bald and ugly, and Macabre's skin was a dull purple, which hinted at his mixed blood.

"Nay, Captain," Macabre said, laughing. "My mother never made one of us with wings."

Skullam stood there in silence while the other two laughed at his expense.

"Where is Incanus Dru'Waith?" Morley asked of the imp, getting back to the matter at hand.

"He's here, Captain," Skullam said, pointing to the hooded figure approaching from the docks.

"You know, Skullam," Morley said, "you're going to have to teach us how you do that one of these days. It still unsettles me."

"Teach you what, my liege?" Skullam asked.

Morley shook his head, learning more clearly that imps understood neither humor nor sarcasm.

The Bone elf climbed aboard, hiding his identity from those in the harbor.

"You must be Morley," Incanus said.

"*Captain* Morley," Macabre said, correcting the assassin.

Incanus looked the captain up and down.

For a moment, Morley was taken aback. He was unremarkable in many ways, of average height and build for a middle-aged human, and he wore the clothes of a merchant ship captain and not a captain of a warship. His sword was tucked into a broad sash around his waist, and he wore a doublet, which was common amongst seamen.

"Never seen a captain before?" he asked.

"I was told to find Kryslexx," Incanus said, ignoring Morley's question.

As if on cue, Kryslexx appeared from below deck.

"There's your man," Morley said, beckoning for the naval wizard to approach.

"I hear you were trained at Thunder Cove and at Halifax," Incanus said, wasting no time.

"You heard correctly," Kryslexx replied, his gaze moving away from Incanus and over to Skullam. "I was trained as a war wizard, focusing on naval tactics." He paused, distracted by the imp's presence. "Is this your familiar? I didn't know you were a man of magic and could summon a creature like this. I was told you were an assassin. You must be fortunate to have secured the services of such a beast."

"I'm no familiar of his," Skullam growled.

"The imp is correct," the assassin said. "He belongs to… another."

"Apologies," Kryslexx offered, half-heartedly. "I just assumed—"

"Captain," Incanus interrupted. He was clearly in no mood to suffer pleasantries. "Are we equipped with the new weapon from Abacus?"

Morley and Macabre both pointed to a brown tarpaulin, which canvassed some clunky shapes on deck, the contents nearly protruding through the cover.

Incanus said nothing and turned to walk away, Skullam joining him at his side.

"Where are you going?" Morley asked.

"To sleep," the assassin said, disappearing below deck.

THE SEAS WERE GENTLE, unlike the events at Thronehelm. *Doom's Wake* was sailing south by southeast after spending the night heading west past the Horn of Seabrooke, Admiral LaBrecque's home.

The admiral didn't bother to disturb anyone during the night. Instead, he watched the distant lanternlights of the city in solitude. He knew their next stretch would be on the open seas and that his passengers needed the sleep. And besides, he enjoyed stealing moments for himself. It never got old. He always felt ambivalent as he passed the Horn, knowing that while his body belonged to Seabrooke, his heart belonged to the salty waves of the Firth of Fury.

That didn't stop him from appreciating the beauty of the city from afar, though.

As dawn peeked over the horizon, the first of his passengers emerged from below deck. It was Sir Ritter Valkeneer, who'd spent the night watching Princess Addilyn from a distance. She and Jessamy had huddled together to share their rage and sorrow.

LaBrecque felt Ritter's reticence from twenty paces. It was palpable. He guessed that Ritter had never been on a ship before and that he was struggling to find his sea legs. He also knew that Ritter possessed a trait that many men suffered from. He saw himself as the white knight to a damsel in distress. LaBrecque didn't know the details, but he guessed that Ritter's relationship with the princess wasn't as close as Ritter thought it was.

As the morning waned, the rest of his passengers slowly emerged. They came up one at a time, with Addilyn bringing up the rear. Only the occasional voices of the crew broke the silence.

By midday, the awkward mood had spread, and the sorrowful silence was only broken by the rhythmic flapping of the waves against the boards of the ship. There was no jovial scuttlebutt, and the only words spoken were murmured reassurances or whispered accounts of the assassination the night before. They were nursing their wounds, both physical and emotional. By late afternoon, it felt to the concerned admiral that they were adrift on a sea of uncertainty.

And then the shriek of a terrified lookout from the crow's nest broke the silence.

"Ahoy!" they shouted. "Ahoy!"

LeBrecque glanced up at the crewman pointing toward the stern and turned frantically to see what was amiss. A charcoal-colored brigantine had seemingly materialized from nowhere, already in range to fire.

LeBrecque raced to the helm to get a better view of the approaching warship. The brigantine flew no flag, which meant it was most likely a mercenary boat, and it was almost on top of them.

There was no time to think.

It was time to act.

KRYSLEXX'S CONCEALMENT SPELL HAD WORKED flawlessly. The war wizard was barely aware of the crew around him, his concentration focused solely on holding his spell in place until the right moment. The energy he channeled, and then cast outward, manifested in an invisible tapestry around the Phantom, rendering it hidden from human vision. The power of the spell had sapped him of nearly all his mental stamina, and he couldn't remember how long he'd maintained it.

"Well done," Captain Morley said, placing his hand on Kryslexx's shoulder.

The touch of the man's hand was enough to distract the war wizard, and the spell dissipated within seconds. He took a deep breath and shook off the effects of the magic. He knew there was no time to rest.

The Phantom had caught up with Doom's Wake undetected and Morley's trained crew had sailed into the perfect firing position. "Now!" Captain Morley cried.

The crew of the *Phantom* could hear the surprise in the voices of the enemy, rising in protest from afar.

The *Phantom*'s first volley came not in the form of a ballista but in a second spell. A stream of flame leapt from Kryslexx's practiced fingers.

"*Ammu sormet,*" Kryslexx uttered in the conjurer's tongue, waving his hands in front of his face. A hale of fiery magic ignited blue-green flames at the tips of his extended fingers. With a gesture toward *Doom's Wake*, the fire leapt from his hands and arced across the expanse between the vessels and struck amidships, spraying into the *Wake*'s full sails.

Captain Morley and Boatswain Macabre looked at Kryslexx with smirks on their faces. The battle against the Seawolf had begun.

LABRECQUE ORDERED HIS SAILORS to battlestations and the veteran crew snapped to the task, scrambling to return fire. Some fought the flames that were crippling the mainmast while others prepared their first volley, spinning their ballistae at the mercenary ship.

The princes and viscounts ran to LaBrecque's side, with Master Cray just a couple of steps behind them. Their faces were twisted with confusion.

"They must have a formidable naval wizard," LaBrecque lamented.

"We have a wizard of our own," Addilyn shouted from astern. With a vengeful stare, she took matters into her own hands and matched Kryslexx's spell with one of hers.

"*Hvit vind matherag fryse!*" Addilyn said in the conjurer's tongue. With a quick incantation, her hands summoned a magical hale of blue wisps. She directed the spell at the flames and a burst of frost jumped from her hands, quickly dowsing the threat.

The crew cheered and the admiral couldn't help smiling. But *Doom's Wake* was far from safe.

FROM THE DECK OF the *Phantom*, Captain Morley and Kryslexx watched on helplessly as their first attack was countered. Undaunted, Morley turned to Boatswain Macabre. "It's time to employ our new toy," he said.

"With pleasure, Captain," Macabre replied with a wry smile. He raised his arm and yelled, "Prepare the fisher's hook!"

LABRECQUE'S CREW WAS READY TO return fire. Sailors were loading their ballistae and working quickly to replace the damaged sails.

From a distance, the crew heard the swift recoil of the miniature catapults bolted to the enemy's deck as they sprang into action. The devices, small but deadly, only worked over short distances. But their enemy had dealt with that problem by catching *Doom's Wake* by surprise.

"Incoming!" LaBrecque bellowed.

Arcing balls of heavy lead rained down, smashing into the hull and deck. LaBrecque and the royals ducked, helpless to stop the falling metal from wreaking havoc. A second, more traditional volley left the brigantine, and a half-dozen ballista bolts bounded out from their casings at the *Wake's* mainmast. The projectiles skittered into the frenzied crew as they ricocheted, sending splinters flying and nearly crippling the *Wake*. This time, their losses were in sailors and not sails.

"LaBrecque!" Montgomery yelled. "What are we doing?"

LaBrecque just grunted, ignoring the young prince, and yelling, "Loose!"

He watched the barrage of metal bolts as it pierced the

morning sky, sending damaged wood and dead sailors from the brigantine into the firth.

"Fire at will!" LaBrecque cried, and the seasoned crew of *Doom's Wake* hurried to obey him.

"Captain, I have a falcon," Ritter said, confusing LaBrecque at an inopportune time.

"And?" LaBrecque replied, sarcastically.

"I can dispatch him. He can fly high above the enemy ship and see great distances. We have a… connection that allows me to see through his eyes."

"Do it, then," LaBrecque replied. "Have it look for their captain and armaments. And find out how many are in their crew."

CAPTAIN MORLEY CONTINUED TO exchange volleys with the enemy, waiting patiently for Boatswain Macabre and Quartermaster Broynwyn to ready the fisher's hook. Standing at the helm, it fell to him to steer the *Phantom* closer to Doom's Wake while giving his gunners time to align the weapon. Both were dangerous, as the maneuvers gave LaBrecque more time to return fire.

Quartermaster Broynwyn emerged from below, her expression telling Morley everything he needed to know. The fisher's hook was ready. He nodded and she disappeared below deck.

As Morley turned, he heard the swoosh of a ballista overhead, forcing him to duck. The bolt sent wooden shards flying past him, nearly damaging the helm.

"Must have been LaBrecque," he murmured, grinning to himself. The admiral had a reputation as a former artilleryman. The bolt had been inches away from adding to the Seawolf's score.

As he stood up, he noticed that Incanus Dru'Waith and his imp had made their way topside. Incanus watched the two ships draw closer, saying nothing to the captain. Skullam climbed on the rigging next to him, getting a better view of the enemy vessel than he'd had from the deck.

"You picked the right time to join us, Dru'Waith," Morley said with a proud smile on his face. He waited for Macabre to find his mark.

Incanus said nothing, barely acknowledging the captain and staring at his prey from afar.

"Damned Bone elves," Morley murmured. He shook his head and got back to the task at hand.

LABRECQUE SMIRKED, BASKING IN the skill and composure of his crew as they leveled the battlefield. He spat on the deck in defiance, proud to see *Doom's Wake* holding its own in the fight. They'd make the privateers pay for their mistake.

As LaBrecque and the royals looked on, the brigantine swung around to reveal a unique porthole at the bow, exposing the tip of a doubled-cased ballista. The porthole was thrice the size of all the others, and the ballista protruded from the opening, pointing at the hull of *Doom's Wake*.

"By the Ancients," Montgomery murmured. "What *is* that?"

LaBrecque had no answer. The two vessels were close enough that they could hear the voices of the enemy crew growling orders below deck.

"Brace for impact!" the admiral yelled.

Then the war machine fired. LaBrecque and his crew watched as a massive grappling hook flew toward them, trailed by two thick chains as dark as the vessel herself. The hook smashed easily through *Doom's Wake*'s hull, lodging itself deep inside the ship. The *Wake* lurched from the impact and several sailors slipped overboard and into the water.

"HEAVE!" CAPTAIN MORLEY CRIED. He was below deck with Boatswain Macabre, who wasted no time putting his crew to work. The fisher's hook was designed to pierce the hull of enemy ships and, like a fishhook, to latch onto the bones of its target.

Morley shook his head. The maritime tool, designed at the High Aldin in Abacus, had worked. He'd been anxious to see it deployed for the first time, and his crew had executed the attack to perfection. With the two ships linked, the crew of the *Phantom* cranked back on the hook, dragging their enemy in for the kill.

"Heave, heave, heave!" Macabre yelled. His artillery crew threw their muscles into the job, turning the dual reels of the monstrosity and slowly dragging their prey closer.

Macabre smiled to himself and then turned, running topside to prepare to board.

LABRECQUE AND THE PRINCES rushed to the rails, looking at the hole the weapon had gored into the *Wake* and surveying the damage to the hull. The fisher's hook had wrapped itself around the *Doom's Wake* like a set of manacles. For one inconceivable moment, LaBrecque almost lost his footing as the mercenary ship started to tow the *Wake* toward them. At first, the tugging was slow, but *Doom's Wake* was crippled and the tethered hook was gathering momentum.

"Admiral, what do we do?" Montgomery blurted.

It was the prince's first naval battle, and LaBrecque could see the mounting panic in his eyes.

The admiral looked at the hook and then back to the rudder, arriving instantaneously at a decision. He knew that fighting the hook by maneuvering the ship would only cause further damage.

"Free us!" LaBrecque bellowed, waving for his carpenters and smithies to rush below deck. Then he took the helm, rallying his crew and bellowing orders.

Instead of struggling against the *Phantom*, he ordered the *Wake* to turn.

MORLEY WATCHED KRYSLEXX READY another spell to counter the *Wake*'s erratic tacking.

"*Ventus imperium!*" the veteran wizard evoked, sending a billowing gust into the sails of the *Phantom*, closing the gap between the two warships. Both crews continued to exchange volleys of ballistae bolts, but they were also close enough to fire arrows.

"What are they doing?" Macabre asked Morley. "Do they mean to board us? We outnumber them three to one."

"The man's insane!" Morley replied without thinking. "He's doing our job for us."

Incanus leaned into a wooden rail, using it as a brace as he readied his longbow.

Skullam leapt from the rigging to the deck and scrambled to find cover.

The Black Rose nocked an arrow and waited for a shot, scanning the deck for Addilyn or one of the princes.

THE CREW AND PASSENGERS of *Doom's Wake* had been galvanized by an unspoken desperation. There was no longer a place for self-pity.

The princes and viscounts were below deck, directing the crew as the carpenters repaired the gaping hole in the side of the ship while the smithies inspected the fisher's hook. Sea sprayed in from multiple holes, making the footing treacherous, but the royals waded into the chaos regardless.

"It's no use!" Joferian yelled to Montgomery. He and Talath were shoulder-to-shoulder with three smithies, trying to cut the fisher's hook free.

"Aye!" shouted one of the smithies, his cries hard to hear over the gushing water. "If we remove it, we'll worsen the flooding."

Montgomery looked closer. The giant hook was attached to chains made of metal, but the hook was pulleyed by bull rope.

"The rope!" Montgomery shouted, pointing to it. "We need to cut it!"

RITTER WAS IN THE crow's nest, brandishing Silencer and communicating with Storm. Storm had begun to circle the brigantine, and Ritter could see through his sharp eyes, spying for activity on the pirate deck. His bow was nearly in range, and he saw a group standing at the helm.

Ritter's shared vision with Storm revealed more than he'd bargained for. The Bone elf from the night before was standing by the helm, an arrow nocked to his bowstring as he scanned the deck of the *Wake* for a target.

"Princess, get down!" Ritter bellowed. She and Jessamy both hit the deck as a black arrow sailed over their heads, narrowly missing the princess, and splintering off a cleat behind them.

Ritter returned fire, but his arrow soared high and wide. The waves made it damn near impossible to snipe. Unaccustomed to the tumble of the ocean, he knew his aim might not be as true, but it didn't matter. He had to try.

"MY LORD!" SKULLAM SAID, pulling on his master's cloak to get his attention.

Incanus whirled around. "You cost me a follow-up shot," he growled.

"My liege, you're a target," Skullam replied, his gnarled finger directing Incanus's eyes to an arrow sprouting from an impaled bailer.

Incanus scrambled for cover and smiled at the growing rivalry with Ritter. Only the trollborn archer would be brave enough—or foolish enough—to target him. Ritter had thwarted him at the Battle of Rillifane's Meander, but Incanus knew he'd foiled himself at the masquerade.

"The man is skillful with that bow," the Bone elf said.

"Sire," Skullam said. "Above."

Skullam pointed to the sky and Incanus shielded his eyes against the sun for a second or two. Even though he was a Bone elf and bred for the surface, the sun was still an enemy. He shrank back beneath the hood of his cloak, his eyes burning as he looked to the skies.

"A falcon," Skullam explained. "No normal bird of prey would be this far out to sea. I suspect our trollborn possesses an animal companion, a *familiar* of sorts. He's watching us from afar."

Incanus tilted his head to seek the spy in the skies above, a hovering speck against the clouds. He grunted.

"Take care of it," Incanus ordered. "It's too high for my arrows."

"With pleasure," Skullam replied. The imp grinned and spread his bat-like wings, then pushed off from the deck and spiraled up toward the falcon.

RITTER WATCHED THROUGH STORM'S EYES as the winged creature that Jessamy had described from the night before approached them, then ordered the falcon to return to *Doom's Wake*. He'd hoped the falcon's return would lure the beast within range of Silencer, but the flapping monster cut off his game of cat and mouse, staying far from Ritter's arrows while circling the *Wake*.

"He won't escape us," Addilyn cried. *"Brann pilar angrep!"* she sounded, conjuring another spell. Instead of blue wisps, Ritter watched her summon a fiery hale that morphed in her hands into three searing bolts of flame, peppering the winged creature in the chest from afar.

The injured beast flipped sideways into a forced barrel roll and tumbled toward the open water, but he caught the air inches from the waves, coasting above the water's surface for a second or two before disappearing from sight.

LABRECQUE WAS WAITING FOR the right moment as the two ships swung on one another. Then he saw an opportunity.

"Sailing Mistress Tamsyn," LaBrecque said, his expression calm. "Take the helm."

Tamsyn stepped to the helm as the admiral hurried away, arriving at a starboard ballista. He ordered his artillerists to step back, and they respectfully did so.

LaBrecque knew his plan was a desperate one, but it *had* to work. The right shot could win the battle. The Seawolf looked through the sights of the giant crossbow and lined up his shot. With the fate of his crew, the princes and a Vermilion princess riding on the outcome, LaBrecque pulled the trigger.

The long metal bolt released from its casing and flew

true, smashing into its target. The bolt struck the base of the *Phantom*'s mainmast, which exploded in a storm of splinters and sent the enemy's crew diving for cover.

The mast lurched for a second, its heavy timber swaying fore then aft. Time stood still. Then it started to groan and with a slow, sustained snap, it crashed down to the deck, crushing sailors and weapons alike. The crew of the *Doom's Wake* erupted in cheers and relieved prayers. The Seawolf had done it again.

LaBrecque disentangled himself from the crossbow and removed his Abacunian spyglass, unfurling it and putting it up to his eye. Over on the *Phantom*, the fallen timber had crippled the brigantine and scattered the crew, buying LaBrecque and his men enough time to cut the *Wake* loose from the fisher's hook.

MONTGOMERY, EVERETT, JOFERIAN, TALATH, Zendel Cray, and a half dozen carpenters and smithies were all hacking away at the hook's tethers. The *Wake* was still being tugged by their crippled opponent and battered by the waves and the winds, making it hard for them to keep their feet. Their swords and hatchets were sharp, but the thick rope had a metal core, dulling their efforts and slowing them down.

Still, they worked frantically to cut the ties. One of the ropes snapped, then a second, followed by the last. When the final rope broke, the crew of the *Wake* lost their footing as the tension disappeared and the ship rolled and then righted itself.

Another shout of elation echoed out from the *Wake*.

"Smithies, bail the water!" Talath ordered. "Carpenters, fix the hole!"

The crew raced to follow Talath's lead. Joferian and Everett joined the effort while Montgomery made his way topside to inform LaBrecque. As he emerged, he saw that LaBrecque was disengaging and sailing away.

"Admiral!" Montgomery protested. "Why aren't we pressing our advantage? Why do we sail away like cowards?"

"We sail away to safety, young prince," LaBrecque said. "Their ship is twice our size and holds thrice the men and war machines. Yes, they're crippled for a few precious moments, but they'll recover before we can sink her. We're already bailing water. A direct hit from one of those ballistae will finish us. We can barely maneuver as it is. We must use this time to put enough distance between us to lose her at sea. It would be suicide to board her."

MORLEY WATCHED FROM THE deck of the broken *Phantom* as their injured quarry limped away. They were close enough to see the crew of the *Wake* making vulgar hand gestures over the rails as the ship slipped free from the fisher's hook.

He surveyed the damage from the helm and spotted Macabre and Kryslexx climbing out from beneath the fallen masts.

"Naval Wizard Kryslexx," Morley said, sarcasm dripping from his tongue. "Do you by any chance have a spell that can stop them from escaping?"

"No, Captain," he said. "They've moved out of my magic's range."

Morley looked ahead at the escaping LaBrecque, not bothering to acknowledge the wizard. Instead, he grunted in disgust and descended to the deck to help his crew to recover.

ADMIRAL LABRECQUE AND THE crew of the damaged *Doom's Wake* attended feverishly to the disabled ship, guiding her to safety. They sailed far out of range of spells and the remaining war machines of the crippled marauding vessel, gaining distance and time and disappearing over the horizon before their adversaries could pursue them.

"Nothos was for and against us in this battle," LaBrecque said through pursed lips. "He brought us fortune enough to escape but teased us by tempting us to stay and fight. But we can't fight. Our damage isn't fully reparable until we reach a safe port."

The royals, still soaked in sea spray, let out a collective groan as they watched the Seawolf inspect the repairs.

"She'll sail," he remarked. "But once they fix their sails, they'll catch us. Especially if their war wizard is as capable as they seem to be."

"Is there anything I can do?" Addilyn asked. "My sorcery may help, but I know little of warships."

"Unless you can keep us from taking on water, my princess, then the answer is no," LaBrecque said. Then he turned to his carpenters and added, "Well done, lads and lasses. You've stemmed the flow of new seawater, but let's work to bail what remains. It'll slow us down, no doubt, and we'll need to lighten our load."

LaBrecque turned to his reliable helmswoman. "Sailing Mistress Tamsyn?"

"Aye, Admiral?"

"Set a course for Castleshire," La Brecque said, "bearing south by southwest."

"I beg your pardon, Admiral," Tamsyn said. "That would take us into the open seas. Should we not stay on our southeasterly course, hugging the shores to save us time?"

"Aye," LaBrecque remarked, "but that's exactly what the captain of that privateer is going to expect. I don't want her sneaking up on us. We'll take our chances in the open seas. Let's see how much of a sailor their captain is. Let them come and find us."

"Aye, Admiral," Tamsyn acknowledged. "South by southwest."

"First Mate Cortez," the admiral continued. "Round up the crew and help me to jettison as much ballast as possible."

"Aye, sir," Cortez answered. "What should we lose?"

"All of it," LaBrecque responded. "We'll need to lighten our load considerably. Anything not bolted to the deck or used in our defense will need to go, and that includes food and personal belongings. Everything, Cortez."

"Aye aye, sir."

LaBrecque turned to Montgomery and reiterated the order, staring into the prince's questioning eyes. Montgomery nodded.

As the crew began to hastily unload ballast, LaBrecque watched from a distance, making calls on anything of import before it went overboard. Anything that could float had to be weighed down so that they wouldn't leave a trail.

"Viscount Joferian and Prince Everett, a word if I may," LaBrecque said. Both approached him with a curious look in their eyes. "Follow me."

The men descended briefly into the hold of the ship, where LaBrecque walked proudly over to a store of dozens of unmarked sacks.

"What is it, Admiral?" Everett asked.

"This, my dear prince, is silver flake," the admiral said with a wry smile. "This was meant as a gift for your father from Abacus. Perhaps Nothos has blessed our voyage after all. This is our salvation. May I ask the two of you to carry these onto the deck? It's time for the hunter to become the hunted."

"Of course," they replied in unison.

The admiral turned away and reemerged topside to scan the deck. He put one hand up to his brow to shade his eyes from the harsh sunlight as it bounced off the water.

"Sir Ritter," LaBrecque called. "Pray, tell me. How does that trick with your bird work?"

CHAPTER TWENTY-FOUR

"Servant leadership is the reason the common
people believe in the goodness of rulership."
—The Worshipful Scrivener's Guild of House Alaric

FAUX AND ARJUN WORKED their way down the cobblestones of Auddinger's Alley, taking a few paces more as Gigerold had suggested. Through the soft glow emanating from the waning candlelight in the windows of the inns in Forecastle's small commerce district, they saw a group of buildings ahead, some of them bearing the coat of arms of the families they served.

Faux had never traveled to Forecastle before, and the orderly and proud compounds surprised her. She paused in the street to better take them in.

"What is it?" Arjun asked.

"I'm not sure," she replied. "I guess I didn't expect the servant compounds to be so well-maintained."

"Just because they serve, it doesn't mean they live as serfs," Arjun said. "The workers of Castleshire take pride in their homes, just like the lords and ladies. It's a tradition and a part of the culture, dating back to the Chessborough family when the city was founded."

The two proceeded down the row, looking for the Alaric sigil. It didn't take them long to find it. The Alaric compound, like many of the Shirelord compounds, was made up of half a dozen buildings housing the servants, or at least those who chose to live there on Alaric laurels. The simple tenements housed a galley, stores for wares, an infirmary, and a small barn and stable for horses and other livestock. A decorative brick wall surrounded the compound with a gate on either side, watched over by two small guardhouses. The Alaric crest was displayed prominently on the gates.

As the two approached, they were greeted by a friendly guard wearing the livery of the Alaric family. He stood proudly in his silver and blue uniform, with the familiar mountain and fox patch emblazoned on his chest.

"Welcome to the Alaric Compound," the guard said, pleasantly. "How may I help you this fine evening?"

Faux looked to Arjun and reached into her rucksack, then presented the guard with Kester's sealed scroll. The guard looked at it and saw that the seal was whole.

"I was told to show this to Ellissio," Faux said.

"Stay here, please," the guard replied, turning and leaving Faux and Arjun at the gate with his fellow sentry. They watched as he made his way through the square to a building near the rear of the residence. He knocked on the door of one of the houses and handed the scroll over. Moments later, a second figure appeared in the doorway.

"Here we go," Faux said, looking to Arjun for support. Her heart told her to stay, but her head told her to run.

"Courage," Arjun urged. "We'll need more of it to enter the gates of Castleshire than we will for Forecastle."

They watched as the guard and the other figure approached the front gate. The guard was still holding the open scroll in his hand.

"I'm the one you seek," the other man said as he approached them. "Please, come with me."

His accent was one that Faux couldn't recognize. The guard swung the gate open and the two followed Ellissio across the square and into the building he'd come from. They found themselves in a small lounge inside an even smaller foyer, barely large enough for the three to fit in.

Ellissio sat in silence for a few minutes more, re-reading the scroll. Faux couldn't help noticing he was advanced in age, and his long face seemed to grow longer as he read. She could tell he was nervous, something that any good rogue who'd played enough tavern games would spot. His reddish-brown hand rubbed the greying bristles of his manicured goatee and every now and then he reached to his eyes to wipe away tears. His hand slumped, almost dropping the scroll in disbelief.

"I'm sorry," Faux said. "Kester was a good man. To me and my family, as well as yours. He'll be sorely missed."

"How did it happen?" Ellissio managed.

"He distracted a clan of trollborn that were tracking us," Arjun said. "Young Daemus saw his death in a vision after we escaped. On the planes of the Vilchor Highgrass."

"Is Daemus alive?" Ellissio asked, without looking up.

"Yes," Faux confirmed. "A little shaken, but we made it back in one piece."

Ellissio let out a sigh of relief and spoke in a tongue that was foreign to Faux's ears. It seemed to be a prayer to the Ancients in thanks for the safe return of the Alarics' only child.

"My name is Ellissio Ramani," he said. "I'm Kester's personal valet. Or at least, I was."

On that sorrowful note, both he and Faux shared a moment of grief. She wrapped the man in her arms to comfort him. After several moments of high emotion, he bent over and managed to stop his tears.

"Kester and I met in the Phontu River Basin, many years ago," he continued. "He saved me when I was a prisoner of war. He purchased me and freed me from my shackles. In return, I helped him to get home safely and chose to stay here with his family to earn my keep. He embodied the very spirit of Castleshire. I'll miss him."

Ellissio broke down again, but just for a moment.

"I too was rescued by a family in Castleshire," Arjun said, breaking the awkward silence. "They bought me from slavery and had me delivered to Abacus, where I was freed. I served them for ten years. I still serve them now."

"Then you must be Arjun Ezekyle."

"That I am," Arjun replied.

"It's been a long time, Captain," Ellissio said. "Age has been kind to you. And you must be the Dauldon, as this message suggests?"

"Aye," Faux said reticently, hoping for a kind reaction.

"Don't worry, my lady," Ellissio said. "I won't sound the alarm. I'll follow Kester's final orders and deliver you and Master Daemus to the Alaric estate. For your safety, until we arrive at the estate, I ask that you allow me to dress you as servants of House Alaric and that you stay quiet as we enter the city gates."

Then he paused again.

"I'm sure his family will want to know the full details of Daemus's return," he said. "You must understand, I'll have no choice but to reveal you for who you are. Your fate will be out of my hands."

"I promised Kester I'd get Daemus home," Faux said. "That home isn't Forecastle, and it's time for me to stop running. If there are consequences, I'm ready to face them. Kester risked his life to save me, smuggling me from Castleshire when I was young. I must now return his nephew to Castleshire to repay my debt."

Ellissio pursed his lips and nodded slightly.

"In that case, welcome home, Faux Dauldon." Ellissio placed his hand on hers. "May your return to Castleshire be happier than the circumstances in which you left it."

THE SUN ROSE OVER Forecastle as Daemus, Faux and Arjun made their way through the narrow streets of the servant city. The morning dew frosted the windows of the buildings in the late autumn air, and Daemus's stomach growled anxiously, knowing what was to come. He could smell crackling bacon as they snuck past the many taverns that called the town square home, but he couldn't imagine keeping anything down.

"Why did we leave Blue and Marquiss back at the Halo?" Daemus asked, as they made their way toward the Alaric compound.

"We need to travel inconspicuously at the moment," Faux said. "Marquiss's ears give him away, and... well, Blue Conney is anything but inconspicuous."

"Besides," Arjun explained, "I've asked them to back-track into the valley and the nearby woods to ensure that we haven't been followed. I don't want to leave anything to chance. There's no telling if Clan Blood Axe has regrouped and decided to seek revenge. Don't worry, Daemus. They have their tasks."

Daemus couldn't argue with that. He knew his family employed no elven or huldrefolk servants. They'd surely be noticed.

Daemus was nervous—not for himself, but for Faux. He knew his parents could be political and guessed he'd have to convince them to help her and Arjun. With her family's past and without his urging, they'd lack the fortitude to do it on their own. He was too young to remember the Dauldon drama that had unfolded in the city, but he wagered that his parents wouldn't want any part of it, even if the lone survivor had brought their wayward son home.

In many respects, his expulsion was the least of his worries. In fact, his father might even welcome the opportunity to bring Daemus back into the Alaric compound and a life of politics in the court of Castleshire. But he carried a grave burden with him. He dreaded telling them of Kester's death. He thought his father would be crushed by the news and his mother self-satisfied, knowing that her predictions of Kester's undoing had finally come true. Even if he did save her only child in the process.

In his eyes, his parents barely accepted him as their son, let alone as a Keeper. They'd only agreed to let him go to the cathedral at the behest of First Keeper Makai once they could no longer deny his Erudian Sight. He remembered their shock when, at the age of five, he'd predicted the death of a servant, which they'd passed off as the babblings of a young child. When he was a little older and told them of a horse's stable burning in town, they'd put him to bed. Then it had happened soon after, and he'd cried for three days.

Then his visions of Graytorris had manifested. Daemus sometimes found himself dreaming through Graytorris's eyes, while other dreams were nightmares of things to come or messages from Erud that he was too young to interpret. These visions were far different to his others, as they attacked him both mentally and physically. To his parents, his blessing was their curse.

Daemus had found direction and a loving uncle in Kester. His parents had known that Kester had a way with Daemus, one that could calm him when his powers flared. Instead of hiding Daemus or ignoring his Sight, Kester had fostered the gift. Even at the cost of his gallivanting and loose lifestyle, Kester would stay with Daemus instead, convincing him that his dreams were a puzzle to solve instead of a plague on House Alaric.

One night, Daemus dreamed of a twerg visitor with a shock of blond hair. His parents had ignored it, thinking it was just another scary man from his nightmares. But Daemus was proven correct when the next day, Aliferis Makai, the First Keeper of Castleshire, had shown up at their estate. The ancient twerg Keeper had shared Daemus's dream and sought his parents' permission to take Daemus under his wing. Aliferis had promised that his sect would teach Daemus to harness his abilities at the Cathedral of the Watchful Eye, making him valuable to Castleshire in a different way.

Daemus recalled the loud protests from Ranaulf, his father, who'd desperately wanted him to follow in his footsteps. But in a moment of rare agreement, Kester had convinced his mother, Mercia, to allow Makai to take him to the cathedral, where he could train as a Keeper.

"Daemus, we're here," Faux said, stirring Daemus from his thoughts. "Are you okay?"

Daemus said nothing. He looked ready to relieve himself of his breakfast, though he hadn't eaten one.

"Steady, lad," Arjun encouraged him. "These are your servants. If you're like this at their door, how will you be at your own?"

Daemus didn't respond again, and Faux threw an arm around him and kissed his forehead. Then she approached the alley where they were to meet Ellissio and watched the guards from a distance. Daemus didn't recognize any of the guards, and so he looked past them to Ellissio, who made his way from the courtyard of the Alaric compound toward them.

A long train of servants dressed in Alaric blue and silver made their way through the front gate. It was almost exactly two miles to Castleshire, far enough for Daemus to ponder his first words when he arrived home.

Ellissio waved for the three to come with him, breaking from the group and ducking into the alley for a quick change. He'd brought Alaric robes for each of them, and after they slipped the uniforms on, Ellissio and Daemus shared a brief hug.

"Master Daemus," Ellissio said. "We're so glad to have you home."

"Thank you," Daemus replied. "But I fear for what's to come."

Ellissio hugged Daemus again and took him by the shoulder as the two began to walk far enough behind the troupe to talk in private.

"They're your parents, Master Daemus," Ellissio said. "They love you and will welcome you back with open arms. I'm sure they'll be happy that you're safe."

"I wish I could say the same for Kester." Daemus looked at his feet and slowed his pace. "I feel as though I've lost a father."

"Kester was a great man," Ellissio continued, "and from what your friends told me, he sacrificed everything to save you. You should honor him by carrying his memory with you for the rest of your days. Don't let his sacrifice be in vain."

Daemus heard the wisdom in Ellissio's words. They strengthened him for his return home.

THE SERVANTS OF HOUSE Alaric arrived at the shining gates of Castleshire and began the trek to the easterly corner of the city and the Alaric estate. Ellissio marched at the rear with Daemus, Faux and Arjun, keeping Daemus and his unmistakeable eyes away from the other servants, at least until they arrived at the front door.

Faux and Arjun did their best to blend in, keeping their heads low to avoid eye contact as they passed guards and civilians alike. Faux was tempted to look around at Castleshire's many wonders, but she willed herself to play the role that had been assigned to her, at least for another few moments.

The smell of the city during the Time of the Bountiful Harvest was unforgettable. The scent of fresh apple pies from the bakeries washed over her nostrils as they passed through town, and memories of her childhood rushed back to her. She peered out from under her hood and watched outdoor cafés serve Castleshire's signature fall dish, a chilled strawberry soup that she'd loved as a child. It wasn't much of a soup, consisting mostly of squashed and sugared strawberries with the consistency of a thick cider, but it reminded her of her younger days.

But while everything seemed as she remembered it, she knew that nothing would be the same for her this time round.

Within minutes, the group arrived at the gates of Daemus's home. Faux noticed that his hands were trembling and reached for his arm to calm him. As the crowd split, heading to their respective duties, Ellissio led them to the front door.

The guards parted at the sight of the chamberlain of the house, and Ellissio led them into the foyer of House Alaric.

"Stay here," Ellissio whispered. "I'll go and find your parents."

Daemus stood like a stranger atop the Alaric sigil that had been carved with great care into the floor of the two-story foyer.

"Ellissio," Mercia said, as the two emerged from the second-floor balcony overlooking the room below. "You know I don't like surprises."

She entered the stairwell above Daemus and looked over the decorative rail and into the hexagonal foyer below.

"My chamberlain said you have a surprise for me," Mercia called into the foyer with a stern tone. "Please tell me what it is so that we can return to our duties."

"Mother," Daemus said, lowering the cowl of his cloak. "I'm home."

MERCIA SPUN TO SEE her son, now grown to near manhood, standing in servant garbs beneath her in the foyer. For a second, she tilted her head in confusion. Her eyes settled on his bandages.

"Why are you traveling in disguise?" Mercia asked, poorly feigning disinterest in his wounds. Her eyelids fluttered.

Daemus and Mercia weren't close, but he was her only child. She'd always been hard on him and had blamed the misfortunes of House Alaric on his "condition." To show him compassion would betray that performance, the one that she'd acted out on the Alaric stage for his entire life.

"Daemus!" Ranaulf exclaimed, as the lord of the house entered the foyer.

Daemus turned to greet him and the two embraced, interrupting the awkward reunion with his mother. Mercia used the time to descend the spiral stairs and join them.

"By the Ancients, what are you doing home?" Ranaulf asked. He stepped back to look at his son. "Are you hurt?"

"I'm fine now, Father," Daemus replied. "Sore, but fine."

"Where's your uncle?" Ranaulf asked. "And who are all of these people?"

"I bring grave news," Daemus started. His voice shook and tears welled in his eyes. "Uncle Kester was killed on our way back from Solemnity."

Ranaulf and Mercia stood still beside their son, unresponsive. Daemus looked up at them, untucking his face from his grieving hands. Neither said anything, but both peered into his eyes, searching for understanding.

"Is this another one of your dreams?" Mercia asked, doubt dripping from her tongue.

"Regrettably, I'm telling the truth," Daemus confided. His eyes drifted back to his feet.

"But he wasn't to leave for Solemnity until—" Ranaulf said. "I mean, why would he—?"

"He was summoned early by the Great Keeper," Daemus said, tears rolling down his cheeks. His voice swelled with emotion and his face reddened. "I was expelled, and so she sent for him to retrieve me."

"Daemus speaks the truth," Arjun said.

"Who are you?" Ranaulf asked.

"We're the ones who brought your son home safely," Arjun said. "And at great cost, I might add."

"Do you expect payment?" Mercia snapped. "Is that why you're still here?"

"They're here because Kester asked them to help me," Daemus retorted. "Two of their companions were also slain on our way home."

Mercia, seemingly unaccustomed to her son's newfound impertinence, bit her tongue.

"Who attacked you?" Ranaulf asked, an air of uncertainty in his question.

"Clan Blood Axe," Daemus said.

"Ha!" Mercia sputtered. "This lunacy has gone on for too long. Where's Kester?"

"Mother, I—"

"Answer her, Daemus," Ranaulf demanded. "Who are these people?"

"Yes, who are these people that brought my failing son home?" Mercia added.

"I'm Faux Dauldon, and this is my captain of the guard, Arjun Ezekyle."

Ranaulf and Mercia fell silent and stared momentarily at each other before turning back to Faux.

"Yes, *that* Faux Dauldon," Arjun confirmed. "Kester met us in a mountain town on his way back from Solemnity with Daemus. The Great Keeper told him that Daemus was in grave danger and that he needed protection on the journey to Castleshire. We learned how important your son truly is, so we agreed to escort him here while Kester distracted a clan of trollborn that were hot on his trail. Unfortunately, he paid with his life, as did two of our comrades, before we made it safely back to Forecastle."

"I saw Kester die," Daemus said, reinserting himself into the conversation while Arjun produced the clan leader's axe and Kester's heirloom sword, hidden on his back under the servant's garb. "Their chieftain killed him with an axe that I took when I avenged him at Homm Hill."

"*You* avenged him?" Ranaulf exclaimed.

"He did," Arjun said. "With a mace I trained him to use."

Mercia turned to walk away in disgust, but then she stopped herself. She called for Ellissio, who returned within seconds.

"Yes, my lady?"

"You brought these fools to me," Mercia said. "Why do you believe their story?"

Ellissio hustled down the staircase and bowed, handing Mercia the handwritten scroll he'd received from Faux the night before. Ranaulf read the scroll over Mercia's shoulder as Daemus looked on.

Mercia's hands trembled as she tried to hide her true feelings for Kester's demise. Always the black sheep, Kester was the source of many of the Alarics' political problems in Castleshire. Mercia had fumbled her relationship with him as much as she had with Daemus. But in the end, family was family.

"It's Kester's seal and handwriting," Ranaulf conceded as he slumped onto a bench. Mercia stepped over to hug her husband. The two shared a mutual moment of grief that allowed Daemus to join them in their sorrow.

"Curse you, Kester," Mercia said, breaking her silence. Daemus backed away from her. "Ellissio, take Master Daemus to his room. I'll be up shortly to speak to him in private."

Mercia watched as Daemus turned to Ellissio and the two shared a mutual look of confusion.

Mercia turned back to the group and continued, "Please wait here until my husband and I have a chance to discuss this matter in private. There's much to mull over."

"Of course," Arjun said.

"Thank you," Mercia replied. "I'll have the servants bring you water and breakfast while you wait."

Mercia and Ranaulf left the foyer and headed deeper into the house. Once they were out of earshot of their visitors, Mercia grabbed a guard by the elbow.

"Don't let them leave," she said. "And quietly summon the jailer."

MARQUISS DAULDON AND BLUE Conney were sharing swigs from a wineskin Marquiss had purchased the night before at the Halo. They stood in the early morning haze, enjoying the errand Faux had asked them to tackle. They were used to retracing their tracks, but sweeping the woods was pleasant at this time of year and seemed like a far better chore than facing the blue bloods in the city.

"This wine is piss," Blue said, taking another swig. "Did you purposefully pick the worst?"

"If you don't like it, Blue, just hand it back," Marquiss said, smiling and reaching for the wineskin.

Blue took two more swigs and handed the skin back to Marquiss.

"Piss enough to leave it half empty, eh?"

The two laughed aloud and entered the woodlands on their

steeds. The first mile of the trek went as planned. There were no signs of spies or pursuers, and that meant more time to themselves.

They soon came upon a narrowing stretch of road with a dogleg turn to the west. The foliage clung to the branches, obscuring the trail as it wound through the thicker trees. Jericho stopped and began to growl.

"What's the matter with your dog, Conney?" Marquiss asked. "That beast can't be hungry again."

"Shh," Conney whispered. The springheel raised his arm toward Marquiss, his face contorted in alarm.

They both turned and looked ahead, seeing only the meandering road, but they heard something move. Something big.

Marquiss's horse neighed and stopped dead in the road.

"What are those elven ears hearin'?" Conney asked, as softly as a springheel could.

"It's what they aren't," Marquiss whispered in return.

Conney understood. The sound of silence was pervasive. No birds chirped; no game ran. The two waited, looking ahead at the curve. This was no tracker or mercenary. The smell of carrion invaded their nostrils, even from afar.

A hulking figure emerged from behind the overgrowth. It was taller on foot than Marquiss was on his horse. The beast lumbered around the bend, its skull and antlers turning toward them. With a thud that shook the leaves from the trees, it dropped heavily onto all fours. Its muscles rippled in anticipation of the chase.

"By the Ancients, what *is* that?" Marquiss managed, daring but a second's glance at Conney. He drew his sword from his scabbard and froze.

"Turn, turn, turn!" Blue yelled, and Jericho responded. Both men spun around and pressed their steeds into action.

The war dog took off like a bolt of lightning, nearly tossing its rider. Conney held his saddle and glanced over his shoulder to see that the monster had leapt to the chase and had narrowed the gap in seconds.

"Split up!" Marquiss yelled to Blue, knowing the fiend could only follow one of them. Conney darted left and into the underbrush with Jericho. Marquiss stayed on the path, his horse's strides now putting distance between them.

The Antlered Man clawked in protest and rambled after Conney, chasing him deeper into the woods. The springheel now had the advantage.

"Run!" Blue commanded, and the war dog knew what to do. The hound darted through the briars and brambles, making him and his rider small. They crested a low hill and used the momentum from the slope to propel themselves down the embankment and across a crooked run of a creek.

Jericho jumped the distance, rider and all, and scampered again to the left, up the other side of the hill.

The Antlered Man maintained its pursuit but stumbled down the hill, turning its slip into a leap. It landed on the other side of the creek, but the beast had lost its momentum and glared up the hill at the mounted dog.

The pair backtracked, circling the crest, and baiting the creature to pursue them. The Antlered Man followed, gurgling and clawking all the way to the crest.

"Now!" Conney yelled at the hound, and the two charged at the Antlered Man, who froze, seemingly dumbfounded at the move.

Conney drew his daggers and Jericho lowered his armored head. The two raced for the creature's legs.

The Antlered Man tried to turn but was too late. The dog lowered his bullish head and rammed their enemy's goat-like legs while Blue's blades sliced into its flesh. The force of the attack felled the Antlered Man, knocking it from its feet and sending it tumbling down the hill.

Conney stopped the war dog at the crest and waved his daggers in the air. The creature grasped futilely at the sprawling leaves and slid to the bottom in a rage.

"You bleed!" Conney yelled into the valley. He looked at his blades for a moment. They were coated in dull, white blood that didn't drip, but instead held its place like a paste on the steel.

Blue tossed the ruined knives to the ground and grabbed Jericho's collar, pushing him to full pace. He resisted every barbaric urge to ride down the hill to glory. He'd found the beast from Daemus's nightmares. Glory could wait.

GHYRR RUGALIS RODE ALONE, cutting his way through the windstorms of the Killean Desolates. Half blinded by the dustbowl conditions and deafened by the ceaseless winds, Ghyrr kept his head low and his face covered with the mask that he'd bought back in Krahe. The mask, which consisted of two lenses of transparent glass sewn together into a leather strap, afforded his eyes a respite. Even so, he had to use his gloves every few minutes to clear the lenses of the dust that was collecting on their surface.

"Idiots," he murmured to himself. "They invent a device to cover your eyes, but nothing to deafen the winds."

He'd had to improvise something himself, plugging his ears with material torn from his scarf. The fabric only lasted for a few hours in the harsh conditions, often blowing from his ears in the wind. Ghyrr guessed that he'd be down to his undergarments by the time he reached Spine Castle. All the rogue could hear was the billowing of the wind across the arid plains and the unrelenting slapping of his tattered scarf.

"How could anything live in this?" he muttered.

Ghyrr had traversed part of the Killean Desolates before, but nothing like this. The Desolates extended from the easternmost part of Foghaven Vale into barren, nearly uninhabitable badlands. The Desolates mostly knew only two seasons, winter and summer. Spring and autumn lasted a mere few weeks between them. In the winter, the Desolates became tundras of snowdrifts and ice storms. In the summer, they suffered from intolerable heat and long droughts. Ghyrr was traveling in what was technically late autumn, but it felt more like a sweltering desert.

He'd pressed on for several days since leaving Dragon Ridge, resting inside caves or finding reprieve from the elements inside canyons. He fed his horse when it was safe and hoarded their water, the lifeblood of the trip. He didn't dare light a fire at night, so he ate only dry rations. Rugalis was a veteran of many trails, and this had to be the worst. He understood why Graytorris had sought solitude in a place like this. No one would dare to look for him here.

On the evening of the fifth day, Ghyrr found a small, uninhabited cave that offered some shelter. He set up camp as best he could and bedded down for the night. Then he saw a shadow move outside the cave.

He swiftly unsheathed his sword and spun to face whatever terror awaited him. Instead of a Killean yeti, he saw a comely woman emerging from the shadowy entrance of the cave. She wore neither armor nor protection from the elements, and her exposed face and hands appeared no worse the wear for it.

"Friend or foe?" Ghyrr demanded, pointing at her with his blade.

"Neither," the woman replied.

Ghyrr sized her up. She held no weapons, and her mere appearance suggested she was a sorceress of some type. He closed the distance between them with a few steps, knowing it would take her precious seconds to conjure a spell and hoping that his blade would be faster if she tried. But the woman didn't move to defend herself.

"Is this your shelter?" he asked.

"No," she replied, taking a couple of steps toward his sword until it was only inches from her face. Ghyrr couldn't help noticing her beauty. Her dark eyes and hair were unfettered by the winds, and her only weapon appeared to be a sickle that hung at her side.

"Why are you here?" he asked, still not lowering his weapon.

"I believe you have something for me, Ghyrr Rugalis," she said. "And I have something for you in return."

"Did Graytorris send you?" Ghyrr asked, already knowing the answer.

"Yes," she replied. "I am Zinzi of the Moor Bog."

"I wasn't expecting you," he said, sheathing his blade.

"What were you expecting?"

"A Killean yeti," Ghyrr offered bluntly. "Or someone… older."

"I'm much older than you think, Rugalis," she said, smiling sweetly. "Have you brought something for me?"

Ghyrr had heard stories of Zinzi's dealings in Dragon Ridge since he was a child, and yet here she stood, untouched by age. She must have been protecting her youth with her magic. His sword would be no good, and he knew it. In an empty gesture, he returned it to his scabbard and opened his saddle bag to retrieve the package.

"Here," he said, approaching her cautiously and handing it over to her. "From my sovereign, my lady."

Ghyrr bowed slightly and stepped back to allow her to examine it as she took it gently from his outstretched hands. She slowly unwrapped the tetrine's horn and held it in her palm, balancing it like a magic wand.

Ghyrr had no idea what the horn could do, but he took a couple of cautious steps back to give her room. She chuckled and lowered the tip of the horn.

"I'm not going to hurt you, Rugalis," she mocked. "I've never held one of these in my hand before."

"Neither have I," the rogue said. "Is it a wand of sorts? A weapon?"

"Careful," Zinzi cautioned. "You shouldn't ask questions that you don't want the answers to. No, it's not a wand, but it could be used as one in the hands of the right person. But my master has something very different in mind..."

CHAPTER TWENTY-FIVE

"Books are as useful to the unwise
as a mirror is to the blind."
—Edict of The Divine Protectorate of Erud

NASYR PEERED THROUGH HER telescope at the distant stars, hoping for a sign from Erud. To her chagrin, no such harbingers rode the constellations, save for a distant shower of shooting stars that danced on the horizon.

Resigned to another day bereft of divination, Nasyr crossed the inner sanctum and approached *The Tome of Enlightenment*. With reticence, she stepped to the Tome and entered a brief reverie, praying for Erud to enlighten her. After a few patient moments, the Tome started glowing for the first time in weeks. A true vision appeared, the pages telling the story of a magical mirror affixed to a dark, weathered wall in the ruins of a stone keep.

Nasyr studied the scene intently, her blood racing in anticipation of an augury from Erud. There was something different this time. She could feel a presence with a different hale emanating from the great book. A mirror?

It was then that the weight of the vision struck her. The mirror looked familiar, almost too familiar. She glanced back across the inner sanctum and saw that its twin was affixed to the wall. It was Graytorris's mirror, Dromofangare. The mirror she'd told Daemus and Kester about weeks before.

She quickly turned to First Keeper Amoss, who was watching her from the far doorway.

"Keeper Amoss," she said in her usual stoic tone. "The Tome has shown us a mirror this evening. One that could lead us to Graytorris. We must summon First Keeper Jhodever. He's our best hand at catoptromancy."

"He's far away," Amoss replied. "He still serves the Barony of Foghaven Vale. Do we have an alternative in Solemnity? We have several strong specularii and scryers on campus."

"Yes, of course," Naysr said. "Bring me Precept Jochem. He's usually skulking around the library stacks at this time of night."

"As you wish," Amoss said, a resolute look upon his face. He departed the inner sanctum to find the bibliophile Jochem, certain he was already lost in his evening's studies.

A few moments passed and Nasyr continued to stare at the vision depicted in the Tome. What was Erud trying to say? Then a moment of lucidity seized her every sense, but it was too late to stop the scene that was about to unfold. Behind her, she felt a magical hale emanating from Dromofangare on the wall across the room. Terror gripped her, and she turned to see a figure emerging from the glowing surface.

Graytorris materialized in her inner sanctum, returning to the scene of his blasphemy from nearly two decades ago. Nasyr stared at the grisly figure, his face smeared in red and his arms balancing his contorted frame on an obsidian staff. His sickening smile petrified her, and she hoped with everything she had that this was a vision from Erud and not the man himself.

The gangly intruder turned her way as she stumbled backward into the altar. His smile widened.

"Nasyr, my Great Keeper," Graytorris mocked, bowing derisively. "I've returned."

"Come no closer," Nasyr warned, trying desperately to gather her thoughts. "You're not welcome in these hallowed halls. Don't forget the curse that befell you the last time you stepped foot in this most sacred of chambers."

Graytorris paused for a second and then continued his approach.

"Let me remind you, Great Keeper, of one of the lessons I learned from reading *The the Tome of Enlightenment* on that dreaded night," he said. "The Tome won't reveal the reader's own future, but it will tell the tale of others."

Nasyr winced as Graytorris approached her and the Tome she guarded.

"These are your final moments, Great Keeper," he said with a toothy snarl. "Use them wisely."

"*Pida paikallan murskaus,*" Graytorris evoked in the conjurer's tongue, and with a quick wave of his obsidian staff, a dark blast of magical energy appeared and engulfed Nasyr. A swirling force descended from the hale and swept her up into the air, rendering her defenseless. She levitated a few feet from the ground. The more she struggled against the force, the tighter it gripped her.

Nasyr struggled to speak, feeling her lungs slowly crushed.

"Graytorris!" she cried. "You're mad!"

Graytorris, now only a foot from her levitating body, leaned ever closer and whispered, "That's it. Graytorris the Mad."

As the force ensnaring Nasyr grew tighter about her chest, Graytorris stepped toward his quarry, lecturing her the way she'd lectured him on that fateful night.

"I was your friend," he said, his demeanor calm and deliberate. "I needed you. Yet you and our sect had forsaken me. I asked Erud for guidance. Again, I was forsaken, and then I was punished."

"You violated our greatest edict," Nasyr replied, struggling to make herself heard. "You fell of your own accord."

Graytorris stepped away from Nasyr and made his way over to the glowing Tome of Enlightenment behind her. Helpless to stop him, she could only watch the inevitable.

"Please... don't..." she moaned pitifully, in a final attempt to stop the fallen Keeper. She watched in dread as the man lifted the Tome from its resting place. He cackled and then slammed the Tome shut.

With the Tome sealed, the ever-present light at the top of the cathedral slowly died, its beaming pillar smothered in vengeance. Nasyr's fading sight adjusted to the darkness, a tear slipping down her cheek.

"Fear not, Great Keeper, for this is almost over," Graytorris said, stepping back to her side. "I just require two more items from you."

Placing the staff and Tome on the ground, Graytorris extended a hand across the Great Keeper's face, searching blindly for her eyes. He produced a sharp dagger from the folds of his robe and held it inches from her face for her to see.

Nasyr tried to cry for help, but Graytorris stopped her feeble lamenting by pressing his hand against her mouth and mercilessly digging into her eyesockets with his blade. She convulsed in pain, trying to escape, but Graytorris's grip was too strong. He slowly finished his fiendish work, cutting the seer's eyes from her skull and stashing them gently in a velvet purse that hung at his side.

As the bloody woman fought through the pain, she sensed Graytorris moving away from her, his vengeance near complete. She heard his staff clacking with every step he took back toward the magical mirror.

Graytorris tapped his staff on the floor and Nasyr twitched one last time, the magical grip crushing her ribs and spine. Her body went limp and the force dissipated slowly, lowering her broken carcass onto the oaken pedestal that had long held *The Tome of Enlightenment*.

GRAYTORRIS STOOD IN FRONT of Dromofangare as the hale of its powerful magic warmed his face. The deed he'd dreamed of all these years was done, yet the accomplishment made him feel no better. His cursed eyes still ached. His sickened frame still wilted.

For a moment, he turned from the mirror toward Nasyr's body, contemplating the scene he was leaving behind. A woman he'd once loved as a sister lay dead by his hand. The coveted Tome rested safely in the crook of his elbow, its weight and power now belonging to him, the fallen Keeper.

Yet he felt nothing.

He turned his eyeless gaze to the heavens, pondering what views he and Nasyr might have shared together if they'd looked up through the mighty observatory's roof. He waved his staff to the stars and then tapped the obsidian rod one last time onto the floor.

"*Ithiel rom Stjerner rymdmeteoris!*" he screamed in the conjurer's tongue. Then he slowly turned and walked back through the mirror, reappearing moments later in his quarters atop Spine Castle.

"It's done," he said.

"May I watch?" Zinzi replied, stirring from the shadows of his room. He didn't respond, but the mirror stayed aglow with magic, allowing her a perfect view of the spectacle to come.

He couldn't see the falling stars, but Zinzi's gasps told the story. Over his turned shoulder, the mirror held the images of streaking balls of flame—stars that Nasyr had watched earlier—showering chaos on Solemnity below. One flaming star streaked across the horizon and rammed into the observatory, decapitating the Cathedral of the Watchful Eye and spraying fiery rubble in all directions.

FIRST KEEPER AMOSS WAS hustling across the campus to the library, on his way to find Precept Jochem. At his age, he watched his feet when he walked. His sandals and his weight weren't ideal for navigating the loose cobblestone walkways that led from building to building, especially at night.

He slowed briefly to exchange pleasantries with several deacons on the way, and as they finished their brief encounter, he noticed that the sky above them was slowly darkening.

He averted his gaze from his feet and turned upward. He and the others observed the cathedral's ever watchful eye dim and finally extinguish. A hush fell over the campus as Keepers from all corners noticed the light of Erud disappearing.

The campus went dark save for several small, ensconced lanterns that lit the way between buildings and the flickering of candlelight through windows. The deacons exchanged glances with Amoss, an unspoken apprehension passing between them.

Then a series of flaming stars lit up the darkness and descended upon the campus. He darted for the doors of the library, turning to guide the nearby deacons to cover. He watched as the first meteor struck the heart of the grounds, exploding in a spray of white heat. After the light dimmed, he saw that the deacons he'd spoken to seconds earlier were no more.

Amoss spun around to look for shelter, but nowhere appeared safe from the incoming swarm. As he made it to the archway to the library, he ducked behind a stone pillar, hoping it would provide some protection. He felt the temperature around him rise as one meteor after another struck home. He closed his eyes for a second and instinctively pulled his hood over his face to stop the heat from boiling the sweat on his skin.

Cries for help and the screams of the dying rose around him, but he could only hide and pray. As the shower of flames halted for a moment, Amoss turned back to the campus to survey the damage and watched as the last falling star collided with the top of the Cathedral of the Watchful Eye, sending a deluge of stone cascading down the side of the tower.

"Nasyr!" he yelled, standing in the shelter of the library doorway. Mad thoughts ran through his mind as he disregarded his own safety to rush through the burning storm to the cathedral. His first thought was of his friend and mentor, Nasyr. But then a haunting and inevitable follow-up question occurred to him: *What of the Tome?*

As he reached the cathedral's entrance, he waved for a group of stunned deacons to climb the burning shrine with him in search of Nasyr. In search of reason.

FIRST KEEPER AMOSS SIFTED through the rubble on the top floor of the cathedral. He and a dozen deacons and disciples had dared to climb the long flight of stairs, not sure if the falling star had damaged the cathedral enough to cause it to collapse. If there was a chance to find and save the Great Keeper, the reward outweighed the risk.

The small group climbed the stairs, clearing rubble and dodging fires as they went. The central elevator would have taken them to the observatory in minutes, but it was too risky to ride it.

When they finished their ascent, they found the observatory in ruin. The roof of the once-glorious tower had been destroyed. The stone floor and several buttresses were miraculously intact, though they were covered with fiery debris. The proud observatory, the crown jewel of the Cathedral of the Watchful Eye, was lost. The hall, used for centuries by generations of star-charting Keepers, stood no more. Amoss found the top floor exposed to the elements like a collapsed tower in an abandoned castle.

"First Keeper!"

Amoss turned to a deacon behind him and saw that their sacred tree obelisk, the pedestal which held *The Tome of*

Enlightenment, remained miraculously unharmed.

Amoss made his way carefully over to the obelisk where the others had gathered. Several of his supplicants prayed aloud to Erud while others searched the nearby debris for signs of the Great Keeper.

The First Keeper touched the sacred pedestal, just to make sure it was there. The polished stump had survived the tragedy and was no worse for wear, but the Tome was gone.

"It's a sign from Erud," Amoss said. "The survival of the tree obelisk portends of good fortune. A phoenix rising from the ashes of the Watchful Eye, perhaps."

"Over here!" Deaconess Humlebaek shouted.

Amoss rushed over to see what the matter was. As he jogged toward the noise, Deaconess Humlebaek dropped to her knees, her hands folded, while two other sisters stood frozen in horror. He rounded a fallen pillar and saw the source of their dismay.

Nasyr's body lay amongst the ruins, twisted from the carnage. Amoss's heart sank and his hands shook as he approached her corpse. A wellspring of grief and love overtook him, and the man fell to his knees beside her. Tears flowed freely from his eyes as he slowly and carefully cleared her body from the stone.

"Help me with this, Caspar," Amoss said, emotion pouring from his swollen throat. He and Daemus's old roommate, Caspar Luthic, heaved a small but weighty stone from on top of her, uncovering her face. Sorrow turned to horror at their grisly discovery. Caspar lurched to the side and dry heaved at the ghastly sight.

"Dear Nasyr," Amoss muttered, covering his mouth with his hand.

Her eyeless countenance, frozen in the moment of her death, revealed the terror of her last seconds. Humlebaek joined the two Keepers and knelt amidst the fallen stone, looking at the Great Keeper's body.

"How?" Amoss asked of the Ancients, looking up at the stars. "Why?"

"Something is amiss, First Keeper," Humlebaek said. Amoss lowered his teary eyes and looked squarely at her. "Her eyes."

Amoss turned to look at her face, but Caspar continued to look away.

"Look here," Deaconess Humlebaek remarked. "There's damage to her skull from the fallen pillar, but there are incisions here. No stone cuts eyes from a body."

Amoss tilted to inspect his dead friend and accepted her theory. Incisions from a sharp object—a knife, perhaps—had removed the eyes from her face.

Amoss wrenched his head back. This discovery washed over him for a few moments and then his grief turned into rage.

"Brothers and sisters," he said, his voice as stout as ever, "our Great Keeper has been murdered. These falling stars were no accident, no sign from Erud. They were an attack on the Cathedral of the Watchful Eye."

"How do you know, First Keeper?" Danton Hague asked. He was the captain of the Knights of the Maelstrom, and his mere presence had steadied the others.

"Deaconess Humlebaek pointed out the incisions," Amoss replied. "Her eyes were taken. They were cut from her."

The group gasped at the torturous thought. The young warrior of faith stepped toward the First Keeper, helping him to his feet.

"Thank you, Captain," Amoss said, resting his hand on Hague's armored shoulder. "My old bones aren't as forgiving as they once were."

"What do you need of me and my knights?" Hague asked. The Knights of the Maelstrom were a small but skilled group of crusaders, templars to their faith and willing to defend the Keepers to the death.

"I need you and your knights to fly to the four corners of Warminster," the First Keeper replied. "Inform the leaders and First Keepers of the realm of what's transpired here tonight. Our Keepers are blind with the closing of the Great Tome and our sect needs to recover it at all costs. Command every Keeper, every Disciple of the Watch, and every Deacon of Erud to find Graytorris. We're at war. No one is safe."

"Of course, First Keeper. We'll flood the skies with our hippogryphs and deliver the word."

"One more thing, Captain," Amoss said. "I need you to personally fly to Castleshire and find Daemus Alaric..He may be our last connection to Erud."

"What should I do when I find him?"

"He'll know," Amoss said.

DANTON HAGUE GATHERED HIS knights in the stables, saddling their gryphs and preparing to depart into the night sky. Hague stood in front of the full contingent of the Knights of the Maelstrom, who rarely gathered in such a group.

"Knights," Hague began, "we carry with us the grim news of what happened here. We fly tonight to all the kingdoms of the realm to tell them a tale of tragedy and treachery. The leaders of Warminster have depended on Erud's visions since the time of the Ancients. We must not fail in our flights. Return here with news once you've met with Warminster's First Keepers, kings and queens. May Erud grant you wisdom on your journeys."

He paused for a moment, taking time to look at each of them, as if enunciating the urgency through his gaze. Finally, he stepped forward, held his arm aloft, and shouted, "To the skies!"

CHAPTER TWENTY-SIX

"I'll never board a ship that doesn't sail fast,
for I intend to sail into harm's way."
—Admiral Valerick LaBrecque

THREE UNEVENTFUL DAYS HAD passed since the battle with the *Phantom*, and *Doom's Wake* had made good progress toward the safety of Castleshire's port. Admiral LaBrecque stood in silence at the helm, pondering the next moves in his cat-and-mouse game with his new rival. The *Phantom* was still out there somewhere.

He and his mariners had crippled the enemy's ship, but the *Wake* was damaged and barely seaworthy. Thanks to the skills of his carpenters and crew, LaBrecque had pressed his luck by chancing a run into the open seas. He hoped the captain of the brigantine would be baited into following the simple charts, staying to the coastline and searching there for his wounded prey.

But if they did pursue them into the open seas, LaBrecque knew he had little chance. They had more weapons and a bigger crew, and they also had a battle mage. Addilyn could counter some of his spells, but naval wizards were trained in seafaring tactics and the use of offensive magic. The brigantine was also equipped with long oars on each side, making it more maneuverable than LaBrecque's barque. The *Wake* was light and fast with a shallow draft, but it was outclassed by the *Phantom*.

LaBrecque didn't care. He knew what the *Wake* could do. He'd outmaneuvered man-o-wars before, and he'd run down faster sloops and emerged victorious against greater odds than these. But the enemy captain was no fool, and he was well-equipped and better prepared. The *Wake* had sailed into

Thronehelm for a party, not a fight. Even the new munitions and provisions they'd taken on did little to prepare the *Wake* for combat on the high seas. LaBrecque was learning a lesson he wouldn't soon forget.

"Admiral," Ritter said, pulling LaBrecque back from his thoughts. "You asked for me?"

"Ah, yes, Valkeneer," LaBrecque replied. "We've lightened our load, but the damage to *Doom's Wake* has slowed us considerably. Once our enemy makes repairs, which they probably already have, they'll be on our tail with all the speed they can muster."

"Seems likely," Ritter replied.

"You're a tracker, are you not?" LaBrecque said. "You must know that the prey never escapes until the hunter forfeits the hunt. I'm ready for the trick that we discussed a few days back."

"Do you think we'll need it?" Ritter asked.

"If their captain is worth his or her salt, we will," LaBrecque replied, putting his hand on the young Longmarcher's shoulder. "I've doubled the watch at night, and we only have two days until we reach Castleshire. If they're going to make their move, they'll do it soon. They still have their wizardry. We must take that advantage away from them."

"Of course, Admiral," Ritter replied. He dispatched Storm high into the air, searching through the dusk skies for traces of an invisible enemy. Storm circled above as Ritter communed with the bird and watched from a distance through his eyes.

Their plan was to watch for mysterious wakes in the waves, looking not for a boat but for the traces of one. Ritter understood the concept and had employed similar tactics when trying to cover his own tracks in the woods. Doing it from several hundred feet at night through the eyes of a falcon was a different story. Ritter hoped that the wake of an approaching ship, albeit an invisible one, would still be too big to miss.

SEVERAL HOURS HAD PASSED, and Addilyn was watching Ritter from afar. His trance with Storm was fascinating to behold, but she knew he was neither here nor there, stuck somewhere between in a shared consciousness with the war falcon.

Her quiet spying on the Longmarcher went unnoticed by Ritter but not by Jessamy, who soon joined her at the starboard rail, staying away from the chatter of the crew and the nobles.

"My princess," Jessamy said, "we're nearly there."

"Don't curse us, Jessamy," Addilyn said with a half-smile. "I'll relax when we get to the city of Castleshire and not a moment before." She turned to rest her back against the rail and looked away from Ritter to avoid arousing Jessamy's suspicions.

"My lady, I wasn't talking about our voyage," Jessamy said, her eyes leading Addilyn back to the young noble whose consciousness was high in the skies above. "I was talking about your time with Sir Ritter. Once we reach the city, he'll return to his duties in Valkeneer, and you'll attend to yours as princess and future coronelle of the Vermilion nation."

"Jessamy," Addilyn said, "you know I can't—"

"He's not fully a Raven elf," Jessamy continued, "but he shares our blood. It's in our nature to obsess about all matters, great and small. It's what drives the Raven elves to perfect their chosen crafts, regardless of the artform."

"I don't think Ritter possesses such a trait," Addilyn said. "His skill as an archer rivals the best Vermilion."

"It's not his mastery of the bow of which I speak," Jessamy continued. "When we Raven elves fall in love, it's for life. I know you have feelings for him, but I also know of your duties as a Vermilion... and as a princess. If you need to end this, you should do so before it truly begins. It will be for his own welfare as much as for yours. He already has eyes for you, even though he knows it cannot be."

Addilyn smiled and threw her arm around her champion.

"Thank you," she said, hugging her tight and feigning agreement. As much as the advice rang true in Addilyn's ears, she couldn't stop her growing feelings for the knight from the borderlands.

AS NIGHT FELL, THE boredom on the deck of *Doom's Wake* ended abruptly. Storm's hawkish vision pierced the night sky as he watched an unnatural parting in the waves. Ritter awoke from his malaise, witnessing the wake of a large object tacking its way toward them on the open seas.

Ritter watched the invisible vessel tell its tale, creating a massive disturbance downstream. The *Phantom* had caught the *Wake*, but this time they were prepared.

With a silent signal, Ritter warned the admiral and LaBrecque set his mariners in motion. The crew moved quietly, maintaining the element of surprise as they dumped LaBrecque's gift to the king overboard. He didn't think Godwin would mind.

It left a floating plume of silver flake spreading wide across the water behind them. Ritter and Addilyn climbed to the crow's nest and waited for the signal.

"Be careful," Jessamy whispered to her princess in the Melexian tongue.

Addilyn didn't respond, concentrating on the task at hand.

When they reached the nest atop the mainmast, they were alone. They squeezed into the bucket, first Ritter then Addilyn. The crow's nest on the *Wake* was made for one, not two. Quarters were tight, but neither seemed to mind. They both ducked, hiding themselves until LaBrecque gave the order.

Ritter knew this was no time for romance, but it was hard to suppress his growing emotions when sitting so close to her. He tried to maintain his focus, but he was flooded by warm memories of her body pressed to his during their momentary dance at the masquerade. For an instant, as they adjusted their places, he felt her breath on the back of his neck. She smiled at him, and the simple gesture sent butterflies fluttering inside him.

They could hear the whispered prayers to Nothos and Koss rising from their friends below. Their hearts raced and their adrenaline pumped. The battle would soon be upon them.

They stared at each other in anticipation of what was to come. Ritter knew the fight was nigh, but it was difficult to think of anything except for the smell of Addilyn's hair and the flecks of pink hidden in the deep crimson of her eyes.

They leaned closer, their elven ears picking up the rushing of the waves against the *Phantom*. They had seconds left to themselves, and Ritter's eyes drifted to Addilyn's lips. She reached out with her hand and placed it on his cheek. Ritter leaned in, his eyes finding hers. She tilted her head to meet his lips.

"Fire!" LaBrecque yelled from the deck below.

The two snapped out of their trance and into the urgency of the present. For a few seconds, Ritter fought the urge to finish the kiss, but LaBrecque's second command to fire was echoing in his ears.

Ritter drew a special arrow from his quiver, one wreathed in cheesecloth and doused in oil. Addilyn closed her eyes and cupped her hands around the arrow's tip.

"*Eldr wyrr orr,*" she whispered in the conjurer's tongue.

A fire sprung from her fingers and leapt onto the shaft of the arrow. Ritter leaned from the nest and aimed at the expanding plume behind them. He released the bowstring and the arrow sailed for its explosive target.

THE PHANTOM SAILED INTO attack position. Kryslexx's concealment spell had worked well in their first encounter, so Morley ordered him to employ it again. Casting his spell on a single person took little energy. Keeping a ship the size of the Phantom invisible nearly tapped the wizard.

Boatswain Macabre and Quartermaster Bronywyn stood next to the captain, as did Incanus Dru'Waith and the ever-present Skullam. The Bone elf had his bow in hand and was staring impatiently at the target.

"We've got her, Captain," Macabre mumbled through his remaining teeth. "By the hip, this time. She's ours."

Morley couldn't disagree.

Then a single flame illuminated in the night sky above them, arcing at first before turning harmlessly over and descending toward the sea.

"What was that?" Incanus asked.

Before Morley could answer, a giant shower of sparks erupted from the waves in front of them. The searing light blinded the crew and created a frothy wall of glittering explosions between the ships. Morley felt the shower of white heat cascade over him and watched Kryslexx struggle to maintain his concentration on his spell. The wizard turned and covered his eyes, and Morley knew the spell would disappear. They'd been exposed.

As the curtain of invisibility fell, the *Phantom* emerged from the cover of magic and into a glittering storm of light. The hapless vessel sailed forward into the radiant plume, illuminated from bow to stern. The crew scrambled to respond to the white fire, but the sparks served their purpose and spotlighted the *Wake's* target, turning night into day while hiding the *Wake* behind it.

A ballista bolt tore across the *Phantom*'s bow, destroying men and machines and sending splinters flying in all directions. The tip of the bolt was laced in the glowing material and set part of the deck aglow. Morley felt panic wash over his crew.

"Return fire!" he yelled, but the screams of his crew drowned out his commands. He ran from the helm toward Kryslexx, who tried to cast a spell to dowse the shower of sparks that was blinding them. Another flaming ballista bolt split the distance between the two men, who were mere yards apart. Morley averted the near miss as the flaming death swept by him, but Kryslexx wasn't as fortunate. He was struck by the streaking bolt and knocked from the *Phantom*, plummeting overboard to his death.

Morley watched the grisly scene, frozen in shock for a few moments. His fiery cloak had started to burn through and he instinctively fell to the deck and struggled to cut his cloak loose.

The advantage, Morley knew, had swung to *Doom's Wake*.

Boatswain Macabre stepped from the debris, running for the stunned Morley. "Captain, we need to sail away from these flames!"

"The sparks are harmless!" Morley yelled over the commotion. "Nothing more than a light show."

"One that exposed us," Macabre shot back. "And we can't see our target! Our crew is firing blind."

Morley knew Macabre was right, but sailing away would let the *Wake* escape again. Time was of the essence.

"Fire, Macabre!" Morley shouted. "That's an order."

Macabre turned from his captain and waved for the gunners to fire blind, as more flaming arrows and ballistae descended upon the deck.

Morley rallied his crew to stay in the fight, but experience told him they'd lost. It was time to peel off and save the ship. He couldn't win while the *Phantom* burned. He could only hope that the *Wake*, in her damaged condition, would choose to sail on, happy with bringing the odds to even.

INCANUS COULD TAKE NO more.

"Skullam, fly to that ship," he commanded in desperation. "Hide as you must. When the opportunity presents itself, sabotage her. We lost this battle before it began. At all costs, you must stop that ship from reaching Castleshire."

"It will be done, my liege," Skullam said. Then he flew invisibly from the stern, circling his way toward *Doom's Wake*.

CHAPTER TWENTY-SEVEN

"Iron Jack rings one final time for you, House Dauldon. We will mourn your victims while we mete out their justice."
—Lord Duncan Alberic of Castleshire's Regent Court

DAEMUS SAT ON THE bed that he hadn't slept in for months. Sleep was the farthest thing from his mind as he was separated from his friends. A few guards were posted at his door, but not to protect him from intruders; it was to stop him from leaving. He was a prisoner in his own home.

He could hear the mumblings of his mother and father filtering through the walls. They were still arguing about his return, somewhere in the far corners of the estate. They didn't know it, but the acoustics had bounced their conversations to him ever since they'd given him his own room when he was three.

He'd listened to them often over the years, learning their true feelings for him. His father, the more loving of the two, worried about his line of succession and the Alarics' role as founders of the city. Daemus's blindness and his dreams made him too volatile for the Caveat and its Regent Court. He wasn't "acceptable" enough for the political crowds. His mother professed her love for him, but she did little to show it. He'd beg her not to drag him to social gatherings and then would hear of her embarrassment after an incident. His powers had been unharnessed at that age, and he'd often interrupted parties with innocent predictions that annoyed, bewildered or even angered those he talked to.

He remembered saying farewell to an uncle and embracing him, knowing he'd never see him again. She'd warned him to stop, but he'd cried, nonetheless. His uncle had died within the week, but confirmations of his wild gift didn't bring forgiveness, just distrust of the kid with the white eyes.

"I don't know what to do," his father was saying. "He's here and alive, thank the Ancients, but his injury... that was of a blade's making. There must be some truth to the story. What if our son is right and Kester is truly dead? You assume our son's visions deceive him."

"He's dishonored our house by bringing those criminals here," Mercia replied. "With or without Kester. Your brother has long meant trouble for this family, and now he's put Daemus in harm's way. We did the right thing by alerting the jailer."

Daemus's ears perked up. He couldn't believe what he was hearing.

"It's wrong, my love," Ranaulf said. "If he speaks the truth, they saved his life. We should at least have offered to have Ellissio take them to Forecastle."

"And what would befall us if we were caught aiding a known criminal?" Mercia replied. "One whose executioner has been waiting these past years? Think, Ranaulf! You're on the Regent Court, for the love of the Ancients!"

Daemus felt sick. He knew that Faux had taken him there at great risk to herself, and he couldn't believe his parents could be so cold as to refuse help or sanctuary to the people who'd saved him. To Daemus, it was unconscionable.

"The guards and jailer should be here shortly," Ranaulf concluded. "They'll decide what to do. It's out of our hands now."

Daemus stood up and looked at himself in the polished mirror near his bed. His white eyes saw the reflection of the boy who'd once lived there, now turned into a man. As he stared at his own reflection, he felt his eyes grow warm, but this time, he had control of the Sight. His reflection changed, the mirrored image moving even though he himself stood still. Again, he saw Faux and Arjun reunited, as he had on the plains of the Vilchor Highgrass.

"She'll see him again," he said to himself.

A rap on the door interrupted his introspection.

"Master Daemus," Ellissio said. "May I enter?"

"Yes," Daemus replied, quickly recovering this time.

Ellissio stepped into the room with a tray of food, the breakfast that Daemus had missed.

"I'm not hungry, Ellisio," Daemus murmured.

"Come now, Master Daemus." Ellissio placed the tray on his table. "The kitchen sent this up just for you."

Daemus approached the tray with no desire to eat. As the door shut behind the chamberlain, Ellissio continued to speak loudly enough that Daemus's guards would be able to hear him.

"Master Daemus, please enjoy." Ellissio lifted the cover on the tray, revealing porridge.

"I told you, I'm not—"

"Master Daemus," Ellissio whispered, "I'm not here to force-feed you. If you want to help your friends as they helped you, you must leave here."

"How?"

Ellissio looked past Daemus, guiding his eyes to the balcony. The small overlook was barely wide enough for one person to stand on and was more ornate than practical. But there was only one floor to the flagstone patio below, and in the darkness, he could sneak by the guards.

Daemus smiled and turned to Ellissio.

"Will you help me?" Daemus asked.

"Of course," Ellissio said. "What do you need?"

Daemus thought for a moment. He knew neither Kester nor Faux would have let their friends down. Kester had sacrificed himself, and it appeared Faux and Arjun were to meet a similar fate, only rendered by a different axe. He knew what he had to do.

"I have a plan to visit Master Jaxtyn Faircloth this evening," Daemus said. "Do you mind going to the jail for me?"

ARJUN AND FAUX WERE waiting impatiently in the foyer of the Alaric estate at the request of Mercia and Ranaulf, who'd accompanied their son to his quarters. Arjun leaned against the marble wall, his arms folded while Faux paced nervously.

"We're prisoners," Faux whispered to Arjun. "In everything but name. You'd think they'd show more gratitude, more empathy."

Arjun didn't respond, and Faux knew that meant he agreed. She'd known him for too long to misread his silence.

"Should we make a run for it?" she asked, not calculating the odds.

"Us?" Arjun choked. "Against formidable house guards on high alert? Without weapons? I think that ship has sailed."

The pair heard booted footfalls from the far end of the corridor that led from the rear of the house. Faux and Arjun watched as Mercia and Ranaulf re-emerged, this time with more guards and a man wearing a cream-colored tunic emblazoned with the seal of the Regent of Castleshire. Faux's heart fell into her stomach. She remembered the uniform, one that had come for her parents a decade before.

Mercia pointed a finger at Faux and said, "She's the exiled Dauldon child, now grown to a woman."

Faux looked at Arjun, knowing that the observation was true. But there were too many guards. It was useless to resist.

"Thank you, my lady," the man said, making his way to Faux. She looked him over and thought him more a legate than a jailer. He was small, with a precisely trimmed moustache and beard that hid the age lines around his mouth and eyes. He held his flat cap in his gloved hand, and he waved it in a deep bow to Faux.

"Good evening, Lady Dauldon," the man began, false kindness oozing from his words. "I'm Zayd Nephale, Castleshire's jailer."

He showed her the symbol of his station, which consisted of a badge with a key in the center wrapped in a sleek gold chain around his neck.

"Do you know why I'm here?"

"To collect the one that got away?" Faux answered.

"Aye," Nephale said with a snide bow. "I'm under orders from Lady Amadeur Chessborough herself to arrest you and your accomplice on behalf of the Regent Court of Castleshire. I assume your companion is Captain Arjun Ezekyle."

"I am," Arjun replied.

"Excellent," Nephale said with a disdainful glance. "I was told to bring a contingent of guards, but I assume you wish to go peacefully?"

"What will become of us?" Faux asked.

"You'll be taken to the dungeons of Castleshire, where you'll await a verdict from the Regent Court. I must confiscate your possessions and chain you. Are you willing to comply without bloodshed?"

Arjun and Faux glanced at each other, and Faux nodded for them both.

"Thank you, my lady. Then consider yourselves under arrest."

He turned to his guards and waved a halfhearted glove in their direction. The guards approached and shackled the pair, then quickly searched them. One of the guards found a scroll on Faux and handed it to Nephale.

"How convenient," he said, mocking her. "I see you've brought your patents of nobility with you as proof of who you are. Unfortunately, they may lead to your death."

Faux didn't reply.

Nephale approached her and got close enough that only she could hear his whispered taunts. "Can you still hear Iron Jack ringing in your ears from long ago?"

"I've been running from death for many years," Faux replied. "I've grown weary of the chase."

Nephale smiled.

"Take them away," he ordered, polite as ever.

He bowed as Lady Dauldon left in irons.

FAUX AND ARJUN WALKED the long mile from the Alaric compound to the dungeons of Castleshire. The route took them past the old Dauldon estate, and Faux wondered if Nephale was deliberately reminding her of her family's misdeeds.

They arrived at the compound and Nephale removed the skeleton key from his badge. He unlocked the iron-banded gate that guarded the jail and led the pair underground to their cells.

"And here you are, my lady," Nephale said, loudly enough for the other prisoners in their shared cell to hear. "And my captain, of course."

He opened the cell door and removed their shackles, then ushered them inside. The cell was populated by a scummy mix of trollborn, thieves, murderers, and other ne'er-do-wells. Then he returned the key to his badge and disappeared down the long hall, his boots clicking distinctively as he left.

"I'm sorry—" Faux started, but Arjun stopped her.

"Enough of that," he said. "We're in this together. Kester warned us of the danger."

Faux turned to sit against the wall, but her self-pity was interrupted by a trollborn prisoner coming to test her and Arjun.

"So, which of you is the lady?" the trollborn asked, getting a chuckle from his cellmates. But their laughter was short-lived. Before he could utter another word, Faux punched him in the throat, leaving him gasping for air. As his hands grabbed at his neck, Faux raised her knee into his face, breaking his nose. He fell in a pathetic lump to the cell floor, unconscious.

"I'm no lady," she said.

Neither she nor Arjun would be bothered again.

FAUX'S ADRENALINE BURNED AWAY WITH the candle-wicks, and as her senses slowly returned to her, the gravity of their situation became clear.

The distant sound of a door opening echoed down the hall, followed by approaching feet. A guard came around the corner, accompanied by a man in a hooded cloak with an Alaric sigil.

"Daemus?" Faux murmured.

"Nay," the voice said, "it's Ellissio."

Faux and Arjun scrambled to the cell door and the guard took a few steps back as Ellissio slipped him a handful of copper sheaves.

"By the Ancients," Faux said. "What are you doing here?"

"We have mere moments," Ellissio said. "I can help you."

"Bail?" Arjun asked, laughing at his own suggestion.

"There's no key for your cell," Ellissio said. "At least, none that's affordable. We need to win your freedom on the floor of the Caveat, where you'll be tried."

"Bribes?

"I need a few hours," Ellissio whispered. "Master Daemus and I have a plan. Keep your wits about you until then."

"All we have is time," Faux said. "We'll wait for a miracle."

DAEMUS WAITED PATIENTLY IN his room, trying not to call attention to himself. Neither of his parents had visited him since he'd been placed under house arrest, and he preferred it that way. As dusk fell over the Alaric estate, Daemus opened the window to his small balcony and climbed over the railing. He squatted on the edge for a brief second and leapt from his quarters to the flagstones below.

His landing, muffled as it was, made a suspicious sound, so he darted for cover in his mother's garden, ducking behind a row of vined beautyberries and hanging lantern flowers. Once he was sure that the coast was clear, he hustled across the patio and around the west quarter of the house. As he snuck by the dining room, he thought of it as it should have been, full of family mourning the loss of his dear uncle and celebrating his safe return. But the hall was as cold as his greeting.

He made his way to the front gates and found the usual two guards manning the wall. In truth, the gate was more decorative than functional. It looked like a formidable barrier, but it was easy to climb. Daemus stayed in the shadows, avoiding the gate and scurrying down the length of the wall, closer to the street.

He paused and looked around, but no one was pursuing him. With a quick jump, he reached the top of the barrier and pulled himself over, then dropped slowly to the other side. Once the coast was clear, he ran from the wall and blended with the night. He was on his way to the Faircloth estate.

THE WALK TO THE Faircloth estate took Daemus fifteen minutes, and it took the same amount of time again to reach the gate. The estate was a sprawling, walled campus with the Faircloth manse at its center. The Faircloths were famous for breeding horses, so their estate was more of a ranch than a palace.

Daemus had never been to the ranch, but he'd visited it in his visions. He recalled the sprawling estate from his dreams, but he couldn't see the stables from the street. He trudged up the small hill and arrived at the gatehouse, where he was greeted by the guards.

"Hello, young lad," one of the guards said from behind the gate. "It's a little late for you to be out."

"It's an emergency," Daemus replied. "I'm here to see Master Jaxtyn Faircloth. Please tell him that Master Daemus of House Alaric is at his front door."

Daemus could tell that the man doubted him, but there was an air of recognition once he noticed his eyes.

"Of course, Master Alaric," he said, gesturing for a second guard to fetch the lord of the estate. A few moments passed and then he returned with word to let Daemus in.

"Thank you, sirs," Daemus said. He followed the first guard to the door, where he was greeted by a man who led him into the foyer.

"Master Faircloth will be down presently," the man said. "We needed to wake him to take your visit."

Daemus smiled in thanks but didn't engage with him any further. After a few moments, Daemus saw a young man approaching. He recognized him from his vision.

"Master Alaric, I'm Jaxtyn Faircloth," the man said, running his hands through his disheveled black hair. "I understand you've—"

"Faux Dauldon is back," Daemus blurted. "She's in the dungeons under the Regent Court, and it's my fault that she's there."

Daemus looked at Jaxtyn, whose blue eyes were taking the measure of him.

"Excuse me?"

"It's true," Daemus explained. "She risked her life and the lives of others to bring me home safely, and now she awaits the executioner's axe because of my family. My mother summoned the jailer. I came here to ask for your help."

"Look, Master Alaric," Jaxtyn said, "my door was only open to you because of your surname. Why should I believe you, a stranger at my door?"

"You love Faux, don't you?"

Jaxtyn leaned away from Daemus for a second, his face contorted in disbelief.

"I saw her save you," Daemus continued.

"What do you mean?"

"I'm a Keeper of the Forbidden," Daemus explained.

"If that's true, then where are your robes?" Jaxtyn asked. "And why weren't you presented to us by Disciple Delling or First Keeper Makai?"

"You were riding." Daemus ignored Jaxtyn's attempts at logic. "I saw you racing and watched her save you from a fall that would have killed you. She told you that she couldn't let the boy she loved die before he asked for her hand. You wanted to profess your love for her at that moment, but you didn't. It's a regret that you carry to this day."

Daemus watched the doubt disappear from Jaxtyn's expression. The man lowered his head and fought back the emotions that were creeping onto his face. He tried to speak, but his voice escaped him. He stuttered, managing only a few indiscernible words, then stopped.

"She saved me, too," Daemus continued. "On the Vilchor Highgrass. She and Arjun fought a clan of trollborn mercenaries that had been hired to kill me. When she risked entering the city, my mother turned her in."

Jaxtyn calmed and looked at Daemus. He let a few moments

pass between them, choosing his words wisely.

"When she grabbed me, she dropped a necklace in the field somewhere," Jaxtyn said. "Apparently, it belonged to her grandmother. It was one of the only things she had to remember her by. She gave it to Faux when she was on her deathbed."

Daemus smiled uncertainly, unsure where this was going.

"Once she realized it had been lost, she made me search for it," Jaxtyn continued. "I knew it was my fault. I think I tore it from her neck when she stopped me from falling. But we couldn't find it."

"What happened?"

"When we finally gave up, we saw your Uncle Kester waiting for us at the stables," Jaxtyn said. "We didn't know it, but he was there to smuggle Faux out of town. We barely had a chance to say goodbye before Kester rode off with her. Your uncle saved her life."

"Aye," Daemus said, "and she risked hers to save mine. My uncle is dead, killed by the same mercenaries that sought my head. Faux saved me from them."

"I'm sorry," Jaxtyn said.

"So am I," Daemus replied. "What happened to the necklace?"

"I searched the field for hours that day," Jaxtyn said, smiling. "I was angry that I was too young to help and that I'd never see Faux again. It was all so sudden. I returned to the field, determined to find the damned thing. I knew it would be the only token I'd have to remember her by."

"Did you find it?"

Jaxtyn smiled and opened his night shirt, then showed Daemus the necklace.

"I haven't taken it off since," he said. "You know, if she hadn't lost this, she wouldn't have returned late to her estate. She would have gone to the executioner's block that day with her family. I like to think of it as her grandmother reaching back from the Hall of the Ancients to save her."

"That same fate awaits her if you don't help me to stop it."

"I'll do anything," Jaxtyn said. "But first, let me find Disciple Delling. I'm sure he'll want to help you both."

CHAPTER TWENTY-EIGHT

*"May the Ancients have mercy on my
enemies, for I shall not."*
—Annals from Halifax Military Academy

THE MORNING SUN PEEKED above the horizon as *Doom's Wake* sailed for Castleshire. LaBrecque knew they'd reach the harbor within a day if the *Wake*'s crew could keep the crippled ship on its current course. But his crew was tired, injured and hungry, and they'd cast most of their food overboard to rid their hobbled vessel of excess ballast. They'd been surviving on rationed water for the last three days, and after this morning, their stores were bare.

LaBrecque stood at the helm, watching the royals appear on deck. The Thorhauers and Maeglens had each been helpful in their own way, but in the grand scheme of things, LaBrecque preferred it when they left the crew alone. They eventually made their way to LaBrecque.

"Admiral," Montgomery said. "We know we're close, but we were wondering if there's anything we can do to help. We want to pull our weight here if we can."

"My prince, while I appreciate the offer, my mariners require nothing save for some fresh water and a meal in their bellies."

"When do you think we'll arrive?" Everett asked.

"By nightfall," LaBrecque replied, "if the winds hold and we don't see our phantom friend again."

"We've seen only open seas for the last few days," Addilyn said. "Do you think we've outrun them?"

"The *Wake* is almost out of ammunition and a quarter of our mariners are dead or injured," LaBrecque said. "Worse, that captain appears to be as determined as I am. They know these facts about us, too. I don't expect them to have sailed away. We'll see them again."

The royals held their tongues. Cray's belly growled and the group laughed at their portly cousin, breaking the tension.

"Do you know who's pursuing us, Admiral?"

"Nay," LaBrecque replied.

"They're after me," the princess said, "and for that, I'm sorry."

"Nonsense, Princess," Montgomery said. "They're the ones who'll be sorry. They've attacked our kingdom, our family, and now you, our friends. We'll fight together to see this through."

"You're too kind," Addilyn replied. "If I hadn't brought the news of the tetrine to you…"

"You did it to warn us," Monty said. "The task of delivering ill omens was your burden."

"The prince is right," the admiral concluded. "The bandits, the assassins, the phantom ship… all of it. We're all targets."

"Aye," Ritter added, "as if they wanted to decapitate the kingdom in one fell swoop. Our answers await us on that phantom ship."

"Let them come, then," Addilyn said.

LaBrecque wasn't so sure.

RITTER WAITED FOR THE group to disperse and walked with Addilyn to the bow, away from prying eyes. Addilyn preempted him before he could speak.

"I wanted to thank you, Sir Ritter, for saving my life at the masquerade ball," she began. "I never had the chance to properly do so."

"And you mine," he said. "Your dagger bought me time to escape the assassin's blade. I was… outmatched."

"How are your wounds?" she asked, grabbing his arm to see for herself. It hurt, but he didn't care about the pain. He was just glad she'd found a way to touch him.

"I'll survive," he replied. "I wish I'd been quicker, for you and for Dacre."

Addilyn turned away and braced herself on the rail. She paused for a second to watch the sunrise.

"I have a question for you," she said, her eyes meeting his. "The golden palmettes that the king offered to you. Were you being sincere when you turned it down in front of the court?"

Ritter felt insulted. His face reddened in embarrassment and his voice was lost. He looked deep into her eyes, wondering why she'd asked such a question.

"Your face tells me all I need to know," she said, disarming him. "Even though you don't see yourself as a noble, that gesture was the noblest thing you could have done."

She leaned in and kissed him on the cheek.

Ritter continued to feel the emotion between them, but he could offer her nothing in front of the crew. He let her walk by him and slowly turned to watch her disappear below deck. His heart told him to follow, but his instincts held him fast.

The ever-present Jessamy shot him a glance that would have stopped a raging dragon it its tracks before she turned to follow her ward below. He strained a smile and half-hearted wave, but the gesture went unreturned.

He looked back to the sea, staring intently at the horizon.

INCANUS SPENT MOST OF his time on the *Phantom* below deck, staying away from the sun when he could and bearing it when he had to. He'd found himself a small corner of the ship near the bilge that offered privacy, as no one dared to brave the smell. He sat meticulously sharpening his blades and checking his arrows, knowing their last chance to attack the *Wake* was coming.

"Dru'Waith," Macabre yelled from topside. "Your pet has returned."

Incanus smiled and put down his whetstone. He knew that if Skullam was back, it was time. He climbed the stairs to find Skullam perched on a rail near Morley and Macabre.

"What do you have for us?" Morley asked, once Incanus had joined them. "What news of the *Wake*?"

"They're just in front of us, over the horizon," Skullam said, pointing to an improvised sea chart. "The Seawolf believes they'll reach the harbor by nightfall."

"What of their condition?"

"They're limping along," the imp remarked. "They're almost out of bolts for their ballistae and they're still taking on water, despite the best efforts of their mariners."

"What of the crew?" Macabre interjected.

"Twenty dead, with the same number nursing wounds."

"And LaBrecque?" Morley inquired.

"Steady," Skullam replied.

"What's the plan, Captain?" Macabre asked.

"They're sailing for the harbor," Morley began, "and from what the imp tells us, we have a shot at catching them by surprise."

"How so?" Macabre asked.

"These waters hide a channel to the west of the harbor," Morley said. "One with friendlier winds but deadlier shores. I've used it many times to sneak in and out of the bay while I was banished. I'll wager that LaBrecque doesn't know about it. We can use the channel to pass them."

"Are you sure, Captain?" Macabre asked.

"Yes." Morley drew an invisible line across the map with his finger. "The sea will move us past them here. We should gain a good hour on them. They'll sail in at the mouth of the bay, and we can hide along the western shores of Lighthouse

Island. With the cover of darkness and the right signal from Skullam, we can catch them before they make the safety of the harbor."

"What do you need me to do, my lord?" Skullam asked.

"Return to the vessel unseen," Morley said. "Then disable their rudder as Macabre has shown you so that they can only sail straight."

"Is that what we want?" Incanus asked. "Another sea battle between two crippled ships?"

"We must stop them from reaching the shore," Morley said. "If they land, they'll have countless allies. The battle must take place in open water if we're to win it."

"How will we escape when it's over?" Macabre asked.

"We won't," Morley replied.

LABRECQUE AND HIS CREW worked feverishly to get everything they could out of the *Wake*, and by nightfall, they'd made the bend into the cape. They could see the lights of Castleshire in the distance. In the foreground, the spectacular Lighthouse Inn stared back at them like a one-eyed beacon of salvation. A cheer rose from the crew, and LaBrecque couldn't hide a smile.

"Admiral," Addilyn said, approaching him at the helm. "I wanted to thank you—"

The distinct grinding of metal on wood stopped Addilyn from completing the thought. LaBrecque looked to Sailing Mistress Tamsyn, who'd already started to run to the stern, following the sound.

"Tamsyn?" LaBrecque yelled, but before she could respond, another louder and more ominous cracking of wood echoed throughout the *Wake* from deep below. Tamsyn pointed to a crew member, who climbed into a rope swing to inspect the matter.

LaBrecque made his way astern and the crew began to follow as Tamsyn slowly lowered the crewman. He nearly hit the surface of the water.

"What do you see, Aurigo?"

"The rudder," he yelled back in desperation. "She's shot."

"How so?" LaBrecque hollered.

"Sabotage!" Aurigo replied. "She's jammed up, Admiral. I can't fix her in the dark!"

Tamsyn and LaBrecque headed back to the helm with Addilyn trailing behind them. The wheel wouldn't respond.

"We can't turn, Admiral!" Tamsyn exclaimed.

"We're gonna sail right into Lighthouse Island."

"We're too close to slow," Tamsyn said. "We could lower the sails… drop anchor?"

Before LaBrecque could respond, a shrill voice from the crow's nest yelled, "Ahoy! Ahoy!"

All heads on deck turned to see the *Phantom* emerging from the darkness in the distance. The privateer was turning toward them, revealing itself from an inlet to the west.

"What are they doing?" Tamsyn yelled. "They'll sink us both."

"Well, Princess," LaBrecque said. "Your wish has been granted. It looks like you'll have a chance to test your steel."

Addilyn looked at the dark vessel as it sailed toward them. The collision was inevitable. Jessamy stood beside her, sword already drawn.

MORLEY HAD TIMED THE arrival impeccably. The *Phantom* had emerged from the darkness and rammed the port side of the *Wake*. The two enemies smashed together, rocking both vessels and sending sailors tumbling overboard.

The roar of the marauders hung over the deck of the *Wake* as the privateers climbed aboard, daggers and broadswords flashing in the glow of the nearby lighthouse. The ships drifted toward the shoals, both listing and taking on water, but that didn't stop either side. The crews wanted to see the whites of their opponents' eyes.

Incanus let the mob of eager sailors jump ahead of him. He slid to the bow of the *Phantom*, standing above the fracas and observing the deck. He scanned for his Vermilion target but spotted a different foe that he couldn't pass up. He jumped to the deck of the *Wake*, then filtered through the crowd toward Everett Thorhauer.

LABRECQUE GRITTED HIS TEETH and drew his cutlass, slashing at the first enemy sailor to approach him. He turned to look to the mass of men flooding onto his deck and knew that his crew was outnumbered.

"Tamsyn," he said calmly, pointing his cutlass to a mass of oncoming pirates.

She nodded and took a small contingent of mariners with her to engage them.

Then LaBrecque turned to see Montgomery and Cray standing next to him. "Gentlemen, with me."

The prince and the master of Hunter's Manor trailed him as he waded into the first wave. Montgomery's sword was bloodied within seconds. LaBrecque parried an onrushing pirate, and his pirouette sent the hapless man stumbling by to meet Monty's steel on the other side. Then Montgomery stepped into the gap and defended LaBrecque's back by engaging with two other sailors.

Cray, not the best of warriors, took a different approach. He waited patiently for LaBrecque to cut through the crowd and grabbed a belaying pin on his way by. He tossed the pin at a marauder, catching him off guard, and then lunged in, stabbing the man in the stomach. The bloody pirate fell to the deck, grabbing at his wound as Cray walked by and finished him off with a flick of his sword.

SKULLAM SKULKED AROUND THE deck, looking for his target. Incanus had given him orders to find Ritter and take him from the fight. Ritter was a wild card with his bow, and one that Incanus didn't want interfering with his hunt.

He flew to the helm, holding his invisibility and surveying the scene. He waited patiently for his moment, watching enemy after enemy pass him by. He knew that as soon as he attacked, he'd lose his concentration, the invisibility would be dispelled, and he'd forfeit the advantage of surprise.

Ritter was nowhere to be found.

Skullam watched a man fall, a feathered arrow sticking from his chest. Then another fell, followed by another. He didn't hear the flight of the arrows, but he saw their effect. He looked up to see his target leaning from the crow's nest, peppering pirates from afar. He pushed off with his feet and ascended as quietly as possible.

THE CHAOS ON DECK made it hard for Joferian and Talath to stick with the princes, and after a throng of mariners split them apart, the two guarded each other's backs like they'd done thousands of times back in Halifax. They pressed forward into the fray.

They found themselves forced against the starboard rail, slowly fighting their way to the bow. It was difficult for them to identify rank, so anyone unfamiliar was a target. Joferian slashed out to create a gap for the two to break free, and they found some space just a few paces ahead.

"Well, don't you look special in your shiny armor?"

The voice rang out above the roar of battle, and Joferian and Talath turned to see a group of pirates led by a purplish trollborn with a cutlass in his hand. Joferian grunted at the group and spun, his sword thrusting outward from his short guard posture and inviting them in. The trollborn smiled, a single fang protruding from his mouth, and steel met steel.

Talath split from Joferian, guarding his flank while engaging two of the pirates. His swordmanship was too much for the pirates, and with a slash combined with a block and a counterattack, the two fell dead at his feet. To his side, Joferian's sword clanged viciously against the trollborn's cutlass as they tested each other.

"Come now, blueblood," the trollborn spat, and the two re-engaged, exchanging heavy blows.

Joferian knew his enemy was strong, and every exchange brought the trollborn's blade closer to him. He had to try something else.

As the trollborn raised his weapon, Joferian ducked the attack and rammed his shoulder into his opponent's chest. The trollborn was heavy and barely moved, but it forced his sword to fall low and Joferian slashed horizontally across his midsection.

His sword hit home and blood flowed from his wound. The trollborn staggered back, grasping at the blood and looking incredulously at Joferian. With a roar, the trollborn raged forward. Joferian was able to block his sword, but the momentum knocked him to the deck. The injured trollborn raised his blade, ready to finish the job.

Talath's blade whirled across from the trollborn's rear and, at the last moment, deflected the attack. Joferian smiled for a second and rolled to one knee, but before he could climb back into the fight, the trollborn spun and tripped Talath, sending him flying onto the rail. With a quick dip, his foe lowered his shoulder and lifted Talath into the air, casting him overboard.

Joferian's eyes widened in rage. He heard the splash and rushed to the rail to see his brother's armored body sink into the sea like a stone.

A clap of steel against his armor did little to wake Joferian from the nightmare. His eyes stared at the unforgiving sea, his ears deaf to the trollborn's steel as it banged against the back of his breastplate. No longer in control of his own senses, he turned to the trollborn and started to swing. His enemy deflected the blows as best he could, but Joferian's fury bent his sword back and sent the pommel slipping from his hand.

Joferian swung again and again, cutting chunks of flesh off the dying trollborn until he stopped moving. He looked futilely overboard again, hoping against hope that Talath had grabbed a net or a rope. But his eyes played no tricks. His brother was gone. All that remained was his bloodied sword, lying ownerless on the deck.

INCANUS WAITED FOR HIS moment. He'd watched from a distance as one of the viscounts was flipped overboard, but the second had killed Boatswain Macabre. Still, that was one less foe for him to worry about.

Then the time was upon him. He saw that the young prince had been separated from the other royals, and he was waiting patiently for his target to get clear.

Everett Thorhauer had killed a group of pirates singlehandedly, and Incanus had watched every parry and every stroke the prince took with his sword. It was a pattern he'd encountered before, a good one to use against the sloppy pirates that lay dead at his feet. But it was no match for Incanus.

Incanus's eyes met with Thorhauer's and he could tell that Everett recognized him. He said nothing but instead raised his sword to defend himself against the Bone elf.

Incanus sheathed his sword and held out a dagger, waving the prince on with its tip. Everett scowled at the hubris of the maneuver and waded in. Incanus knew he could bait the young prince, but he was still shocked at his speed. Everett ducked a sword thrust and quickly leapt from a clever thumb grip maneuver, fanning his sword to the right and barely missing the assassin. The move impressed Incanus.

Everett stepped away and switched to a boar's tooth guard, his right foot leading and his sword tip pointing down and forward.

"What's next, young prince?" Incanus taunted. "A cut upward to my face?"

The prince growled and Incanus took some joy in frustrating the talented but inexperienced warrior. But he'd had enough of playing with his prey. It was time to move in for the kill.

Everett fell back into a high guard as Incanus inched forward and feigned a direct attack. Everett swung down to block the Bone elf's dagger, but Incanus had already rolled away to the side.

Dru'Waith's dagger slid between the cracks in Everett's armor, burying itself deep in his armpit. The prince cried in anguish and lurched to the side to escape. Incanus left the blade in, watching the prince flail to remove it.

The prince pulled at the pommel, which was fashioned in the shape of a black rose, but his strength and breath had left him and he collapsed slowly to the deck. He struggled to move, and Incanus kicked his sword from his hands for good measure.

"You're already dead," the assassin said. "But you've died with honor."

"I'll await you in the Hall of the Ancients," Everett managed, gargling blood as his eyes went black.

"You'll have to wait in line," Incanus replied.

ADDILYN AND JESSAMY STOOD at the helm of the ship, defending themselves from the onslaught of marauders. Several small waves of combatants had challenged them, and all of them had failed. They stood amongst a group of dead pirates, adding to the pile with their swords.

With a final slash of her sword, Jessamy killed the last of the latest wave and the two found a moment to breathe. Addilyn surveyed the deck for the Bone elf and found him slowly picking his way toward her through the morass. She took a deep breath and pointed at him with her sword, alerting Jessamy to their enemy.

The Bone elf stepped onto the platform among the dead and slowly drew his sword. He reached into the pile of bodies and found a dagger to balance his attack. His eyes never left the Vermilion.

"I'll finish the fight, this time," the Bone elf said. "My steel is still stained with the blood of your father."

Addilyn grunted, nearly losing her composure, but Jessamy steadied her, stopping her advance by slipping her blade in front of Addilyn.

"Let him come to us," she said, and Addilyn listened.

The Bone elf drew closer and switched his sword hand to face Jessamy, the dagger pointing at Addilyn. He stepped over the final few corpses and then lunged ferociously.

Addilyn watched Jessamy block the sword at the last moment while she herself averted the swipe of his dagger with a twist of her own.

"Ljusstralen lichte!" Addilyn growled, feeling the hale of her magic appear in her hand, and then a flash of light left the tips of her fingers.

The spell erupted in the assassin's face, briefly blinding him. He growled and instinctively reached to cover his eyes, setting him back on his toes.

Jessamy used the precious seconds to close the gap, lunging at his sword hand. The blinded elf deflected her blow, but the blade of her sword rode up his forearm, cutting into his flesh.

The assassin roared in anger and quickly twisted his sword, unwittingly blocking Jessamy's follow-up attacks. Addilyn darted to the left, crossing behind Jessamy and nicking the Bone elf's shoulder with a quick thrust.

The assassin surprised the women by pressing his attack, running through their blades with wide swings. He forced them back and away for long enough to shake off some of the spell's effects.

Jessamy dared an attack and ducked beneath his sword. She lifted her blade, catching the Bone elf on the chin. He turned his neck in the nick of time, but blood flowed from his jaw as he regathered himself.

"Andioth lumistae!" Addilyn screamed, manifesting an arc of flames this time and launching it at the assassin. The spell was done in desperation, and it was a greater version of the trick she'd shown Ritter in the garden of Thronehelm. She grunted as the energy she expelled from herself hastened the magical bolt, but the toll it took on her body was telling. She nearly dropped to a knee as the evocation tapped her strength.

The Bone elf dodged the burning bolt, but the edge of the fire seared his side and hip before exploding behind him against the wheel.

Addilyn was prepared for him, this time.

LABRECQUE STOOD STALWART IN the middle of the fray, his sword arm striking and parrying as his eyes scanned for the captain of the *Phantom*. In a chance clearing of the mob, he saw a figure emerge, carrying a bloody cutlass in his hand.

"Valerick LaBrecque," the man yelled, flashing his steel.

"And you are?" LaBrecque replied, stepping toward the man.

"I'm Captain Eruduel Morley of the *Phantom*," the man said, circling the admiral in a small clearing amidships.

"Well done, Captain," LaBrecque said. "You're going to sink us both."

Morley shrugged, and the two exchanged glancing blows of steel, the first dance in a longer performance. Morley snickered and arced a swing above LaBrecque's head, allowing the admiral to twist away and counter with a swift swipe, cutting a small wound in Morley's side.

Morley groaned and charged in, his sword clashing against the admiral's until they parted, each blade sliding down the other's and bouncing harmlessly off their quillons. The two stepped away from each other, both regathering their thoughts and waiting for the right time to strike.

Then the battle was interrupted by the loud crash of the entwined vessels pummeling the rocky shoreline of Lighthouse Island. The two ships lurched in different directions, separating in the foam. The *Phantom* had taken the worst of the damage and stopped dead, parting from *Doom's Wake* and floating adrift.

The *Wake* turned starboard and began to list. The combined crews, most of them stranded on the *Wake*, leaned into the tilt, some tumbling overboard.

LaBrecque and the captain fell into each other, both rolling over the starboard rail and into the shallows below.

RITTER SWAYED BACK AND forth inside the crow's nest and took a moment to regain his senses. He peered out of the barrel and nocked an arrow. The listing of the ship tilted Ritter's position, but the swaying had stopped.

His first thought was of Addilyn. His eyes scanned the deck for the Vermilion princess and caught her facing off at a distance with the assassin. He was raising his bow to shoot when pain tore through his back.

He spun around, dropping his bow to the deck below, and found that the assassin's little creature had slashed him with his claws. The beast hissed his forked tongue, and his sharp tail whipped by Ritter's face, smacking the mast pole behind him. Ritter drew his dagger and grabbed at the creature, his hand wrapping around the imp's neck.

The demon fought back with a strength Ritter wasn't expecting, slashing away and wrapping his tail around Ritter's arm. He tried to tug free of Ritter's grip, but Ritter slashed at the tail, slicing it open and forcing the foul creature to let go. With a push of his legs, the creature leapt into the sky, his bat-like wings beating against Ritter's face and shoulders. The damned thing wanted to escape, and Ritter was having none of it. As the beast gained the slightest of altitudes, Ritter slashed again, cutting one of its razor-sharp claws free.

The imp howled in pain. It was a scream that Ritter would never forget. The sound was otherworldly, a spectral wail that froze him for a split second, which was all the imp needed to coast to the deck.

Ritter jumped from the crow's nest and slid down the rigging. He watched as the imp staggered through the battle, holding his severed talon close to his chest. As Ritter reached the deck, he saw the imp run toward Addilyn and the assassin, but then he jumped to the rail, launching himself to safety. With his bloody arm tucked, he flapped his wings violently, briefly interrupting the melee as he soared above the Vermilion.

Ritter grabbed Silencer off the deck and drew an arrow from his quiver. As the creature lifted off into the night sky, Ritter fired, piercing through one of the wing's membranes and sending the crippled beast spiraling into the rocky shoals.

INCANUS WATCHED AS SKULLAM spun uncontrollably overhead, disappearing over the rail. The princess and her champion had fought hard, and it had taken his all just to keep them at bay. With Ritter on deck, he knew the fight was lost.

In desperation, Incanus turned to the rail and threw his dagger at the master swordswoman. The Raven elf swung her blade and deflected the projectile, but the move bought Incanus the time and space he needed to jump.

He heard the Vermilion casting another hurried spell as he leapt, and then he felt the fiery pain of flames searing through his leather armor onto his back. As he splashed into the shallow waters, the fire was extinguished. Even underwater, he could hear the hissing of the magical fire and feel the burn of steam on his exposed skin.

He swam submerged, blind in the darkness, waiting for a second attack from an arrow that never came. He knew he wasn't far enough from the ship to be safe from the mage's spells or the trollborn's bow, so he let the weight of his studded armor hold him down. He only surfaced enough to take a quick breath.

A few minutes went by. He drifted farther from the ship, hiding himself in the flotsam and jetsam. He could hear the cries and clangs of the battle, and he raised his head high enough to take an account of his situation.

It seemed safe.

When he looked to the rail, he saw no Vermilion, no Raven elf, and no magical bow. He watched for a few moments more and then scanned the waters to see if they'd followed him overboard. But there was no sign of them, just the distant sounds of a scattered melee. His elven eyes, accustomed to the darkness, spotted a small figure on the shore lying crumpled against the rocks. It was Skullam.

The creature had smashed into a shore rock, and Incanus couldn't tell if he was alive or dead. He swam softly toward Skullam and saw that the imp still lived, though he was unconscious from the impact. Incanus gently moved the broken creature, carrying him into the dark waters. He swam on his back, resting Skullam on his chest as he made his way to a lifeboat that had been cast off one of the ships during the battle. He carefully lifted his only friend onto the boat and then climbed aboard himself.

Paranoid as always, Incanus looked around to see if anyone had seen them.

Convinced he was safe, he crouched low and rowed gently away, assured that the enemy's suspicious eyes wouldn't notice them.

ADDILYN AND JESSAMY RAN to the rail to look for the assassin. Addilyn could make out the ripples where he'd entered the water, but it looked as though he'd never surfaced. Jessamy jumped from the deck to the rail, ready to dive in.

"Wait," a garbled voice called from behind them. "I... shoot."

They both turned to see Ritter staggering toward them, his bow clutched at this side. His other hand held an imaginary arrow that he was trying to string to Silencer while his eyes rolled to and fro. After one final step, he fell flat to the deck.

Addilyn rushed to his side. She heard Jessamy dive into the water behind her, but her mind had drifted from the assassin to the collapsed Longmarcher in front of her. She saw claw marks on his back, some of which had cut through his armor. She guessed that the assassin's winged fiend had attacked him.

She worked quickly to stave off the blood and dragged him clear of the battle, hiding him against the rail. She wasn't thinking of Jessamy, and nor was she thinking of the Bone elf. She only thought of protecting Ritter.

She raised her sword, waiting for the next pirate to attack her, but none came. There were scattered screams and small fires lit by the marauders, but from Addilyn's little corner of the *Wake*, it appeared as if the battle was over.

LABRECQUE CRAWLED TO SHORE, never taking his eyes off the enemy captain. The two struggled to climb the rocks, finding level ground to resume their duel. The lighthouse illuminated their personal battlefield. LaBrecque flipped his wet hair out of his face and stared at his opponent.

"You've been a worthy opponent," Labrecque said, calmly. "I'll now make you part of my legend."

The man sneered and lifted his blade, signaling that he was ready to fight. The two engaged. Their swords tangled in a fierce exchange, crossing steel in countless swings, blocking, and sliding for position. LaBrecque dodged to the left and the captain followed, both climbing onto an uneven stone that jutted from the shore.

The captain swung his cutlass at LaBrecque's feet, but he was too quick and leapt the maneuver, returning with a lunge of his own. The captain dodged the maneuver, but LaBrecque stepped into it and punched the man with his quillon. LaBrecque felt the weight of the blow, and he carried through with a kick, knocking the man from his perch. Once he'd recovered from the fall, LaBrecque saw he had a bloodied jaw. The man spat loose teeth and wiped his face on his sleeve, waving LaBrecque on.

The admiral jumped down from the rock to attack. Sparks flew from their swords as LaBrecque pressed his charge, forcing the captain backward. Then the captain lunged forward, lifting his cutlass and stabbing at his opponent's heart.

But LaBrecque was faster.

With a spin to his left, LaBrecque dodged the blade and returned the maneuver, striking the captain in the chest and running him through. The man fell to his knees, his eyes widening. He stared at the admiral. LaBrecque withdrew his sword and watched his opponent collapse to the ground.

A round of cheers and applause rose, and LaBrecque turned to see that he'd drawn a crowd. The patrons of the famous Lighthouse Inn had lined the front of the tavern to watch the duel.

Without missing a beat, LaBrecque pulled himself to attention, then clicked his heels together and swiped his cutlass in front of him for effect. He took a deep bow, bringing more cheers from his impromptu audience.

Soaked to the skin and limping as he began to feel his injuries, LaBrecque was approached by a balding, bearded old man who had stomped out of the inn that stood on the cliff. Joining him was a skinnier man who wore the cassocks of a disciple from the Cathedral of the Watchful Eye.

"Good evening, Captain," the man with the beard called, guessing incorrectly at his rank. "Congratulations on your victory."

LaBrecque gave another exhausted bow, half-amused and half-irritated by the man's sardonic tone.

"May I ask why you're dueling in front of my inn?"

"Master Innkeeper," LaBrecque replied with a small smile, wringing out his shirt as he spoke, "my apologies for entertaining your customers while they sat in comfort. I can see how it might have posed a problem, given that such a spectacle would naturally raise their expectations for future visits."

The man's eyes narrowed and LaBrecque decided to back off.

"My name is Admiral Valerick LaBrecque, and my ship was attacked by this pirate and his crew." He jerked his head to gesture behind him.

"That was Captain Morley," the innkeeper said, relaxing a little. "A longtime scoundrel from around these parts. You've bested a man of ill repute, and I imagine you'll have the regency's thanks."

"I'd rather have their help," LaBrecque said. "Although the battle is over, my passengers are in need of sanctuary."

"Who do you sail with?"

"The prince of Thronehelm," LaBrecque replied, "and a princess of the Vermilion elves."

The innkeeper squinted at him. "Weren't there two princes from Thronehelm?"

LaBrecque's expression answered him, and the man sighed heavily.

"I'll help you, Admiral," he said at last. "My name's Greyson Calder. And this is Disciple Delling of the Watch, of course. I sent for the constables and healers before I came down to talk to you, and they should be here directly. Delling has also offered his training in the art of healing for your crew."

"Thank you," LaBrecque said. Relief flowed through him, somehow making him feel wearier. He had to pause for a moment to summon the energy to say, "May I ask two more favors?"

Calder looked at him, brows raised, and Delling chuckled, turning away from Calder.

"Can you send someone to find the harbormaster? My ship is badly damaged, and I'm sure they won't want it to founder in the bay."

Calder inclined his head. "She's among the crowd that watched you defeat Morley, so I'm sure she'll be glad to help. And the second item?"

"Can you scrounge up a bottle of wine for an old sea dog?" LaBrecque asked, a hint of the smile returning. "I can think of nothing better than a drink after a battle."

The two men laughed and Calder's belly shook. "I'm sure we can find something to your liking, Admiral."

MONTGOMERY STOOD ABOVE HIS brother's body. Everett's corpse still clung to the dagger that had killed him, the one with a black pommel in the shape of a rose. Monty shook with a blend of sorrow and rage as he dropped his sword to the deck.

Cray, injured as he was from the conflict, threw his arm around his prince, and the two wept openly over Everett's body.

Montgomery heard booted feet against the deck and looked up to see Joferian standing alone. His eyes were wet with tears, and his countenance told Montgomery the news with no need for him to ask.

"How?" That was all Monty could muster as he lifted and hugged his dead brother, pulling the dagger from him and casting it across the deck in disgust.

"The sea," Joferian said. "He was cast overboard. He saved me, but I couldn't save him."

Joferian dropped to his knees, letting go of first his own sword and then his brother's. It was all that remained of Talath.

Cray shifted over to hug the viscount, and the three shared several minutes of grief as they contemplated their losses.

"Where's LaBrecque?" Montgomery asked, finally breaking the silence. He didn't really want to know, but he had to say something. His mind was flooded with the hows and whys of the battle, and he still wasn't sure how he'd lost track of Everett.

"Overboard."

They turned to see Princess Addilyn, her sword still drawn.

"Alive?" Cray asked.

"I don't know."

"This wasn't supposed to happen," Montgomery said to both no one and everyone. "We were supposed to rule Warminster together. He wasn't meant to die. Not like this…"

Monty's voice trailed off, and his eyes drifted from Everett to the blade that had killed him. Then, calmly, he asked, "Where is he?"

"Who?" Cray replied.

"Where is he?" Montgomery repeated, shouting this time.

"The assassin jumped overboard," Addilyn replied. "Jessamy is hunting him now. We think he swam to shore."

Montgomery reached hastily for his sword and struggled to stand upright. Cray and Joferian both helped the injured prince to his feet, but they also held him back.

"I must find—"

"We will," Addilyn assured him, gently putting her hand on his breastplate. "Given time. But right now, you're chasing a shadow at night."

DISCIPLE DELLING SQUEEZED THE blood from the rag before replacing it on one of the sailor's wounds. The bleeding hadn't abated, and Delling knew the end was upon him.

"You there," Delling yelled to the Raven elf in front of him, who appeared no worse for wear. "Put some pressure on this wound."

Jessamy knelt near the dying sailor and did as he'd asked. Delling shifted to his feet and moved along to the next sailor, who was unconscious but who'd survive his wounds.

A door opened, and the light of dawn warmed the room. Delling hadn't realized he'd been up all night and that the new day was upon them. A tall, rotund figure stepped into the doorway.

"Disciple," the figure said, "take some water and get some rest."

Delling recognized Greyson Calder's distinctive baritone voice and smiled up at his friend. They'd spent many nights together sharing spirits in this very hall.

"Thank you, Grey," Delling said, quaffing the chilled water. "I'll be upstairs in a few minutes to check on the rest."

Calder had let Delling convert the first floor of the Lighthouse Inn into a makeshift triage unit. Those who didn't fit there were taken downstairs into the wine cellar.

"No need, my friend," Greyson said. "The wounded have all been tended to and many are resting under the care of volunteers from the Temple of Ssolantress. Let's take a walk."

Delling wiped his hand on the stained rags and looked back at Jessamy.

"Is he...?" Delling asked.

"Yes, Disciple," Jessamy said, and with his unspoken permission, she released the pressure on the man's chest. Delling put his hands on his hips and turned his head in disgust. They'd saved many, but not all.

"Thank you, soldier," he said to her. "May the light of Erud shine upon you."

Jessamy nodded respectfully.

Calder and Delling made their way from the cellar into the restaurant, which looked more like a butcher's block than the high society establishment it usually was. They strolled outside the lighthouse building and onto the rocky shoals of the island for some privacy.

"The Caveat has called for an emergency session to address the events of the evening," Calder said in an even tone. "They're going to want a full account."

"Aye." Delling's hands remained on his hips. "As they should. I spoke to Prince Montgomery and tended to his wounds before he left for the First Embassy."

"How was he?"

"He has a few injuries, but the wound that cut the deepest was the loss of his younger brother, Prince Everett."

Calder let a moment pass between them and glanced over at the listing ship in the harbor. The second vessel had already sunk, its mainmast barely visible above the surface of the water.

"What do you think happened here?" Calder asked. "Why was he so desperate?"

"The prince told me that the Vermilion's father was assassinated in the halls of Thronehelm," Delling said. "They were on their way here to warn us. They said something about finding a man that had helped the princess's father."

"Morley was hunting a Vermilion princess?" Calder asked. "I know the man's been desperate, but that seems extreme even for him. What web has he tangled himself in this time?"

Delling shrugged.

"If there were ill omens," Calder pressed, "wouldn't First Keeper Makai have seen something?"

Delling stood silently by, looking at his bloody boots. Then he decided to come clean.

"Makai has been blind to the blessings of Erud for several months," Delling began. Calder's face twisted in confusion, but he let Delling continue. "It's not just him. This blindness has cursed the entire order. The Erudian Sight has been slowly fading. It doesn't surprise me that the Vermilion rode to warn us."

"And what of your order?" Calder asked.

"The Disciples?" Delling replied. "My sect is different, my friend. We don't have the Sight like the Keepers. We spread the good word of Erud to the masses."

They paused, enjoying a moment of silence away from the screams of the night.

"The city's already stirring with rumors and innuendo," Calder said. "Castleshire is full of news, and I'm sure that word of this has already left on the tongues and scrolls of messengers. It's already on its way to the four corners of Warminster."

"News like this travels fast." Delling laughed bitterly at the politics of it all. He crouched down and grabbed a loose stone, flicking it into the ocean.

"It does, my good man," Calder said. "I'll have to ask Makai about this in front of the Caveat. It's my duty as tribune. I'm sorry if that puts your order in a tough position."

Delling stood and turned to his friend, frowning. He left Calder standing on the rocks and patted him knowingly on the shoulder as he walked away. It wasn't going to be a good day.

CHAPTER TWENTY-NINE

*"I swear to the Ancients that I shall bear true
faith to the Regent Court of Castleshire."*
—Oath of Obligation to the Caveat

FAUX AND ARJUN HAD been moved to a private cell, as Zayd Nephale, always the gentleman, had given them special treatment after the run-in with the trollborn prisoner. She was still a noble, even if she was a Dauldon. Nephale wasn't going to have her killed in his dungeons before her head could find the executioner's block. She'd be afforded the same rights as all nobles and landed gentry under Shirian law until her final sentence had been discharged.

To Faux, the scenery was the same. Bars and locks in a gilded cage made no difference to her.

"Arjun," she said, deliberately waking the captain. "How in the name of Koss are you able to sleep in this place?"

Arjun sat up from his cot and looked at her.

"It's better than the floor in the other hold." The captain opened his eyes but remained prone. "I've slept in worse conditions. This, compared to some, is pleasant. I have my own cot."

Faux stared daggers at Arjun for the poor attempt at humor. Then she heard a door unlock down the hall, followed by footsteps coming their way. The clack of Nephale's boots was becoming all too familiar. Lanternlight spilled around the corner as he held the lamp to their cage.

"Five minutes, Master Faircloth," Nephale warned, pocketing a purse that Jaxtyn held out for him to take. "Five minutes only."

Jaxtyn didn't waste time responding to the bribed jailer and instead leaned into the cage to see Faux. Faux's eyes brightened, her features softening as she saw her childhood love.

For a moment, she forgot about the iron bars that separated them. She rushed to the gate to embrace him, catching herself at the last second. *Would he still feel the same way? And why was he here?*

Their eyes met for the first time since she'd absconded from Castleshire. He was as dashing as the day she'd left, leaving her lost for words.

"Hello, Faux Dauldon," Jaxtyn whispered. "How did the red-headed rogue find her way into this predicament?"

"Jax—" Faux managed at length, but she couldn't finish her thought. She smiled and he smiled back. "How did you know I was here?"

"I received a visit in the middle of the night from your Alaric friend," Jaxtyn said. "He and his valet, Ellissio, told me I'd find you here."

"Then you know what we've done?"

"I didn't believe him at first," Jaxtyn admitted. "But then he told me about a vision he'd had. It was all I needed."

"They're going to execute us, Jax. Daemus's family turned us in."

"Not if I have anything to do with it," Jaxtyn promised, a resolute timbre in his words. "I'm on the Regent Court now. I have the position my father abdicated three years ago when he retired from the Caveat. We're meeting today to consider your... situation."

"But—"

"All I can ask for is a little more time." Jaxtyn smiled and knelt at the bars that separated him from her. "And perhaps some faith."

"We've lost too much time already, you and I," Faux said, only remembering after she'd already spoken that Jaxtyn might no longer feel the same way.

To her disappointment, he didn't reciprocate, focusing instead on the task at hand. "We assemble this afternoon. There's much for the Caveat to discuss. I'll fight for your redemption if I must. I pray that the others will see your sacrifice as I do."

"Thank you," she said, a small tear forming in the corner of her eye. "For trying to rescue us."

"Do you remember that ride?" Jaxtyn asked. "You saved me... once."

"Of course," she said, a smile briefly returning to her face.

"Do you remember what you said to me?"

"I told you that I couldn't let the boy I loved fall and die before he had the chance to marry me."

Jaxtyn reached through the bars and at first, Faux thought he was going to touch her. Instead, he handed her a token. When she offered up her hand, he placed her grandmother's necklace in her palm. Faux, lost in quiet love, didn't hear Nephale coming to fetch Jaxtyn.

"Your time is up, my lord," Nephale announced, loudly enough to subtly sting Faux, as was his way.

"You're correct, good jailer." Jaxtyn rose from his knees, not breaking from Faux's gaze. "But ours has just restarted."

She smiled, letting go of his hand and putting her faith in love.

AS THE DAY WANED, the nine members of the Caveat gathered in the domed halls of the Regent Court to hear news of the battle in the harbor. The crowd buzzed with anticipation while Addilyn waited patiently for her time to speak.

There was also news of an outlaw Dauldon who was sitting in the dungeons beneath the Caveat. With hundreds of members of Shirian society in attendance, the Regent Court was brimming with hearsay and conspiracies. The main chambers of the rounded building held nearly a thousand seats, none of which was empty. The hall contained a center dais, matching the design of the building where the regency held court. The members of the Caveat sat behind a crescent-shaped table, its open end facing the main doors of the building.

"My ladies, my lords, please take your seats," Lord Callum Darcy announced. Addilyn recognized him from their short meetings in the past, mostly from Dacre's affairs of state. He was the Caveat's superior, and he lifted Iron Jack from the desk and gently clanged the shield that hung behind him. He took a quick roll call of all members of the Regent Court, including Lady Amadeur Chessborough, the Regent of Castleshire.

"I call this emergency meeting of the Regent Council of Castleshire to order," Darcy began. "I know that many of us have heard rumors of the events that transpired last night. We're gathered here today to learn the truth and to decide how to react as a city, representing all the governments of Warminster."

As Darcy and the other members of the Regent Court waxed poetic on the virtues of Shirian culture, Addilyn watched Montgomery stare at the floor, clearly a mixed bag of emotions.

"Gather yourself, Prince," Addilyn urged, reminding him of his station. Ritter, Jessamy, and Joferian all sat directly behind the prince and princess, and Joferian patted his cousin on the back.

"Prince Montgomery Thorhauer," Darcy called. "As the Thorhauers are one of the founding families of Castleshire, you're called upon to speak first. The Caveat will hear from you now. Will you please offer us your understanding of last night's events?"

Montgomery stood slowly and walked to the floor. Before he could open his mouth, a voice raised itself from the audience.

"Point of order, Lord Darcy," Thessica Camber said, making her way to the Caveat floor. She was a Von Lormarck niece and a comely cousin to Montgomery.

"And what would that be, Lady Camber?" Lord Darcy asked.

"The kingdom of Foghaven Vale and the Barony of Gloucester no longer recognize the Thorhauers as our sovereigns, Lord Superior," Camber reminded him. "Before the good prince offers his remarks, I want to ensure that my king's voice is heard through my own. We've ceded from Warminster and neither Prince Montgomery nor his father can speak for us any longer."

Addilyn could see rage boiling in Montgomery's eyes. His face flushed and he stepped closer to Camber, who pretended to ignore him.

"Lady Camber, this is out of order," Lord Darcy said. "We're yet to address the issue of your secession. I believe you've jumped the line. Please have a seat while Prince Montgomery speaks. The events of last night brought great tragedy to his family and the Kingdom of Warminster. I believe he's earned the right to speak first with the blood of his brother and cousin."

All eyes turned back to Montgomery, and Addilyn knew that Camber's charade had unbalanced him even more. His mouth opened, and Addilyn watched his emotions overwhelm him. His head sank. As tears welled in his eyes, Addilyn rose and walked over to him, comforting him with a hug.

"Lord Darcy," Addilyn said. "I was with the prince during the events of last night. May I speak in his stead?"

Darcy looked to his table for objections. Seeing none, he said, "Proceed."

"My father and I were sent beyond the walls of Eldwal by Coronelle Fia Elspeth to warn Warminster of a coming calamity." Addilyn turned to face the regency. "And, sir, I believe we're already beyond the precipice."

"Explain," Tribune Greyson Calder said from his seat on the dais. "Your vessel lists in the waters yards from my restaurant, and many of my guests witnessed the events unfold over dinner. A Vermilion visit is rare, so take as much time as you require."

"About a month ago, I saw a tetrine."

The crowd reacted with groans of both shock and disbelief, as she'd thought they would, but Darcy gaveled them down.

"I understood that sightings of the fabled horses are rare," Addilyn continued, "so I came to Castleshire to meet with Anselm Helenius. I sought advice from the great cryptid hunter. He told me that what I saw was the rarest of the rare and that despite his many years, he knew of no such spectacle in the annals of the Vermilion legacy and perhaps the entire realm."

"What did you see, Princess?" asked Lady Chessborough.

"I saw a lone tetrine fall into the trap of a spellcaster, who magically charmed the horse and rode off on it."

Again, the crowd interrupted, and again, Darcy gaveled them into silence.

"Go on."

"Then I saw a harrass of tetrine appear from the treeline. They were looking for the missing stallion and a great mare spoke to me."

"She *spoke*?" Darcy asked, his eyes crossing at the thought.

"Yes, she spoke," Addilyn confirmed, her voice full of conviction. "In her own way, at least. We didn't share a language, but I saw and felt her fear."

"If you weren't a Vermilion princess…" Darcy shook his head in doubt.

"Yet I am, Lord Superior," Addilyn countered, her voice steady.

"So how are the sightings linked to the battle in the harbor?" Ranaulf Alaric asked.

"My father and our wing traveled to Thronehelm. The sighting took place in the Dragon's Breath Mountains, and they were the closest kingdom to the encounter. We surmised that the tetrine's arrival had something to do with Thronehelm. From what legend tells us, the sightings usually take place close to a coming tragedy."

"And what did you find?"

"Death," Montgomery finally managed. The masses gasped at the word.

"My father was assassinated in Castle Thronehelm by a Bone elf posing as a jester," Addilyn explained as she struggled to maintain her poise. "A group of assassins dressed as minstrels also attacked the princes, but fortunately they failed to kill them."

Again, the crowd moaned and gasped at the revelation.

"Silence," Darcy ordered. "What happened next, Princess?"

"We left the following morning, sailing for Castleshire so that we could find Helenius and discover the meaning of the tetrine sighting."

"This council shares your grief," Lord Darcy said. "We were made aware of these tragedies just last night."

"Thank you, Lord Darcy."

"Then pray tell," Calder said, "what happened in the harbor?"

"We sailed from Thronehelm the morning after the incident. But we were followed by an unidentified ship, one employing the services of a powerful naval wizard. We were attacked several times and Admiral LaBrecque of the royal navy was able to stave them off until we reached your shores. They rammed us, my lord. That's how desperate they were to stop us from reaching you."

"The Bone elf was with them," Montgomery interjected. "He must have set sail with the other ship."

"That ship was captained by Eruduel Morley," Calder added, his eyes scanning his fellow regents. "He and the admiral fought to the death last night on the shoals of the Lighthouse Inn. Morley was slain."

At this, the crowd nearly erupted, and Darcy had to bang Iron Jack to gavel them down once again.

"Morley did this?" Lady Chessborough asked once silence was restored. "It was that traitor? He who smuggled the Dauldon girl out of our city?"

"I'm afraid so, my lady," Calder confirmed. "He sailed with a crew of mercenaries."

"Did any of the crew survive?" Darcy asked.

"Yes, we have about a dozen of Morley's crew in the dungeons," Calder answered. "But they knew little of their mission and Morley's intentions. Please continue, Princess."

"Let them rot," Montgomery hissed.

"What happened to the assassin?" Darcy asked. "This, uh, Bone elf?"

"The Bone elf was injured in the battle," Addilyn continued. "But unfortunately, he killed Prince Everett and many others before he escaped into the night."

"He leaves a black rose on his victims." Montgomery dropped the bloody dagger that had been left in Everett's corpse to the floor of the Caveat as evidence. It echoed nearly as loudly as Iron Jack. "We've also seen his token left in the form of a flower on Ambassador Dacre's body and roses carved into arrow shafts during an ambush not far from where Princess Elspeth saw the tetrine."

"Bone elves are a rare and dangerous breed," Darcy bemoaned, staring at the stained blade. "They were bred into their form by their evil cousins, the Shadow elves, who dwell in darkness and who venture out only at night. Bone elves were created to do their bidding during the day."

"No one has heard of him," Addilyn added. "But whoever he is, he's hunting me. Unfortunately, he's left a wake of chaos in his path."

"Did he escape to our city?" Lady Chessborough asked.

"We don't know," Addilyn said, while waving at two of her companions in the front row of the hall. "Sir Ritter injured his companion, but its body was never recovered. Jessamy and I wounded the Bone elf, but he escaped back into the sea, where we couldn't follow."

"Why haven't the Keepers seen this?" Lady Chessborough asked, loudly enough for everyone in the chamber to hear. She stood and looked around. "The tetrine? The assassinations? Where's First Keeper Makai?"

Darcy whispered down from the dais to Lady Chessborough, who was sitting next to him. Within seconds, the Regent Court began conferring while Addilyn and Montgomery waited impatiently for their next remarks. Master Jaxtyn Faircloth stood up from the table for a moment and signaled to two cloaked figures in the crowd, who made their way to the Caveat floor.

"Master Faircloth," Darcy waved. "You have the floor."

"Thank you, Lord Darcy." Jaxtyn rose from his seat and motioned to his companions. "Please allow me to introduce Disciple Delling of the Divine Protectorate of Erud, as well as Daemus Alaric, a Keeper of the Forbidden."

DAEMUS LOOKED NERVOUSLY AROUND as he lowered the cowl of his cloak. He was standing opposite a prince and a princess in front of the most influential people in Castleshire. Even though he stood with Delling, the pressure weighed heavily upon him. Jaxtyn joined the pair on the floor and greeted them warmly.

"Disciple Delling," Jaxtyn began. "Tell the chamber of your order. Why haven't the Keepers divined the threats that have befallen us?"

"My lord, I'm no Keeper," Delling began. "But the Keepers' visions have been… limited in these past months. We've been unable to identify the source of the trouble."

An unfriendly susurrus rose in the hall and Delling waited for the voices to calm.

"However," Delling continued, "I've brought Master Daemus Alaric of House Alaric with me. He's a Keeper of our faith. I believe he has the answer."

"A blind child?" one of the nameless rabble yelled from the back of the hall. "What chicanery is this, Delling?"

"He's no child," Delling replied, slowly scanning the Regent Court. "And nor is he blind, I assure you. He's the only one of his order *with* the Sight."

"I made the acquaintance of Master Alaric last night," Jaxtyn added. "He came to my door after midnight, looking for my help. He was sent here, to Castleshire, by the head of his order, the Great Keeper Nasyr. At the time, he didn't know why he was being sent home, but Delling and I believe it was in anticipation of this very moment. For him, it was a long and arduous journey from Solemnity. One that cost Lord Kester Alaric, Daemus's uncle and the brother to Ranaulf Alaric, his life."

The crowd gasped at the news and Jaxtyn's gaze fell upon Ranaulf. The elder Alaric avoided the stare.

"Kester knew of the dangers on the road," Jaxtyn said, as Daemus felt the room hanging on his every word. "And the Great Keeper implored him to guard Daemus with his life. So, he recruited the help of an old friend. A friend who, at great risk to herself, survived the road and brought Daemus home. And now that brave woman sits in our dungeons. Her name is Faux Dauldon."

Again, the crowd responded to Jaxtyn's tale, but his voice fought its way through the grumblings.

"Hear me!" he shouted. "She and her companions risked their lives. They fought their way across the Vilchor Highgrass and faced down the same trollborn mercenaries that killed Kester. Without Dauldon, they would have done the same to Master Alaric. She knew what returning to Castleshire would mean for her and her friends, and she put the needs of the realm in front of her own well-being."

The crowd quieted.

"But first, let's deal with the issue of Daemus's visions," Jaxtyn said, adroitly turning the conversation to the matter at hand. "I've politely requested that our First Keeper stays silent until Daemus shows us what we've all been blind to."

"Jaxtyn, I—" Daemus began, but Jaxtyn's stare stopped him.

"This is your time, my friend," Jaxtyn encouraged. "Do what you did for me and they'll believe."

Daemus stepped back from Jaxtyn and Delling and looked momentarily at the crowd, which was waiting for him to speak. He swallowed hard and then looked at his father, who was sitting on the dais. Jaxtyn was correct. It was his time.

"I've had visions of a man," he began. "A blinded man. He came to me in my dreams every night. We'd meet at the edge of a lake that I didn't recognize. He'd emerge from a distant bank of fog, hiding faraway mountains. Blood dripped from his eyes and trickled down his face. When I screamed, he knew who I was, yet we've never met."

The great hall remained silent.

"Once the man knew I was there," Daemus continued, "my

dreams left the lake and dropped me into a forest of white, where the trees were both dead and alive. I could hear ghostly whispers, like an echo from a long-ago battle, but I was never close enough to understand their cries. Then a great creature chased me from the woods, standing twice my height and smelling of carrion. He chased me out of my dreams and I could no longer see the blinded man."

The prince urged a figure in the audience to step to the floor. Daemus watched a trollborn make his way toward him with a bow of white wood slung across his back.

"Your bow, sir," Daemus said, pointing at the weapon. "It looks like it's hewn from the dead forest I saw in my visions."

"It may well be," the trollborn replied. "This bow comes from the Ashen Hollows, a petrified forest near the Dragon's Breath Mountains, where Princess Elspeth saw the tetrine. It seems it may also be where the cloaked figure was leading you. The locals call it Ghostwood. The whispers you heard in your nightmares can be heard by those who stay too long in the hollows. My father, Sir Hertzog, forbids his subjects from entering Ghostwood."

"Who are you, sir?" Daemus asked.

"I'm Sir Ritter Valkeneer," he said, handing Daemus the bow to inspect. "What's the significance of Ghostwood in your dreams?"

"I don't know," Daemus replied. "Not yet, at least."

"First Keeper," Delling said. "Perhaps it's time for you to speak?"

A venerable old twerg rose from behind the dais. He was wearing the robes of the second highest station in Daemus's sect. His flaxen hair had never lost its color, and his cloak bore the sigil of his old clan, a shield with crossed warhammers. He'd been the First Keeper of Castleshire for as long as anyone could remember.

As the twerg drew closer, a pulse of energy rode through Daemus's body and the twerg paused in his approach for a second. Daemus wondered if the First Keeper had felt it.

Daemus had only met First Keeper Makai once. Makai had come to House Alaric when Daemus was still a child to usher him off to the Cathedral of the Watchful Eye. They'd had mutual dreams of one another the night before, and Makai had urged the family to allow Daemus to become an Initiate of the Keepers of the Forbidden.

"Daemus, this is Aliferis Makai, First Keeper of Castleshire," Delling said.

"We're acquainted," Daemus replied as he shook the First Keeper's hand and another spark of unseen magic passed between them. Makai reached for his beard, revealing a near-toothless smile.

"You've brought more than just yourself from Solemnity," Makai announced. "I can sense the presence of Erud for the first time in many moons."

The First Keeper turned to face the crowd, his cheeks rosy with hope.

"People of Castleshire, hear me," he commanded. "The Sight had left me, as it's left so many of my brothers and sisters. But now as I stand with this Keeper, I can feel the Sight again. Erud is with him."

Makai turned back to Daemus, their eyes meeting for a moment.

"You've seen more than you've said, lad. Tell us more."

Daemus paused, hoping that Makai would yield, but the twerg held firm, his anxious tail waving back and forth beneath the folds of his robe like an excited puppy caught under a blanket.

"I saw the same cloaked man, holding our sect's most holy

item, *The Tome of Enlightenment,*" Daemus said. "His dead eyes were aglow with the power of Erudian Sight, and he levitated above the pool of water where we stood. The once-pristine water was contaminated."

"Who *is* this man?" Lady Chessborough barked.

"Nearly two decades ago," Delling explained, "he was a Keeper of the Forbidden. He tried to cheat death by using *The Tome of Enlightenment* to see his own future. In our faith, there's no greater sin. Erud punished him by melting his eyes and stealing his Sight. He fled the cathedral with his magic but was pursued by a group of Keepers, Knights and Disciples, who feared he'd seek revenge."

"Go on," Lady Chessborough pressed. "We need more than that. Is this our man?"

"They found the fallen Keeper in a remote part of Ravenwood," Delling said. "At the base of the Dragon's Breath Mountains. In a rage, the fallen Keeper killed the others in a magical battle of such force that when the fog of war had lifted, the forest around them was petrified. It appears that Sir Ritter knows that battlefield as Ghostwood."

Daemus listened to Delling as he pieced his dreams together, and he began to feel a wellspring of emotions in his stomach. He fought the urge for a moment, trying not to fall into a trance.

"The fallen Keeper's name is Graytorris," Makai said. "He was nearly killed in his exchange with the Keepers and the Disciples of the Watch, and he disappeared after that. Most believed Graytorris was dead. When Nasyr assumed control of the cathedral, she searched for him with all the tools of our faith, but part of his curse made him invisible to scrying, including with the great Tome of our order. Since that night, his story has been erased from the Tome. It's as if he never existed. And it seems that Daemus is the only one who can see him."

The room fell silent again. Then a sound arose from outside the Caveat's halls. A raised voice could be heard through the closed double doors and the guards scrambled to high alert.

The doors swung open, and the masses turned to see who dared to interrupt the Regent Court. A man rode into the great hall on a hippogryph, carrying the banner of the Cathedral of the Watchful Eye. He sat high on his steed and lowered his lance.

"What's the meaning of this?" Darcy yelled from his place atop the dais.

"I'm Captain Danton Hague of the Knights of the Maelstrom," the rider replied. "I've flown all night to reach Castleshire with grave news. The cathedral's light shines no more over the skies of Solemnity. Falling stars have destroyed much of the campus, and Great Keeper Nasyr is dead."

The halls of the Caveat erupted in terror, and Lord Darcy rose to quiet the crowd, banging Iron Jack on its shield until peace had been restored.

"Captain Hague," Darcy said, "this is grave news indeed. Falling stars? By what manner of the Ancients—?"

"I haven't finished," Hague interrupted, with a desperate tone. "*The Tome of Enlightenment* is gone. The beacon of light and knowledge for all the realm… is missing."

Gasps and panicked wailing filled the hall as Darcy slumped back into his chair. The panic burned itself out after several minutes, and the chamber returned to a dead silence. All eyes turned to the last Keeper.

"It looks like the Great Keeper saved your life twice," Jaxtyn said to Daemus. "She knew what she was doing all along."

"Daemus," Makai began, "if the Tome is closed, our sect is blind to the knowledge of Erud until it's reopened. Do you still possess the Sight, lad?"

Daemus felt the pressure of the room squeezing against him, and the wellspring he'd been suppressing became unstoppable. He felt a vision coming and lost track of First Keeper Makai's words. His gaze drifted slowly to the dome of the Caveat, his head wrenching backward as his body grew stiff. A glow emanated from the corners of his eyes.

The Sight had taken over.

CHAPTER THIRTY

"Many look, but not all can see."
—Trillias, the Ancient

THE HALLS OF THE Caveat were deathly silent. Daemus' eyes radiated in a hale of soft gold and his jaw yawned open. A foreign voice emanated from within.

Ihm throlla mochal lemm.
kastus whyrren zzaknolen.
Viram kondast, regar vonnpast.
Puna toonch paprashash.
Florescu solamash.
Ihm throlla zzaknolen.

First Keeper Makai inched his way toward Daemus, whose whispers grew louder as he repeated the verse again. The chorus had a pleasant meter and strummed in a tongue unfamiliar to the room.

"Daemus," the twerg called, "what do you see?"

Lord Darcy stood from his seat and pointed to the First Keeper. "Makai, what are you—?"

Makai merely raised a hand to silence Darcy and entreated Daemus again, who was still seizing. His muscles were tensed, bulging unnaturally, but he was aware of the First Keeper's approach.

"Daemus!" Makai ordered. "Answer me! What do your eyes see?"

Daemus struggled to tilt his head toward Makai as he fought for control of his body. Two voices spoke as one from the keeper's bowels in a simultaneous refrain. "A... hallowed... ground," Daemus muttered. "A tree... of books. A... broken... poem."

Daemus turned from Makai, his body contorting as the voice from within grew stronger, this time forcing him to sing the refrain. For some reason, he looked to the Vermilion they called Princess Addilyn, and he saw her face twitch in recognition.

"First Keeper," the princess said in a hurried voice, "I recognize the melody, but not the language. The words may be of Vermilion origin. A dialect perhaps, but one I've never heard. But I have no doubt that it's a Melexian tongue at its roots."

Makai's face contorted in confusion.

"It's from an old lullaby," Addilyn hastened to explain. "One that every Vermilion child has sung to them. It's an ancient Vermilion poem, and when put to song, it's used to quiet our young."

"Tell me quickly, what's it's significance?" Makai asked, as he kept an eye on Daemus.

Daemus still held the Sight, but a lapse in its control allowed him to catch his breath. He slumped forward and wrapped his arms around his torso, trying to calm himself.

"The poem is about a woman sitting under a tree," Addilyn uttered, a perplexed look painted on her face. "She reads verses to a group of children. But what does that have to do with this?"

A sudden rush of energy welled up in Daemus and he knew better than to fight it. He let the surge guide him, and his song grew louder, echoing softly in the halls of the Caveat.

Some took cautious steps back. Others leaned in closer as Daemus dropped to his knees, his mouth now shut.

As the words resonated in the hall, Ranaulf stood and hustled from the dais to his son's side.

"Daemus," Delling said, "are you—?"

With a quick twitch, Daemus cast his arms into the air, forcing Makai, Jaxtyn and Delling back on their heels. The singing continued without him, and Daemus extended a finger to his mouth, quieting the men. His other arm raised to halt his father's advance.

None spoke.

The distant sound of hoofbeats rose gently over the dis-embodied refrain of the Melexian verse. Jaxytn, Makai and Ranaulf exchanged anxious glances.

"What's that?" Jaxtyn asked, a confused look on his brow. His eyes scanned the hall for its source.

The echoes grew closer until they were loud enough for all in the Caveat to hear.

"Guards!" Darcy called, as the sounds of the spectral stampede drew nearer. He stood from his chair and pointed to the closed double doors of the chamber. "Hold the portal!"

The doors flung open wide and the sound of the angry rush of horse hooves barreled through the hall, sending spectators diving for cover. A gust of wind followed the invisible intruders, sending parchment scattering and hair flying. Only Daemus knelt stoically, unaffected by the ghostly stampede that rode through the Caveat's marbled halls.

The room fell silent once again in a pregnant pause as confused regents recovered and shot glances at one another. Makai pulled himself back to his feet and reached for Daemus.

A giant thunderclap reverberated through the Caveat, cracking its painted dome and breaking the silence. The crowd ducked in shock.

"Son," Ranaulf whispered, after a long pause, his voice desperate. "Daemus?"

Daemus took a moment, his white eyes returning, and then looked up into his father's caring countenance. He was flustered and exhausted, as the Sight had taken its toll on his body. It always did, but this time was different. It was far worse.

"Where am I?" he asked. "Am I home?"

"Yes," Ranaulf affirmed as he fought back tears. "You're home." He hugged Daemus tightly.

Daemus leaned into Ranaulf and pulled himself to his feet. He glanced around at the staring eyes of the Caveat and the hushed crowd. A concerned look emerged on his face as he turned back to his father.

"What...?" he started. "What did I do?"

"You did well, son," Ranaulf replied. "You did very well."

ADDILYN HAD REMAINED SILENT throughout the spectacle, but her mind raced with thoughts of Daemus's message. She'd felt the presence of the stampede like everyone else, but she knew there was something different to it.

"Horses?" Darcy managed, gathering the courage to peek from beneath the table.

"I don't think the sound was of mere horses." Addilyn gathered her thoughts. She knew that what she was about to say could be controversial, and she subconsciously turned to Ritter and Jessamy for affirmation. "I believe the Sight brought us the echo of tetrine hooves."

The Caveat, still reeling from the scene, offered no response.

Thessica Camber made her way to the floor. She sneered and her head shook as she approached. "My lady," she began, her voice dripping in doubt, "we'll remember what we witnessed here for the rest of our lives. But do you honestly expect us to believe that you can tell the difference between horses and tetrine by the sound of their *hoofbeats*?"

A thin laughter echoed out from the crowd, and Addilyn took a moment before facing Camber.

"I know how it sounds," Addilyn remarked, turning from Camber to address first the crowd and then the Regent Court. "But that's why I'm here, and I believe Daemus's vision connects our stories, mine of the tetrine and his of Ghostwood."

Darcy sat back in his chair and offered no words as Camber bowed and gave the princess the floor.

"My people came to Castleshire a month ago to search for a champion for me," Addilyn explained, her voice stern and clear. "My father understood the gravity of my encounter with the fabled horses, as well as the dangers that would follow. He was correct, and now he lies in a grave because of it."

Makai stepped closer to Addilyn, and she allowed him to speak.

"It's true," the crusty twerg grumbled. "When Daemus was presented by Master Faircloth, it was the first time in several moons that I felt the touch of Erud. We all witnessed his powers. His auguries are undeniable. Erud has spoken and given us clues to the paths we must follow."

"When I saw the leader of the tetrine, she was looking for a lost stallion," Addilyn added. "The cloaked man that used magic to trap the creature... could it have been Graytorris?"

"It's possible," Makai replied. "He still lives."

Camber took a few purposeful steps toward Addilyn. "There's no doubt about the manifestation we just witnessed. If the First Keeper of Castleshire says it was the Sight, then please accept my apologies for questioning your judgement, my lady."

Addilyn accepted the apology with a nod.

"However," Camber continued, turning back to the regency, "these ill omens concern the kingdom of Foghaven Vale. On behalf of my uncle, King Dragich Von Lormarck, we offer our assistance."

Montgomery took a half step toward her, clearly insulted by the inference that Von Lormarck was a king, but Addilyn's outstretched arm stopped any rash act.

"We thank you," Montgomery said in feigned civility. "But on behalf of King Godwin Thorhauer, let me remind you that neither the Caveat nor the kingdom of Warminster recognizes your independence. Therefore, Thronehelm will seek the Regent Court's advice and *their* support, and not the support of your treasonous uncle."

"Princess Addilyn," Lady Amadeur Chessborough began, returning the conversation to what had just been witnessed. "What do you require of Castleshire?"

"I believe I can answer that, in part," Makai said.

"Continue."

"If the princess is correct," Makai said, "then Daemus's vision carved a direct path to the scholar city of Abacus."

"How so?" Lord Darcy asked.

"The Sight shows us the way," Makai continued. "First, the poem, sung to a Vermilion lullaby. No one here but Addilyn would have been able to recognize its origins. That message was clearly meant for her."

"Intriguing, First Keeper," Lady Chessborough said. "Perhaps the keeper and the princess were destined to meet here in our halls today. But how does that guide us to Abacus?"

"While in the throes of Erudian Sight, Daemus talked of a tree of books and a broken poem. There's a venerable Dale elf, Vorodin the Ageless, who seeded and nurtured a sapling in the center of Abacus on the day of the city's founding. Over the years, with Vorodin's care, the sapling grew to a tree of enormous size, known to the Abacunians as the Fey Tree. Parts of the Fey Tree have become a hidden library of sorts, where he still dwells. It's known in the city of Abacus as Vorodin's Lair. I surmise that if we find Vorodin the Ageless, he could help us to interpret the meaning of the Melexian dialect."

"Go on, Makai," Lady Chessborough urged.

"The princess told us that the poem was about a woman reading to children under a tree," Makai said. "I believe this woman to be your counterpart in Abacus, Lady Chessborough. The Athabasica of Abacus is a poetess. There's only one key that grants entry to those worthy of Vorodin's Lair, and the Athabasica possesses it."

"Helenius departed Castleshire to seek answers in Abacus for you and your father," Darcy said. "It rings true."

"First Keeper." Mirth Ashrem of the Regency stood to speak. "I see the wisdom in your *perception* of all this, but Athabasica the Poet rarely entertains audiences. We of the Regent Court struggle to have her return our communications. The woman is an eccentric, unlike many of her predecessors. If she were Athabasica the Nomad or Athabasica the Pious, the princess and the Keeper would be welcomed with open arms. But Athabasica the Poet? Does anyone in this great chamber know her well enough to secure an audience?"

"Perhaps no one here can help us," Jaxtyn said. "But I know of someone in our dungeon."

FAUX LEANED AGAINST THE unwelcoming walls of the jail cell. She was staring at Arjun, who'd made a pillow from his cape and who'd somehow found sleep. The two were alone in the cell, and Faux was lamenting ever coming to Castleshire.

She heard a distant rumble of thunder as Arjun stirred from his slumber.

"It must be raining." Faux looked to the dark ceiling of their cell as if it were the sky. "The perfect weather for a swift trial and execution."

Arjun sat up and the two stared at each other for a few moments.

"Have faith," Arjun said. "Daemus and Jaxtyn won't let us face the executioner's axe. We brought an Alaric home safely, and at great peril. I'm sure they'll grant some mercy for that. Perhaps a gentle exile is in order?"

They both laughed out loud but then fell back into an anxious silence. Time passed slowly, and Faux looked to her grandmother's necklace, thinking back to the day that she'd lost it, only to be interrupted by the opening of a distant door. Nephale's familiar footsteps reached their cell and they both stood up as he rounded the corner and made his way to their cell door.

"My lady," Nephale began in his usual polite tone, "I'm here to escort you to the chambers of the Caveat. You've been summoned by Lady Chessborough herself. You too, Captain."

Nephale snapped his fingers and several jailers made their way into the cell, slapping shackles on their wrists and ankles and connecting them together in a two-person chain gang.

"Is it time for our sentencing?" Faux asked, the ringing of Iron Jack in the back of her mind.

"You'll learn shortly, my lady," Nephale replied.

Faux and Arjun were escorted from their cell into a long, poorly lit hallway. Faux tried not to struggle against her bonds, but the cheap metal cut at her wrists and ankles with every step. Arjun was trying to keep an even pace for her, but his longer strides made it a painful trek. As they reached the end of the hallway, they came to a set of closed doors. The murmurs of a crowd drifted out from behind it.

"My lady, Captain," Nephale said, "your fate lies beyond this door. You're to remain silent unless addressed by myself or a member of the Regent Court. Is that understood?"

Both Faux and Arjun nodded.

"Good. Then let us proceed."

Nephale opened the door and light flooded the hallway, catching the two off-guard. Faux raised her hand to shade her eyes and could feel Nephale pulling their chains and urging them forward.

The halls of the Caveat were brimming with attendees.

Faux gazed at the crowd as she was led to the center of the hall, her head swirling as she tried to process the many faces looking down at her. Her heart raced in anticipation as she turned her eyes to the Regent Court, looking for Jaxtyn Faircloth. Jaxtyn's eyes met Faux's, and he nodded at her. Faux's eyes widened at the spectacle and her nostrils flared as they always did when she was happy or surprised. She hoped that Jaxtyn's subtle nod was a good sign.

A man rose from the center of the dais and grabbed Iron Jack before turning to tap the shield behind his chair. Faux closed her eyes and lowered her head, feeling the weight of its ominous tone wash over her.

"Silence!" the man ordered, and a hush quickly fell over the Caveat chamber. "My name is Lord Callum Darcy of House Darcy, and I'm the Caveat Superior. You, as the accused, have the right to know your judges. To my left sits Duke Ottomar Ivanhower of the Duchy of Ivanhower, Master Jaxtyn Faircloth of the Faircloth family and guild, Father Mirth Ashrem, the freely elected High Priest of Castleshire, and last, but not least, Lord Dariam Callanwind."

Faux locked gazes with Jaxtyn again, reaching out with unspoken hope as Darcy continued his roll call.

"To my right," Darcy continued, "we have Tribune Greyson Calder, elected freely by the people of Castleshire, Lady Helisent Shivall of the Shivall family, and Lord Ranaulf Alaric of the Silvercroft Mountains. Presiding over the Caveat is Lady Amadeur Chessborough, the city's regent."

Darcy rang the shield with Iron Jack once more and then they all took their seats. Arjun turned to Faux. With every toll of the shield, her spirit grew weaker.

"Are you all right?" Arjun whispered, earning himself an angry nudge from Nephale.

"The accused have been informed of those who sit in judgement," Darcy said. "It's now time for them to announce themselves."

Nephale nudged Arjun a second time and he took an involuntary step forward.

"I'm Arjun Ezekyle," he said, "former captain of the guard for the Dauldon family."

The hush was broken by whispers, and Darcy gaveled Iron Jack on the desk, calling for silence.

"And you?" Darcy asked.

Faux paused for a second, but she didn't wait for a friendly push from Nephale.

"I'm Faux Dauldon of House Dauldon."

The restless crowd moaned aloud.

"Enough," Darcy commanded, gaveling the crowd back to silence as Zayd Nephale handed over Faux's patents of nobility.

"My lady," Lord Darcy began, "these patents prove who you are. You've been on the run from justice these past twelve years."

He paused, sharing the patents as evidence with the rest of the Caveat.

"Before I permit you to speak on your own behalf," Lord Darcy continued, "Master Jaxtyn Faircloth and Master Ranaulf Alaric have asked me to allow them to offer some remarks in your defense. Master Alaric, you may proceed."

Ranaulf stood up to address the council and the crowd. "My ladies, lords, and citizens of Castleshire," he said. "I rise today to tell you of a great miscarriage of justice, one perpetrated when my wife and I summoned the jailer. My son was returned to me at great cost. His uncle died trying to save him. As Captain Danton Hague from the cathedral has informed us, many died there, too."

Faux and Arjun shot sideways glances at each other. The

tragedy at the cathedral was news to them.

"Kester sought out Faux and Arjun and asked for their help," Ranaulf continued. "They agreed to do so, and at great peril to themselves. Now they stand in front of us because I didn't believe them."

Ranaulf turned and locked eyes with Daemus.

"I didn't believe my own son," he said, lowering his head in shame and sniffing back tears. "Daemus, I ask for your forgiveness."

"Of course, Father," Daemus replied. "It was a difficult tale to tell, let alone to believe."

Ranaulf nodded with a smile and turned back to Faux and Arjun. "I ask the same of you. Will you pardon my rash actions? My petulance?"

"We do," Faux said. "I would have done the same if the roles were reversed. Thank you for asking."

Ranaulf slunk back into his seat, pursing his lips and bowing to the prisoners.

"Master Faircloth," Darcy urged.

Jaxtyn stood up and paused.

"Lady Dauldon, Captain Ezekyle," he began, "I rise today in your defense. I was moved by the bravery of Daemus Alaric, demonstrated here just moments ago, for whom you risked your lives. We now know how important it was to return him here, and he's already recalled your heroic deeds and your perilous journey from the Hearth, a journey that claimed the life of his beloved uncle and this chamber's devoted friend."

Jaxtyn paused again to looked around, as the chamber had fallen silent during his soliloquy.

"We all know the risks you took coming back here," he continued, "and we're grateful for your act of selflessness in escorting Daemus home. He told me of the kindness you showed and that you asked for nothing in return."

"Yes," Faux said. "And we lost two additional friends defending Daemus at Fort Homm."

A slight murmur floated above the crowd, but Jaxtyn continued. "What happened at Fort Homm?" he asked. "I thought it was abandoned."

"It was," Arjun said, "but the mercenaries who killed Kester caught up with us on the plains. We had no choice but to stop and fight. Daemus himself delivered the killing blow to their leader."

Heads spun from Faux and Arjun back to Daemus. Ranaulf sat up in his chair and stared at his son from afar.

"It was his vision that guided us," Faux explained. "If not for his Sight, we would all have been meals for horsehounds."

Again, the murmurings in the hall grew louder and Darcy raised his hand to quell them.

"Continue," Lord Darcy ordered, hushing the crowd with a scowl.

"We'd been running for days and our horses were spent," Faux began. "Daemus had a vision that Kester had fallen to Clan Blood Axe, the mercenaries, on the plains. He also saw the fort at the end of his reverie. He knew then that Erud was guiding us to Blood Ridge."

"How did seven stand against so many?" Jaxtyn asked.

"I'm a veteran of the High Aldin," Arjun explained. "I'm also a survivor of the first battle of Blood Ridge and very familiar with the fort. We refortified it as best we could and made our last stand there."

"At the cost of your friends?"

"Yes," Faux dropped her head at the thought. "We paid the price in blood."

"Daemus Alaric," Jaxtyn called. "Is this true?"

Daemus rose from his seat near the floor and nervously

adjusted his cassock.

"Yes, Master Faircloth, save for one detail."

"And what would that be?" Darcy asked.

"After the clan broke through the defenses," Daemus recalled, "Faux urged me to flee through the escape tunnels. She wanted me to run so that I'd be saved. She knew that the trollborn would kill them, but she hoped they could hold them off for long enough for me to sneak away to the horses."

"A deed worthy of honor," Jaxtyn said, his somber voice rising. Faux could tell that he wanted the entirety of the Caveat to hear it. Jaxtyn's eyes scanned the crowd before turning back to Daemus. "Why did you stay?"

Daemus looked around at the Caveat and raised his voice, the voice of an Alaric and one that belonged in the hall.

"Because they're my friends," Daemus said. "I couldn't leave those I loved behind."

The hall fell back into silence, save for the occasional sniffling of those who were fighting back tears at the story. Jaxtyn maintained the silence and nodded to Daemus.

"Thank you for your testimony," he said, his voice cracking. He tapped the table and sat down, signaling to Darcy that he was done. Lord Darcy tapped Iron Jack gently on the table and turned to his fellow members.

"We'll discuss your sentences in private," he announced to Faux and the crowd. "Jailer, please keep the accused here while we retire to our quarters."

"Aye." Nephale bowed to the superior, tugging on their chains and forcing them to sit on a nearby bench.

As the nine members of the Regent Court retired to their quarters, several shouts for mercy rang through the Caveat's halls. Faux looked around at the crowd and acknowledged Daemus's kind words with a nod from across the floor. He smiled back at her.

THE CROWD HAD ONLY been waiting for a few minutes when the Regent Court returned. Faux scanned the group for Jaxtyn, but he hadn't returned with the rest. She and Arjun exchanged worried glances, but before they could say anything, Nephale pulled at their shackles and they stood up. Lord Darcy gaveled and stood to deliver their sentences.

"Ladies and lords of the Caveat," he started. "It falls to me as Caveat Superior to render judgement on the accused. Faux Dauldon, Arjun Ezekyle, you've avoided justice for over a decade, escaping from this very city the night before sentencing. But here you stand, willfully returning and finding yourselves at the mercy of this court."

Lightning darted through every nerve in Faux's body. Her eyes glazed with anxiety. As Darcy droned on, her attention was glued to the empty chair, the one vacated by Jaxtyn Faircloth. Had the vote gone so wrong that he couldn't bear to witness her fate? A pit formed in her stomach, sapping her of strength and faith. She started to swoon but caught herself leaning forward and stopped before she fell.

"Guilty," Lord Darcy said.

The words punched Faux in the face, harder than she'd ever been hit in battle. Her cheeks reddened and she couldn't lift her head for fear of the empty chair on the dais. She felt Arjun's hands tugging on their entwined manacles, but she didn't dare look at him. She barely heard the shocked protestations of the crowd or Daemus crying to her from across the room. But she clearly heard the ringing of Iron Jack in her ears. She closed her eyes, a lone tear escaping.

"Faux Dauldon, Arjun Ezekyle," Lord Darcy continued, "the Regent Court sentences you to death by beheading."

EPILOGUE

*"When mortals presume to know the will of the Ancients,
they are found not omniscient, but diabolical."*
—Erud, The Ancient of Knowledge

THE PALE HORSE BORE its crooked rider to the gates of
Spine Castle, trudging through the elements of the Killean
Desolates. The rider slipped from his saddle and was greeted
at the gates by Zinzi, his incantatrix.

"Master."

"Was the exchange made?" Graytorris asked, not bothering
to raise his head as he shuffled by her, feeling his way through
the crooked gates.

"Yes, Master," Zinzi replied. "The horn awaits you in the
laboratory. All of the components are in hand."

"Then let's waste no time," Graytorris said.

The two turned to the doors of the twisted tower and made
their way to the top floor. Zinzi entered before her master,
lighting the room for her own purposes. The small flame revealed
a gnarled table at its center. A pestle and mortar rested on its
surface alongside several stoppered jars and a small iron cauldron.

Zinzi retrieved a small chest from a shelf against the
far wall and emptied its contents on the bench in front of
Graytorris. His bony hands searched through the items and
seized on the wrapping containing the tetrine's horn.

A rare smile appeared on Graytorris's face as he unwrapped
the horn and held it in his hand. The horn was cold to the
touch but intact, and his fingers followed the deep curves along
its spindle to its point. He could feel the magical hale inside
the horn. He hoped to soon release it.

"How long will this take?"

"I need to prepare the concoction one step at a time," she replied. "It must be exactly prepared or it could be tainted with unintended side effects. Now, give me your arm."

Graytorris extended his grey arm and Zinzi produced a two-tined fork from the chest. She grabbed his wrist and held his arm over the cauldron, then skillfully stabbed the fork into his forearm. Graytorris didn't flinch.

Blood dripped slowly from the holes in his arm. Once she'd leeched enough for the concoction, she let go of his wrist and swirled the blood at the bottom of the cauldron to coat its surface. Graytorris waited, his dead eyes staring into the darkness as she prepared the other ingredients for the potion.

"First, the eyes of a seer," she said to her master, so that he could follow her progress. She emptied the bloody pouch containing Nasyr's eyes into the pot. "Next, the blood of a dragon, freely given."

She reached into the chest and pulled out an ample bottle of black blood, which she uncorked and poured into the cauldron. Graytorris felt the heat from the dragon's blood and could smell Nasyr's eyes melting into a primordial soup. The cauldron began to boil.

"Then, we add the rarest of the rare," Zinzi continued. "A red sea urchin."

She reached for one of the stoppered jars on the table and emptied it into the vat. The urchin splashed into the vessel and the smell turned, leaving a harsh, astringent bite at the back of Graytorris's throat. Zinzi fell silent for a moment and tussled with the talon of a vrykar, one that she'd cut directly from the winged creature's claw.

"This one almost cost me my life," she mumbled, but Graytorris didn't care.

She used the pestle and mortar to grind the talon to

a rough powder and then dumped it into the bubbling pot. The talon grist crackled as the remainder dissolved.

"And now for the final ingredient," Zinzi said. She slipped on a pair of thick leather gloves and grabbed some darkened pliers from the tabletop. She used the pliers to hold the tetrine horn carefully by its tip. Cautiously, she dipped the base of the horn into the contents of the cauldron, lowering it slowly.

The horn hissed in magical defiance, releasing a heat that Graytorris felt on his face. He sensed the magic seeping from the horn and baptizing the liquid in the vat.

"Steady, witch," he said. "Or else this will all be in vain."

Zinzi didn't answer, concentrating instead on her task. She watched while the horn slowly liquefied, turning the black mixture to a golden hue.

"Well done," Graytorris said, rising from his seat. The first step would be complete once the dragon's blood had cooled.

"Thank you, master," Zinzi said, putting the pliers down and removing her gloves. "The potion will take several weeks to ferment before it can be used. Even at that, its effects may only last a month."

"A month will be long enough for what I have in mind," Graytorris said, cackling and rubbing his hands together with glee. "Let the leaders of Warminster and the pretenders to the throne sleep soundly in their beds tonight. Yesterday was the light and today was the twilight. Tomorrow will mark the beginning of a time of darkness."

ACKNOWLEDGEMENTS

I COULD NEVER SUFFICIENTLY EXPRESS my never-ending gratitude to my family and friends for their continued support and encouragement.

Nevertheless, thanks are in order to the many people who've helped me along in this journey. To Dane Cobain, my literary compass; Andrew Jackson, my mentor; Shai Shaffer, my development sherpa; Larch Gallagher, Jeff Jarrett, James Stillwagner and Luke Bruss, my illustrators; Ann Howley, my honest professor; Jordan Messineo, Lizzy Schinkel and Tom Beresnyak, my social media gurus; Phil Athans and Pam Harris, my fantasy wordsmiths; Victor Bevine the voice of Warminster; Jan and Susan Dickler, my media giants; Jim Stefanyak, my plotter and mirror; Dave Kuklis, my trailblazer; and Joey Davis and my Howley classmates, my beta everything. To you, I'm eternally indebted. As a novice author, I needed a "party of hearty adventurers" to walk the path with me as we took The Last Keeper over the finish line. You have my sincere appreciation for your borrowed skills, your precious time, and the golden opportunities that you provided for me to learn from your wisdom and combined experience.

The Last Keeper wouldn't exist without the support of three decades of Dungeons & Dragons player characters. Together, we lived (and died) in the realm of Warminster, as well as many others.

Ramincere the Dark Mage, Johonnem Incarnate, Incanus Dru'Waith, Rufus Crag, Windrider the Demonist, Magnus the Bearslayer, Lord Moreland, Borhai the White Paladin, Sir Talath Maeglen, Ruven Nightstar, Til Aarron and many others—for your dedication, tenacity, and desire to live through a game, I salute you. Or, as Admiral Valerick LaBrecque would say, "I toss my oars to you."

Finally, to my loving, understanding and supportive wife Andrea, I offer my deepest gratitude. I can't express in words and love how much your encouragement and support meant to me when times got rough. It was a great comfort to know you were willing to sacrifice for our small family to work your fingers to the bone, allowing me to live out this dream. I love you.

ABOUT J. V. HILLIARD

BORN OF STEEL, FIRE and black wind, J.V. Hilliard was raised as a highlander in the foothills of a once-great mountain chain on the confluence of the three mighty rivers that forged his realm's wealth and power for generations.

His father, a peasant twerg, toiled away in industries of honest labor and instilled in him a work ethic that would shape his destiny. His mother, a local healer, cared for his elders and his warrior uncle, who helped to raise him during his formative years. His genius brother, whose wizardly prowess allowed him to master the art of the abacus and his own quill, trained with him for battles on fields of green and sheets of ice.

Hilliard's earliest education took place in his warrior uncle's tower, where he recovered from grievous wounds that were suffered in a forgotten war. He learned his first words there, and his uncle, who'd sacrificed so much both for him and for others, helped him to learn the basics of life—and, most importantly, creative writing.

After years of education at the hands of the highlanders and at the great cathedral, Hilliard ventured to a place of wonderment in the capitol of all capitols, where he trained to defend his homeland and help his people.

It was then that he met his lady, a Ranger of the Diamond, and over the chords of an orchestra, he fell in love with her. Once his time serving the kings and queens of his Camelot had come to an end, he returned home to gather his own band of merry men. Together, they served the underserved—those without a voice—and rode to Camelot, fighting for those who couldn't defend themselves.

Unfortunately, Hilliard was injured and could no longer serve the people of the highlands. It was time for him to move on from the battlefield and to take up something mightier than a sword. He lifted a pen that would scribe the tale of the realm of Warminster, filled with brave knights, harrowing adventure and legendary struggles. He returned home for the last time to the city of silver cups, hypocycloids and golden triangles. He built his castle not far into the countryside, guarded by his own two horsehounds, Thor and MacLeod, and resides there to this day.